OXFORD WORLD'S CLASSICS

GUSTAVE FLAUBERT

Madame Bovary
Provincial Manners

Translated by
MARGARET MAULDON

With an Introduction by
MALCOLM BOWIE

and Notes by
MARK OVERSTALL

OXFORD
UNIVERSITY PRESS

OXFORD

UNIVERSITY PRESS

Great Clarendon Street, Oxford OX2 6DP

Oxford University Press is a department of the University of Oxford.
It furthers the University's objective of excellence in research, scholarship,
and education by publishing worldwide in

Oxford New York

Auckland Bangkok Buenos Aires Cape Town Chennai
Dar es Salaam Delhi Hong Kong Istanbul Karachi Kolkata
Kuala Lumpur Madrid Melbourne Mexico City Mumbai Nairobi
São Paulo Shanghai Taipei Tokyo Toronto

Oxford is a registered trade mark of Oxford University Press
in the UK and in certain other countries

Published in the United States
by Oxford University Press Inc., New York

Translation © Margaret Mauldon 2004
Introduction © Malcolm Bowie 2004
Notes © Mark Overstall 1981

British Library Cataloguing in Publication Data

Data available

Library of Congress Cataloging in Publication Data

Data available

ISBN 978–0–19–953565–1

10

Typeset in Ehrhardt
by RefineCatch Limited, Bungay, Suffolk
Printed in Great Britain by
Clays Ltd, St Ives plc

MADAME BOVARY

GUSTAVE FLAUBERT was born in 1821 in Rouen, where his father
was chief surgeon at the hospital. From 1840 to 1844 he studied law
in Paris, but gave up that career for writing, and set up house at
Croisset in 1846 with his widowed mother and niece. Notwithstand-
ing his attachment to them (and to a number of other women),
Flaubert's art was the centre of his existence, and he devoted his life
to it. His first published novel, *Madame Bovary*, appeared in 1856 in
serial form, and involved Flaubert in a trial for irreligion and
immorality. On his acquittal the book enjoyed a *succès de scandale*,
and its author's reputation was established.

Flaubert is often considered a pre-eminent representative of
'realism' in literature. It is true that he took enormous trouble over
the documentation of his novels. Even his historical novel *Salammbô*
(1862), set in Carthage at the time of the Punic Wars, involved a trip
to North Africa to gather local colour. But Flaubert's true obsession
was with style and form, in which he continually sought perfection,
recasting and reading aloud draft after draft.

While enjoying a brilliant social life as a literary celebrity, he
completed a second version of *L'Éducation sentimentale* in 1869. *La
Tentation de Saint Antoine* was published in 1874 and *Trois contes*
in 1877. Flaubert died in 1880, leaving his last (unfinished) work,
Bouvard et Pécuchet, to be published the following year.

MARGARET MAULDON has worked as a translator since 1987. For
Oxford World's Classics she has translated Zola's *L'Assommoir*,
Stendhal's *The Charterhouse of Parma*, Maupassant's *Bel-Ami*, Con-
stant's *Adolphe*, Huysmans's *Against Nature* (winner of the
Scott Moncrieff prize for translation, 1999), and Diderot's
Rameau's Nephew.

MALCOLM BOWIE was Master of Christ's College, Cambridge, and
previously Marshal Foch Professor of French Literature in the
University of Oxford. His publications include *Henri Michaux: A
Study of his Literary Works* (1973), *Mallarmé and the Art of Being
Difficult* (1978), *Freud, Proust and Lacan: Theory as Fiction* (1987),
Lacan (1991), *Psychoanalysis and the Future of Theory* (1993), *Proust
among the Stars* (1998), and the jointly written *A Short History of
French Literature* (2003).

MARK OVERSTALL taught French at Winchester College.

OXFORD WORLD'S CLASSICS

*For over 100 years Oxford World's Classics have brought
readers closer to the world's great literature. Now with over 700
titles—from the 4,000-year-old myths of Mesopotamia to the
twentieth century's greatest novels—the series makes available
lesser-known as well as celebrated writing.*

*The pocket-sized hardbacks of the early years contained
introductions by Virginia Woolf, T. S. Eliot, Graham Greene,
and other literary figures which enriched the experience of reading.
Today the series is recognized for its fine scholarship and
reliability in texts that span world literature, drama and poetry,
religion, philosophy and politics. Each edition includes perceptive
commentary and essential background information to meet the
changing needs of readers.*

CONTENTS

INTRODUCTION

*Readers who do not wish to learn details of the plot will prefer
to treat the Introduction as an Epilogue.*

I

Flaubert's approval rating among his fellow writers has always been
exceptionally high, and for many of them *Madame Bovary* (1857) has
been a particular object of veneration. 'It has a perfection that not
only stamps it, but that makes it stand almost alone,' wrote Henry
James in 1902; 'it holds itself with such a supreme unapproachable
assurance as both excites and defies judgment.' Nearly twenty years
later, Proust pointed to the 'grammatical beauty' of Flaubert's style
in *Madame Bovary* and elsewhere, and to the new vision of the
world, comparable to the philosophy of Immanuel Kant, that Flaubert had achieved by way of an artfully reinvented imperfect tense.
Vladimir Nabokov, lecturing to students at Wellesley College in
Massachusetts in the immediate aftermath of the Second World
War, picked up the refrain, and performed a dazzling close analysis
of the novel. 'Stylistically it is prose doing what poetry is supposed
to do,' he announced, before setting out to expose the compressed
layers of poetic implication that Flaubert had packed into his most
celebrated work. For well over a century, this approving chorus has
sounded internationally, and brought together a range of otherwise
dissimilar critical voices.

Great writers cannot be expected to approve unreservedly of their
predecessors' efforts, however, for each has his own slant of vision to
find, and his own battery of stylistic effects to nurture and perfect.
Emma Bovary, for James, was a limited 'reflector and register' of the
real world, and suffered from the selfsame poverty of consciousness
that his own heroines were uniformly spared. Proust was rude about
Flaubert's style, finding in it something of the moving pavement and
the mechanical digger, and he entertained a further subversive
thought: perhaps Flaubert was a great writer who had schooled
himself out of writing well. Even Nabokov, the most admiring of
these three witnesses to Flaubert's genius, spends a delicious page

itemizing the avoidable implausibilities that the master had incorporated into his text. What all Flaubert's fellow professionals agree on, despite their reservations, is that *Madame Bovary* marks a moment of decisive discontinuity in the history of the European novel, and that prose fiction produced in its wake, and under the influence of Flaubert's singular style, could move in directions that were quite new.

In part, the surprise that Flaubert sprang on the first readers of *Madame Bovary*, and that many readers coming to him for the first time at the beginning of the twenty-first century are still likely to experience, has to do with the banality of his subject matter and the relentless microscopic vision that he brought to bear on it. Emma and her provincial neighbours are little in moral stature, limited in intelligence, stunted in their ambitions, sordid in their private thoughts, and ridiculous in their public prating and posturing. Around his centrally placed married couple, locked into their miseries, Flaubert has laid out a gallery of unedifying stereotypes: Homais the self-seeking pharmacist, who represents secularism and republican virtue at their lowest ebb; Bournisien the fleshly priest, much given to empty ecclesiastical exhortation; Rodolphe the well-to-do landowner and full-time rake. No trade or profession escapes Flaubert's derision. No individual represents true decency. How can a serious novel, a work of high art, be made from material of this kind? And how can an artistic project aiming so low be sustained over hundreds of pages? These are genuine sources of puzzlement, and even when Flaubert's astonishing ironic gift has been recognized many readers are likely to find themselves wondering how it was ever possible to expend so much irony on targets such as these. With undimmed malice, Flaubert has Bournisien and Homais watch over Emma's corpse at the end of the novel, one of them sprinkling her room with holy water and the other with chlorine. This double gibe, although delivered in exquisite symmetrical syntax, surely comes too late in the day, and after too many sallies of the same sort.

If we follow various of the tourist trails through modern Normandy, looking out for the legacies of Emma, Charles, Homais, and Bournisien as we go, we are likely to be confirmed in the view that Flaubert has misjudged the task of the novelist and the wishes of his audience. The secluded world of Yonville-l'Abbaye and its surrounding hamlets exists to this day. The river Andelle still flows, and sudden vistas still guide the eye across the fields to an isolated church or chateau. The modern Ry, with its long main street, prides itself on being the prototype for Flaubert's imaginary village, and reminders of the novel, down to its tiniest descriptive phrases, are everywhere in the locality: the grey-white cliffs in the area are streaked with brick-red, as described at the beginning of Part II, and flowers grow on the roofs of thatched cottages, exactly as Flaubert specifies towards the end of the book (p. 301). For the modern visitor, as for Emma herself, the metropolis of Rouen is at once nearby and as remote from this quiet rural landscape as Jerusalem or Constantinople. Finding the topography of the novel still largely intact, preserved in a green museum just north of the N31, those who worry about such things are likely to begin worrying all over again about realism in fiction. Surely novelists of note must have better things to do with their time than to tell their readers what they already know, or can easily discover elsewhere. If one is going to map the contours of *la France profonde*, or trace out the flat expanses of an average bourgeois marriage or adulterous affair, one needs the leaven of metaphor, or ideas, or speculative adventure. The writing must crackle with invention at some level. One cannot just preside, poker-faced, over the everyday world, setting it down as a procession of precisely observed details, and expect one's reader to stay the course.

Flaubert certainly wanted to create a first impression of himself as the author of a guileless guidebook to a region and its manners. The flat, deadpan tone mattered to him, and he returned to it at intervals throughout the work. But other impressions are soon superimposed on this one. The miracle of Flaubert's writing is in the stealth with which he adjusts its focus from one word to the next, or from sentence to sentence. Proust's excavating machine is often to be heard in the background, and there are entire paragraphs of *Madame Bovary* that seem to be made of constricted telegrammatic utterances placed end to end, but even here the enumeration of details has a living pulse to it:

As there were not enough stable boys to unharness all the horses, the gentlemen rolled up their sleeves and got down to it themselves. Depending on their social position, they wore dress coats, frock coats, jackets both short and long: good-quality dress coats, treated with great respect by the entire family, and brought out of the wardrobe only on solemn occasions;

frock coats with voluminous tails that flapped in the breeze, cylindrical collars, and big pockets like miniature sacks; jackets of coarse cloth, generally worn with a brass-banded peaked cap; very short-skirted jackets with, at the back, two buttons close together like a pair of eyes, and tails that might have been hacked straight from a single piece of cloth with a carpenter's hatchet. (pp. 25–6)

These are the male guests arriving for the wedding of Emma and Charles, or rather this is their attire come loose from their bodies and recorded as a series of shapes and sociological meanings. On the one hand, the narrator seems to be having fun at the expense of his country folk, and to be suggesting, by way of a determined transfer of attention from persons to clothing, that local festivities of this kind are nothing but show and pantomime: all right if you live in a village, as Gertrude Stein once remarked, but if not, not. Failures of dress sense have been sorted into a jeering catalogue by one who clearly knows better about such matters than his Norman neighbours. On the other hand, however, something more akin to a musical exposition is also going on in this paragraph. There are three thematic kernels—dress coats, frock coats, and jackets—and each of them is no sooner stated than subjected to an elaborate process of variation. Flaubert's prose speaks of an ordinary world that is becoming fantastical even as each separate notation is set down: these country-dwellers are beginning to flap like birds and to grow eyes in the back of their jackets. And it speaks, too, of a playful, self-delighting intelligence at work upon whatever undistinguished fragments of the real world it finds to hand.

It will be plain to many readers of *Madame Bovary*, from its first page onwards, that this is a novel in which something strange and undeclared is going on, and that Flaubert has other than 'realist' designs upon us. Charles's famous cap—'Ovoid in shape, its curves enlarged with whalebone, it began with three circular sausage-shaped layers'—is already much more than a preliminary indicator of its owner's character. To be sure this exercise in ponderous description does tell us about the clumsiness and ill-fittingness of Charles himself, but it introduces us at the same time to another major tendency of Flaubert's imagination, by which he devalues and simultaneously revalorizes the objects that fall beneath his gaze. The cap is a concoction and a contraption, a bundle of heterogeneous components, yet at the same time it resembles a complex measuring device, a theodolite or an astrolabe perhaps, designed for use in two or more dimensions at once. In its concoctedness it resembles a work of art, and in its intersecting planes and conjoined materials it resembles an instrument of intellectual enquiry. This strange, stranded piece of headgear is a warning of excitements and provocations to come, and the first in a long Flaubertian series of uncanny, proto-surrealist assemblages.

By far the commonest, and most acclaimed, device used by Flaubert to float his own and his reader's attention between incompatible value-systems is the one known to critics of the novel as 'free indirect style'. This is a familiar enough feature of many literary works, and of everyday conversation for that matter, but Flaubert uses it with a persistence and range of implication that are quite new. Sometimes it simply involves a momentary discord, a single word that switches us from an impersonal to a personal viewpoint: 'And her husband, knowing that she enjoyed going for drives, found a second-hand gig which, once it was fitted with new lamps and splash-boards of quilted leather, looked almost like a tilbury' (p. 31). The conveyance named at the end of this sentence takes us from a no-nonsense narrative viewpoint, in which the refurbishment of shabby vehicles can be mentioned without shame, to the very heart of Emma's impatient aspirations. A tilbury, even an approximate one, would mark the beginning of an upward gradient in Emma's social life.

More telling, however, are those extended passages in which two systems seem to be cross-hatched, or in which two ways of looking at the world each provide the other with a distorting gravitational field. In this slightly later account of Emma's fantasies in full self-dramatizing swing, for example, narrator and character enter into a rapturous dialogue. Emma is already making damaging comparisons between her own marriage-partner and those that others are likely to have found for themselves:

For indeed not all husbands were like this one. He might have been handsome, witty, distinguished, attractive, as were no doubt the men her old school friends from the convent had married. What must they be doing now? In the city, with the noises of the streets, the hum of the theatres, and the bright lights of the balls, they were leading lives where the heart had space to expand, the senses to blossom. But her life was as cold as an attic with a skylight facing north, and boredom, like a silent spider, was weaving its web in every shadowy recess of her heart. (p. 41)

This is an impulsive interior monologue, a moving picture of day-dreaming as it happens, and at first the narrator's voice edits it only lightly. Emma speaks for herself, and is discreetly nudged from time to time towards symmetry in her phrasing or precision in her diction. But in the last sentence there is a change of gear. The narrator both wants and does not want to share her view of things. The meagre skylight, the northern prospect, and the busy spider are borrowed from Emma's favourite adolescent reading. They are literary hand-me-downs, the prefabricated parts of a Gothic stage-set. Yet *ennui*, that special, virulent sub-species of boredom, was a badge of honour for certain of Flaubert's poetic contemporaries, and for the novelist himself at times. Baudelaire praised its repulsiveness highly, and imagined with relish a hideous population of spiders at work in the bored individual's brain. Emma, using her own version of the image, has become a woman of her time, and a poet of sorts. Her still adolescent habits of imagination have brought her into radical company, and the commentator who seemed to despise her a moment ago has suddenly found in her a soul-mate, and a fellow devotee of extreme emotional states.

There is, then, a counter-current of poetic suggestion running through Flaubert's portrait of the Normandy landscape and its desperate middle-class inhabitants. On the face of it everything in the human realm is flat and drab, and the beauties of nature can do little to enliven or elevate the minimal life-stories that unfold here. Yet the voice of the narrator, as it shrinks and then suddenly expands its range of sympathies, proves to be a very unreliable guide to this supposedly worthless rural scene. That voice absorbs and re-inflects other people's points of view, and in so doing becomes mobile and accommodating. 'What will he do next?', the reader begins to ask of this capricious narrator. There can be no real doubt, for example, that Rodolphe, the first lover Emma finds outside her marriage to Charles Bovary, is a cad and a boor, and the following passage certainly begins by emphasizing his lack of discrimination. Rodolphe is reacting to Emma's declarations of love and admiration, all of which he has heard before, from earlier mistresses:

He could not see—this man of such broad experience—the difference of feeling, beneath the similarity of expression. Because wanton or venal lips had murmured the same words to him, he only half believed in the sincerity of those he was hearing now; to a large extent they should be disregarded, he believed, because such exaggerated language must surely mask commonplace feelings: as if the soul in its fullness did not sometimes overflow into the most barren metaphors, since no one can ever tell the precise measure of his own needs, of his own ideas, of his own pain, and human language is like a cracked kettle on which we beat out tunes for bears to dance to, when what we long to do is make music that will move the stars to pity. (p. 170)

With the words 'as if the soul in its fullness' a halt is called to the flow of Rodolphe's self-justifying reverie on the language of lovers. The narrator takes Rodolphe's views seriously, thinks of them indeed as a fledgling philosophy of language, and enters into debate with them. Even a scoundrel may be worth arguing with. The narrator corrects an imperceptive character, and offers a superior philosophical basis for any future enquiry into amorous speech. The arbitrariness of the verbal sign, much discussed in modern linguistic theory, is already here, as is the importance of considering context in seeking to understand any communicative act. A hinge in the middle of the paragraph thus connects the views of a cad with a fine tragic insight into the limitations of human language. Abruptly, in the last sentence, a universal sorrow and rage sing out, and mere Rodolphe has acted as the pretext for their song.

Flaubert clearly enjoys the company of fools, and beats the drum with relish for his dancing bears. But there is much more to the design of the book, and to the virtuosity of its execution, than these singular moments of collusion between a storyteller and his cast of characters. Such moments are distributed throughout the novel and together create a pattern of long-range echoes and refrains, but much of the internal architecture of Flaubert's narrative involves a smaller and more elastic series of supporting struts. For many readers of the text in its original French the first inkling of this quality will come not from large movements of recurrence, but from the fall of sounds and phrases within individual sentences. Flaubert has a predilection for things, actions, or attributes that come at him in threes, and the shoes worn by the young Charles Bovary on the first page of the novel—'heavy, badly shined, and studded with nails'—offer a foretaste of countless formulations of the same three-fold kind. He also enjoys assonance, alliteration, rhyme, and near-rhyme, and these features can descend as a seemingly gratuitous sound-texture upon any incidental observation: 'L'air, passant par le dessous de la porte, poussait un peu de poussière sur les dalles' ('A draught of air from under the door stirred a little dust on the flag-stones', p. 22). On occasion the triadic obsession and the sound-play coincide to produce a bizarre effect of motiveless emphasis: 'Un peu plus bas, cependant, on était rafraîchi par un courant d'air glacial qui sentait le suif, le cuir et l'huile' ('But just a little further away, refreshing gusts of chilly air smelling of tallow, leather, and oil could be felt', p. 196). Emma is about to see Donizetti's *Lucia di Lammermoor* for the first time, and the air of Rouen is already alive with a premonition of tunes and harmonies. In both these cases, it is the silent air that suddenly breaks into sound inside the Flaubert sentence, but any neutral or characterless medium can be turned into sensory stuff in the same way. At this local level, the novelist's self-appointed task is clearly that of bringing ordinary things together into an enchanted interlace. Even agriculture can be musicalized by verbal art: Emma's father, visiting the young couple at their first home together, talks insistently of 'veaux, vaches, volailles' ('calves, cows, poultry', p. 60).

The web of connections operating on a larger scale between the separate phases of Flaubert's plot is the novel's most extraordinary feature. Moreover, one of these combined patterns of sound and sense comes close to offering Flaubert's own commentary on his narrative technique. It concerns the passage of meaning across space and time, and the waning of meaning that sets in as the novel moves towards its bleak denouement. The key terms in the miniature lexi-con concerned are 'loin', 'lointain', 'éloigner', 'vague', and, bringing with them a further series of events that unfold in empty air, 'vibra-tion' and its synonyms. This language of distance and remoteness, of far horizons and reverberating sound, cuts across the exact technical languages—of farming, pharmacy, medicine, and commerce—that Flaubert also exploits exhaustively. Flaubert's dry-goods store of useful objects has a current of vagueness and inscrutability running through it.

II

Emma Bovary is one of European literature's most celebrated dreamers and fantasists, and she is introduced to us as a specialist in long perspectives that end mistily. In Part I of the novel, this note is struck often, and with no more than a tinge of disapproval on the narrator's part. Looking into the distance may, after all, be the sign of a forward-flung creative mind at work:

And in her thoughts she followed them, up and down the hills, through the villages, racing along the highway by the light of the stars. Then, always, after an indeterminate distance, things became a blur, and her dream died away. (p. 52)

But, very gradually, the circle whose centre he was grew larger round him, and that halo he wore shifted away from him, to shine its radiance on other dreams. (p. 52)

They lived on a higher plane than other people, somewhere sublime between heaven and earth, among the storm clouds. As for the rest of the world, it was lost in shadows, it was nowhere, it seemed not to exist. Indeed, the closer things were to Emma, the more her thoughts avoided them. (p. 53)

In the first of these extracts, Emma is imagining the travels of a fish-vendor's cart, in the second remembering the mysterious Vicomte with whom she had danced at the ball of La Vaubyessard, and in the third dreaming of superior people at large. But in all three cases, her mind, for all its lack of self-aware analytic power, is presented as an active force. It builds possible worlds. It projects itself into realizable futures. And even when a blur sets in and dreams die away, Emma is in good company—that of all strenuous thinkers who have had exactly this sensation of an intellectual limit being reached.

Flaubert's heroine is soon to be firmly censured for her distance-seeking habits of mind and for the cult of vagueness that they seem to foster, and her error is linked with the misuse of the printed word. Léon, a clerk who has a serious passion for prose fiction, has just praised books for the fantasies they encourage, and for the passions they allow readers to savour at second hand:

'That's true! That's true!' [she said.]

'Have you ever had the experience', Léon continued, 'of finding, in a book, some vague idea you've had, some shadowy image from the depths of your being (*de loin*), which now seems to express perfectly your most subtle feelings?'

'Yes, I have,' she replied. (p. 75)

Passages of this kind are theatricalized exercises in literary criticism and have two principal targets: literary authors who promote either

sentimentality or mental slackness generally, and readers who do not
know how to read. Flaubert assails both groups with acerbity and
irrepressible comic invention. If Emma had read better books, and
read them better, he seems to imply, she would not now be in her
advanced delusional state. Second-rate books have rotted her judgement, and undermined her survival instinct. If only she had been
able to keep a clear eye on things close at hand—been more of a
realist, as one might say—she could have achieved intellectual
coherence, self-control, and a worthwhile role in the community.

Yet Flaubert's criticism of poor reading habits does not in fact
take him very far in this direction. His tenderness towards Emma is
intense, and all the more moving for having no loose sentiment in it.
The plain facts of her case are what matters, and the material
medium in which her life is led. And this is where resonance and
reverberation enter his drama, offering their own view of distance,
disappearance, and the ending of the human life-span. Bells ring
often in *Madame Bovary*. Their sound carries over long distances,
and expires slowly. They join forces with other resonating chambers,
man-made and natural, to create an animated acoustic picture:

She sank into that kind of brooding which comes when you lose something for ever, that lassitude you feel after every irreversible event, that
pain you suffer when a habitual movement is interrupted, when a long-
sustained vibration is suddenly broken off. (p. 110)

Then she heard, in the distance, from the other side of the wood, on those
other hills, a vague, long-drawn-out cry, a voice that seemed to linger in
the air, and she listened to it in silence, as it blended like a melody with the
last vibrations of her tingling nerves. (p. 143)

The chill of the night spurred them to more passionate embraces; the
sighs on their lips seemed to them more ardent; their eyes, dimly seen,
seemed to them larger, and, in the silence, low-spoken words dropped into
their hearts with a crystalline ring, echoing there with an ever-growing
resonance (*en vibrations multipliées*). (p. 150)

These are all sexual as well as sonorous vibrations: the first passage
refers to Léon's departure from Yonville, and to the state of semi-
arousal that his presence had recently provoked in Emma; the second
and third concern her lovemaking with Rodolphe, and its afterglow
of sympathetic sound-echoes from the natural world around them.
But in all such cases Flaubert's scientific reminder is clear: the
human organism vibrates, for its nerve-structure ordains that it

should, and that quality of rhythm or periodicity inside the individual connects him or her to the larger process of nature. This imagery is perhaps closer to Franz Anton Mesmer's recently fashionable doctrine of universal 'animal magnetism' than to the latest physiological discoveries of Flaubert's own day, but its force is of an entirely this-worldly kind: humans are excitable organisms, however much they try to spiritualize and etherealize themselves, and it is in the nature of things that such entities should come into being, flourish for a while, and then cease to be. Vibrations in due course stop. Bells fall silent. At the hands of nature, or by their own hand, people die.

If Emma behaves self-defeatingly in her choice of reading matter, therefore, and is rather contemptible in her taste for far-off things, she is altogether admirable in her creaturely self-assertion. She is a sexual being, a vibratory power-source, and seeks to fill the empty space of reverie with the spasms and transports of her own desire. She is a fully sentient everywoman and everyman, and, while bringing a characteristic touch of stage-management to her own dying, understands her own mortality as part of the natural order:

They were behind her forever, thought Emma, all the betrayals, the infamies, and the myriad cravings that had tormented her. She did not hate anyone, now; a twilight confusion was settling over her thoughts, and, of all the world's sounds, Emma heard only the intermittent sobbing of that poor man, soft and faint, like the fading echo of an ever-more distant symphony. (p. 283)

Flaubert is closer here to sentimentality than anywhere else in the novel, and these sentences, read in isolation, may seem to offer a coyly consoling view of death. Occupying their proper place in the elaboration of the text, however, they bring Flaubert's natural history of human feeling to a cogent culminating point. Emma is dying, Charles is lost in grief, and the sounds of nature are continuing to vibrate around them. Her extinction has been many times foretold in the sound-world of the novel, and the 'intermittent sobbing' of Charles and its gradual falling away into silence are the last premonition of what is soon to occur. Just as the sound of a struck chord decays, or as biological processes reach their term, so Emma dies. An 'ever-more distant symphony' connects her not only to the noise of nature but to the cadenced prose and the acoustic artifice of her creator.

III

Flaubert became famous in his lifetime for the supposed extreme cruelty with which he described his heroine's downfall and death. He was depicted in a cartoon of the day as a bloodstained surgeon, triumphantly butchering his own fictional creature. And those commentators on the novel who dwell at length on Flaubert's irony have tended in their own quieter way to suggest that the art of dissection is his main business. Madness is everywhere, they point out, from the preposterous forenames of the Homais offspring to the three coffins, one inside the next, in which Emma Bovary is eventually laid to rest. Irony is the instrument—by turns lancet, scalpel, and surgical saw—by means of which the intricate anatomy of human folly is exposed to view. Such an account of the novel's tone and manner does fit certain of the textual facts rather well, and we would not be reading it with the imaginative absorption it demands if we did not sometimes find ourselves wincing, cringing, or laughing aloud at the performance. But the emotional texture of Flaubert's book is much richer than this suggests, even in its bravura pieces for the ironic imagination.

The following, for example, is one such piece, in which Emma dreams of eloping with Rodolphe to the sun-drenched south:

Often, from a mountaintop, they'd catch a sudden glimpse of a magnificent city with domes, and bridges, and ships, and forests of lemon trees and cathedrals of white marble, whose slender steeples were capped by storks' nests. Their carriage had slowed to walking pace because of the enormous flagstones; the ground was strewn with bouquets of flowers that women in red bodices held up to you as you passed by. You could hear the ringing of bells and the whinnying of mules, blending with the murmur of guitars and the sound of fountains, the moisture from which, carried on the breeze, was cooling pyramids of fruit heaped below pale statues that smiled through the flying spray. And then, one evening, they'd come to a fishing village, where brown nets lay drying in the wind along the cliff and in front of the cottages. This was where they'd stop and make their home: they'd live in a low, flat-roofed house shaded by a palm tree, in the shelter of a bay, by the sea. They'd ride in gondolas, they'd laze in swaying hammocks, and their life would be free and flowing like their silken garments, warm and star-studded like the soft night skies they'd gaze at. (p. 174)

At one level this is a simple caricature of the Mediterranean landscape as seen by residents of the chilly north. In a succession of tiny snapshots Flaubert seems to acquire clairvoyant knowledge of the modern tourist industry, complete with its package holidays and gleaming brochures, and Emma's *vita nuova* proves to be wondrously tawdry and novelettish. The syntax in which the whole survey is conducted is enumerative rather than hierarchical, as befits the continuous gliding of desire from one fantasy gratification to the next. All of us who have taken lazy journeys south stand accused by those fishing nets, gondolas, and hammocks.

Yet this is also a portrait of fiction being born, and Flaubert is too self-conscious an artist to miss the points of comparison between his own calling as a novelist and the plot-making in which Emma indulges. The story she tells herself has an abrupt beginning, an eventful middle, and a reposeful end; it has protagonists and minor characters; it has adventure, surprises, and colourful incidents, and edges the interwoven human sense-fields towards a dizzying neurological overload. The occupants of the ever-changing scene are magically attuned to the sounds and rhythms of nature.

The echoes that pass between Flaubert's own performance as a writer and the doomed self-inventions of his protagonist are such as to make Henry James's talk of Emma's 'poverty of consciousness' seem, for a great critic, oddly wide of the mark. If we imagine that consciousness isolated for a moment from the feints and ruses of Flaubert's literary style, it proves to be an unusual, multiform thing: Emma, after all, is a person who can desire at one and the same time, and with no sense of contradiction, to die and to move to Paris (p. 54). But as soon as we put this active changeable mind back into the force field of Flaubert's writing, matters become altogether more complex. The 'grammatical beauty' that Proust described, and the poetry that Nabokov found in Flaubert's prose, create diffraction patterns across the textual surface of the book, and these patterns, in their turn, create a continuous lattice of cross-references between the novelist at work and the life led by his principal character. At the risk of making a grave category mistake, we could say that Emma and Flaubert share a mind, and an art, and that their joint consciousness suffers not at all from poverty.

Madame Bovary contains countless comments on stylistic questions, and many implicit comparisons between the style of the novel we are reading and the verbal habits, many of them objectionable, of its characters. Homais, for example, holds up a mirror to his creator while preparing to break the news to Emma of her father-in-law's death: 'He had pondered over what to say, making his phraseology more orotund, more polished, and more harmonious; it was a masterpiece of prudence, judicious transitions, subtle wording, and delicacy' (p. 222). For a moment, Flaubert's own meticulous crafts-manship is in the dock, charged with hypocrisy and bad faith. Yet the complicity between Emma and Flaubert is much more intimate and revealing than passing self-commentaries of this kind. Emma, as we have noted, is alert to echoes and resonances in the world around her, and is presented as a fragile and destructible component of the nat-ural order. Flaubert's writing, beyond the apparent dryness of its many clipped formulations, becomes an echo-chamber in its own right. Assonance, alliteration, rhyme, the syntactic mirroring of sen-tence in sentence, and the long-distance play between images all combine to produce the sympathetic word-web in which Emma is enfolded. When it comes to the originality of Flaubert's narrative technique these patterns of repetition and recall deserve particular mention, for they not only connect phase to phase within an unfold-ing tragic tale but they give narrative itself a role in Flaubert's nat-ural history of the human imagination: we live our creaturely lives in the sentences we place end to end, and in the stories we wish them to tell. We live at the mercy of the fictions we ourselves create.

For many critics and historians of French literature, Flaubert is by far the most modern of the great nineteenth-century novelists, and it is easy to see why. While being an originator of 'realism' in prose fiction, and one of its touchstones, he also looks beyond the realist dispensation, and rejoins the playful, self-reflexive tradition of Cer-vantes, Rabelais, and Sterne. What makes his writing in *Madame Bovary* distinctively modern, however, rather than the simple con-tinuation of an earlier self-conscious literary manner, is the extreme vulnerability that Flaubert ascribes to writers in the exercise of their craft. They live with the arbitrariness of language, and make it their own. The wordscapes they create for themselves are porous and transitory. The sounds they make reverberate in the empty air. Small wonder, therefore, that Flaubert should have felt so close to his chronically deluded heroine, and that his best-known remark about her should have been 'Madame Bovary, c'est moi!'

NOTE ON THE TEXT

Flaubert was 30 years old when he set to work on *Madame Bovary*, had published almost nothing, and, beyond his immediate circle, had little by way of reputation. Starting in 1851, he laboured for almost five years on the manuscript of his novel and, in an extraordinary series of letters to friends, produced a simultaneous chronicle of the creative process. Although he was conscious of his own singular talent, and had already written a great deal, he was beset by doubts at every stage, and complained at length about the sheer drudgery of literary composition. In a letter to his mistress and fellow writer Louise Colet, for example, written in January 1852, he describes 'les affres du style' ('the agony of style'):

Work had not gone well; I had reached a point at which I really did not know what to say. It was all nuances, all finesse, and I couldn't see a thing myself, and it is very difficult to express clearly something which is still only a vague thought. I have sketched and botched, floundered and fumbled. Perhaps I shall find my way again now. What a devil of a thing it is, style! I do believe you have no idea what sort of book this is. Slovenly as I was in my other books, in this one, I am trying to be neatly buttoned up and to follow a geometrically straight line. No lyricism, no reflection, author's personality absent. It will make melancholy reading; there will be things atrociously distressing and fetid.[1]

Two years later, his mood has changed, and he is now in the throes of an astonishing erotic infatuation with his heroine:

Since two in the afternoon (apart from about 25 minutes when I was having supper) I have been writing *Bovary*. I've reached the Big Fuck, I'm right in the middle of it. We are in a sweat, and our heart is nearly in our mouth. This has been one of the rare days of my life which I have spent in a state of complete Enchantment, from beginning to end. Just now, around six o'clock, at the moment when I wrote the phrase *a nervous attack*, I was so carried away, I was making such a racket, and feeling so intensely what my little woman was feeling, that I began to fear I was about to have one myself. I stood up from my writing-table and I opened the window to calm myself down. My head was spinning. I still have sharp

---

[1] Quotations from Flaubert's correspondence are from *Selected Letters*, trans. and ed. Geoffrey Wall (London: Penguin, 1997).

pains in my knees, in my back and in my head. I am like a man who has just come too much (if you will forgive me the expression). I mean a sort of lassitude which is full of exhilaration. And since I am *in the midst of love*, it is most appropriate that I do not go to bed before sending you a caress, a kiss, and all the thoughts that are still on my mind. (23 December 1853)

Although the scenes of lovemaking in the novel itself are a great deal more restrained than this account of the artist's solitary aches and pleasures, the novel attracted the attention of Napoleon III's censors as soon as it began to appear, and it was duly prosecuted as an offence against religion and morality.

Madame Bovary was published in the autumn of 1856 in the *Revue de Paris*, and in book form the following April. Flaubert dedicated his work to Marie-Antoine-Jules Sénard, the barrister who had successfully defended him during his trial. This dedication, reprinted in the present volume, still has its eloquence, and serves as reminder of just how dangerous *Madame Bovary* was thought to be by certain of its earliest readers. Even today the *Bovary* trial serves as a major reference point in discussions of literary censorship.

The texture of Flaubert's writing in *Madame Bovary* is remarkable for its economy and precision, and throughout he seems intent on vindicating the aesthetic principle 'less is more'. These qualities are all the more remarkable when one sets the novel against Flaubert's earlier works of prose fiction, in which rhapsodizing exuberance had been to the fore, and against his personal letters, which are often freewheeling, ranting, and hyperbolic in manner. 'Having to say everyday things simply and clearly', he wrote to Colet in March 1853, 'It's atrocious!'

NOTE ON THE TRANSLATION

This translation of *Madame Bovary* is based on the Garnier-Flammarion edition of 1986, cross-referenced with other editions.

Flaubert used italics to foreground, and to distance himself from, certain cliché-like phrases that represent a collective, anonymous voice expressing popular lore or conventional judgments, and French editions, as well as most translations, preserve these italics. In the present version such phrases appear in quotation marks.

Whenever possible, I have respected Flaubert's idiosyncratic paragraphing, which he used for emphasis and to slow down the narrative flow at appropriate junctures. Apart from the suppression of an occasional 'he/she said,' my only intentional departure from Flaubert's text occurs in Part III, ch. 5, p. 235, where I substituted 'our slippers' for 'my slippers', to conform to the logic of the sentence. I could find no way to preserve a number of regional expressions such as *boc, masure, érifler* that Flaubert wove into his narrative, the better to embed it in the Normandy countryside; however I know only too well that there are other, more crucial, elements that have also been 'lost in translation'. I can only say that I have done my utmost to be faithful to Flaubert.

Many people have helped me during my work on this translation. My warm thanks go to my editor Judith Luna for entrusting me with *Madame Bovary* and for her sensitive support; to Ron Rosbottom and his students at Amherst College for some lively discussions about translation; to my neighbours at Applewood for their genuine interest; to my life-long friend Elizabeth Chadwick for our wonderful trip round 'Bovary' country; to computer wizard Edward O'Connor; to my son-in-law David Wheeler and all my dear family for technical advice (sorely needed), encouragement, and love. This translation is in memory of Jim, and for Jane, Matthew, Maria, and Lucy.

Margaret Mauldon

SELECT BIBLIOGRAPHY

Editions

Two editions of the French text of *Madame Bovary* may be recommended:

(i) ed. Mark Overstall (London: Harrap, 1979), introduction and notes in English
(ii) ed. Claudine Gothot-Mersch (Paris: Garnier, 1971), the standard French critical edition

Those wishing to study the genesis of the French text should consult *Madame Bovary: nouvelle version, précédée des scénarios inédits*, ed. Jean Pommier and Gabrielle Leleu (Paris: Corti, 1949) and *Plans et scénarios de Madame Bovary*, ed. Yvan Leclerc (Paris: CNRS, 1995).

Readers who have enjoyed *Madame Bovary* should go on to try *L'Éducation sentimentale, Trois contes*, and *Bouvard et Pécuchet*; all are available in paperback English translations. *Salammbô* and *La Tentation de Saint Antoine* are for devotees.

Biographies and Letters

A selection of Flaubert's letters is presented in Francis Steegmuller, *The Letters of Gustave Flaubert 1830–1857* (Cambridge, Mass., and London: Harvard University Press, 1980). The most up-to-date and informative biographies of Flaubert are Herbert Lottmann, *Flaubert: A Biography* (London: Methuen, 1989), and Geoffrey Wall, *Flaubert: A Life* (London: Faber, 2001). See also Enid Starkie, *Flaubert: The Making of the Master* and *Flaubert the Master: A Critical and Biographical Study* (London: Weidenfeld and Nicolson, 1967 and 1971), and *Gustave Flaubert: Selected Letters*, trans. and ed. Geoffrey Wall (London: Penguin, 1997).

Critical Studies

Three essays on Flaubert by Henry James, first published in 1876, 1893, and 1902, provide a good starting point for critical reading on Flaubert and an interesting picture of the development of James's ideas. The whole of the substantial 1902 essay, originally an introduction to a translation of *Madame Bovary*, and sections of the other two relevant to this novel, may be found in *Henry James: The Critical Muse. Selected Literary Criticism* (London: Penguin, 1987). All three essays are to be found complete in Henry James, *Literary Criticism*, ii (New York: The Library of America,

1984). Among more recent studies in English, the following (in chronological order of publication) are recommended:

Thorlby, Anthony, *Gustave Flaubert and the Art of Realism* (London: Bowes and Bowes, 1956)

Ullmann, Stephen, *Style in the French Novel* (Oxford: Blackwell, 1960)

Fairlie, Alison, *Flaubert: Madame Bovary* (London: Edward Arnold, 1962)

Levin, Harry, *The Gates of Horn: A Study of Five French Realists* (New York: Oxford University Press, 1963)

Bart, B. F., *Madame Bovary and the Critics: A Collection of Essays* (New York: New York University Press, 1966)

Brombert, Victor, *The Novels of Flaubert: A Study of Themes and Techniques* (Princeton: Princeton University Press, 1966)

Steegmuller, Francis, *Flaubert and Madame Bovary*, rev. edn. (London and Melbourne: Macmillan, 1968)

Sherrington, R. J., *Three Novels by Flaubert* (Oxford: Oxford University Press, 1970)

Nadeau, Maurice, *The Greatness of Flaubert*, trans. Barbara Bray (London: The Alcove Press, 1972)

Culler, Jonathan, *Flaubert: The Uses of Uncertainty* (London: Paul Elek, 1974)

Tanner, Tony, *Adultery in the Novel: Contract and Transgression* (Baltimore and London: The Johns Hopkins University Press, 1979)

La Capra, Dominick, *Madame Bovary on Trial* (Ithaca, NY, and London: Cornell University Press, 1982)

Lowe, Margaret, *Towards the Real Flaubert* (Oxford: Clarendon Press, 1984)

Haig, Stirling, *Flaubert and the Gift of Speech: Dialogue and Discourse in Four 'Modern' Novels* (Cambridge: Cambridge University Press, 1986)

Prendergast, Christopher, *The Order of Mimesis: Balzac, Stendhal, Nerval, Flaubert* (Cambridge: Cambridge University Press, 1986)

Knight, Diana, *Flaubert's Characters* (Cambridge: Cambridge University Press, 1989)

Roe, David, *Gustave Flaubert* (London: Macmillan, 1989)

Lloyd, Rosemary, *Madame Bovary* (London: Unwin Hyman, 1990)

Heath, Stephen, *Gustave Flaubert: Madame Bovary* (Cambridge: Cambridge University Press, 1992)

Further Reading in Oxford World's Classics

Flaubert, Gustave, *A Sentimental Education*, trans. and ed. Douglas Parmée.
—— *Three Tales*, trans. and ed. A. J. Krailsheimer.

A CHRONOLOGY OF GUSTAVE FLAUBERT

1802   Achille Flaubert, Gustave's father, comes to Paris to study medicine.

1810   Achille Flaubert moves to Rouen to work as deputy head of the hospital (the Hôtel-Dieu).

1812   Achille Flaubert marries the adopted daughter of the head of the Hôtel-Dieu.

1813   Gustave's brother Achille-Cléophas born.

1819   Achille Flaubert appointed head of Hôtel-Dieu on the death of his superior.

1821   12 December: Gustave Flaubert born.

1824   July: Gustave's sister Caroline born.

1836   While at school in Rouen, writes several stories. On holiday at Trouville, falls in love with Elisa Foucault, a woman of 26, who shortly afterwards marries Maurice Schlésinger. The image of Elisa Schlésinger recurs in a number of Flaubert's writings: in particular, she is said to be the model for Madame Arnoux in *L'Éducation sentimentale*.

1837   More stories. One of these, *Une leçon d'histoire naturelle, genre Commis*, is published in a local journal; another, *Passion et vertu*, anticipates the story of *Madame Bovary* in certain respects.

1838   *Mémoires d'un fou*, an autobiographical narrative; *Loys XI*, a five-act play.

1839   Completes *Smarh*, a semi-dramatic fantasy which may be considered an embryonic version of *La Tentation de Saint Antoine*.

1841   November: registers as law student in Paris, though continuing to live at home.

1842   *Novembre*, another autobiographical narrative. Passes his first law examination.

1843   Begins the first version of *L'Éducation sentimentale*. Fails his second law examination.

1844   Has a form of epileptic seizure. Gives up law. April: Flaubert's father buys a house at Croisset, near Rouen. June: the Flaubert family moves to Croisset.

1845 *L'Éducation sentimentale* (first version) completed.

1846 Flaubert's father and sister die. He sets up house at Croisset with his mother and niece. Meets Louise Colet in Paris; she becomes his mistress.

1847 *Par les champs et par les grèves*, impressions of his travels in Brittany with his literary friend Maxime Du Camp.

1848 Together with Louis Bouilhet (another literary friend) and Maxime Du Camp, witnesses the 1848 uprising in Paris; he will later draw on these memories for scenes in *L'Éducation sentimentale*. Begins *La Tentation de Saint Antoine* (first version).

1849 Reads *La Tentation* aloud to Bouilhet and Du Camp, who consider it a failure. Leaves for a tour of the Near East with Du Camp.

1850 February: they journey up the Nile. May: they cross the desert by camel. August: death of Balzac; Flaubert and Du Camp reach Jerusalem. September: they abandon plans to travel to Persia and turn west. October: Rhodes. November: Constantinople. December: Athens.

1851 April: Flaubert in Rome; Du Camp returns to Paris. May: Flaubert returns to Croisset; resumes relations with Louise Colet. 19 September: begins writing *Madame Bovary*.

1852 While working on *Madame Bovary*, recalls his earlier project for a *Dictionnaire des idées reçues*.

1854 End of affair with Louise Colet.

1856 *Madame Bovary* completed and published in serial form in *La Revue de Paris* (from 1 October). Begins to revise *La Tentation*.

1856–7 Fragments of *La Tentation* published in *L'Artiste*.

1857 Flaubert and *La Revue de Paris* prosecuted for irreligion and immorality; acquitted. The trial attracts a great deal of attention and makes *Madame Bovary* (now published as a complete novel) a *succès de scandale*. Begins work on *Salammbô*.

1858 Visits North Africa to gather material for *Salammbô*.

1862 *Salammbô* completed and published: an enormous success. Flaubert by now a famous literary figure.

1863 January: first letter to George Sand. February: first meeting with Turgenev.

1864 Begins work on *L'Éducation sentimentale*. In the course of the next five years gathers material for his novel, and at the same time enjoys a brilliant social life.

1866   August: nominated Chevalier de la Légion d'honneur.
           November: George Sand's first visit to Croisset.

1869   *L'Éducation sentimentale* (definitive version) completed and
           published. Death of Louis Bouilhet.

1870   Works on yet another version of *La Tentation de Saint Antoine*.
           August: Franco–Prussian War begins. December: victorious
           German troops arrive in Rouen.

1871   January: armistice signed with Prussia. May: insurrection in
           Paris. July: German troops leave Rouen.

1872   Flaubert's mother dies. Third version of *La Tentation*
           completed.

1874   *La Tentation* published. Begins work on *Bouvard et Pécuchet*.

1875–7   Writes *La Légende de Saint Julien l'Hospitalier, Un Cœur simple*,
           and *Hérodias (Trois contes)*.

1877   *Trois contes* published. Returns to *Bouvard et Pécuchet*.

1877–80   Works on *Bouvard*, which will remain unfinished.

1880   8 May: dies.

1881   *Bouvard et Pécuchet* published. House at Croisset sold and later
           demolished to make way for a distillery.

1882   January: death of brother, Achille Flaubert.

MADAME BOVARY

TO

MARIE-ANTOINE-JULES SÉNARD*

Member of the Paris Bar

Ex-President of the National Assembly and

Former Minister of the Interior

Dear and Illustrious Friend,

allow me to inscribe your name on the first page of this book, which I dedicate to you as having been chiefly responsible for its publication. As a result of the magnificent way in which you conducted my case, my work has conferred upon me, its author, an authority which I had no reason to anticipate. I should like you, therefore, to accept this token of my gratitude. However great it be, it can never adequately repay either your eloquence or your devoted loyalty.

GUSTAVE FLAUBERT

Paris, 12 April 1857

PART ONE

CHAPTER I

We were at prep* when the Headmaster came in, followed by a 'new boy' not wearing school uniform, and by a school servant carrying a large desk. Those who had been asleep woke up, and we all rose to our feet as though we had been interrupted at our work.

The Headmaster motioned to us to be seated; then, turning to the master on duty:

'Monsieur Roger,' he said in a low voice, 'this is a pupil I'm putting in your hands. He's starting in the fifth. If his work and his conduct warrant it, he'll be moved up to the "seniors", which is where he should be, given his age.'

Still standing well back, in the corner behind the door, so that he was almost invisible, the 'new boy' was a country lad of about fifteen who towered over the rest of us. He wore his hair in a straight fringe across his brow, like a village choirboy, and he looked sensible and very ill at ease. Although his shoulders were not particularly broad, his green cloth jacket with black buttons seemed tight round the armholes, and revealed, through the slits of his cuffs, sun-reddened wrists unaccustomed to being covered. His legs, clad in blue stockings, stuck out below a pair of yellowish trousers that were hitched up very high by his braces. His shoes were heavy, badly shined, and studded with nails.

We began reciting our lessons. He listened attentively, concentrating as though listening to a sermon, not daring even to cross his legs or lean on his elbow, and, at two o'clock, when the bell rang, the master had to tell him to line up with us all.

We were in the habit, on entering our classroom, of flinging our caps onto the floor, so as to leave our hands free; you had to stand at the threshold and hurl your cap under the bench, hitting the wall and raising clouds of dust; it was 'the thing' to do.

But, either because he had not noticed this manoeuvre or because he did not dare try it, prayers were over and the 'new boy' was still holding his cap on his knees. It was one of those head coverings of composite order, in which one recognizes features of a military busby, a lancer's cap, a bowler hat, an otter-skin cap, and a cotton nightcap, one of those pathetic objects, in fact, whose mute ugliness reveals great depths, like the face of a halfwit. Ovoid in shape, its curves enlarged with whalebone, it began with three circular sausage-shaped layers; then, after a band of red, came alternating diamond-shaped patches of velvet and rabbit fur; next there was a kind of bag, its top a stiffened polygon covered in intricately frogged braid, from which hung, at the end of a long, skinny cord, a little knot of gold threads, in place of a tassel. It was new; the peak shone.

'Stand up,' said the master.

He stood up; his cap fell down. The whole class began to laugh.

He bent over to pick it up. A boy beside him knocked it down again with his elbow; he picked it up again.

'I suggest you disencumber yourself of your helmet,' said the master, a man of wit.

A roar of laughter came from the class and disconcerted the poor lad, who could not decide whether he should keep his cap in his hand, put in on the floor, or place it on his head. He sat down again and put it on his lap.

'Stand up,' repeated the master, 'and tell me your name.'

The 'new boy' mumbled something completely unintelligible.

'Again!'

The same mumbled syllables emerged, drowned by the jeering of the class.

'Louder!' cried the master. 'Louder!'

With desperate resolve the 'new boy' opened his mouth stupendously wide and bellowed at the top of his lungs, as if shouting for someone, the word: '*Charbovari*.'*

The ensuing hullabaloo began instantaneously and grew louder and louder, punctuated by shrill shrieks. They howled, they bayed, they stamped, repeating '*Charbovari! Charbovari!*' again and again. The din rumbled along, with occasional isolated bursts of sound, dying away only with extreme reluctance and occasionally starting up afresh along one of the benches where, like a half-spent squib, a smothered laugh would suddenly erupt.

Little by little, however, a deluge of penalties restored order in the classroom, and the master, finally grasping the name of Charles Bovary after having it dictated and spelled out and then rereading it himself, promptly ordered the poor devil to go and sit on the dunce's seat at the foot of the rostrum. He began to get up, but then hesitated.

'What are you looking for?' asked the master.

'My ca . . .' replied the 'new boy' timidly, glancing round uneasily.

'The entire class gets five hundred lines!' This infuriated declaration, like Neptune's '*Quos ego*,'* quelled a fresh storm. 'Silence!' continued the indignant teacher, mopping his brow with a handkerchief he had taken from inside his cap. 'And as for you, "new boy",' he said, 'you'll copy out the entire conjugation of *ridiculus sum* twenty times!'

Then, in a gentler voice:

'You'll get it back, your cap; no one's stolen it!'

All was calm once more. Heads bent over copy-books, and for two hours the conduct of the 'new boy' was exemplary, despite the occasional paper pellet, launched from a quill, that spattered his face. But he wiped his cheeks with his hand and continued sitting quietly, with lowered eyes.

That evening, in prep, he took his cuff-protectors from his desk, set out all his little belongings, and ruled his paper with great care. We watched him working conscientiously, looking up everything in the dictionary and taking a lot of trouble. This display of assiduity was probably why he was not moved down to the lower form, for, although he showed a reasonable knowledge of the rules, his style lacked elegance. The village curé had given him his grounding in Latin, for his parents, to save money, had delayed sending him away to school until as late as possible.

His father, Monsieur Charles-Denis-Bartholomé Bovary, a former assistant army surgeon, had been forced to resign from the service about 1812 because of a conscription scandal in which he was involved. Turning his personal advantages to good account, he bagged a sixty-thousand-franc dowry attached to a hosier's daughter who had lost her heart to his good looks. Handsome and boastful, given to jingling his spurs, growing his moustaches long enough to meet his side-whiskers, loading his fingers with rings, and sporting flashy clothes, he looked like an adventurer and had the glib tongue of a travelling salesman. Once married, he lived on his wife's money for two or three years, dining well, sleeping late, smoking big porcelain pipes, coming home at night only after the theatres had closed, and spending his days in cafés. His father-in-law died and left very little; filled with indignation, he 'went into textiles', lost some money at this and retired to the country, intending to 'make a bit' from the land. But as he knew no more about farming than he did about calico, rode his horses himself instead of using them for the plough, drank his bottled cider instead of selling it by the cask, ate the best poultry in his yard, and polished his hunting boots with the lard from his pigs, he soon realized he had better abandon any thought of making money.

For a couple of hundred francs a year, therefore, he found a place to rent in a village situated close to the border between Normandy and Picardy. It was part farm, part gentleman's residence; and there, morose and malcontent, cursing heaven and envying everyone, he shut himself away at the age of forty-five, declaring himself disgusted with his fellow men, and resolved henceforth to live in peace.

His wife had been wild about him at first; she had treated him with an amorous servility that had turned him against her all the more. Vivacious, effusive, and very loving in the early days, over the years she had, like a stale wine that turns to vinegar, grown ill-humoured, waspish, and nervy. She had suffered so much, without, at first, a murmur of complaint, watching him chase after all the village drabs and then having him come home to her at night from any one of a score of filthy places, surfeited and stinking drunk! Then her pride had rebelled. So she withdrew into silence, stifling her rage in a mute stoicism that she maintained until her death. She was always on the go, dealing with one thing or another. She was forever consulting lawyers, or the magistrate, remembering when an account was due and negotiating an extension; at home she ironed, sewed, laundered, kept an eye on the workmen and paid their wages, while Monsieur never worried his head about a thing, engulfed in a surly drowsiness from which he roused himself only to mutter some nasty remark, as he sat all day long by the fire, smoking and spitting into the ashes.

When she had a child, he had to be sent out to a wet-nurse. Once home again with his parents, the lad was pampered like a prince. The mother stuffed him with sweet things; his father let him run about barefoot, and, affecting a philosophical pose, declared that he'd like the child to go entirely naked, the way a young animal did. To offset maternal protectiveness he tried to bring up his son according to a certain virile ideal of childhood that advocated a tough, Spartan regimen aimed at producing a robust constitution. He made him sleep in an unheated room, taught him to swallow great swigs of rum and make fun of religious processions. But the child was of a peaceful disposition, and responded poorly to his endeavours. His mother kept him tied to her apron strings; she cut out pictures for him, told him stories, and treated him to never-ending monologues full of bitter-sweet whimsy and beguiling chatter. In the isolation of her existence, she transferred onto this childish head all her crushed and scattered vanities. She dreamed of high positions, and could already visualize him as tall, handsome, witty, established in the civil service or the magistrature. She taught him to read, and even, on an old piano of hers, to sing a few sentimental ballads. But of all these efforts Monsieur Bovary, who set little store by culture, would remark that 'it wasn't worth the bother!' Would they ever have enough money to send him to one of the professional colleges, buy him a practice, or set him up in business? In any case, 'given sufficient nerve, a man can always make his mark in the world'. Madame Bovary bit her lip and the child wandered at will in the village.

He followed the farm workers about and flung clods of earth at the crows until they flew away. He ate blackberries growing alongside the ditches; armed with a stick, he watched over the turkeys; and he helped with the haymaking, ran about in the wood, played hopscotch in the shelter of the church porch when it rained, and, on church festivals, begged the sexton to let him toll the bell, so that he could hang with his weight dangling from the big rope and feel himself pulled off his feet by it as it swung in its arc.

He grew like a young oak; his hands were strong, his cheeks ruddy.

When he turned twelve, his mother managed to get him started on his studies. The curé was entrusted with his education. But these lessons were so short and so spasmodic as to be of little use. They were given in a hurry, with both of them standing in the sacristy, in the few moments the curé might spare between a baptism and a funeral; or else the curé would send for his pupil after the angelus, when he was not called out. They would climb up to his bedroom and settle down to work; midges and moths would be fluttering round the candle. It was warm, the child would fall asleep, while the old man, dozing off with his hands folded across his belly, would very soon start to snore, his mouth wide open. At other times when, returning with the viaticum after visiting a sick parishioner, the priest caught sight of Charles larking about in the fields, he called him over, read him a bit of a lecture, and took the opportunity to make him conjugate a verb right there on the spot, under a tree. Rain would interrupt them, or a passing acquaintance. In any case he was always pleased with the boy's progress, saying that the 'young fellow' had a good memory.

But all this was by no means good enough for Charles. Madame was determined. Ashamed, or more probably exhausted, Monsieur gave way without a struggle; and they waited a further year until the boy had made his first communion.

Six more months went by; and finally, the next year, Charles was sent to the lycée in Rouen.* His father delivered him personally, towards the end of October, at the time of the Saint-Romain fair.

It would be impossible, now, for any of us to remember anything about him. He was an ordinary sort of boy, who played during recess, worked during prep, paid attention in class, slept well in the dormitory, and ate well in the refectory. His local guardian was a wholesale ironmonger from the Rue Ganterie, who took him out once a month, on a Sunday, after his shop closed, sent him off to the harbour to look at the boats, then brought him back to the lycée by seven, before supper. Every Thursday evening, he wrote a long letter to his mother, in red ink, sealing it with three seals; then he revised his history notes or read an old volume of *Anacharsis** that was lying about in the prep room. When the boys went out for a walk, he always chatted to the servant, who, like him, came from the country.

By dint of working hard, he always managed to maintain his position in the middle of the class; on one occasion, he even won a 'highly commended' in natural history. But, at the end of his third year, his parents removed him from the lycée so that he could begin studying medicine;* they were confident he could satisfy the final secondary-school requirements without outside help.

His mother found a room for him in the house of a dyer she knew, on a fourth floor, overlooking the Eau-de-Robec.* She arranged for his board, acquired some furniture—a table and two chairs—had an old cherry-wood bed sent from home, and also bought a little cast iron stove and a supply of wood to keep her poor child warm. Then, at the week's end, she departed, after endless admonitions to behave well, now that he was being left to look after himself.

The lecture list that he read on the notice board made his head swim: courses in anatomy, pathology, physiology, pharmacy, chemistry, as well as botany, and clinical medicine, and therapy, not to mention hygiene and *materia medica*—all titles of unfamiliar etymology that he thought of as portals to holy places full of sacred mysteries.

In vain did he listen; he understood nothing whatsoever, he simply could not get his head round it. But even so he worked; he kept bound notebooks. He attended every lecture, he never missed a hospital visit. He completed his modest daily task after the fashion of a mill horse, plodding round and round blindfolded, unaware of what he is grinding.

Every week, to save him expense, his mother sent him a piece of roast veal by the stagecoach. This was his lunch, which he ate on his return from the hospital, banging his feet against the wall to keep them warm. Afterwards he had to rush off to more lessons, to the lecture hall, to another hospital, and then walk home again, along all those streets. In the evening, after the meagre dinner doled out by his landlord, he climbed up to his room and went back to work, his clothes, still damp, steaming on him as he sat by the red-hot stove.

On fine summer evenings, when the warm streets are deserted and the servant girls play at shuttlecock in the doorways, he would open his window and lean out on the sill. The river, which turns that part of Rouen into a squalid little Venice, flowed along down there below him, yellow, violet, or blue, between its bridges and railings. Workmen crouched on the banks, washing their arms in the water. On poles that protruded from attic windows, skeins of cotton were hung out to dry in the open air. Opposite, above the rooftops, he could see the vast, pure sky, and the red sun setting. How wonderful to be in the country! How cool it must feel, in the beech wood! And, his nostrils wide, he would take deep breaths, hoping to smell those good country smells that never ever reached his window.

He grew thinner, he grew taller, and his face took on a kind of plaintive expression that made it almost interesting.

Inevitably, out of apathy, he gradually came to abandon all the good resolutions he had made. The first time, he missed hospital rounds, the next, his lecture, and then, finding idleness to his taste, little by little he gave up his studies entirely.

He began to frequent bars, and developed a passion for dominoes.

To shut himself away in a grubby public room and spend his evenings clinking bits of mutton bone marked with black spots about on a marble-topped table seemed to him a precious affirmation of his freedom, and raised him in his own estimation. He saw it as a rite of passage into the real world, a way of attaining to forbidden delights; and, upon entering, he would take an almost sensual pleasure in grasping hold of the door knob. Now much that had been repressed in him began to come alive; he learned songs that he sang at student gatherings, became an admirer of Béranger,* learned how to make punch, and, at long last, discovered love.

Thanks to this style of preparation, he failed very thoroughly in his examination for *officier de santé*.* And he was expected in the village that very same evening, to celebrate his success!

He set off on foot, and stopped at the approach to the village, where he sent for his mother and told her the truth. She forgave him, blaming his failure on the unfairness of the examiners, and braced him up a bit by promising to take care of everything. It was not until five years later that Monsieur Bovary learnt the truth; by then she was old, and he accepted it, being unable, in any case, to imagine that any son of his could be stupid.

So Charles settled down to work again and crammed unremittingly for his examination, learning all the required material by heart. He passed quite respectably. What a proud day for his mother! They gave a splendid dinner.

Where should he set up his practice? In Tostes.* The only doctor there was old. For a long time now Madame Bovary had been waiting for him to die, and even before the old boy had turned up his toes Charles had moved in across the road, as his successor.

But it was not enough to have brought up her son, arranged for his training in medicine, and chosen Tostes for him to practise it in; he needed a wife. She found one for him: the widow of a bailiff in Dieppe, forty-five years old, with twelve hundred francs a year.

Although she was ugly, thin as a rake, with more pimples on her face than a tree has buds in springtime, Madame Dubuc certainly did not lack for suitors. In order to achieve her objective, Charles's mother had to eliminate them all, even managing with great skill to foil the machinations of a pork-butcher whose candidature was backed by the priests.

Charles had pictured marriage as the start of a better life, imagining that it would bring him greater freedom, and more control over what he did with himself and his money. But his wife was the boss; she told him what he ought and ought not to say in public, insisting that he fast on Fridays, dress as she thought fit, and dun those patients who were slow in paying. She opened his letters, watched everything he did, and listened through the dividing wall when he was seeing a female patient in his consulting room.

She had to have her hot chocolate every morning, and made him dance attendance on her all the time. She complained endlessly of her nerves, of her bad chest, of her low spirits. The sound of anyone moving about grated on her nerves, so people left her alone, but then she could not bear solitude; if they did happen to come back it must surely be just to 'watch her dying'. When Charles returned home at night she would poke her long skinny arms out from under the sheet, wrap them round his neck, make him sit down on the bed beside her, and embark on her tale of woe: he was neglecting her, he was in love with someone else! People had warned her, indeed they had, that she'd be unhappy! It always ended with her demanding a tonic to pep her up, and a bit more love.

CHAPTER II

One night, at about eleven, they were woken by the sound of a horse stopping just outside their door. The maid opened the attic window and had a lengthy exchange with a man down below, in the road. He had come for the doctor; he had a letter. Shivering, Nastasie climbed down the stairs and first undid the lock, then drew the bolts. Leaving his horse, the man quickly followed the maid and came into the room behind her. He wore a woollen cap with grey pompoms, and from inside it he took a letter wrapped in a piece of rag; this he handed gingerly to Charles, who propped himself up on the pillow to read it. Nastasie stood by the bed, holding the light. Madame lay facing the wall, modestly turning her back to the company.

This letter was sealed with a small blue seal and begged Monsieur Bovary to go immediately to the farm of Les Bertaux,* to set a broken leg. Now from Tostes to Les Bertaux is a distance of at least six leagues, by the road through Longueville and Saint-Victor. The night was very dark. Young Madame Bovary was afraid her husband might have an accident, so it was decided that the stable boy would go on ahead. Charles would leave three hours later, when the moon rose. A boy would be sent to meet him, to show him the way to the farm and open the gates.

Towards four in the morning Charles, well wrapped up in his cloak, set off for Les Bertaux. Still drowsy with the warmth of slumber, he let himself be lulled by the peaceful trotting of his horse. Whenever it stopped of its own accord at one of those holes bordered with thorns that farmers dig along the edge of their ploughed land, Charles, waking with a start, would quickly remember the broken leg, and try to recall all the fractures that he knew. It was no longer raining; day was breaking, and, on the leafless branches of the apple trees, birds sat motionless, fluffing out their tiny feathers in the cold morning wind. The flat landscape extended as far as the eye could see, the clumps of trees round the farms making widely spaced splashes of dark purple on that vast grey surface which, at the horizon, merged with the dreary tones of the sky. Charles, from time to time, would open his eyes; then, his mind growing weary and sleep returning unbidden, he would fall into a kind of doze in which, his recent sensations mingling with his memories, he saw himself as double, at once a student and a married man, lying, as he had just been doing, in his bed, and walking across a surgical ward as in the past. In his head the warm smell of the poultices blended with the fresh clean smell of the dew; he could hear the rattle of the iron curtain rings on the bars above the beds and the sound of his wife sleeping . . . As he passed through Vassonville, he caught sight of a young boy sitting in the grass on the edge of a ditch.

'Are you the doctor?' asked the lad.

And, at Charles's answer, he picked up his clogs and began to run along in front of him.

As he rode, the medical officer gathered from his guide's remarks that Monsieur Rouault was a farmer, and comfortably off. He had broken his leg the previous evening while returning home after celebrating Twelfth Night at a neighbour's house. His wife had been dead for two years. He only had his 'young lady' living with him; she helped him keep house.

The ruts grew deeper. They were nearing Les Bertaux. The little boy vanished through a gap in the hedge, then reappeared to open the farmyard gate. The horse kept slipping about on the wet grass;

Charles had to bend low to pass under branches. The watchdogs in their kennel barked, pulling on their chains. When he entered Les Bertaux his horse took fright, and shied violently.

It was a prosperous-looking farm. Through the open half-doors of the stables you could see huge draught horses placidly feeding from brand-new mangers. A stream of vapour arose from the big manure-heap that flanked the buildings, and, standing out among the hens and turkeys, five or six peacocks—that luxury of Pays de Caux farm-yards—were pecking for food. The sheep-run was long and the barn tall, with walls as smooth as the back of your hand. In the shed he saw two big carts and four ploughs, complete with whips, yokes, and all their equipment, the blue-dyed fleeces dusty with the fine powder that drifted down from the lofts. The farmyard, planted with evenly spaced trees, ran uphill, and resounded with the cheerful honking of a flock of geese over by the pond.

A young woman in a blue woollen dress trimmed with three flounces came to the door of the house to welcome Monsieur Bovary; she showed him into the kitchen, where a great fire blazed. The farmhands' breakfast, in small pots of varying sizes, stood bubbling all round it. Wet garments had been hung up to dry within the chimney area. The shovel, the tongs, and the nozzle of the bellows, all of gigantic proportions, glistened like polished steel, while on the walls hung a great many pots and pans, on which the bright firelight, mingling with the first rays of sun shining through the window panes, gleamed fitfully.

Charles went up to the first floor to see the patient. He found him in his bed, sweating under the covers, his cotton nightcap flung far away. He was a short, fat man of fifty, with white skin, blue eyes, and receding hair; he wore rings in his ears. Beside him on a chair stood a large carafe of brandy from which he helped himself from time to time to bolster his courage; but, the moment he saw the doctor, all his animation vanished, and, instead of swearing as he had been doing for the past twelve hours, he began moaning feebly.

It was a simple fracture, without any kind of complication. Charles could not have dared hope for an easier one. So then, recollecting the bedside manner of his teachers, he comforted his patient with all sorts of little jokes—professional caresses that are like the oil used on surgical instruments. A bundle of laths was fetched from the cart-shed to make splints. Charles chose one, cut it into lengths, and smoothed it with a piece of glass, while the servant tore up sheets to make bandages, and Mademoiselle Emma tried to sew some pads. As she was slow finding her needle case her father lost patience with her; she did not answer him but, as she sewed, she kept pricking her fingers, which she then put in her mouth and sucked.

Charles was surprised at the whiteness of her nails. They were lustrous, delicately pointed, cleaner than the ivories of Dieppe, and almond-shaped. Yet her hand was not beautiful, not pale enough, perhaps, and rather dry round the knuckles; also, it was too long, and its shape had no softness of outline. But her eyes were indeed beautiful; although they were brown, they appeared black because of the lashes, and she looked straight at you with a gaze that was candid and bold.

Once the dressing had been completed, Monsieur Rouault himself invited the doctor to 'take a bite' before leaving.

Charles went down to the main room on the ground floor. Silver beakers stood at two places which had been set on a small table there, at the foot of a big canopied bed hung with calico printed in a pattern of Turkish figures. A smell of orrisroot and damp linen came from the tall oak press opposite the window. Sacks of wheat were stacked upright on the floor in the corners. This was the overflow from the adjacent granary, to which three stone steps gave access. As decoration the room had, hanging from a nail in the middle of a wall whose green paint was flaking from the damp, a black chalk drawing of the head of Minerva, in a gilded frame, inscribed in Gothic lettering along the bottom 'To my dear Papa'.

They talked first of the patient, then of the weather, of the periods of bitter cold, of the wolves that roamed the fields at night. Mademoiselle Rouault did not find it much fun living in the country, especially now that she was almost solely responsible for running the farm. As the room was chilly she shivered as she ate, revealing her rather full lips that she tended to nibble when she was not speaking.

Her neck rose from a white, turned-down collar. The two black bands in which her hair was arranged, each so smooth that it seemed an indivisible unit, were separated in the middle of her head by a finely drawn parting, which dipped slightly following the curve of her skull; at the back her hair was caught up into a very full chignon, showing just the tip of the earlobe, and falling at the temple into a faint wave—something which the country doctor now found himself noticing for the first time in his life. Her cheeks were pink. Like a man, she carried a pair of tortoiseshell-rimmed glasses tucked between two buttons of her bodice.

When Charles, having gone upstairs to say goodbye to old Rouault, came back into the room before leaving, he found her standing with her head against the window pane, gazing at the garden, where the beanpoles had been blown down by the wind. She turned round.

'Are you looking for something?' she asked.

'My riding crop,' he replied.

And he began hunting on the bed, behind the doors, under the chairs; it had fallen on the floor, between the sacks and the wall. Mademoiselle Emma noticed it and bent over the sacks of wheat. Charles hurried forward politely and, reaching down with his arm in a similar movement, felt his chest brush against the back of the young girl, who was bent over beneath him. She straightened up, blushing, and looked at him over her shoulder as she handed him his whip.

Instead of calling back at Les Bertaux in three days, as he had promised, it was the very next day that he came again, then regularly twice a week, not counting the unexpected visits that he paid from time to time, as though by chance.

Everything, in any case, went well; the recovery proceeded in textbook fashion, and when, after forty-six days, old Rouault was seen trying to walk round his farmyard all on his own, people began to consider Monsieur Bovary an exceptionally able man. Rouault declared that he could not have been better cared for by the best doctors in Yvetot* or even Rouen.

As for Charles, he never stopped to ask himself why he loved going to Les Bertaux. Had he thought about it he would probably have attributed his zeal to the gravity of the case, or perhaps to the profit he hoped to make. But was that really why his visits to the farm formed such a delightful exception in the humdrum routines of his life? Those days he would get up early, set off at a gallop and urge his horse on, then dismount to wipe his shoes on the grass and slip on his black gloves before entering the house. He loved riding into the farmyard, feeling the gate swing open under the pressure of his shoulder, hearing the cock crow from the wall, and seeing the lads hurry to meet him. He loved the barn and the stables; he loved old

Rouault, who would give him a smacking handshake and call him his saviour; he loved Mademoiselle Emma's tiny clogs on the scrubbed flagstones of the kitchen; their high heels made her a little taller and, when she walked in front of him, their wooden soles, rising quickly, gave a sharp click against the leather of her ankle-boots.

She always saw him to the top of the front steps. If his horse had not yet been brought over, she would wait there. They had already said their goodbyes, and stood in silence; the fresh air would blow round her, ruffling the unruly little hairs at the nape of her neck, or tossing her apron strings about her hips, where they rolled and twisted like streamers. One day there was a thaw; in the yard the bark on the trees streamed with moisture and the snow lay melting on the roofs of the outbuildings. She had come to the door; she went back for her parasol, and opened it. The sun, filtering through the iridescent dove-grey silk of the parasol, cast flickering reflections on the white skin of her face. As she smiled from beneath it at the soft warmth of the morning, you could hear the drops of water falling, one by one, on the taut surface of the silk.

At first, when Charles made a call at Les Bertaux, Madame Bovary the younger never failed to ask after the patient; in the ledger that she kept in double entry she had even set aside a lovely clean page just for Monsieur Rouault. But when she heard that he had a daughter, she wanted to learn more; she discovered that Mademoiselle Rouault, who had been brought up at an Ursuline convent,* had had what is called 'a fine education', and had, consequently, learnt dancing, geography, drawing, tapestry work, and the piano. It was the last straw!

'So,' she said to herself, 'that's why he's all smiles when he's going to see her, and he puts on his new waistcoat even though the rain might spoil it! Oh, that woman, that woman!'

Instinctively, she loathed her. At first she relieved her feelings with innuendoes that Charles did not understand; then, later, with parenthetical remarks that Charles ignored for the sake of a quiet life; and finally with point-blank reproaches which he had no idea how to answer. Why did he keep going back to Les Bertaux, since Monsieur Rouault was cured and those folks hadn't paid up yet? It was because of a certain person, oh yes, someone who could chat pleasantly, and embroider, and be witty. So that was what he fancied, was it, town-bred young ladies! And she went on:

'Old Rouault's girl, a town-bred young lady! Oh, come on! Their grandfather was a shepherd, and they've a cousin who nearly got taken to court for some dirty trick he got up to, in an argument. There's no point in her putting on such fancy airs, or showing herself in church on Sunday all done up like a countess in a silk dress. Besides, the old boy's badly off, he'd have been hard put to it to pay his back rent if it hadn't been for last year's rape crop!'

Wearying of this, Charles stopped going to Les Bertaux. After a tremendous scene full of sobs and kisses and passionate protestations, Héloïse had made him swear, with his hand on his missal, not to return there. So he obeyed; but the boldness of his desire rebelled against this abject behaviour and, by a kind of ingenuous hypocrisy, he felt that being forbidden to see her gave him almost a right to love her. And then the widow was skinny; she was long in the tooth; and regardless of the season she wore a skimpy black shawl with its point falling between her shoulder-blades; her unyielding body was encased in stiff dresses that were too short, revealing grey-stockinged ankles criss-crossed by the ribbons of her big shoes.

From time to time Charles's mother visited them, but, after a few days, it was as if the daughter-in-law had transmitted some of her own sharpness to her. Then, like a pair of knives, they would go at him with their cutting remarks and observations. He oughtn't to eat so much! Why must he always offer a drink to anyone who dropped in? And what pigheadedness, to refuse to wear flannel underclothes!

It so happened that early in the spring, a notary in Ingouville* who administered the widow Dubuc's property decamped one fine morning, carrying off all the money in his office. True, Héloïse did still own—aside from a share in a ship valued at six thousand francs— her house in the Rue Saint-François; yet even so, out of this fortune which had been so much vaunted, nothing, other than a few odds and ends of furniture and clothing, had been seen in the Bovary household. It was time to bring the facts into the open. The house in Dieppe turned out to be mortgaged to its foundations; God only knew how much she had deposited at the notary's, and the share in the ship was certainly less than five thousand francs. So the good lady had lied! In his fury Monsieur Bovary senior smashed a chair on the flagstones and accused his wife of ruining his son's life by hitching him to a skinny old nag like that, whose harness was as worthless as her hide! They came to Tostes. Things were said. There were scenes. Weeping, Héloïse flung herself into her husband's arms, calling on him to defend her against his parents. Charles tried to stand up for her, and they departed in a rage.

But 'the damage was done'. A week later, as she was hanging out washing in her yard, she began to cough up blood, and the next day, while Charles, with his back turned, was drawing the curtains at the window, she cried: 'Oh, my God!' gave a sigh, and fainted. She was dead! How astonishing!

When it was all over at the cemetery, Charles returned home. There was no one downstairs. He went upstairs, to the bedroom, and saw her dress still hanging at the foot of the bed-recess; then, leaning on the writing desk, he stayed there until dusk, lost in a painful reverie. She had loved him, after all.

CHAPTER III

One morning, old Rouault came to pay Charles for setting his broken leg: seventy-five francs in two-franc pieces, and a turkey. He had heard about his misfortune, and comforted him as best he could.

'I know what it's like!' he told him, slapping him on the back; 'I've been through it myself! When I lost my late-lamented, I used to go off into the fields to be alone; I'd fling myself down under a tree, and weep, and call on the good Lord, and curse him; I wanted to be like the moles I saw hanging on the branches with worms crawling in their bellies; in a word, dead. And when I thought that at that very minute, other men were hugging and kissing their dear little wives, I'd thump on the ground with me stick. I nearly went crazy, I nearly stopped eating; would you believe it, the very idea of going to a café turned me stomach. And then, ever so slowly, as one day followed another, spring came after winter and autumn after summer, it slipped away, little by little, bit by bit; it went away, disappeared, it went down into me, I mean, because there's always something left deep down inside, like . . . a kind of weight, here, on me chest! But since it comes to us all, in the end, we mustn't let ourselves waste away and, because other folks have died, want to die ourselves . . . You must pull yourself together, Monsieur Bovary; this'll pass. Come and see us; me daughter thinks of you now and again, you know, and says you've forgotten her. It'll soon be spring; we'll do a bit of rabbiting, to take your mind off things.'

Charles did as he suggested. He returned to Les Bertaux. Everything was just as he remembered; his last visit could have been yesterday, instead of five months ago. The pear trees were already in bloom, and old Rouault, now recovered, was forever on the go, so that the farm seemed more full of life.

Thinking it appropriate, in view of the doctor's unhappy circumstances, to be as polite to him as possible, Rouault begged him not to remove his hat, spoke to him in a low voice as though he were ill, and even pretended to be annoyed because something a little lighter—baked custards, perhaps, or stewed pears—had not been prepared for his enjoyment. He told stories. Charles caught himself laughing; but then he suddenly remembered his wife, and relapsed into gloom. Coffee was brought in; he thought no more about her.

He thought about her less and less as he grew used to living alone. The unfamiliar pleasures of independence soon made him find solitude easier to bear. He could change the times of his meals now, come home or go out without giving any explanation, and, when he was very tired, stretch out right across the bed. So he pampered and coddled himself and accepted whatever solace came his way. In any case, the death of his wife had done him no harm professionally; for a whole month people kept saying: 'That poor young man! What a terrible thing!' His reputation had spread, his practice had grown; and now he could go to Les Bertaux whenever he chose. He was filled with an unspecified hope, a vague happiness; he thought his face more attractive when he brushed his whiskers in front of the mirror.

He turned up one day at about three; everyone was in the fields; he went into the kitchen but did not, at first, see Emma; the shutters were closed. The sunlight, shining through the slats in the wood, fell across the flagstones in long narrow stripes that broke where they came up against the furniture, and flickered on the ceiling. On the table, flies were crawling up the used glasses left from the last meal, and buzzing as they drowned in the remaining dregs of cider. The light that filtered down the chimney lent a velvety bloom to the soot on the fireback and tinged the burned-out embers with hints of blue. Emma sat between the window and the fireplace, sewing; she was not wearing a neckerchief, and on the bare skin of her shoulders you could see little beads of sweat.

As was the custom in the country, she offered him something to drink. He refused, but she insisted, and finally asked him, with a laugh, to join her in a glass of liqueur. So she fetched a bottle of curaçao from the cupboard, reached down two tiny glasses, filled one to the brim, poured just a drop into the other and then, after clinking glasses with him, raised it to her mouth. As it was almost empty, she leaned right back to drink and, with her head tilted, her lips pushed forward and her neck taut, she laughed at finding nothing, while the tip of her tongue, poking between her beautiful teeth, delicately licked at the bottom of the glass.

She sat down and resumed her work, a white cotton stocking she was darning; she sat with her head bent over it, not speaking. Charles did not speak either. A draught of air from under the door stirred a little dust on the flagstones; he watched it slowly move, hearing only the pounding inside his head and the distant cry of a laying hen in the yard. From time to time Emma would freshen her cheeks with her palms, which she then cooled on the knobs of the huge iron firedogs.

She complained that ever since the beginning of the hot weather she had been suffering from dizzy spells, and enquired whether sea bathing might help her; she chatted about the convent, and Charles about his college; they began to talk more freely. They went upstairs to her room. She showed him her old music books, the small volumes she had received as prizes, the wreaths of oak-leaves lying forgotten in the bottom of the wardrobe. Then she talked about her mother and about the cemetery, and even pointed out the flower bed in the garden where she picked flowers, the first Friday of every month, to put on her grave. But their gardener was no good with flowers; it was so hard to get reliable help! She would have liked, even if just during the winter, to live in town, although the long fine days made the countryside even more tedious, perhaps, in summer; and, depending on what she was saying, her voice was clear and high-pitched or else, suddenly full of languor, would modulate to a drawl then almost to a whisper, when she was talking to herself—sometimes she seemed joyful, with her eyes innocent and wide, and sometimes she was lost in boredom, with her eyelids half closed and her thoughts wandering far away.

Going home that evening, Charles went over the things she had said one at a time, trying to remember them, to complete their meaning, so as to create for himself that part of her existence which she had lived during the years before he met her. But never was he able, in his imagination, to see her as different from how he had seen her the first time, or how she had looked when he had just left her. Then he began to wonder what would become of her, whether she would marry, and whom? Her father, alas, was very rich, and she! . . . she was so beautiful! But Emma's face would always reappear before his eyes, and his ears were filled with a monotonous buzzing like the drone of a top: 'But what if you were to marry! if you were to marry!' That night he could not sleep, his chest felt tight, his throat dry; he got up to take a drink from his water jug and opened the window; the sky was covered with stars and a warm breeze had risen; dogs were barking, a long way off. He turned his head towards Les Bertaux.

Telling himself that, after all, he had nothing to lose, Charles decided he would ask for her hand when the opportunity arose; but, every time it did, the fear of not finding the right words paralysed his tongue.

Old Rouault would not have been sorry to have his daughter taken off his hands, for she was not much use to him in the house. Deep down he made excuses for her, believing that she had too good a mind for farming, an occupation that must surely have been cursed by heaven, since no one had ever seen a farmer who was a millionaire. Far from having made his fortune, the old fellow was losing money every year: for although he excelled in the market place, where he delighted in the tricks and ruses of bargaining, the actual work of farming the land and of managing the farm, by contrast, could not have suited him less. He never willingly took his hands out of his pockets, and he spared no expense when it came to his personal comfort, liking good food, a warm fire, and a soft bed. He wanted his cider strong, his meat rare, his coffee well laced with brandy. He had his meals in the kitchen, alone, in front of the fire, on a small table that was brought to him already laid, as in the theatre.

So, noticing that Charles went red in the face when he was near his daughter, which meant that one of these days he would ask for her hand, he pondered the whole matter in advance. It was true he thought him a bit of a loser, and not what he'd have chosen as a son-in-law; but people said he was a steady young man, careful with his money, and very learned; and probably he wouldn't haggle too much

over the dowry. Now, as Monsieur Rouault was going to have to sell
twenty-two acres of 'his place', and he owed a lot to the mason, a lot
to the harness-maker, and the shaft of the cider-press needed
replacing, he said to himself:

'If he asks me for her, I'll let him have her.'

At Michaelmas, Charles came to stay at Les Bertaux for three
days. The last day passed like those preceding it, in postponing the
question from one quarter of an hour to the next. Rouault saw him
off; they were walking down a sunken lane and were about to part; it
was now or never. Charles gave himself as far as the corner of the
hedge, and finally, when they had passed it:

'Maître Rouault,' he murmured, 'There's something I want to tell
you.'

They stopped. Charles said nothing.

'Well come on, out with it! As if I didn't know what's on your
mind!' old Rouault replied with a soft chuckle.

'Père Rouault . . . Père Rouault,' stammered Charles.

'There's nothing I'd like better,' continued the farmer. 'I'm sure
me little girl feels the same, but still, I'd better ask her. So off you go;
I'll be getting back to the house. If it's "yes"—listen carefully now—
you'd best not come back, because there's people about, and besides,
it'd be too much for her. But so you don't eat your heart out, I'll
push the big shutter of the window wide open: you'll be able to see it
by looking back, if you lean over the hedge.'

And off he went.

Charles tied his horse to a tree. He ran to the footpath; he waited.
Half an hour passed, then he counted nineteen minutes by his watch.
All of a sudden he heard something hit the wall; the shutter had been
folded back, the latch was still vibrating.

Next morning he was at the farm by nine. Emma blushed when he
came in, although she tried to cover her embarrassment with a little
laugh. Père Rouault embraced his future son-in-law. They put off
any discussion of money matters, there was plenty of time for that,
since the marriage could not decently take place before the end of
Charles's mourning, that is to say, not until the following spring.

The winter passed in waiting. Mademoiselle Rouault busied herself with her trousseau. Part of it was ordered from Rouen, and she
made herself nightgowns and nightcaps with the help of fashion-
plates which she borrowed. During the visits Charles made to the

farm they talked about the preparations for the wedding, wondering which room they'd use for the wedding feast, how many courses they'd have, and what particular dishes they'd serve.

Emma, on the other hand, longed to be married at midnight,* by torchlight; but old Rouault couldn't make anything of such a notion. So there was a wedding celebration attended by forty-three guests; they sat round the table for sixteen hours, began all over again the next day, and went on celebrating on and off for a few days after that.

CHAPTER IV

The guests arrived early, in carriages, one-horse carts, two-wheeled traps, ancient open gigs, and wagonettes with leather curtains; the young people from the nearest villages travelled standing up in wagons, packed closely together and holding onto the rails so as not to fall as they jolted along at a smart pace. People came from twenty-five miles away, from Goderville, Normanville, and Cany. All the relatives on both sides had been invited; broken friendships had been mended, and letters written to acquaintances not spoken to in years.

From time to time, the crack of a whip sounded from behind the hedge; soon the gate would open; a horse and cart was arriving. Driving at a gallop right up to the bottom of the front steps, it would stop dead and eject its passengers, who emerged from all sides rubbing their knees and stretching their arms. The ladies, in bonnets, wore city dresses, gold watch chains, and capes with the ends crossed at the waist, or else little coloured neckerchiefs fastened behind with a pin, leaving the nape of the neck bare. The small boys, dressed like their papas, seemed ill at ease in their new suits (indeed many of them were that day wearing their first ever pair of boots). Beside them, not daring to open her mouth, would be a lanky girl of fourteen or sixteen, an older sister, perhaps, or a cousin, her white first communion dress let down for the occasion, her face red and bewildered, her hair plastered with rose-scented pomade, very anxious lest she get her gloves dirty. As there were not enough stable boys to unharness all the horses, the gentlemen rolled up their sleeves and got down to it themselves. Depending on their social position, they wore dress coats, frock coats, jackets both short and long: good-quality dress coats, treated with great respect by the entire family, and brought out of the wardrobe only on solemn occasions; frock coats with voluminous tails that flapped in the breeze, cylindrical collars, and big pockets like miniature sacks; jackets of coarse cloth, generally worn with a brass-banded peaked cap; very short-skirted jackets with, at the back, two buttons close together like a pair of eyes, and tails that might have been hacked straight from a single piece of cloth with a carpenter's hatchet. There were even some guests (though they, of course, would be relegated to the bottom of the table) who were wearing their Sunday-best smocks, smocks, that is, with the collar turned down over the shoulders, the back gathered into narrow pleats, and stitched-on belts very low on the hips.

And their shirts! They ballooned out like breastplates! All the men were freshly shorn; their ears stuck out, their cheeks were newly shaven; in fact some, who had risen before dawn and not been able to see properly to shave, displayed diagonal gashes below the nose or abrasions as big as a three-franc piece along the jaw. The cold air on the drive had inflamed the scratches, marbling with rosy blotches all those big, beaming white faces.

As the Mairie was barely more than a mile from the farm, they went there on foot and, when the ceremony at the church was over, returned in the same manner. At first the procession was a compact unit, a single coloured scarf winding through the countryside along the narrow track that snaked its way between the fields of green corn; but soon it began to stretch out, and then to break into different groups as people stopped to chat. The fiddler led the way, his violin garlanded with multicoloured ribbons; then came the bridal couple, followed by their relatives, then their friends in no special order, and finally the children, who amused themselves pulling off the ears of the sprouting oats, or playing games together, well away from adult eyes. Emma's dress was rather long and the hem trailed a bit; from time to time she would stop and lift it up, then, with gloved fingers, delicately remove the wild grasses and tiny thistle burrs, while Charles stood empty-handed, waiting for her to finish. Père Rouault, with a new silk hat on his head and the cuffs of his black dress coat covering his hands right down to his nails, was escorting Madame Bovary senior. As for the groom's father, he, to show his profound contempt for the company, had come dressed in a simple frock coat of military cut with a single row of buttons; he kept showering a young fair-haired country lass with bar-room gallant-ries. She, curtsying and blushing, had no idea how to answer him. The other wedding guests were talking business or playing jokes on one another, getting into the swing of the fun that lay ahead; and, if you listened carefully, you could always hear the fiddler scraping away across the open fields. Whenever he noticed that he had left the company far behind, he would stop to catch his breath, thoroughly wax his bow with rosin so as to get a sharper screech from the strings, and then set off again, alternately raising and lowering the neck of his violin to help himself keep time. The distant sound of the instrument put all the small birds to flight.

It was in the wagon shed that the table had been set up. On it stood four sirloins, six fricassees of chicken, a casserole of veal, three legs of mutton, and, in the centre, a fine roast sucking pig, flanked by sorrel-flavoured pork sausages. The brandy, in carafes, had been placed at the corners of the table. Bottles of sweet cider foamed thickly round their corks and all the glasses had been filled to the brim, in advance, with wine. Huge dishes of yellow custard, which the slightest bump to the table set quivering, displayed on their smooth surfaces the initials of the newly-weds, picked out in sugared almonds. The tarts and nougats had been ordered from a pastry-cook in Yvetot. As he was new to the area, he had gone to a great deal of trouble, and he himself brought to the table, at the dessert stage, an elaborate confection which drew cries of admiration. The base was a square of blue cardboard representing a temple with, round its sides, porticos, colonnades and stucco statuettes in niches spangled with gold-paper stars. The main tier consisted of a medieval castle made of sponge cake, surrounded by tiny battlements of angelica, almonds, raisins, and orange segments; and, finally, on the topmost layer—a green meadow with rocks, lakes of jam, and hazelnut-shell boats—a little Cupid sat on a chocolate swing, the uprights of which were finished with real rosebuds in the place of knobs.

They ate until nightfall. When they grew tired of sitting, they would take a stroll in the courtyard or play a game of cork-penny in the barn, then return to the table. Towards the end, some fell fast asleep there, snoring. But everything livened up when the coffee was served; they embarked on songs, and displays of strength; they lifted weights, played 'Under my Thumb', tried to raise the carts onto their shoulders, exchanged dirty jokes, and kissed the ladies. That night, when it was time to leave, the horses, stuffed to the ears with oats, could hardly squeeze between the shafts; they kicked and reared and broke their harnesses as their masters laughed and cursed. And all night long, in the moonlight, there were runaway carts galloping madly along the country lanes, bounding over the ditches, leaping over the piles of gravel, running up the banks, with women leaning out of the doors and trying to grab hold of the reins. Those who stayed at Les Bertaux spent the night drinking in the kitchen. The children had fallen asleep under the benches.

The bride had begged her father that she be spared the traditional horseplay. Even so, a cousin of theirs who was a fishmonger (and who had even brought a pair of soles as a wedding present) was on the point of blowing water through the keyhole with his mouth, when Rouault arrived just in time to stop him, explaining that such improprieties were out of place, in view of his son-in-law's import-ant position. The cousin complied, but with some reluctance. In his heart he accused Rouault of being proud, and took himself off into a corner with four or five other guests who had been served, more than once, with inferior cuts of meat and felt that they too had been shabbily treated. There, in whispers, they exchanged veiled remarks at their host's expense, wishing him ill.

Madame Bovary the elder had not opened her mouth throughout the entire day. She had been consulted neither about her daughter-in-law's wedding dress nor about the arrangements for the wedding feast; she went up to bed early. Instead of accompanying her, her husband sent to Saint-Victor for cigars and spent the night smoking and drinking punch made with kirsch—a mixture his fellow guests had never heard of, and which inspired still greater respect for him.

Charles had no talent for repartee, and had not shone during the festivities. He made only lame replies to the digs, puns, double mean-ings, compliments, and dirty jokes that they all felt in honour bound to level at him from the moment the soup was served.

The next morning, by contrast, he seemed a different man. He was the one you would think had been a virgin, whereas the bride gave absolutely no sign that meant anything to anybody. Even the shrewdest could make nothing of it, and stared at her, whenever she came near them, with intense concentration. But Charles hid nothing. He called her 'my wife', addressed her by the familiar 'tu', was always asking everyone where she was and looking for her everywhere, and often he would take her outside into the grounds, where he could be glimpsed from afar, among the trees, walking half bent over her with his arm round her waist and his head crushing the front of her bodice.

Two days after the wedding the couple departed: because of his patients, Charles could not be away any longer. Père Rouault sent them off in his own trap, himself going with them as far as Vassonville. There, he kissed his daughter one last time, got down and started for home. When he had gone about a hundred paces, he stopped and, seeing the trap disappearing into the distance, its wheels turning in the dust, he gave a heavy sigh. Then he remembered his own wedding, his own youth, his wife's first pregnancy; he, too, had been so happy, the day he had taken her from her father's house to his own. She had sat behind him as their horse trotted across the snow; it was almost Christmas and the fields were completely white; she had clung to him with one arm, while the other held her basket; the wind whipped about the long lace streamers of her Normandy headdress, sometimes blowing them across his mouth; when he turned his head, he could see, over his shoulder, her little rosy face close behind him, smiling silently beneath the golden ornament on her bonnet. From time to time she would warm her fingers by slipping them under his coat, against his chest. How long ago all that was! Their boy would have been thirty now! He looked back along the road: there was nothing to be seen. He felt as desolate as an empty house; and, tender memories mingling with black thoughts in a brain befuddled by his hangover from celebrating, he felt a momentary urge to go round by the churchyard. However, as he was afraid that such a sight would make him feel still gloomier, he went straight home.

Monsieur and Madame Charles reached Tostes about six. The neighbours went to their windows to take a look at their doctor's new wife.

The old servant appeared, curtsied, apologized because dinner was not ready, and suggested that in the meantime Madame might like to take a look at her house.

CHAPTER V

The brick front of the house stood flush with the street or, more precisely, the road. Hanging behind the door were a cloak with a short cape, a bridle, a black leather cap, and, in a corner on the floor, a pair of gaiters still caked with dried mud. To the right was the parlour, the room that served for eating in, and for sitting. A canary-yellow paper, set off along the top by a border of pale-coloured flowers, hung in wrinkles on its badly stretched canvas backing; white calico curtains, edged with red braid, criss-crossed the windows, and, on the narrow mantelpiece, a clock adorned with a head of Hippocrates stood in state between candlesticks of plated silver under oval glass shades. On the other side of the passage was Charles's consulting room: a small room—about six paces in width—containing a table, three straight chairs, and a desk chair with arms. The volumes of the *Dictionary of the Medical Sciences*,* their pages uncut but their bindings shabby from being handled by so many different owners, were virtually the only books on the six shelves of a pine bookcase. Cooking smells filtered through the wall during consultations, and, from the kitchen, you could hear the patients coughing in the consulting room and describing all their symptoms. Next, opening directly onto the yard, with its stable, was a large dilapidated room with an oven in it, and which now served for keeping wood and wine and for storage; it was crammed with bits of scrap iron, empty barrels, disused garden implements, and a lot of other things that defied description and were thick with dust.

The garden, longer than it was wide, ran between two walls of clay and wattle on which espaliered apricots were growing, down to a thorn hedge that divided it off from the fields. In the centre was a slate sundial on a stone pedestal. Four beds of scrawny dog roses were arranged symmetrically round a more utilitarian plot devoted to vegetables. Down at the far end, under some spruces, a plaster priest stood reading his breviary.

Emma went upstairs to the bedrooms. The first had no furniture in it, but the second, the conjugal bedroom, contained a mahogany bedstead in an alcove with red hangings. A box covered in seashells adorned the chest-of-drawers and on the writing desk near the window, in a carafe, stood a bouquet of orange blossoms tied with white satin ribbons. It was a bride's bouquet, the other one's bouquet! She stared at it. Charles, noticing this, picked it up and took it away to the attic. While her belongings were being arranged round the room, Emma sat in an armchair, thinking about her own bouquet packed in its box, and wondering dreamily what would be done with it if she were to die.

She spent the first few days planning changes in the house. She took the shades off the candlesticks, had new paper hung, the stairs repainted, and benches placed round the sundial in the garden; she even made enquiries about installing a fish pond, with its own fountain. And her husband, knowing that she enjoyed going for drives, found a second-hand gig which, once it was fitted with new lamps and splash-boards of quilted leather, looked almost like a tilbury.

So he was happy, without a care in the world. A meal alone with her, a stroll along the road in the evening, her hand smoothing down her hair, the sight of her straw hat hanging from a window hasp, and many other things in which he had never imagined he would find pleasure, now made up the even tenor of his happiness. In bed, in the morning, by her side on the pillow, he would watch the sunlight moving over the golden down on her cheeks, half-hidden by the scalloped flaps of her nightcap. Seen from so close, her eyes seemed to him to have become larger, especially when she blinked her lids repeatedly on waking; black in the shadows and dark blue in daylight, they seemed to be made of successive layers of colour which were denser at the bottom and grew progressively lighter towards the surface of the enamel. His own eye would lose itself in these depths, and he could see himself, in miniature, down to his shoulders, with his scarf on his head and his nightshirt unbuttoned. He would get up. She would go to the window to see him off, and remain there, leaning on the sill, between two pots of geraniums, her dressing gown hanging loosely round her. Below, in the road, Charles would put his foot on the mounting block to buckle on his spurs while she, up at the window, went on talking and blowing down at him a bit of petal or leaf that she had torn off with her teeth. It would flutter and float through the air, sketching half-circles like a bird, and, before landing on the ground, would catch in the unkempt mane of the old white mare, standing motionless at the door. Charles would mount and blow her a kiss; she would wave in reply and close the window, and off he would go. And then, on the endless dusty ribbon of the highway, or in the sunken lanes under bowering trees, on paths where the grain stood knee-high, with the sun on his shoulders and the morning air in his nostrils, his heart full of the night's bliss, his spirit at peace, and his flesh content, he would ride along ruminating his happiness, like someone who, after dinner, goes on savouring the taste of the truffles he has eaten.*

Up until now, what happiness had he had in his life? His school-days, shut in by those high walls, lonely among those boys who were richer than he was or better at their lessons, who laughed at his accent and made fun of his clothes, and whose mothers came to visit them with their muffs full of cakes? Or later, when he was studying medicine and never had enough money in his purse to go dancing with some little seamstress who might have become his mistress? Then for fourteen months he had lived with the widow, whose feet, in bed, were like blocks of ice. But now he possessed, for always, this pretty woman whom he adored. The universe, for him, was bound by the silken circle of her petticoat; and, reproaching himself for not loving her enough and longing to be with her again, he would hurry back and, his heart pounding, climb up the stairs. Emma was in her bedroom, at her dressing table; tiptoeing up to her, he would kiss the back of her neck; she would give a startled cry.

He could not resist constantly touching her comb, her rings, her scarf. Sometimes he gave her great smacking kisses on the cheeks, sometimes a row of tiny kisses all along her bare arm, from her fingertips to her shoulder; she would push him away, half-laughing, half-irritated, as one might push away a clinging child.

Before her marriage, she had believed that she was in love; but since the happiness she had expected this love to bring her had not come, she supposed she must have been mistaken. And Emma tried to find out what exactly was meant, in real life, by the words 'bliss', 'passion', and 'ecstasy', words that she had found so beautiful in books.

CHAPTER VI

She had read *Paul et Virginie*,* and had dreamed of the bamboo hut, of Domingo the black man and Fidèle the dog, but above all of the sweet friendship of a dear little brother who'd pick crimson fruit for you from great trees taller than steeples, or come running barefoot over the sand to bring you a bird's nest.

When she was thirteen, her father took her to the city, to place her in a convent. They stopped at an inn in the Saint-Gervais quarter, where their supper was served on painted plates depicting the story of Mademoiselle de la Vallière.* The explanatory captions, obliterated here and there by knife scratches, all glorified religion, refinement of sentiment, and the splendours of the court.

Far from being unhappy at the convent in the early days, she enjoyed the company of the nuns who, to keep her amused, used to take her into the chapel, through a long corridor that led from the refectory. She hardly ever played during recreation, she understood the catechism well, and was always the one who answered the visiting priest's difficult questions. So, living continuously in the cloistered warmth of the classrooms, among those white-faced women whose rosaries bore copper crucifixes, she was gently lulled into a mystical languor by the scents on the altar, the coolness of the holy-water stoups, and the radiance of the candles. Instead of following the mass, she would study, in her missal, the pious illustrations with their sky-blue borders, and she loved the sick lamb, the Sacred Heart pierced by sharp arrows, and poor Jesus, stumbling under the burden of his cross. She attempted, as a mortification, to go a whole day without eating. She tried to think of some vow she might fulfil.

When she went to confession, she used to invent petty sins so as to stay there longer, kneeling in the darkness, her hands together and her face against the grille, listening to the murmuring of the priest. The analogies of betrothed, spouse, heavenly lover, and eternal marriage that she heard repeatedly in sermons excited an unwonted tenderness deep in her soul.

In the schoolroom, before evening prayers, there was always a reading from some work of piety. During the week it would be an abridged biography of a saint or the Abbé Frayssinous's *Lectures*,* and on Sundays, for relaxation, excerpts from *Le Génie du christianisme*.* How intently did she listen, the first times, to those plangent lamentations of romantic melancholy, which all of nature and eternity seemed to echo and re-echo! Had her childhood been spent in the back room of some city shop, she might perhaps have been receptive to the lyrical appeal of nature, which normally only reaches us through the intermediary of literature. But she knew the country too well; she was too familiar with bleating sheep, with milking, with ploughing. Accustomed to the tranquil side of nature, she sought the dramatic in its stead. She loved the sea only for its storms, and the green grass only when it grew in patches among ruins. She had to derive a kind of personal profit from things, and rejected as useless anything that did not contribute directly to her heart's gratification—for her temperament was sentimental rather than artistic, and she longed for emotion, not scenery.

There was, at the convent, an elderly spinster who came for a week every month to mend the linen. Protected by the archdiocese because she belonged to an ancient aristocratic family that had been ruined by the Revolution, she ate in the refectory with the nuns, and after the meal would always stay for a little chat with them before going back upstairs to her work. The girls often slipped out of the classroom during the study hour to see her. She knew by heart love songs from the last century, and would sing them softly as she sewed. She told the girls stories, passed on bits of news, ran errands for them in the town and, surreptitiously, would lend the older ones the novel which she invariably carried in her apron pocket, and which the good lady herself, in her spare moments, devoured in large chunks. These novels were solely concerned with love affairs, lovers and their beloveds, damsels in distress swooning in secluded summerhouses, postilions slain at every posting-house, horses ridden to death on every page, gloomy forests, wounded hearts, vows, sobs, tears, and kisses, gondolas by moonlight, nightingales in woods, and 'gentlemen' brave as lions, meek as lambs, unbelievably virtuous, always immaculately turned out, who weep buckets of tears. So, when she was fifteen, Emma spent six months breathing the dust of old lending libraries. Later, with Walter Scott, she became enthralled by things historical and would dream of oaken chests, guardrooms, and minstrels. She would have liked to live in some old manor house, like those ladies in long-waisted gowns who, leaning chin in hand on the stone ledge of a window, spent their days gazing from beneath its trefoil arch at a white-plumed cavalier, mounted on a black steed, riding towards them from the distant horizon. At that period she idolized Mary Queen of Scots, and felt a passionate admiration for women who were famous or ill-starred. Joan of Arc, Héloïse, Agnès Sorel,* La Belle Ferronnière,* and Clémence Isaure* shone like comets, for her, against the vast grey backdrop of history, where here and there also appeared—though more shadowy in outline, and totally unrelated to one another—St Louis under his oak,* Bayard* as he lay dying, some dreadful deeds of Louis XI,* odd scenes from the Massacre of St Bartholomew,* Henri IV's* plumed crest, and, always, the memory of the painted plates glorifying Louis XIV.*

In music class, the ballads that she sang were solely about little angels with golden wings, madonnas, lagoons, and gondoliers: soothing compositions which allowed her to glimpse, behind the inanity of the words and the incongruity of the music, the seductive illusion of emotional realities. Some of her companions brought back to the convent the 'keepsakes'* they had received as New Year gifts. These albums had to be kept hidden, which was no easy matter; the girls used to read them in the dormitory. Handling their handsome satin bindings with great care, Emma stared in dazzled amazement at the names of the unknown authors, most of whom had used a title— count or viscount—when signing their contribution.

She shivered as she blew the tissue paper off each engraving; it would lift up half folded, then gently fall back against the opposite page. There, behind the balustrade of a balcony, a young man in a short cloak would be clasping in his arms a young girl wearing a white dress, with a purse at her girdle; or else there would be a portrait of an unnamed English noblewoman with golden curls, her large pale eyes staring at Emma from beneath a round straw hat. Some ladies reclined in carriages gliding through parks, with a grey-hound bounding along in front of the trotting horses, which were driven by two little postilions in white knee breeches. Others lay dreaming on sofas, an opened letter beside them, as they gazed at the moon through a half-open window partly concealed by black drapery. Innocent maidens with tear-stained cheeks blew kisses at turtledoves through the bars of Gothic birdcages or, smiling, heads coyly bent to one side, plucked petals off a daisy with tapering fingers that curved up at the tips like Turkish slippers. And of course there were also sultans with long pipes, lolling in arbours in the arms of dancing girls, and Giaours,* and Turkish sabres, and fezzes; and, above all, the monochrome landscapes of Dithyrambia, where palms and pine trees often grow side by side, with tigers on the right and a lion on the left, Tartar minarets in the distance and in the foreground Roman ruins, with a kneeling camel or two beyond; all of this framed by a neatly groomed virgin forest, and showing a great

perpendicular sunbeam shimmering on the water where—white
scratches on the steel-grey background—a few carefully spaced
swans are floating.

And the shaded lamp on the wall above Emma's head shone on all
these images of the world,* as one after another they passed before
her eyes in the silent dormitory, where the only sound came from
some distant, belated cab still driving along the boulevard.

When her mother died, at first she wept profusely. She had a
mourning picture made for herself from the dead woman's hair, and,
in a letter that she sent home, full of sad reflections on human life,
she asked to be buried, when it was time, in the same grave. Her
father thought she must be ill, and came to see her. Emma was
secretly pleased to have so rapidly attained that rare ideal of ethereal
languor to which the commonplace heart can never aspire. So she let
herself drift along the meanders of Lamartinian melancholy,* her ear
attuned to the music of harps echoing over lakes, to all the songs of
dying swans, to all the falling leaves, to the pure virgins rising up to
heaven, and to the voice of the Everlasting intoning in the valleys.
Growing bored with this, though reluctant to admit it, she continued
out of habit and then out of vanity, and eventually was surprised to
find herself soothed, with no more sadness in her heart than she had
wrinkles on her brow.

The good sisters, who had been so certain of her vocation, were
astonished to observe that Mademoiselle Rouault seemed to be slipping from their grasp. They had, indeed, so deluged her with
masses, retreats, novenas, and sermons, preached so well the veneration due to saints and martyrs, and given so much good advice
about modesty of the body and salvation of the soul, that she did as
horses do when reined in too tightly: she stopped dead and the bit
slipped from between her teeth. With a mind that was practical in
pursuit of its enthusiasms, that had loved the church for its flowers,
music for the words of its sentimental songs, and literature for its
power to stir the emotions, she rebelled against the mysteries of
faith, just as she became increasingly impatient of discipline, to
which her temperament was ill suited. When her father removed her
from the convent, they were not sorry to see her leave. The Mother
Superior even thought that she had, of late, shown less than proper
respect towards the community.

At first, after returning home, Emma enjoyed managing the

servants, but then she began to dislike country life, and to miss the convent. By the time Charles first appeared at Les Bertaux she thought of herself as profoundly disillusioned, with nothing more to learn, and nothing more to feel.

But the desire for a change in her life, or perhaps the nervous excitation produced by this man's presence, had sufficed to persuade her that, at long last, she held within her grasp that marvellous passion which until then had hovered like a great rosy-plumaged bird in the splendour of poetic skies—and she now could not believe that this placid existence of hers was the happiness of which she had dreamed.

CHAPTER VII

Sometimes she would reflect that these were, after all, the most beautiful days of her life, the honeymoon, as it was called. Probably, in order to savour their sweetness, you had to travel far away, to those lands with legendary names, where the first days of marriage were filled with a sweeter indolence.* In the post-chaise with its blinds of blue silk you'd slowly climb up the steep mountain roads, listening to the song of the postilion as it echoed over the mountains and mingled with the tinkling of goats' bells and the muffled roar of the waterfall. At sunset, you'd stand above a bay breathing in the scent of the lemon trees; then, in the evening, you'd sit alone together on the terrace of some villa, your fingers intertwined, gazing at the stars and making plans. It seemed to her that certain places on earth must produce happiness, like a plant native to that soil which grows poorly anywhere else. Why could she not be leaning over the balcony of some Swiss chalet,* or nursing her melancholy in a cottage in the Highlands, with a husband wearing a long-skirted coat of black velvet, soft boots, a pointed hat, and ruffles at the wrist!

Perhaps she would have liked to confide all these feelings to someone. But how to speak of so elusive a malaise, which changes its form like the clouds and whirls about like the wind? She lacked the right words, the opportunity, the self-assurance.

Still, if Charles had only tried, if he had guessed her feelings, if his eyes, just once, had read her thoughts, it seemed to her that her heart would suddenly have let drop a great bounty, as ripe fruit drops from a tree at the touch of a hand. But, even as the intimacy of their life bound them ever more closely together, an inward detachment grew in Emma, separating her from him.

Charles's conversation was as flat as any pavement, and everybody's ideas plodded along it, garbed in pedestrian style, inspiring no emotion, no laughter, no reverie. He had never felt tempted, he said, while living in Rouen, to go to the theatre to see the actors from Paris. He did not know how to swim, or fence, or shoot a gun, and he was unable, one day, to explain to her a term in riding that she had come across in a book.

But a man, surely, should know everything, should excel at many different things, should initiate you into the intensities of passion, into the refinements of life, into all its mysteries? But this man taught nothing, knew nothing, desired nothing. He believed she was happy; and she resented him for this settled calm of his, for his untroubled dullness, for the very happiness she brought him.

She used to draw sometimes; and Charles found it most entertaining to stand there at her side, watching her concentrate on her sketch, screwing up her eyes to see her work more clearly, or rolling breadcrumbs into little erasers with her thumb. As for the piano, the faster her fingers flew about, the more was he amazed. She struck each note with a confident touch, sweeping across the whole keyboard from top to bottom without a pause. The old piano with its badly stretched strings shook under her hands and could be heard, if the window was open, right across the village; often the bailiff's clerk, shuffling along the road with his head bare and his feet in slippers, would stop to listen, holding the document he was delivering in his hand.

Furthermore, Emma knew how to run her house. She sent Charles's patients details of what they owed in nicely phrased letters that did not sound like bills. When they invited a neighbour to dinner on a Sunday she would make a point of providing some special dish; she knew how to arrange plums in a pyramid on vine leaves, how to serve pots of fruit preserve turned out onto a plate, and she even spoke of buying finger bowls for use at dessert. All this helped Charles's reputation greatly.

Charles came to think more highly of himself because of having such a wife. He would proudly show off, in the parlour, two little pencil sketches of hers which he had had framed in wide frames and hung on the wallpaper from long green cords. When people came out of mass they would see him standing on his doorstep wearing a handsome pair of carpet slippers.

He came home late, at ten o'clock, sometimes midnight. Then, as he would want a meal and the maid had gone to bed, it was Emma who served him. He would take off his coat so as to be more comfortable while he ate. He would list, one by one, every person he had met, every village he had visited, every prescription he had written, and, well pleased with himself, he would eat the remains of the meat stew, pare the rind off his cheese, munch an apple, finish the wine, then take himself off to bed, where he lay down on his back and snored.

As he had long been used to a cotton nightcap, his silk scarf would never stay properly on his head, so that in the morning his hair was all over his face and white with down from his pillow, which often came undone during the night. He always wore thick boots which had deep creases running obliquely from instep to ankle, while the rest of the upper was as rigid and taut as if it encased a piece of wood. He said they 'did perfectly well for the country'.

His mother approved of his thriftiness, for she still came to see him as she had done in the past, whenever there was a particularly violent row in her own home; yet it appeared that the elder Madame Bovary was prejudiced against her daughter-in-law. She thought 'her tastes too fancy for folks like them'; they went through firewood, sugar, and candles 'as fast as in a great house', and the amount of charcoal burnt in the kitchen would have done to feed twenty-five! She arranged the linen in the cupboards and taught Emma to keep a close eye on the butcher when he brought the meat. Emma listened to her lectures; Madame Bovary did not stint them; and all day long the words 'daughter' and 'mother' flew back and forth between them, issuing from lips that quivered slightly as each uttered soft words in a voice that shook with anger.

In the days of Madame Dubuc, the old lady had still felt she was the favourite; but now, Charles's love for Emma seemed to her a betrayal of his affection, an encroachment on something that belonged to her; and she observed her son's happiness in a mournful silence, like a pauper who gazes through a window at people sitting down to a meal in her former home. Pretending to reminisce, she reminded him of the hardships and sacrifices she had endured for his sake and, comparing them to Emma's careless ways, concluded that it was quite unreasonable of him to worship her so exclusively.

Charles did not know how to answer her; he respected his mother, but he adored his wife; he believed that the judgement of the one was infallible, yet considered the other as above reproach. When Madame Bovary had left he made a faint-hearted attempt to repeat, using the same expressions, some of the more innocuous remarks his mother had made; Emma curtly proved him mistaken, and sent him back to his patients.

Nevertheless, faithful to the theories she believed in, she tried to make herself experience love. In the garden, by moonlight, she would recite all the passionate lines of verse that she knew by heart and, sighing, would sing him melancholy airs; but afterwards she felt just as calm as she had felt before, and Charles seemed neither more in love, nor more deeply moved.

Having tried a few times without success to ignite a spark of passion in her heart, and being, moreover, incapable of understanding what she did not experience, or of believing anything that did not manifest itself in conventional form, she soon came to the conclusion that there was no longer anything extraordinary about Charles's love for her. His transports had become routine; he embraced her at certain times. It was a habit like any other, a dessert to look forward to after a humdrum dinner.

A gamekeeper cured by Monsieur of an inflammation of the lungs had given Madame a small Italian greyhound; she took it with her on walks, for she did go out occasionally, in order to be alone for a while, and no longer have to gaze at that eternal garden and that dusty road.

She would go as far as the beech avenue at Banneville, to the derelict lodge at the corner of the wall on the field side. In the ditch, among the grasses, grew tall reeds with razor-sharp leaves.

First she would look all around, to see if anything had changed since the last time she was there. She would find the foxgloves and the wallflowers still in the same spots, the clumps of nettles still growing round the large stones, and the patches of lichen along the three windows whose permanently closed shutters were rotting away on their rusty iron hinges. Her thoughts, at first unfocused, would stray aimlessly about, like her greyhound, who was running in circles over the fields, yapping at yellow butterflies, chasing field mice, and nibbling at the poppies that grew at the edge of the wheat. Then, gradually, her ideas would take form and, sitting on the grass, jabbing at it with the tip of her sunshade, Emma would ask herself again and again:

'Why in the world did I ever get married?'

She would wonder whether there might not have been some way, through some different set of circumstances, for her to have met a different man; and she tried to imagine what they might have been, those circumstances which had not arisen, that different life, that unknown husband. For indeed not all husbands were like this one. He might have been handsome, witty, distinguished, attractive, as were no doubt the men her old school friends from the convent had married. What must they be doing now? In the city, with the noises of the streets, the hum of the theatres, and the bright lights of the balls, they were leading lives where the heart had space to expand, the senses to blossom. But her life was as cold as an attic with a skylight facing north, and boredom, like a silent spider, was weaving its web in every shadowy recess of her heart. She remembered the prizegivings, when she would go up on to the stage to receive her little wreaths. With her hair in braids and her prunella slippers showing below her white dress, she made a charming picture, and as she walked back to her seat the gentlemen would lean forward to pay her compliments; the courtyard was full of carriages, people were calling goodbye through the carriage windows, the music master waved as he passed by, carrying his violin case. How far away all that was! How far, far away!

She would call Djali and, holding her between her knees, stroke her long delicate head and say:

'Come on, give me a kiss, you've no worries, have you?'

Djali yawned lazily and Emma, touched by the slender creature's mournful expression, would liken herself to her pet and speak to her out loud, as though comforting someone in distress.

Occasionally, squalls would blow up, winds from the sea that whipped right across the plains of the Pays de Caux, bringing a salt-laden chill to the distant fields. Down near the ground the reeds hissed, and the rapidly quivering leaves of the beeches rustled as the treetops gave their vast sighs, swaying endlessly back and forth. Emma would draw her shawl round her shoulders and stand up.

In the avenue a green glow, muted by the foliage, lit up the smooth moss which creaked softly beneath her feet. The sun was setting; the sky showed red between the branches, and the identical trunks of the trees planted in their straight rows stood out like a dark brown colonnade against a golden background; suddenly she would feel afraid, call Djali, and, returning quickly to Tostes along the highway, sink into an armchair and not say a word all evening.

But, towards the end of September, something extraordinary happened: she was invited to La Vaubyessard, the home of the Marquis d'Andervilliers.

Secretary of State under the Restoration, the Marquis wanted to return to political life, and was preparing the ground, well ahead of time, for his candidature to the Chamber of Deputies. In winter he made regular distributions of firewood, and at departmental council meetings argued eloquently for new roads for his district. In the middle of the summer he had developed an abscess in his mouth that Charles had cured, miraculously, it seemed, with a neat touch of the lancet. His steward, sent to Tostes to settle the account, reported that evening that he had seen some superb cherries in the doctor's modest garden. Now cherries grew poorly at La Vaubyessard, so the Marquis asked Bovary for a few grafts, and, as he made a point of thanking him personally, he saw Emma, and observed that her figure was pretty and her manner of greeting him quite stylish. Consequently it was decided, at the chateau, that an invitation to the young couple would exceed neither the bounds of condescension nor those of social acceptability.

At three o'clock one Wednesday Monsieur and Madame Bovary set off for La Vaubyessard in their gig, with a large trunk tied on behind and a hat-box in front. There was also a cardboard box jammed between Charles's legs.

They arrived at dusk, just as lanterns were being lit in the park, to guide the carriages.

CHAPTER VIII

The chateau, a modern building in the Italian style* with two projecting wings and three flights of steps, spread out across the far side of a huge expanse of green, on which a few cows stood grazing among widely spaced groups of big trees; clusters of shrubs, rhododendrons, syringas, and guelder roses displayed their irregular bushy greenery in borders that edged the curved gravel drive. A stream flowed under a bridge; and through the mist you could just make out the thatched roofs of a scattering of buildings in the meadow and, beyond, two thickly wooded hillsides that sloped gently up. Behind the house, in the trees, arose the parallel structures of the stables and the coach houses—all that remained of the original chateau, now demolished.

Charles's gig halted in front of the central flight of steps. Several servants approached, then the Marquis, who offered his arm to the doctor's wife and escorted her into the hall.

The hall had a very high ceiling and a floor of marble tiles, so that footsteps and voices echoed as if in a church. Opposite the entrance rose a straight staircase; to the left a gallery looked out over the garden and led to the billiard room, from whose door came the clink of ivory balls. As she walked through the billiard room on her way to the drawing room, Emma saw, grouped round the table, solemn-looking men with cravats tied high under the chin; they all wore decorations and were smiling as they silently wielded their cues. On the dark wood of the panelling hung large gilded frames that bore, along the bottom, names inscribed in black letters. She read: 'Jean-Antoine d'Andervilliers d'Yverbonville, Comte de la Vaubyessard and Baron de la Fresnaye, killed at the battle of Coutras, 20 October 1587.' And on another: 'Jean-Antoine-Henry-Guy d'Andervilliers de la Vaubyessard, Admiral of France and Knight of the Order of St Michael, wounded at the battle of Hougue-Saint-Vaast, 29 May 1692, died at La Vaubyessard 23 January 1693.'* Then the next names were almost impossible to read, for the lamplight had been aimed onto the green felt surface of the table, filling the rest of the room with shadow. The row of canvases hanging round the walls glowed dimly, the light casting a delicate tracery of lines that followed the cracks in the varnish; here and there some paler detail of a painting would stand out from all those big dark squares edged in gold: a white forehead, two staring eyes, a wig coiling over a scarlet powder-flecked shoulder, or perhaps the buckle of a garter above a shapely calf.

The Marquis opened the drawing room door. One of the ladies (the Marquise herself) stood up; she came over to Emma, made her sit with her on a small sofa, and began to talk companionably to her as though she had known her for years. She was a woman of about forty, with beautiful shoulders, an aquiline nose, and a drawling voice; that evening her chestnut-brown hair was covered by a simple piece of lace that fell down her back in a point. A fair-haired young woman sat close beside her in a high-backed chair; and, all round the fireplace, gentlemen with flowers in their buttonholes stood chatting to the ladies.

At seven o'clock, dinner was served. The men, who were the more numerous, sat at the first table, in the hall, and the ladies at the second, in the dining room, with the Marquis and the Marquise.

As she walked in, Emma felt herself enveloped by warm air in which the fragrance of flowers and fine linen mingled with the smell of roast meat and the aroma of truffles. Candles flaming in the sconces shone taller on the rounded silver dish-covers; cut glass, its facets clouded by steam, gleamed palely; vases of flowers were aligned down the length of the table, and, on the wide-bordered plates, each napkin, shaped into a bishop's mitre, held between its folds a tiny oval roll of bread. Red lobster claws hung over the rims of platters, magnificent fruits reposed on layers of moss in openwork baskets, quail lay in their plumage, enticing smells filled the air; and, solemn as a judge in knee breeches, silk stockings, white cravat, and frilled shirt front, the butler, as he passed the ready-carved dishes between the shoulders of the guests, would with a deft flick of his spoon serve you the slice you indicated. Atop the great copper-banded porcelain stove, the statue of a woman, draped to the chin, gazed unmoving down at the crowded room.

Madame Bovary noticed that several of the ladies had not put their gloves in their wine glasses.*

At the head of the table, alone among all these women, an old man sat eating, hunched over his well-filled plate, his napkin knotted round his neck like a child's; sauce kept dribbling from his mouth. His eyes were bloodshot and he wore his hair in a little pigtail bound with black ribbon. It was the Marquis's father-in-law, the old Duc de Laverdière, once the favourite of the Comte d'Artois, in the days of the hunting parties given by the Marquis de Conflans at Le Vaudreuil; he was said to have been the lover of Marie-Antoinette, between Monsieur de Coigny and Monsieur de Lauzun.* He had led a tempestuous, dissipated life, filled with duels and wagers and abductions, had squandered all his money and terrified all his family.

A servant standing behind his chair shouted into his ear the names of the dishes that he pointed to, mumbling; and Emma's eyes kept returning involuntarily to this old man with pendulous lips, as if to something extraordinary and majestic. He had lived at Court, and slept in the bed of a queen!

Chilled champagne was served. Emma shivered all over when she felt this sensation of cold in her mouth. She had never seen a pomegranate, or tasted a pineapple. Even the powdered sugar seemed whiter and finer than elsewhere.

Then the ladies went up to their rooms to prepare for the ball.

Emma dressed herself with the painstaking care of an actress making her debut. She arranged her hair as the hairdresser had advised, and then slipped into her sheer silk gown which had been laid out on the bed. Charles's trousers were too tight round the waist.

'These foot-straps will be a nuisance when I dance,' he said.

'Dance?' repeated Emma.

'Yes!'

'Are you out of your mind? People would laugh at you; you'd better stand and watch. That's more suitable, anyway, for a doctor,' she added.

Charles said nothing. He was walking up and down, waiting for Emma.

He could see her from behind, in the mirror, between two candles. Her dark eyes seemed even darker. Her hair, dressed so that it belled gently out over her ears, shone with a blue lustre; in her chignon a rose trembled on a flexible stem, its leaves tipped with artificial dewdrops. She was wearing a dress of pale saffron, set off by three bunches of button roses with sprays of green.

Charles came up to kiss her on the shoulder.

'Leave me alone!' she said, 'You'll rumple me.'

They heard a violin playing a ritornello, then the sound of a horn. She went down the stairs, trying not to run.

The quadrilles had begun. People kept arriving. They were crowding into the ballroom. She took a seat near the door, on a small sofa.

When the dance finished, the floor was left to the groups of men standing about chatting, and to the liveried servants carrying large salvers. Along the row of seated women, painted fans fluttered, smiling lips almost disappeared behind bouquets, and gold-stoppered scent bottles turned over and over in half-open hands whose tight white gloves outlined the shape of fingernails and clung snugly round the wrist. Ruffles of lace, diamond brooches, bracelets with medallions quivered at necklines, glittered on breasts, jingled on bare arms. Hair, dressed close and smooth over the forehead, was twisted into a knot at the nape of the neck; every coiffure held a garland or a bunch or a spray of flowers—forget-me-nots, jasmine, pomegranate-blossoms, wheat-sprays, cornflowers. Sullen-looking mothers in scarlet turbans* sat composedly in their places.

Emma's heart beat a little faster as, with her partner leading her by the fingertips, she took her place in the line and waited for the violin to play the opening note. But her nervousness quickly vanished, and she glided forward, swaying to the rhythm of the music and gently nodding her head. Her lips broke into a smile at certain delicate flourishes of the violin, which sometimes played solo, while the other instruments remained silent; you could clearly hear the ringing of gold coins being flung down onto the baize-covered gaming tables in the next room; then the instruments would all start up again together, with a resounding blare of the cornet. Feet picked up the rhythm once more, skirts swung out and swished against each other, hands joined, then parted; those same eyes that had looked down looked up, meeting your gaze intently.

About fifteen or so of the men, aged between twenty-five and forty, who were mingling among the dancers or chatting in the doorways, stood out from the crowd because of a sort of family resemblance, despite their differences of age, dress, or feature.

Their coats were better cut, and seemed to be made of a more supple cloth, and their hair, combed into curls at the temples, seemed to glisten with more subtle pomades. They had the complexion that betokens wealth, that pale complexion which is enhanced by the translucence of porcelain, the sheen of satin, the patina on fine furniture, and which is kept in perfect condition by a discriminating regimen of exquisite foods. Their necks turned confidently above their low cravats; their long side-whiskers flowed over their turned-down collars; they dabbed their lips on softly scented handkerchiefs monogrammed with large initials. There was something youthful about those that were beginning to age, while the faces of the younger ones displayed a kind of maturity. Their coolly indifferent gaze revealed the calm that comes of passions promptly gratified; and, beneath their courtly manners, they exuded that particular brutality born of relatively facile conquests, those that demand physical strength, or titillate men's vanity: the handling of thoroughbred horses, the pursuit of loose women.

A few steps from Emma, a blue-coated gentleman was talking of Italy with a pale young woman wearing pearls. They praised the size of the pillars in St Peter's, Tivoli, Vesuvius, Castellamare, and Cascina, the roses in Genoa, and the Colosseum by moonlight. With her other ear Emma was listening to a conversation full of words she did not understand. People were crowding round a very young man who, just the week before, had beaten Miss Arabelle and Romulus, and won two thousand *louis* by jumping a ditch, in England.* One man was grumbling about his racers putting on weight, and another about misprints that had garbled the name of his horse.

The ballroom was stifling; the lamps were growing dim. People were moving out into the billiard room. A servant climbed onto a chair and broke a couple of panes; at the sound of the shattering glass, Madame Bovary looked round and saw, in the garden, pressed against the window panes, the faces of peasants, staring in. Suddenly she thought of Les Bertaux. She saw the farm, the muddy pond, her father in his smock under the apple trees, and she saw herself in earlier days, skimming cream with her finger from the earthenware milk pans in the dairy. But, in the dazzling splendours of the present moment, her past life, always until then so vivid, was vanishing completely, and she almost doubted that she had ever lived it. Here she was, at the ball; beyond it, now, everything else was veiled in shadow. Here she was eating a maraschino ice, holding in her left hand the scalloped silver-gilt saucer, her eyes half-closed, the spoon between her teeth.

Near her, a lady dropped her fan. A dancer was passing.

'Would you be so very kind, Monsieur,' said the lady, 'as to pick up my fan from behind the sofa?'

The gentleman bowed, and as he stretched his arm down Emma saw the hand of the young woman drop something white, folded in a triangle, into his hat. The gentleman returned with the fan and politely handed it to the lady, who thanked him with a nod and bent her head to smell her bouquet.

After the supper, which included a great many Spanish and Rhine

wines, shellfish bisques* and almond-milk soups, Trafalgar puddings,*
and a wide variety of cold meats set in aspic that quivered on the
plates, the carriages, one after the other, began to leave. Drawing
aside a corner of the muslin curtain, Emma could see the light of
their lanterns slipping away into the darkness. The sofas emptied; a
few people still lingered round the gaming tables; the musicians were
cooling the tips of their fingers on their tongues; Charles, half asleep,
stood leaning against a door.

At three in the morning the cotillion* began. Emma did not know
how to waltz. Everybody was waltzing, even Mademoiselle d'Andervilliers herself, and the Marquise; by now there remained only the
guests staying at the chateau, about a dozen in all.

But one of the waltzers, whom everyone addressed simply as
'Vicomte' and whose very low-cut waistcoat seemed to be moulded
to his chest, came over to Madame Bovary and asked her to dance
with him a second time, assuring her that he would lead her and she
would manage perfectly.

They began slowly, then went faster. They were turning; everything round them was turning—lamps, furniture, walls, floor—like a
disc on a spindle. As they went past the doors the hem of Emma's
dress caught on her partner's trousers; their legs became entwined;
he looked down at her, she looked up at him; a languor came over
her, she stopped. Starting again, the Vicomte, his pace faster now,
swept her away to the far recesses of the gallery where, panting, she
almost fell, and for an instant rested her head against his breast. And
then, still whirling round and round, although more slowly, he led
her back to her seat; she leant against the wall and covered her eyes
with her hand.

When she opened them a lady was sitting on a stool in the middle
of the salon, with three partners kneeling at her feet. She chose the
Vicomte, and the violin struck up again.

Everyone watched them. They danced round and round the
room, she keeping her upper body motionless and her head slightly
bent, he with the same posture as before, his shoulders back, his arm
curved, his lips thrust forward. Now there was a woman who knew
how to waltz! They went on for a long time and wore out everyone
else.

People chatted for a few more minutes and then, after saying
goodnight, or rather good morning, the guests went off to bed.

Charles dragged himself up the stairs; his knees 'were killing him'. He had spent five solid hours standing near the tables watching people play whist, without grasping a thing about the game. So he heaved a great sigh of relief when he pulled off his shoes.

Emma wrapped a shawl round her shoulders, opened the window and leaned out on the sill.

The night was dark. A few drops of rain were falling. She breathed in the damp wind; it felt soothing to her eyelids. The music from the ball was still throbbing in her ears, and she tried hard to stay awake, so as to prolong the illusion of this life of luxury that she would soon have to leave behind.

Day began to break. She gazed for a long time at the windows of the chateau, trying to guess which were the rooms of the people she had particularly noticed during the evening. She longed to know all about their lives, to penetrate into them, be part of them.

But she was shivering with cold. She undressed and snuggled down between the sheets, against a sleeping Charles.

There were a great many people at breakfast. The meal lasted ten minutes; to the doctor's surprise, no liqueurs were served. Then Mademoiselle d'Andervilliers collected the remains of the brioches in a basket to feed the swans on the lake, and they all went for a stroll through the hothouse, where pyramids of weird prickly plants were arranged beneath hanging containers which, like so many over-flowing snakes' nests, trailed long, intertwining tendrils of green. From the orangery, at the end, a covered passageway led to the outbuildings. To amuse the young woman, the Marquis took her to see the stables. Above the basket-shaped racks, porcelain plaques bore the names of the horses, in black letters. Each animal stirred restlessly in its stall as the visitors passed close by, making clicking sounds with their tongues. The floor of the tack room shone like the parquet floor of a salon. Carriage harnesses hung on two revolving posts in the centre, while the bits, whips, stirrups, and curbs were arranged in rows along the wall.

Charles, meanwhile, asked a servant to harness his gig. It was brought round to the front steps, and when all the boxes had been stowed away, the Bovarys said their farewells to the Marquis and the Marquise, and set off for Tostes.

Emma sat in silence, watching the wheels turn. Charles, perched on the very edge of the seat, drove with his arms spread apart, and the little horse ambled along between the shafts, which were rather too wide for it. The slack reins flapped against his rump, soaking up frothy sweat, and the corded box tied on the back kept hitting against the body of the gig with a heavy, rhythmic thump.

They had reached the rise near Thibourville when suddenly a group of horsemen rode across in front of them, smoking cigars and laughing. Emma thought she recognized the Vicomte; she turned round, but could only see, on the horizon, heads bobbing up and down to the irregular cadence of gallop or trot.

Half a mile further on, they had to stop to repair a broken harness strap with a piece of rope.

But Charles, as he was giving the harness a final check, saw something on the ground between his horse's legs; and he picked up a cigar-case with green silk round the edges and a coat of arms in the centre, like a carriage door.

'There's even a couple of cigars in it,' he said; 'I'll have them tonight, after dinner.'

'You mean you smoke?' she asked.

'Sometimes, when I get the chance.'

He put his find into his pocket, and gave the pony a flick with the whip.

When they reached home the dinner was not ready. Madame lost her temper. Nastasie retorted insolently.

'Leave the room!' said Emma. 'I won't stand for it, you're sacked.'

For dinner there was onion soup, and some veal with sorrel. Charles, sitting opposite Emma, remarked happily, rubbing his hands together:

'It's so nice to be home again!'

They could hear Nastasie crying. He was rather fond of the poor girl. In the past, after he was widowed, she had kept him company through many an empty evening. She was his first patient, his oldest acquaintance in the place.

'Do you really mean to sack her?' he said finally.

'Yes. Why shouldn't I?' she replied.

Then they warmed themselves in the kitchen while their room was being prepared. Charles began to smoke. He smoked with his lips thrust out, spitting repeatedly, recoiling at every puff.

'You'll make yourself ill,' she said scornfully.

He put down the cigar, and rushed outside to the pump for a glass of cold water. Emma grabbed the cigar-case and flung it into the back of the cupboard.

The hours dragged, the next day. She walked in her small garden, round and round the same paths, stopping at the flower beds, at the fruit trees, at the plaster curé, staring in amazement at all those things from her past that were so familiar. How far away the ball seemed, already! How did it come about that so vast a distance could separate the morning of the day before yesterday from the evening of today? Her visit to La Vaubyessard had left a chasm in her life, like those great crevasses that a storm sometimes hollows out in the mountains, in a single night. She resigned herself, however; reverently she stowed away in the chest of drawers her beautiful ball gown and even her satin slippers, their soles yellowed by the beeswax on the dance floor. Her heart was like them: contact with riches had left something on it that would never rub off.

Remembering the ball became for Emma a daily occupation. Every time Wednesday came round, she told herself when she woke up: 'Ah! One week ago . . . two weeks ago . . . three weeks ago, I was there!' And, little by little, in her memory, the faces all blurred together; she forgot the tunes of the quadrilles; no longer could she so clearly picture the liveries and the rooms; some details disappeared, but the yearning remained.

CHAPTER IX

Often, when Charles was away, she would go to the cupboard and take out, from between the folded linen where she had left it, the green silk cigar-case.

She would look at it, open it, and even sniff its lining, which smelled of verbena and tobacco. Whose was it? The Vicomte's. Perhaps it was a gift from his mistress. She had embroidered it on some rosewood frame, a charming little object kept hidden from all eyes, and which had filled many hours for the pensive needlewoman as she sat with her soft curls bent over it. Sighs of love had passed through the meshes of the canvas, and every thrust of the needle had stitched a hope or a memory into them; all those intertwined threads of silk were simply the continuing expression of the same silent passion. And then, one morning, the Vicomte had taken it away with him.

What had they talked about, while it was lying on one of those broad mantelpieces, between the vases of flowers and the Pompadour* clocks? She was in Tostes. Whereas he, now, was in Paris, far away! What kind of place was it, this Paris? What an immeasurable name! Again and again she would repeat it under her breath, delighting in the sound; it echoed in her ears like a great cathedral bell, it blazed before her eyes, even on the labels of her jars of pomade.

At night, when the fishmongers in their wagons passed under her windows singing 'La Marjolaine',* she would wake up; and, as she listened to the noise of their iron-rimmed wheels, which quickly died away when they reached the dirt track beyond the village, she would tell herself:

'Tomorrow, they'll be there!'

And in her thoughts she followed them, up and down the hills, through the villages, racing along the highway by the light of the stars. Then, always, after an indeterminate distance, things became a blur, and her dream died away.

She bought herself a street-map of Paris, and with her fingertip went on expeditions in the capital. She walked along the boulevards, stopping at every corner, between the lines representing the streets, in front of the white squares that marked the houses. At length, her eyes growing tired, she would close them and see, in the darkness, the gas-lamps flickering in the wind as the folding steps of carriages were let down with a great clatter at the theatre entrances.

She began subscribing to *La Corbeille*, a woman's magazine, and to *Le Sylphe des salons**. Never missing a single detail, she devoured all the accounts of first nights, race meetings, and evening parties; she was fascinated by the debut of a singer, or the opening of a new shop. She knew about the latest fashions, the addresses of the good tailors, the right days for the Bois* or the Opéra. In the novels of Eugène Sue* she pored over descriptions of furniture; in those of Balzac* and George Sand,* she searched for vicarious gratification of her own secret desires. She would even bring her book to the table and turn over the pages while Charles ate and talked to her. The memory of the Vicomte was always present in her reading. She made connections between him and the fictional characters. But, very gradually, the circle whose centre he was grew larger round him, and that halo he wore shifted away from him, to shine its radiance on other dreams.

Paris, vaster than the ocean, shimmered before Emma's eyes in a rosy haze. But its teeming, tumultuous life was divided into compartments, classified into separate tableaux. Of these Emma was aware of only two or three, which hid all the others from her, and by themselves represented the whole of humankind. The world of high diplomacy moved about on gleaming parquet floors, in drawing rooms panelled with mirrors, round oval tables covered by gold-fringed velvet cloths. It contained dresses with trains, impenetrable mysteries, anguish concealed by smiles. Then came the world of the duchesses; its women were pale, stayed in bed until four, and wore— poor angels!—petticoats hemmed with English lace, while the men, their true worth never recognized behind their masks of frivolity, rode their horses till they dropped just for the fun of it, spent the summer season in Baden, and then, at about forty, married heiresses. From the private rooms of restaurants, after midnight, came the laughter of the mixed crowd of writers and actresses who gathered there to dine by candlelight. They were prodigal as kings, full of idealistic ambitions and wild fantasies. They lived on a higher plane than other people, somewhere sublime between heaven and earth, among the storm clouds. As for the rest of the world, it was lost in shadows, it was nowhere, it seemed not to exist. Indeed, the closer things were to Emma, the more her thoughts avoided them. Everything in her immediate surroundings, the boring countryside, the stupid *petits bourgeois*, the mediocrity of life, seemed to her the exception, a freak accident that had befallen her alone, whereas somewhere else, beyond all this, the vast realm of joy and passion stretched on and on forever. In her longing she confused the sensual pleasures of luxury with the rapture of love, and elegance of manners with sensitivity of feeling. Did not love, like tropical plants, require a specially prepared soil, a particular temperature? Sighs by moonlight, long embraces, tears streaming over hands surrendered to a lover, all the fevers of the flesh and the languors of love—these were surely inseparable from the balcony of a great castle where days pass in idleness, from a silk-curtained, thick-carpeted boudoir with flower-filled window boxes and a bed on a dais, from the sparkle of precious stones, and from livery with braided frogging.

The lad from the post-house who came every morning to groom the mare would tramp along the passage in his thick clogs; he wore a ragged smock, and his legs were bare. This was the groom in knee breeches with whom she had to be content! When his work was finished he left, and did not come back that day, for Charles himself, on his return, would stable his horse, unsaddle her, and put on the halter, while the maid fetched a bundle of hay and tossed it as best she could into the manger.

To replace Nastasie (who eventually left Tostes, weeping copiously) Emma hired a sweet-faced girl of fourteen, an orphan. She forbade her to wear cotton caps, taught her to use the third person when addressing her, to hand a glass of water on a salver, to knock on the door before entering, and to iron and starch and help her dress, in the hopes of turning her into a lady's maid. The new servant, fearful of losing her job, obeyed without complaint; and, as Emma generally left the key in the sideboard, Félicité would take upstairs, every night, a small supply of sugar to eat alone, in bed, after saying her prayers.

Sometimes, in the afternoon, she would go across the road to chat with the postilions. Madame remained upstairs, in her room.

She would wear an open-necked dressing gown that revealed, between its softly draped lapels, a pleated bodice fastened by three gold buttons. Her belt was a cord with big tassels, and her tiny garnet-red slippers bore rosettes of wide ribbons that cascaded over the instep. She had bought herself a blotter, a writing case, a penholder, and some envelopes, although she had no one to write to; she would dust her shelves, look at herself in the mirror, pick up a book, and then, as daydreams replaced the lines of print, let it fall on to her lap. She longed to travel; she longed to go back to her convent to live. She wanted to die, and she wanted to live in Paris.

Charles rode about the country lanes in rain and snow. He ate omelettes at farmhouse tables, stuck his arm down into damp beds, felt warm blood spatter his face when he bled a patient, listened to death rattles, scrutinized the contents of basins, and turned back plenty of dirty linen; but every evening he returned to a blazing fire, a well-set table, a comfortable chair, and a charming, fastidiously dressed wife, who smelled so sweet that he never really knew where this fragrance came from, or whether it wasn't her skin that was perfuming her bodice.

She enchanted him with countless delicate refinements: a new way, perhaps, of making paper drip-rings for the candles, or else a flounce that she had altered on her dress, or the extraordinary name of a perfectly simple dish that the maid spoiled, but which Charles relished to the last spoonful. In Rouen she saw some ladies with sets of charms hanging from their watches; she bought some charms. She wanted, for her mantelpiece, a pair of large vases in blue glass and then, a little later, an ivory workbox with a silver-gilt thimble. The less Charles understood these elegancies, the more seductive he found them. They added something to the pleasure of his senses and the sweetness of his home. They were like a scattering of gold dust along the humble pathway of his life.

His health was good, he looked well; his reputation was firmly established. The country folk were fond of him because he was not proud. He was affectionate with children, never went into a bar, and, indeed, inspired confidence by his morality. He was particularly successful with catarrhs and ailments of the chest. In fact, terrified of killing his patients, Charles rarely prescribed anything other than sedatives or, occasionally, an emetic, footbaths, or leeches. Not that he was frightened of the knife; he would bleed you with a heavy hand, like a horse, and he had the 'devil of a grip' when it came to pulling teeth.

And then, 'to keep up with the latest', he took out a subscription to the *Ruche médicale*, a new publication for which he had received the prospectus. He would read it for a while after dinner, but the warmth of the room and the meal he was digesting combined to send him to sleep after five minutes; and there he would sit, his chin resting on his hands and his hair spread out like a mane under the table lamp. Emma would gaze at him, shrugging her shoulders. Why couldn't she at least have for a husband one of those silent, dedicated men who pore over their books all night long, and finally, when old age and rheumatism come upon them, are awarded a cross to display on their badly cut black coat? She'd have liked this name of Bovary, which was her own, to be illustrious, to see it displayed by booksellers, quoted in newspapers, famous throughout France. But Charles had no ambition! A doctor from Yvetot, who had recently called him in on a consultation, had humiliated him at the very bedside of the patient, in the presence of the assembled family. When, that evening, Charles told her about the incident, Emma was vehement in her condemnation of the colleague. Charles was touched. With tears in his eyes, he kissed her on the forehead. But she was filled with raging mortification; she wanted to strike him and, going into the corridor, she opened the window and breathed the fresh air to calm herself.

'What a pitiful creature! What a pitiful creature!' she muttered, biting her lip.

She was, indeed, finding him more and more irritating. With age, he was developing coarse habits: at dessert he would whittle the cork of the empty wine bottle; after meals he would run his tongue over his teeth; he made a gurgling sound each time he swallowed a mouthful of his soup and, as he was beginning to put on weight, his eyes, already tiny, seemed to be pushed up towards his temples by the pudginess of his cheeks.

Sometimes Emma would tuck in the red border of his sweater under his waistcoat, adjust his necktie, or discard the soiled gloves that he had been about to put on; and it was not, as he supposed, for his sake; it was for herself, out of an overflow of egocentricity, out of nervous exasperation. Sometimes, too, she talked to him of things that she had read, about a passage in a novel, perhaps, or a new play, or some anecdote concerning the 'upper crust' that she had seen in the paper. Charles was, after all, always there, he always listened, he always approved. She confided a great many secrets to her grey-hound! She would have confided in the logs in the fireplace and the pendulum of the clock.

But deep in her soul she was waiting for something to happen. Like a sailor in distress, she cast her eyes in desperation over the solitude of her life, searching the mists of the horizon for some distant white sail. She did not know what this chance event would be, what wind would blow it towards her, to what shores it would bear her, whether it was a small boat or a great three-decker, laden with affliction or crammed to the gunwales with joy. But each morning on waking she expected it that day, and she would listen to every sound, leaping to her feet, astonished that it did not come; then, as each day ended, she felt still sadder, and longed for tomorrow.

It was spring again. She suffered from breathlessness at the start of the hot weather, when the pear trees blossomed.

From the beginning of July, she counted on her fingers the number of weeks remaining before October, thinking that the Marquis d'Andervilliers might perhaps give another ball at La Vaubyessard. But September passed without letters or visits.

After the pain of this disappointment her heart once more stood empty, and the succession of identical days began again.

So now they'd go on and on like this, numberless, always the same, bringing nothing! The lives of others, however dull they might be, did at least hold the possibility of an event. Sometimes a chance occurrence led to endless changes and reversals, and the scenery would shift. But, for her, nothing ever happened; God had willed it so! The future was a dark corridor, with a firmly closed door at the end.

She gave up music. Why play? Who'd listen to her? Since she'd never be able to play at a concert, on an Erard* piano, wearing a short-sleeved velvet dress, and hearing, as her fingers lightly struck the ivory keys, ecstatic murmurs sighing round her like a breeze, there was no point in taking the trouble to practise. She left her drawing portfolio and her tapestry work in the cupboard. Why bother? Why bother? Sewing got on her nerves.

'I've read everything,' she told herself.

And she would poke the tongs into the fire until they glowed red, or sit watching the rain come down.

How sad she felt on Sundays when Vespers were being rung! She would listen in dazed concentration to each clang of the cracked church bell. A stray cat, making its leisurely way over the rooftops, arched its back in the pale rays of the sun. The wind kept blowing trails of dust along the highway. Now and again, in the distance, a dog howled; and the regular, monotonous tolling of the bell went on and on, drifting away across the meadows.

Now they were coming out of church. Women in their polished clogs, farmers in their new smocks, little children skipping about bare-headed in front, they were all returning home. And, until nightfall, five or six men, always the same ones, stayed behind to play tip-penny in front of the main door of the inn.

It was a cold winter. The window panes, each morning, were thick with rime, letting in, as if through frosted glass, an opaque whitish light that sometimes did not change throughout the entire day. By four, the lamp had to be lit.

On fine days she would go down into the garden. The dew had draped the cabbages in silvery lace, stretching long gleaming filaments from one to the next. No birds were singing, everything seemed asleep, the straw-covered espaliers and the vine like a great sick snake coiled under the coping of the wall where, if you went up close, you could see woodlice crawling on their many feet. Among the spruces near the hedge the curé in his tricorn hat, reading his breviary, had lost his right foot, and even had a few milky scabs on his face where the plaster had flaked off in the frost.

Then, returning upstairs, she would close her door, poke the coals, and, faint from the heat of the fire, feel boredom bearing down upon her again, even more oppressively. She would gladly have gone to the kitchen to chat to the maid, but a sense of propriety held her back.

Every day, at the same hour, the schoolmaster in his black silk cap would open the shutters of his house, and the village policeman would walk past, his sword strapped over his smock. Every evening and every morning the post horses, three by three, would cross the road to drink from the pond. Now and again the bell of a tavern door would jangle and, when it was windy, you could hear grating against their rods the little copper bowls that served as a sign for the wig-maker's shop. By way of decoration, this had an ancient fashion print stuck against a window pane, and a wax bust of a woman with yellow hair. The wig-maker, he too mourned for his blighted career, his vanished prospects, and, his head filled with dreams of a shop in some big city, Rouen, perhaps, on the waterfront, near the theatre, he would spend the whole day walking gloomily to and fro between the Town Hall and the church, waiting for customers. When Madame Bovary looked up, she invariably saw him there like a sentry on duty, in his twill jacket, with his smoking cap over one ear.

Occasionally, in the afternoon, a man's head appeared at the sitting-room window: a weather-beaten face, with black side-whiskers and a slow smile, a big gentle smile that revealed white teeth. Then a waltz would begin and, on top of the barrel organ, in a tiny drawing room, dancers no taller than your finger—ladies in pink turbans, Tyroleans in jackets, monkeys in black tailcoats, gentlemen in knee breeches—circled round and round among the armchairs and tables and sofas, mirrored in pieces of glass held together at the edges by a band of gold paper. The man would crank the handle, looking to the right, then to the left, then over to the windows. From time to time, as he fired a long jet of brown saliva onto the kerbstone, he would raise his knee to support the instrument and ease the burden of its hard strap on his shoulder. And the music, now mournful and languid, now jubilant and fast, came throbbing out of the box through a pink taffeta curtain held by an ornate copper grill. They were tunes that were being played in other places, in the theatres, that were being sung in the salons, and danced to in the evenings under lighted chandeliers: they were echoes of the world filtering through to Emma. In her head sarabands played endlessly, and her thoughts, like some exotic dancing girl on a flowered carpet, went leaping about with the notes, swinging from dream to dream, from sorrow to sorrow. When the man had caught in his cap the coins she threw, he would pull down an old blue wool cover, hoist his organ onto his back, and plod heavily away. She always watched him go.

But it was at mealtimes, especially, that she could not bear it any longer, in that small ground-floor room with its smoking stove, its squeaking door, its sweating walls, and its damp flagstones; it seemed to her that all the bitterness of life was served up to her on her plate and that, along with the gusts of steam rising from the boiled beef, she could feel a kind of stagnant dreariness rising from the depths of her soul. Charles was a slow eater, and she would nibble a few nuts or, leaning on her elbow, amuse herself drawing lines on the oilcloth with the point of her knife.

Now she just let everything in the house go, and the elder Madame Bovary, when she came to stay for part of Lent, was amazed at the change. In fact Emma, always in the past so fastidious and refined, now spent whole days without dressing properly, wore grey cotton stockings, and lit the house with tallow candles. She kept saying that they had to economize, as they weren't rich, adding that she was perfectly contented, perfectly happy, that she really liked Tostes, and making other surprising statements that effectively silenced her mother-in-law. Moreover Emma no longer seemed receptive to her advice: indeed on one occasion, when Madame Bovary took it upon herself to assert that employers ought to keep an eye on their servants' religious practices, she replied with such an angry look and such a glacial smile that the good woman never again raised that topic.

Emma was becoming difficult, capricious. She would order herself a dish and then not touch it, would drink nothing but plain milk one day and then, the next, cups of tea by the dozen. She would often refuse to stir from the house, but then would say she was stifling, open the windows wide, and put on a thin dress. After thoroughly browbeating her servant she would give her presents or send her off to visit the neighbours, just as she would sometimes throw all the small change in her purse to beggars, although she was not at all tender-hearted or sensitive to other people's feelings; in this she was like most children of country stock, whose souls retain some of the calluses of their parents' hands.

Towards the end of February, to mark the anniversary of his cure, Père Rouault himself brought his son-in-law a splendid turkey, and stayed in Tostes for three days. Charles was busy with his patients, and Emma kept him company. He smoked in her room, spat on the andirons, talked farming, calves, cows, poultry, and parish council, so that she shut the door on him when he left with a sense of satisfaction that she herself found surprising. But then she no longer concealed her contempt for anything or anyone; and she would sometimes advance extraordinary opinions, criticizing what was generally praised, and praising things that were perverse or immoral: views which made her husband's eyes start out of his head in amazement.

Would this misery go on forever? Was there no escape? And yet she was every bit as good as all those other women who led happy lives! At La Vaubyessard she had seen duchesses with thicker waists and coarser manners, and she cursed God for his injustice; she would lean her head on the wall and weep, her thoughts dwelling enviously on lives full of drama, masked balls, orgiastic revels, and all the extremes of pleasure that these must surely offer, and that she had never known.

She grew pale, and suffered from palpitations. Charles gave her valerian, and camphor baths. Everything he tried seemed to exacerbate her condition.

Some days she chattered on and on with febrile energy; this over-excitement would then suddenly give way to a state of torpor, when she would lie without speaking or stirring. To revive herself, she would drench her arms with eau de Cologne.

Since she was constantly complaining about Tostes, Charles supposed that her illness might well be due to something in the area, and, settling on this idea, he began seriously to consider setting up his practice elsewhere.

She promptly began drinking vinegar to lose weight, developed a dry little cough, and completely lost her appetite.

It was not an easy decision for Charles to leave Tostes, after four years there and just 'when he was beginning to do nicely'. Still, if that was what it took! He drove her to Rouen, to see his former professor. It was a nervous complaint: she should have a change of air.

After looking into various possibilities, Charles heard of a fairly large town, Yonville-l'Abbaye,* in the Neufchâtel district, whose doctor, a Polish refugee,* had decamped just the week before. So then he wrote to the local pharmacist to find out the size of the population, how far away was the nearest doctor, how much a year his predecessor had made, etc., and, on receiving satisfactory answers, he decided to move in early spring if Emma's health did not improve.

One day when she was sorting a drawer in preparation for departure, she pricked her fingers on something. It was the wire round her wedding bouquet. The orange-blossom buds were yellow with dust, and the edges of the silver-trimmed satin ribbons had frayed. She threw it on the fire. It blazed up faster than dry straw. Then it looked like a red bush on the embers, gradually consuming itself. She watched it burn. The tiny pasteboard berries burst open, the brass wire twisted, the braid melted; and the shrivelled paper petals, after hovering like black butterflies against the fireback, finally flew away up the chimney.

When they set out from Tostes in March, Madame Bovary was pregnant.

PART TWO

CHAPTER I

Yonville-l'Abbaye* (so named for an ancient Capuchin abbey of which even the ruins no longer exist) is a market town twenty miles from Rouen, between the Abbeville and Beauvais roads, in the valley of the Rieule. Before it joins the Andelle, this minor tributary turns the wheels of three mills that stand near its mouth; the trout in its waters provide entertainment for boys who like to fish there on Sundays.

You leave the road at La Boissière and continue straight on, climbing up to the top of the Côte des Leux, where you can see the entire valley. The river, as it were, divides the valley into two quite distinct areas: everything to its left is grazing, everything to its right is plough. The meadows extend beneath a row of low hills to merge at the far end with the pasture land at Bray, while to the east the plain rises gently, growing wider, and unfurling its golden fields of grain as far as the eye can see. The water flowing along the edge of the pasture makes a white stripe separating the colour of the fields from the colour of the plough, so that the landscape resembles a great spread-out cloak, its collar of green velvet edged with silver braid.

Ahead on the horizon, as you draw nearer, you can see the oaks of the forest of Argueil, and the steep slopes of the Côte Saint-Jean streaked from top to bottom by long irregular red lines; these are channels formed by the rain, narrow stripes of a brick-red shade which, contrasting sharply with the greys of the mountain, comes from the iron content of the water in the numerous springs of the surrounding area.

It is here that the boundaries of Normandy, Picardy, and the Île-de-France meet, a bastard region where the dialect and the scenery are equally characterless. The worst Neufchâtel cheeses of the entire district are made in this area, and indeed farming is a costly undertaking, as large quantities of fertilizer are needed to enrich this friable soil, full of sand and pebbles.

Until 1835 no passable route into Yonville existed, but about that time a 'connecting highway' was built linking the Abbeville and

Amiens roads, and this is occasionally used by wagoners travelling from Rouen into Flanders. Nevertheless, for all its 'new marketing potential', Yonville-l'Abbaye has stood still. Instead of improving their farming techniques, the locals stick to their pastures, despite the poor condition of the latter, and the sleepy town, turning its back on the plain, has simply followed its natural inclination to develop towards the river. You can see it from far off, stretched out along the river bank like a cowherd taking a nap by the water's edge.

Beyond the bridge, the foot of the hill marks the beginning of a road lined with young aspens which leads you directly to the first of the houses. These are enclosed by hedges, and stand in yards strewn with outbuildings—cider-presses, cart-sheds, and distillery sheds—that are scattered among bushy trees with ladders, poles, or scythes hooked onto their branches. The thatched roofs, like fur caps pulled down over someone's eyes, hang a third of the way down over the low windows, whose thick convex panes have a knot in the centre like the bottom of a bottle. Here and there the plastered walls, crossed diagonally by black beams, support a straggly pear tree, and at the doors of the houses are miniature swinging gates, to keep out the baby chicks that cluster round the step to peck at crumbs of brown bread soaked in cider.

Meanwhile, the yards are growing smaller, the houses closer together, the hedges are disappearing; a bundle of fern tied to a broomstick hangs from a window; you pass the blacksmith's forge and then the wheelwright's shop, with two or three new carts outside, partly blocking the road. Then, through its railings, you can see a white house standing beyond a circular lawn adorned by a Cupid, holding a finger to his lips; a pair of cast-iron urns decorate either side of the steps up to the entrance; brass plates gleam on the door; this is the notary's house, and the finest in the area.*

The church is the other side of the road, twenty paces further on, as you enter the square. The small cemetery surrounding it, enclosed by a waist-high wall, is so crammed full of graves that the old gravestones lying flat on the ground form a continuous paved surface patterned with tidy green squares, where the grass has pushed up on its own between the stones. The church was entirely rebuilt during the last years of the reign of Charles X. The wooden vaulting is beginning to rot at the top; here and there, black pits have appeared in the blue paint. Above the door where the organ would normally be, there is a gallery for the men, with a spiral staircase that resounds under their clogs.

Daylight shining through the windows of plain glass falls obliquely on the pews set at right angles to the wall; here and there a few are covered with straw-stuffed buttoned pads and bear a label, underneath, in large letters: 'Monsieur So-and-so's pew.' Ahead, where the nave narrows, stands the confessional, opposite a statuette of the Virgin; she wears a satin gown and a tulle veil sprinkled with silver stars, and her cheeks are painted scarlet, like an idol from the Sandwich Islands; lastly, a reproduction of *The Holy Family: Presented by the Minister of the Interior* surmounts the high altar between four candlesticks, completing the prospect. The choir stalls, made of pine, have been left unpainted.

The market—that is, a tiled roof held up by twenty or so pillars— takes up about half the space of the main square of Yonville. The Town Hall, built 'to the design of a Paris architect', is a kind of Greek temple, and occupies one corner of the square, next to the pharmacy. It boasts, at street level, three ionic columns, and, on the next level, a semicircular balcony, while the pediment that crowns it displays the figure of a Gallic cockerel, one claw resting on the Charter* and the other grasping the scales of justice.

But what draws the eye most powerfully is opposite the Lion d'Or: the pharmacy of Monsieur Homais. Particularly so in the evening, when his lamp is lit, and the red and green jars that decorate his window cast their colourful glow far out across the pavement; it is then that, peering through this glow as if through Bengal flares, you catch a glimpse of the shadowy figure of the pharmacist, leaning over his desk. His house is plastered from top to bottom with notices handwritten in different scripts—cursive, round, and block capitals—'Vichy, Seltzer, and Barèges Waters;* purgative syrups; Raspail's Remedy; Arabian Raccahout; Darcet's lozenges; Regnault's ointment; bandages; baths; laxative chocolates, etc.' And the sign, which stretches across the entire width of the shop, declares in letters of gold: 'Homais, pharmacist.' Then, at the rear of the shop, behind the large scales that are secured to the counter, the word 'laboratory' unfurls above a glass door where, halfway up, the name 'Homais' appears once more, written in gilded letters against a black background.

There is nothing more to be seen in Yonville. The street (the only street), about the length of a gun-shot, with a few shops along either side, stops short where the road bends. If you leave it on your right and follow the base of the Côte Saint-Jean, you soon reach the cemetery.

At the time of the cholera,* to enlarge it, part of the wall was knocked down and three acres of adjacent land purchased; but the whole of this new area is almost unoccupied and, just as in the past, the graves go on being jammed together near the gate. The caretaker, who is also gravedigger and church sexton (thus netting a double profit from the corpses of the parish), has used the empty ground to plant potatoes. Year by year, however, his little plot grows smaller, and when an epidemic strikes he does not know whether to rejoice at the deaths or to lament over the graves.

'You're living off the dead, Lestiboudois!' the curé finally said to him one day.

This lugubrious remark made him think, and for a while put a stop to his activity; but today he is still cultivating his tubers, and even coolly maintains that they come up on their own.

Since the events that we are about to record nothing, in fact, has changed in Yonville. The tinplate tricolour* still turns on top of the church steeple; above the fancy-goods shop a couple of calico banners still flutter in the wind; the pharmacist's foetuses, like lumps of pale sponge, steadily rot away in their murky alcohol; and, over the inn's main door, the old golden lion, faded by the rains, still displays its poodle's curly mane to the passer-by.

On the evening the Bovarys were to arrive in Yonville, Madame Lefrançois, the widow who kept this inn, was so wildly busy that she dripped with sweat as she stirred her pots and pans. Tomorrow was market day. Everything had to be prepared in advance—the joints of meat cut, the chickens drawn, the soup and coffee made. She also had dinner to prepare for her 'regulars', and for the doctor, his wife, and their maid; roars of laughter were coming from the billiard table; three millers in the small parlour kept calling for brandy; the log fire blazed, the charcoal crackled, and on the long kitchen table, among the quarters of raw mutton, the jolting of the board on which the spinach was being chopped kept shaking the stacks of plates. From the yard came the squawks of chickens as the servant girl chased after them to slit their throats.

A man wearing green leather slippers, his face slightly

pock-marked, his head covered by a velvet cap with a gold tassel, was warming his back at the fire. His face expressed nothing but self-satisfaction, and he seemed as untroubled by life as the goldfinch in the wicker cage above his head; this was the pharmacist.

'Artémise!' shouted the innkeeper, 'chop some kindling, fill the carafes, bring some brandy, get a move on! Oh, if only I knew what dessert to serve these people you're expecting! Lord! Those moving-men of theirs playing billiards are starting their racket again! And they've left their cart right in the entrance! The Hirondelle might easily bash into it when it arrives. Give 'Polyte a shout to put it in the shed . . . Would you believe it, Monsieur Homais, since this morning they've probably played fifteen games and drunk eight jugs of cider . . . They'll tear my cloth,' she added, eyeing them from across the room, her skimmer in her hand.

'That'd be no great loss,' replied Monsieur Homais. 'You'd buy another.'

'Another billiard table!' exclaimed the widow.

'Because that one's falling apart, Madame Lefrançois. I've told you before, you're not doing yourself any kind of favour, really you're not! These days billiard players want narrow pockets and heavy cues. It's not "marbles" they play now; everything's changed. We must keep up with the times. Look at Tellier, now . . .'

The innkeeper went red with annoyance. The pharmacist added:

'Say what you like, his billiard table's nicer than yours; and sup-posing, for example, that someone thought of sponsoring a neigh-bourhood tournament—in aid of Poland,* say, or the flood victims in Lyon . . .'*

'Who cares about good-for-nothings like him!' interrupted the innkeeper, shrugging her heavy shoulders. 'Believe me, Monsieur Homais, as long as the Lion d'Or's here, the customers will come. We've a nice bit put away, we have. But one of these fine days you'll see the Café Français closed, with a big 'For Sale' notice on the shutters . . . Get a new billiard table,' she went on, talking to herself, 'when this one's so handy for folding my wash! And I've slept as many as six on it in the hunting season! . . . But why hasn't that old slowcoach Hivert turned up yet?'

'Are you going to wait for him, to serve your gentlemen their dinner?' enquired the pharmacist.

'Wait for him? And what about Monsieur Binet then! He'll be

walking in here at six on the dot; there's no one like him when it comes to being on time. And he must always sit in the same place in the small parlour. He'd rather die than have his dinner anywhere else! And so finicky! So fussy about his cider! Not a bit like Monsieur Léon; he sometimes turns up at seven, or even half-past; and then he pays no attention to what he's eating. Such a nice young man! Always so civil and soft-spoken!'

'But there's a vast difference, you know, between someone with a proper education, and an old soldier turned tax collector.'

Six o'clock struck. Binet walked in.

He was dressed in a blue frock coat that hung down limply round his skinny body; his leather cap, its flaps tied together by strings on the top of his head and its peak raised, revealed a hairless forehead flattened by years of pressure from a helmet. He wore a black cloth waistcoat, a stiff collar, grey trousers, and, whatever the season, well-polished boots which had two parallel bulges where his big toes jutted up. Not a hair was out of place in the short pale beard that outlined his jaw and, like the edging round a flower bed, framed his long pasty face with its tiny eyes and hooked nose. He was expert at all card-games, an excellent hunter, and wrote a fine hand. He kept a lathe at home and, as jealous as an artist and as self-centred as a bourgeois, spent all his spare time turning napkin rings with which he cluttered up his house.

He made for the small parlour, but first the three millers had to be ejected from the room; and, during the time it took to lay his place, Binet stood silently by the stove, then he removed his cap and went in, as usual shutting the door behind him.

'*He*'ll not wear out his tongue being civil!' remarked the pharmacist, as soon as he was alone with the innkeeper.

'Never says a thing,' she replied; 'we had a couple of salesmen in cloth here last week, they were an absolute riot, told such a string of jokes that night that I laughed till I cried, well! He just sat there, like a clam, never opened his mouth.'

'Yes,' declared the pharmacist, 'no imagination, no repartee, quite devoid of social graces.'

'Still, they say he has ability,' objected the innkeeper.

'Ability!' replied Monsieur Homais. 'Him! Ability? In his own line, perhaps so,' he added in a calmer tone.

And he went on:

'Ah! If a business man with important connections, a magistrate, a doctor, a pharmacist, were so absorbed in their affairs that they became odd or even churlish, now that I understand: history is full of such examples! But at least it's because they're thinking about something. Take me, for example: I couldn't tell you how many times I've looked all over my desk for my pen, to write a label, only to find in the end that I'd stuck it behind my ear!'*

Madame Lefrançois, meanwhile, went to the door to see if the Hirondelle was coming. She gave a start as a man dressed in black suddenly walked into the kitchen. By the fading light of dusk you could make out his ruddy face and athletic figure.

'What may I offer you, Monsieur le Curé?' enquired the innkeeper, reaching up to the mantelpiece for one of the candles in a brass candlestick that stood there in a row; 'would you care for something to drink? A drop of cassis, a glass of wine?'

The priest declined with great civility. He had come about his umbrella, which he had left the other day at the Ernemont convent; and, after asking Madame Lefrançois to send it round to him at the presbytery during the evening, he left for the church, where the angelus was being rung.

As soon as the pharmacist could no longer hear his footsteps in the square, he remarked that the priest's behaviour had been highly impolite. That refusal to accept a drink was, in his opinion, the most revolting kind of hypocrisy; all priests were secret boozers, and they were trying to bring back the tithe.

The innkeeper sprang to her curé's defence:

'Anyway, he could lay four of your size across his knee. Just last year, he gave our men a hand bringing in the hay; he could carry as many as six bales at a go, he's that strong!'

'Great!' said the pharmacist. 'So send your daughters for confession to strapping young fellows like him! If I were in the government, I'd see that priests were bled once a month. Yes, Madame Lefrançois, once a month, a nice copious phlebotomy, in the interests of public order and morality!'

'Shame on you, Monsieur Homais! That's blasphemy! You've no religion!'

The pharmacist replied:

'No, quite the contrary, I do have a religion, my own religion, and in fact I'm more religious than all of them, with their charades and their mumbo-jumbo. Yes indeed, I do worship God! I believe in a Supreme Being,* a Creator, whoever he may be, it's of no importance to me, who put us here on earth to do our duty as citizens and fathers; but I don't need to go into a church and kiss silver platters and dig into my pocket to fatten up a lot of humbugs who eat better than you or I do! Because he can be worshipped just as well in a wood, or a field, or even just gazing at the ethereal vault, like the ancients. My God is the God of Socrates, of Franklin, of Voltaire, and of Béranger!* I believe in the credo of the *Vicaire savoyard** and in the immortal principles of '89!* I've no time for an old dodderer of a god who goes round his garden with a walking stick, quarters his friends in the bellies of whales, dies giving a shriek, and then comes back to life after three days: things not only absurd in themselves but which are, furthermore, flatly contradicted by every law of the physical universe; which only goes to prove, by the way, that priests have always wallowed in the most profound ignorance, in which they do their best to engulf the entire populace along with themselves.'

Pausing, he looked around for an audience, for in his excitement the pharmacist had fancied, for a moment, that he was addressing a session of the municipal council. But the innkeeper was no longer listening to him; she could just make out a distant rumbling. Then came the sound of a carriage mingled with the clatter of loose chains hitting the ground, and the Hirondelle, at long last, drew up at the door.

It was a yellow box-like affair mounted on two large wheels that came up to the roof-cover, blocking the passengers' view of the road and spattering their shoulders with dirt. The tiny panes of its narrow windows shook in their frames when the carriage was closed, and were daubed with mud in places, on top of the ancient encrustation of dust which even heavy rainstorms never completely washed off. It was drawn by three horses—a leader and a pair—and when travelling downhill the underside of the carriage would bump on the road.

A handful of townsfolk had gathered in the square; they were all talking at once, asking for news, for explanations of the delay, and for their hampers: Hivert didn't know which way to turn. It was he who ran all the errands in the city for the locals. He called in at the shops, bringing back rolls of leather for the shoemaker, iron for the blacksmith, a barrel of herrings for his employer, Madame Lefrançois, bonnets from the milliner's, wigs from the hairdresser's; and all along the road on his way back he would distribute his parcels, standing up in his seat and yelling at the top of his lungs as he hurled them over the farmyard gates, while his horses trotted on unattended.

An accident had delayed him: Madame Bovary's greyhound had run off across country. They had spent more than a quarter of an hour whistling for her. Hivert had even driven back for over a mile, expecting to see her any moment; but in the end they had had to press on. Emma had burst into tears, and lost her temper; she had blamed Charles for this misfortune. Monsieur Lheureux, the fancy-goods merchant, who happened to be in the carriage with her, had tried to comfort her with lots of examples of lost dogs that had recognized their master after many years. There was a story about one, he said, that had returned from Constantinople to Paris. Another had travelled over a hundred miles in a straight line, swimming across four rivers; and his very own father had owned a poodle that, after a twelve-year absence, had suddenly jumped up on him in the street, one evening, as he was going out for dinner.

CHAPTER II

Emma emerged first, followed by Félicité, Monsieur Lheureux, and then a nurse; they had to wake up Charles, who had fallen fast asleep in his corner as soon as it was dark.

Homais introduced himself; he presented his compliments to Madame, his respects to Monsieur, declared himself delighted to have been of service to them, and added in a cordial tone that he had taken the liberty of inviting himself to dine with them, as his wife was away.

Upon entering the kitchen Madame Bovary made for the fire-place. With the tips of two fingers she took hold of her dress at knee level and, raising it ankle-high, stretched out to the flames, above the roast of lamb turning on the spit, a foot encased in a small black boot. The firelight fell fully on her, its fierce glare penetrating the weave of her dress, the smooth pores of her white skin, and even the lids of her eyes, which from time to time she blinked. Now and again, fanned by the draught blowing through the half-open door, the flames mantled her in a great glow of red.

On the other side of the fireplace, a young man with fair hair stood silently watching her.

Being very bored in Yonville, where he worked as clerk to the notary Maître Guillaumin, Monsieur Léon Dupuis (the second of the Lion d'Or's 'regulars') often came late for dinner, hoping that some traveller would appear at the inn with whom he might chat during the evening. On days when he had completed all his work, he was obliged, for lack of anything else to do, to arrive punctually, and endure a tête-à-tête with Binet from the soup right through to the cheese. So he had been delighted to accept the innkeeper's sugges-tion that he should have dinner with the newcomers, and they went into the large parlour where Madame Lefrançois had set a table for four in honour of the occasion.

Homais requested permission to keep his cap on his head: he was very nervous of developing rhinitis.

Then, turning to his neighbour: 'Doubtless Madame is feeling a trifle weary? Our Hirondelle jolts one about so mercilessly!'

'That's true,' replied Emma, 'but I always enjoy an upheaval; I love a change of scene.'

'It's so depressing,' sighed the clerk, 'to be forever stuck in the same old place!'

'If you were like me,' said Charles, 'obliged to be always on horseback . . .'

'But', Léon went on, addressing Madame Bovary, 'nothing could be more delightful, in my opinion; when you have the opportunity, that is,' he added.

'Besides,' the apothecary was saying, 'the practice of medicine is not particularly arduous in our area; for the condition of the roads permits the use of a gig, and as a general rule the fees are fairly good, the farmers being comfortably off. Speaking from the medical point of view, apart for the usual cases of enteritis, bronchitis, biliousness etc., we have a few cases of marsh-fever at harvest time; but, in a word, very little that's serious, nothing of particular note apart from a considerable number of cases of scrofula, which doubtless are a consequence of our farm labourers' deplorably unhygienic living conditions. Ah! You'll encounter a great many prejudices to contend with, Monsieur Bovary; an obstinate adherence to traditional ways, with which all your scientific efforts will come into conflict every day; people still rely on novenas, and relics, and the curé, rather than finding it natural to go and see the doctor or the pharmacist. However the climate is not, in point of fact, a bad one, and we even number some nonagenarians among our inhabitants. The thermometer (as I myself have personally observed) drops in winter as low as four degrees and in high summer reaches twenty-five—thirty centigrade at the very most—which gives us a maximum of twenty-four Réaumur, or expressed differently fifty-four Fahrenheit* (English scale), not any more! And, indeed, we are sheltered from the north winds by the forest of Argueil on the one hand, and from the west winds, on the other, by the Côte Saint-Jean; however this warmth, because of the water vapour that rises off the river and the presence of a considerable number of cattle in the meadows, which exhale, as you are aware, a vast quantity of ammonia, that is to say nitrogen, hydrogen, and oxygen (no, only nitrogen and hydrogen), absorbing the humus from the soil into itself, mixing together all these different emanations, making them into a bundle, so to speak, and spontaneously combining with the electricity present in the atmosphere, when there is any, might eventually, as occurs in tropical climes, engender insalubrious miasmas—this warmth, as I was saying, is in actuality moderated in the quarter wherein it originates, or rather wherein it would originate, that is to say in the south, by the winds from the south-east, which, themselves having been cooled by crossing the Seine, sometimes burst upon us all of a sudden, like winds from Russia!'

'Are there at least some pleasant walks round here?' Madame Bovary asked the young man.

'Oh, very few,' he replied. 'There's a place they call the Pasture, up on the hill, at the edge of the forest. I sometimes go there on a Sunday and take a book, and stay to watch the sunset.'

'I don't believe there's anything as wonderful as a sunset,' she went on, 'particularly by the sea.'

'Oh, I adore the sea,' said Monsieur Léon.

'And then,' continued Madame Bovary, 'does it not seem to you that the mind takes wing more freely, over that boundless expanse, whose contemplation uplifts the soul, inspiring thoughts of the infinite, of the ideal?'

'Mountain scenery has the same effect,' Léon replied. 'A cousin of mine went to Switzerland last year, and he told me that no one can have any idea of the poetry of its lakes, or the charm of its waterfalls, or the vast proportions of its glaciers. You see unbelievably huge pine trees growing over mountain streams, chalets built on the edge of precipices, and, when the clouds separate, whole valleys, lying a thousand feet below you. Such spectacles must surely inspire feelings of rapture, incline the heart to prayer, to ecstasy! So now I can well understand that famous musician who, the better to fire his imagination, used to play the piano within sight of some striking view.'

'Do you play an instrument?' she enquired.

'No, but I love music,' he replied.

'Oh, don't listen to him, Madame Bovary,' interrupted Homais, leaning forward across his plate, 'It's sheer modesty. Come on, Léon, what about the other day, in your room, you were singing 'L'Ange gardien'* quite beautifully. I could hear you from my laboratory, your delivery sounded really professional.'

Léon, in fact, lodged at the pharmacy, where he had a small room on the second floor, overlooking the square. He blushed at this compliment from his landlord, who had already turned back to the doctor and was naming, one after another, all the principal citizens of Yonville. He told anecdotes about them and provided a great deal of information. No one really knew how rich the lawyer was; and then 'there was that Tuvache tribe', who gave themselves such airs.

'And what is your favourite music?'

'Oh, German, it sets one dreaming.'

'Have you seen the Italians?'

'No, not yet, but next year I will, when I'm in Paris, to finish my law.'

'As I just had the pleasure of informing your husband,' said the pharmacist, 'on the subject of that unfortunate Yanoda who vanished from our midst: thanks to his spendthrift ways you will find yourselves in possession of one of the most comfortable houses in Yonville. What is particularly convenient for a doctor, is that it has a door opening onto the Lane, which enables people to come and go without being seen. Furthermore, it's equipped with everything one might consider desirable in a home: laundry, kitchen with pantry, sitting room, storeroom for fruit, and so on. He was quite a character, spent money like water. He had an arbour built, down by the river, at the bottom of the garden, just so he could drink beer there, in the summer, and if Madame likes gardening, she'll be able to . . .'

'My wife rarely gardens,' said Charles; 'although she's been advised to take exercise, she much prefers to stay in her room and read.'

'So do I,' said Léon; 'indeed what could be better than spending the evening by the fireside with a book, while the wind beats against the window panes and the lamp glows brightly?'

'Yes, yes, you're right!' she said, gazing at him with her great dark eyes open wide.

'You empty your mind,' he went on, 'and the hours fly past. Without stirring from your chair, you wander through countries you can see in your mind's eye, and your consciousness threads itself into the fiction, playing about with the details or following the ups and downs of the plot. You identify with the characters; you feel as if it's your own heart that's beating beneath their costumes.'

'That's true! That's true!'

'Have you ever had the experience', Léon continued, 'of finding, in a book, some vague idea you've had, some shadowy image from the depths of your being, which now seems to express perfectly your most subtle feelings?'

'Yes, I have,' she replied.

'That's why I particularly love the poets,' he said. 'I find poetry more affecting than prose, it's more likely to bring tears to my eyes.'

'In the long run, though, poetry can be rather wearying,' Emma answered; 'Nowadays, actually, what I really love are stories that keep you turning the pages, stories that frighten you. I loathe commonplace heroes and temperate feelings, the kind of thing you find in real life.'

'Yes indeed,' said the clerk; 'since works like that leave the heart unmoved, they seem to me to deviate from the true purpose of Art. It's so sweet, amid life's disillusionments, to let your thoughts dwell on noble characters, pure affections, and scenes of happiness. For me, living here, cut off from the world, it's my only distraction; there's so little to do in Yonville!'

'Just like Tostes, I suppose,' remarked Emma; 'which is why I always belonged to a lending library.'*

'If Madame would do me the honour of using it,' interrupted the pharmacist, who had caught Emma's last words, 'I myself can place at her disposal a library composed of the best authors: Voltaire, Rousseau, Delille, Walter Scott,* *L'Écho des feuilletons*, etc., and furthermore I subscribe to a number of periodicals every day, among them *Le Fanal de Rouen*,* having the good fortune to be the local correspondent for the districts of Buchy, Forges, Neufchâtel, Yonville, and vicinity.'

They had been at table for two and a half hours; Artémise, the servant girl, shuffled listlessly back and forth over the tiles in her cloth slippers, bringing in the dishes one at a time, forgetting everything, paying no attention to what she was told, and constantly leaving the billiard room door ajar so that its latch kept banging against the wall.

Without realizing it, Léon, as he talked, had rested his foot on one of the rungs of Madame Bovary's chair. She was wearing a little blue silk scarf that kept her frilled batiste collar standing straight up like a ruff; and, depending on how she moved her head, the lower part of her face would sink inside her collar, or rise sweetly above it. Sitting side by side in this manner while Charles and the pharmacist chatted, they had drifted into one of those vague conversations in which every chance remark invariably leads you back to a fixed core of shared feelings. Plays on in Paris, titles of novels, new dance tunes, the world of high society of which they knew nothing, Tostes, where she had lived, Yonville where they now were, they went into everything, talked about everything, until dinner was over.

When the coffee had been served, Félicité went to prepare the bedroom in the new house, and the party soon rose from the table. Madame Lefrançois was dozing beside the dying fire, while the stable lad, holding a lantern, waited for Monsieur and Madame Bovary, to show them to their home. He had bits of straw stuck in his red hair, and he limped with his left leg. He picked up the priest's umbrella in his other hand, and they set off.

The little town was fast asleep. The pillars in the market place cast long shadows. The ground looked silver-grey, as on a summer's night.

But, because the doctor's house was only some fifty yards from the inn, they had to say goodnight and go their separate ways almost immediately.

As soon as she stepped into the hall, Emma felt the chill of the plaster walls fall on her shoulders like a damp cloth. The walls were freshly whitewashed and the wooden stairs creaked. In the bedroom, upstairs, a whitish light shone through the uncurtained windows.

She could make out the tops of trees and, in the distance, meadows half submerged in mist that rose up like steam in the moonlight, following the course of the river. In the middle of the room lay a chaotic heap of bureau drawers, bottles, curtain rods, and gilt bed-posts, with mattresses thrown over chairs and basins lying on the floor—the two men who had delivered the furniture had simply left everything there, in total disarray.

This was the fourth time that she had spent the night in a strange place. The first had been when she entered the convent, the second when she arrived at Tostes, the third at La Vaubyessard, and this was the fourth. Each time had, in a way, marked the start of a new phase of her life. She did not believe that things could turn out to be the same in different places, and since that part of her life that she had already lived had been bad, surely what still lay ahead would be better.

CHAPTER III

The next morning, when she got up, she saw the clerk standing in the square. She was wearing her dressing gown. Looking up, he bowed. She gave him a quick nod and closed the window.

Léon waited all day long for six o'clock to arrive, but when he walked into the inn, he found only Monsieur Binet seated at the table.

For him, that dinner the previous evening was a momentous event; for never before had he conversed, during two entire, uninter-rupted hours, with a 'lady'. How then had he been able to tell her, and with such eloquence, so many things about which he had never previously spoken so well? By nature he was shy, with a reticence compounded of both modesty and dissimulation. In Yonville his manners were thought 'quite the thing'. He listened to the opinions of his elders, and appeared to hold no extreme political views, a remarkable quality in a young man. And then, he was talented, too, he painted in watercolours, knew how to read music, and after dinner always picked up a book, unless he was playing cards. Monsieur Homais respected him for his education, and Madame Homais was fond of him for his good nature, as he would often look after her children, in the garden. They were a perpetually grubby brood, very badly brought up and, like their mother, rather lethargic. They were left in the care of the maid or of Justin, a distant cousin of Monsieur Homais. Justin had been taken into the household out of charity and worked both as the pharmacy apprentice, and as a general servant.

The apothecary proved to be the best of neighbours. He advised Madame Bovary about the tradesmen, arranged for his cider merchant to make a special call, tasted the cider himself, and supervised the proper placing of the cask in the cellar; he also told her how to get butter at a good price, and made an arrangement with Lestiboudois, the sexton, who in addition to his ecclesiastical and funerary responsibilities, took care of the principal gardens in Yonville, working by the hour or by the year, as the client preferred.

All this deferential friendliness on the part of the pharmacist was not prompted purely by his love of meddling; there was a purpose behind it.

He had infringed Article One of the Law of 19 Ventôse of the year XI,* which forbids the practice of medicine to anyone not holding a diploma; as a result, Homais had been denounced anonymously, and summoned to Rouen, to appear before the Royal Prosecutor in his private chambers. The magistrate had received him standing, wearing his robes, with his ermine on his shoulder and his tall official cap on his head. This was in the morning, before the start of the court session. Homais could hear the tramp of policemen's heavy boots along the corridor, and what sounded like enormous locks being turned somewhere far away. The ringing in his ears was so loud that he thought he was about to have a stroke; in his mind's eye he could see deep dungeons, his family weeping, his pharmacy sold, his display bottles all dispersed, and he had to go into a café for a glass of rum and seltzer water, to calm himself down.

Little by little the memory of this reprimand had faded, and he continued, as before, to give innocuous consultations in his back room. But the mayor had it in for him, some of his colleagues were jealous of him, he must be constantly on his guard; he hoped, by these courteous attentions, to ingratiate himself with Monsieur Bovary, so that later, were he to notice anything, he would keep quiet. Every morning, therefore, Homais brought him 'the paper', and often, in the afternoon, would leave the pharmacy for a while, to go for a little chat with the medical officer.

Charles was depressed; the patients were not coming. He would sit in his chair, not speaking, for hours on end, or doze in his consulting room, or watch his wife sew. To pass the time, he did odd jobs about the house, and he even tried to paint the attic with some spare paint the decorators had left behind. But he was worried about money. He had spent so much on the repairs at Tostes, on Madame's wardrobe, and on the removal, that the entire dowry, more than three thousand écus, had melted away in two years. And then, so many of their things had been damaged or lost on the journey from Tostes to Yonville, not least the plaster curé which, when the cart gave a particularly violent jolt, had fallen onto the road at Quincampoix and shattered into a thousand pieces!*

But he had a more agreeable concern to distract him—his wife's pregnancy. As her time drew closer, she became more and more dear to him. It was another physical bond linking them together, the ongoing expression, as it were, of a more complex union. When he saw, from a distance, her languid walk, and the way her body swayed gently on her uncorseted hips, and when they were sitting opposite one another and he could freely gaze at her, and see how wearily she sat in her chair, he was overwhelmed with happiness. He would go up to her, kiss her, stroke her face, call her 'little mother', try to make her dance and, half crying, half laughing, shower her with every nonsensical endearment that came into his head. The thought of having begotten a child enchanted him. Now he lacked nothing. He knew all of human existence, and he settled serenely down to enjoy it.

Emma, at first, felt great astonishment, then longed to be delivered, to know what it was like to be a mother. But since she could not afford to buy the things she wanted—a swing-boat cradle with pink silk curtains, embroidered caps for the baby—she lost interest in the layette and in a fit of resentment ordered the whole thing from a village seamstress, without choosing or discussing anything. So she never engaged in those preparations that stimulate maternal love, and this may perhaps have blunted her affection from the start.

Nevertheless, since Charles, at every meal, talked about the baby, she was soon thinking about it almost constantly.

She wanted a son; he would be strong and dark; she would call him Georges, and this idea of bearing a male child was like an anticipated revenge for all the powerlessness of her past life. A man, at

least, is free, free to explore all passions and all countries, to sur-
mount obstacles, to indulge in the most exotic pleasures. But a
woman is constantly thwarted. At once passive and compliant, she
has to contend with both the weakness of her body and the subjec-
tion imposed by the law. Her will, like the veil attached to her hat,
flutters with every breeze; always there is desire inviting her on, and,
always, convention holding her back.

She gave birth one Sunday, about six in the morning, as the sun
was rising.

'It's a girl!' said Charles.

She turned away her head, and fainted.

Almost at once, Madame Homais rushed in to give her a kiss, as
did Madame Lefrançois from the Lion d'Or. Monsieur Homais,
being a man of the world, merely offered some provisional congratu-
lations through the half-open door. He asked to see the child and
pronounced it well formed.

During her convalescence, she thought a great deal about what
to call her daughter. First she went through all the names with
Italian endings, like Clara, Louisa, Amanda, Atala;* she rather liked
Galsuinde, and Yseult or Léocadie,* even more. Charles wanted the
baby named after his mother, but Emma would not agree. They went
through the church calendar from end to end and asked everyone for
ideas.

'Monsieur Léon,' said the pharmacist, 'when we were talking
about this the other day, was extremely surprised that you haven't
chosen Madeleine, which is so very much in the fashion at the
moment.'

But Madame Bovary senior objected vociferously to this sinner's
name. As for Monsieur Homais, he liked all names that recalled great
men, glorious deeds, or noble ideas, and he had christened his four
children in accordance with this principle. Thus Napoléon stood for
glory and Franklin for liberty; Irma* was perhaps a concession to
Romanticism, while Athalie* paid tribute to the most immortal masterpiece of the French stage. For his philosophical convictions in no
way conflicted with his artistic appreciation; in him the thinker did
not stifle the man of sensibility; *he* knew how to discriminate, where
to draw the line between imagination and fanaticism. In the case of
this tragedy, for example, he condemned the ideas, but applauded
the style, abhorred the conception, but praised every detail, found

the characters infuriating, while their speeches sent him into raptures. When he read the famous passages he felt transported, but
when he considered that those canting clerics used them to peddle
their wares, he was appalled; and so confused was he by these con-
tradictory emotions that he would have liked, with his very own
hands, to crown Racine with a wreath of laurel, and then embark on a
good long argument with him.

In the end, Emma remembered that at La Vaubyessard she had
heard the Marquise address a young woman as Berthe; from that
moment the name was decided and, as Père Rouault could not
come, they asked Monsieur Homais to be godfather. His christen-
ing presents all came out of his stock, namely: six boxes of jujubes,
a whole jar of racahout, three containers of marshmallow paste
and, in addition, six sticks of sugar candy that he had come across
in a cupboard. The evening after the ceremony they gave a big
dinner which the curé attended; the party grew quite lively. When
the liqueurs appeared Monsieur Homais broke into 'Le Dieu des
bonnes gens',* Monsieur Léon sang a barcarole,* and the elder
Madame Bovary, who was godmother, a ballad from the days of
the Empire; finally, Charles's father insisted that the baby be
brought down, and he set about baptizing her with a glass of
champagne that he poured from high up onto her head. This
mockery of the first sacrament incensed the Abbé Bournisien, old
man Bovary retorted with a quotation from *La Guerre des dieux*,*
and the Abbé started to leave; the ladies entreated, Homais inter-
vened, and they managed to get the priest back to his seat, where
he calmly picked up his cup and saucer again and finished off his
half-drunk coffee.

Monsieur Bovary senior stayed on for another month in Yonville,
dazzling the locals with his magnificent silver-braided military cap
that he wore every morning while smoking his pipe in the town
square. Being in the habit of drinking a great deal of brandy, he often
sent the maid to the Lion d'Or to buy him a bottle which was
charged to his son's account; and, to perfume his silk cravats, he used
up his daughter-in-law's entire supply of eau de Cologne.

Emma certainly did not dislike his company. He'd seen the world;
he could talk about Berlin, and Vienna, and Strasbourg, about his
days as an officer, the mistresses he'd had, the splendid dinners he'd
attended; and then he could be quite charming and sometimes,

perhaps on the stairs, or in the garden, he would even grasp her round the waist, exclaiming:

'Better watch out, Charles!'

Then Madame Bovary senior began to worry about her son's happiness, fearing that in the long run her husband might have a bad influence on the young woman's ideas; so she hastened their departure. Perhaps she had more serious concerns. Monsieur Bovary was a man who respected nothing.

One day, Emma felt a sudden urge to see her baby daughter,* who had been put out to nurse with the carpenter's wife; and without bothering to look in the almanac to confirm that the six weeks of the Virgin* had elapsed, she set out for Rollet's cottage which stood at the end of the village, at the foot of the hill, between the highway and the meadows.

It was noon; the houses had their shutters closed; the slates on the roofs, glittering under the harsh glare of the blue sky, seemed to be sending showers of sparks from the gable-tops. A sultry wind was blowing. As she walked along, Emma felt faint; the pebbles on the path hurt her feet, and she wondered whether to turn back, or go inside somewhere to sit down.

At that moment, Monsieur Léon emerged from a nearby door, carrying a bundle of papers under his arm. He came over to greet her and stood in the shade in front of Lheureux's shop, under the grey awning.

Madame Bovary said that she was on her way to see her baby, but that she was beginning to feel tired.

'If . . .' Léon replied, not daring to go on.

'Are you going somewhere in particular?' she asked.

And, on hearing the clerk's reply, she begged him to accompany her. By evening, all of Yonville knew about this, and Madame Tuvache, the mayor's wife, declared in front of her maid that 'Madame Bovary was compromising herself.'

To reach the wet-nurse's house, they had to turn left after the road ended, as if heading for the cemetery, and then go past cottages and yards, following a narrow path bordered with privet. The privet was in flower, as were the veronica, the wild roses, the nettles, and the slender bramble shoots that had sprung from the blackberry bushes. Through gaps in the hedges, they could see, beside the ramshackle cabins, an occasional pig on a dunghill, or a few cows in wooden yokes rubbing their horns against tree trunks. The two of them walked slowly side by side, she leaning on him, he slowing his step to keep pace with her; in front of them a swarm of flies danced about, buzzing in the heavy air.

They recognized the house by an old walnut tree that gave it shade. It was low, with a brown tile roof, and had a string of onions dangling outside from an attic skylight. Bundles of brushwood propped up against the thorn fence protected a small plot where lettuces, a few clumps of lavender, and some sweet peas on training poles were growing. Dirty water was trickling over the grass and various odd garments lay scattered around, knitted stockings, a red calico jacket, a big coarse linen sheet spread out along the hedge. At the sound of the gate the wet-nurse appeared, holding a nursing infant at her breast. With the other arm she was dragging along a frail little chap with sores all over his face—the son of a Rouen knitted-goods merchant whose parents, too involved with their business, had left him to board in the country.

'Come in,' she said; 'your baby's over there, asleep.'

The room—the only room in the house—was at ground level, with a big uncurtained bed standing against the back wall. The kneading-trough occupied the side with the window, one pane of which had been mended with a round of blue paper. In the corner, behind the door, under the stone slab for washing, stood a row of stout boots with gleaming hobnails beside a bottle of oil with a feather in its mouth. A *Mathieu Laensberg** almanac lay on the dusty mantelpiece among gun flints, candle stumps and bits of tinder. As a final superfluous touch the room boasted a picture of Fame blowing her trumpets, no doubt cut out of some perfumery advertisement; it was nailed to the wall with six cobbler's tacks.

Emma's baby lay sleeping in a wicker cradle on the ground. Picking her up in her blanket, she began singing softly as she rocked her.

Léon was pacing about the room; he found it strange to see this fine lady in her nankeen dress in the midst of all this poverty. Madame Bovary blushed, and he turned away, fearful lest his glance might perhaps have been too bold. The baby had just vomited on the collar of her dress, and she put her down again in the cradle. The wet-nurse quickly came over to wipe up the mess, assuring Emma that it wouldn't show.

'She's forever doing that,' she said, 'I do nothing but clean her up! Now if you was so obliging as to leave word with Camus, the grocer, to let me have a bit o' soap when I'm short? That would be handier for you, 'cause I wouldn't need to bother you.'

'Yes, yes, all right!' said Emma. 'Goodbye, Mère Rollet.'

And she went out, wiping her feet on the sill of the door.

The woman walked beside her through the yard, talking about how hard it was, getting up in the night.

'Sometimes I'm that worn out I nod off in me chair; so how about letting me have just one pound o' ground coffee, it'd do me for a month and I'd have it with milk in the mornings.'

After enduring her thanks, Madame Bovary walked off; she'd gone a little way down the path when the sound of clogs made her look round; it was the nurse.

'What is it now?'

So then the peasant woman, drawing her aside under an elm, started telling her about her husband: he just had his trade, and six francs a year that the captain . . .

'Get on with it,' said Emma.

'Well!' the nurse continued, heaving a sigh between every word, 'I'm afeard he'll not be too pleased, seeing me drink me coffee all on me own; I mean, well, you know, men . . .'

'Yes, yes, you can have it,' Emma said again, 'I'll see you both get your coffee! That's enough, you're bothering me!'

'Oh, dear me, you see, Madame, it's like this, he's—on account he's got these wounds—he's these dreadful pains in 'is chest. Says even cider makes 'im go all weak . . .'

'Do hurry up, Mère Rollet!'

'So,' continued the woman, curtsying, 'if it wasn't asking too much . . .' (another curtsy), 'if you wouldn't mind . . .' (with a beseeching gaze at Emma) 'a little jug o' brandy,' she said at last, 'and I'll rub your little one's feet with it, they're as tender as your tongue is.'

When she was finally rid of the wet-nurse, Emma took Léon's arm again. For a while she walked quickly, but then she slowed her pace, and her eyes, wandering from the path ahead, focused instead on the young man's shoulders. His frock coat had a black velvet collar, upon which his carefully combed chestnut hair fell smoothly. She noticed his nails, which were longer than was normal in Yonville.

Manicuring his nails was one of the clerk's chief occupations, and he kept a special penknife for this purpose in his desk.

They returned to Yonville along the river bank. In the warm weather the level of the river fell, uncovering the bottom of the garden walls. From these, short flights of steps led down to the water, which was moving silently and fast, and looked cold. In it grew tall, thin grasses that were all bent in the same direction by the current, and spread out in the limpid water like freely flowing, green-ish hair. At times, on the tip of a reed, or on a water-lily pad, some delicate-footed insect crawled about or rested. Sunbeams shone through the tiny blue bubbles of air that kept forming and breaking on the ripples; the old pollarded willows gazed at their bark-grey reflections in the water; beyond, on all sides, the meadows seemed deserted. It was the time of the midday meal on the farms, and as they walked along the young woman and her companion could hear only the rhythm of their own steps on the dirt path, the words they were exchanging, and the murmur of Emma's dress rustling about her.

The garden walls, their copings covered with glass from broken bottles, were as hot as greenhouse glass. Wallflowers had taken root in the bricks, and the edge of Madame Bovary's open sunshade, as she walked past, crushed a few of their faded petals into yellow dust; or else an overhanging spray of honeysuckle or clematis would trail for an instant across the silk, catching in the fringe.

They chatted about a troupe of Spanish dancers who were expected soon at the theatre in Rouen.

'Are you going?' she asked.

'If I can,' he said.

Had they nothing else to say to one another? Their eyes, at least, were full of more urgent messages, and, while forcing themselves to utter commonplaces, each of them felt overcome by a similar lan-guor; it was like a murmur of the soul, profound and unceasing, audible above the sound of their voices. Astonished by this hitherto unknown sweetness, they had no thought of speaking of it to one another, or of discovering its cause. Future joys, like tropical shores, project a natural indolence that drifts like a perfumed breeze across the vast spaces that precede it, and those who journey there are lulled by its enchantment, and never even wonder what lies beyond the unseen horizon.

In one place the surface of the path had been trampled down by cattle; they had to step on large green stones set down across the mud. Often, she had to pause an instant to see where to place her boot, and, teetering on her wobbly perch, her elbows akimbo and her body bent forward as she gazed about indecisively, she would give a nervous laugh, fearful lest she fall into a puddle.

When they were alongside her garden, Madame Bovary opened the little gate, ran up the steps, and disappeared.

Léon went back to his office. His boss was out; he glanced at some documents, sharpened a fresh quill, and in the end picked up his hat and left.

He walked to the Pasture, high up on the Côte d'Argueil, at the edge of the forest. He lay down on the ground under the pines, and gazed at the sky through his fingers.

'God, I'm bored!' he kept muttering, 'so terribly bored!'

He felt very sorry for himself, having to live in this village, with Homais for a friend and Monsieur Guillaumin for a boss. Wholly taken up with his work, Guillaumin, with his gold-rimmed spectacles, red side-whiskers, and white cravats, was impervious to all intellectual subtlety, although the starchy English style he affected had greatly impressed the clerk at first. As for the pharmacist's wife, she was the best wife in all Normandy, placid as a cow, devoted to her children, her father, her mother, her cousins, weeping over the misfortunes of others, careless and easygoing in the house and a firm enemy of corsets—but so slow-moving, so boring to listen to, so ordinary in appearance and in conversation so limited, that it had never entered his head, although she was thirty and he twenty, they slept in adjacent rooms, and he spoke to her every day, that anyone might think of her as a woman, or that she might possess any attributes of her sex other than her skirts.

And who else was there? Binet, a few shopkeepers, two or three tavern-keepers, the curé, and lastly Monsieur Tuvache, the mayor, and his two sons, well-off, boorish blockheads who worked their own land, never invited outsiders to their family blowouts, and anyway were pious goody-goodies whose company he found intolerable.

But, against the humdrum background of all these human faces, Emma's stood out, isolated from the others and also much more distant; for he sensed that some indefinable abyss existed between himself and her.

He had, at first, occasionally gone to her house with the pharmacist. But Charles had evinced no particular interest in seeing him, and Léon could not see what to do next, torn as he was between his fear of behaving rashly, and his longing for an intimacy that he considered virtually impossible.

CHAPTER IV

As soon as it turned cold, Emma moved out of her room into the parlour, a long, low-ceilinged room where a many-branched piece of coral stood on the mantel in front of the mirror. Seated in her armchair near the window, she would watch the villagers as they walked along the pavement outside.

Twice each day, Léon went from his office to the Lion d'Or. Emma heard him approaching from far away; she would lean forward, listening, and the young man would glide past the curtained window, always dressed in exactly the same clothes, never turning his head. But when, in the twilight, she was sitting with her chin in her left hand, and her unfinished embroidery abandoned on her lap, the sudden appearance of this gliding shadow often made her start, and, rising from her chair, she would tell the maid to set the table.

Monsieur Homais generally turned up while they were having dinner. Smoking cap in hand, he would come in on tiptoe so as not to disturb anyone, with the invariable greeting: 'Evening, all!' Then, when he had settled down at the table between them, he would enquire after the doctor's patients, and Charles would consult him on the likelihood of getting paid. Next they would chat about what was 'in the paper'. By that time of day Homais knew it practically by heart; he would quote it word for word, complete with editorial commentaries and reports of every single calamity that had taken place in France or abroad. Then, when these topics ran dry, he never failed to remark on the dishes he could see before him. And sometimes, half rising from his chair, he would even delicately point out, to Madame, the tenderest morsel, or, addressing the maid, advise her on the preparation of her stews, or the health-giving properties of condiments; his command of such subjects as aromas, osmazomes,* gastric juices, and gelatine was positively dazzling. With more recipes in his head than there were bottles in his pharmacy, Homais excelled at making many different jams, vinegars, and sweet cordials; he was also an authority on the latest fuel-saving stoves, not to mention the arts of preserving cheeses and correcting spoiled wines.

At eight, Justin came to fetch him to lock up the pharmacy. Monsieur Homais would give him a knowing look, especially if Félicité was there, for he had observed that his pupil seemed fond of the doctor's house.

'That fine young fellow of mine's beginning to get ideas,' he would say; 'I'll be damned if he's not fallen for your maid!'

But Justin was guilty of something worse, for which Homais constantly reprimanded him: he *would* listen to their conversation. On Sundays, for instance, when Madame Homais summoned him in to take away the children, who were nodding off in their armchairs, and disarranging the baggy calico slip covers, it seemed impossible to get him to leave the parlour.

Not many guests came to these evening gatherings of the pharmacist, whose slanderous tongue and political opinions had successively antagonized quite a number of respectable people. The clerk never failed to attend. The moment he heard the bell, he would hurry down to greet Madame Bovary, take her shawl, and stow away, under the pharmacy desk, the thick cloth overshoes she wore in snowy weather.

First they had a few hands of *trente-et-un*, then Monsieur Homais played *écarté* with Emma; from behind her, Léon would give her advice. Standing with his hands on the back of her chair, he stared down at the teeth of her comb, sunk deep into her chignon. Each time she reached forward to play a card, the right side of her dress rode up. The coil of hair at the nape of her neck cast a brownish reflection down her back, which grew paler and paler until it gradually disappeared into deeper shadow. Below, her dress flowed out on either side of her chair, its many voluminous folds reaching to the floor. Sometimes, when Léon felt the sole of his boot touch it, he would quickly move back as though he had stepped on someone.

When the card game ended, the apothecary and the doctor usually played dominoes, and Emma, changing her seat, would lean her elbows on the table and leaf through *L'Illustration*. She brought her fashion magazine with her. Léon sat beside her; together, they studied the pictures and waited for one another before turning a page. Often, she would ask him to recite her some poems; Léon declaimed them in a drawling voice, which he carefully let die away in the love passages. But the noise of the dominoes distracted her; Monsieur Homais was an expert, and he could beat Charles by a full double six. When they reached three hundred, they would both stretch out in front of the fireplace and promptly fall asleep. The fire was nearly out; the teapot had been emptied; Léon still read on, and Emma listened to him, abstractedly twirling the lampshade round and round; its gauze was painted with clowns driving carts and tightrope walkers holding balancing poles. Léon, gesturing towards his sleeping audience, would stop; and then they would talk to one another very quietly, their conversation seeming all the sweeter for not being overheard.

So there developed between them a kind of bond, a regular interchange of books and ballads. Monsieur Bovary was not a jealous man, and thought it perfectly natural.

For his birthday he received a fine phrenological bust, numbered all over down to the thorax and painted blue. This was a thoughtful attention of the clerk's, and by no means the only one, for he even ran errands for the doctor in Rouen; and then, a new novel having launched a craze for succulents, Léon bought some for Madame, bringing them back on his lap in the Hirondelle, and pricking his fingers on their spikes.

She had a railed shelf put up outside her window to hold her flower pots. The clerk also had his little hanging garden; and they could see each other at their windows, watering their flowers.

Of the windows in the village, one was occupied even more frequently; for, from dawn to dusk on a Sunday, and every afternoon when the weather was clear, Monsieur Binet's scrawny profile could be seen at his attic window, bent over his lathe. Its monotonous drone reached as far away as the Lion d'Or.

When he came home one evening Léon found, in his room, a wool and velour rug with a pattern of leaves on a pale ground. He called Madame Homais, Monsieur Homais, Justin, the children, the cook; he mentioned it to his employer; everyone wanted to see the rug; why was the doctor's wife giving the clerk 'presents'? It looked very odd, and everyone was positive that she must be 'his sweetheart'.

He himself encouraged this idea, for he was perpetually praising her charms and her wit, so much so that Binet, one day, turned on him violently, saying:

'Why should I care, *I'm* not one of her special friends!'

He agonized over how to go about 'declaring himself'; and, eternally torn between the fear of displeasing her and the shame of being such a coward, he wept tears of despair and desire. He would resolve on some decisive step, and write a letter that he would then tear up, or fix on a date that he would then postpone. Often he would set out determined to risk everything, but this determination quickly evaporated in the presence of Emma, and when Charles came in and suggested he accompany him in his buggy to visit some patient in the neighbourhood, he would immediately accept, make his farewells to Madame, and leave. After all, wasn't her husband part of her?

As for Emma, she never asked herself whether she loved him. Love, she believed, should come upon you suddenly, with thunderclaps and blinding flashes of lightning, bursting like a hurricane out of the skies and into your life, turning everything upside down, sweeping your will along like a leaf in the gale, and carrying with it into the void the whole of your heart. She did not know that when the gutters of a house are blocked up, the rain collects in pools on the roof; and so she would have gone on feeling perfectly safe had she not suddenly discovered a crack in the wall.

CHAPTER V

It was a snowy Sunday afternoon in February.

They all—Monsieur and Madame Bovary, Homais, and Léon— had gone to look at a flax mill* that was being built about a mile or so from Yonville, in the valley. The apothecary had brought Napoléon and Athalie with him, to give them some exercise, and Justin accompanied them, carrying some umbrellas on his shoulder.

Nothing, however, could have been less curious than this curiosity. In the middle of a large tract of empty ground, littered with a few cogwheels that lay, already rusting, among piles of sand and pebbles, stood a long rectangular structure pierced by a number of tiny windows. It was not yet completely finished and you could see the sky between the joists of the roof. Fastened to the joist of the gable was a bunch of straw and wheat-ears tied with tricolour ribbon* that made a snapping sound in the wind.

Homais was holding forth. He was explaining to 'those present' the future importance of this establishment, calculating the strength of the floors, the thickness of the walls, and deeply regretting the fact that he did not possess a metric* measuring rod, like the one owned by Monsieur Binet for his personal use.

Emma had taken his arm, and was leaning lightly against his shoulder as she stared at the far-off disc of the sun, its dazzling whiteness shining through the mist; but then, turning her head, she saw—Charles. He had his cap pulled right down to his eyebrows and his thick lips were quivering, which somehow gave his face a stupid look; even his back, that placid back of his, irritated her, and she felt that the very surface of his overcoat summed up all the banality of his being.

While she was studying him and savouring, in her exasperation, a kind of depraved gratification, Léon stepped forward. The cold had washed the colour from his face, but in its place seemed to have left a sweeter languor; the neck of his shirt, rather loose, revealed, between cravat and collar, his bare skin; the tip of an ear showed below a lock of hair, and his large blue eyes, as they gazed up at the clouds, looked to Emma more limpid and more beautiful than mountain lakes mirroring the sky.

'You little devil!' the apothecary shouted suddenly.

And he ran to his son, who had just jumped into a heap of lime, to make his shoes white. Severely scolded, Napoléon began to howl, while Justin wiped his shoes with a bundle of straw. But the job required a knife: Charles offered his.

'Oh!' she thought, 'he carries a knife in his pocket, like a peasant!'

It was starting to freeze, so they walked back to Yonville.

Madame Bovary did not go to her neighbours' house that evening, and, when Charles had left, when she felt herself alone, the comparison returned, with the clarity of an almost immediate sensation yet with the deeper perspective that memory bestows on objects. Gazing from her bed at the bright fire burning, she could still see Léon standing, as he had been standing down there, flexing his cane with one hand and with the other holding Athalie, who was quietly sucking a piece of ice. She thought him charming; she could think of nothing else; in memory she saw him doing other things, at other times, she recalled the words he had used, the tone of his voice, everything about him; and she said again, thrusting out her lips as if for a kiss:

'Yes, charming! . . . charming! . . . Surely he must be in love?' she wondered. 'But who with? Why of course . . . it's me!'

Suddenly all the evidence was clear to her, and her heart gave a leap. The flames in the grate cast a flickering, jubilant light on the ceiling; she turned onto her back and stretched out her arms.

Then came the age-old lament: 'Oh, if only heaven had willed it! Why didn't it? What was to prevent it?'

When Charles came in at midnight she pretended to wake up and, as he made a noise getting undressed, she complained of a migraine, then asked casually what had happened during the evening.

'Monsieur Léon', he told her, 'went up to his room early.'

She could not help smiling, and fell asleep, her spirit filled with a new delight.

The following evening, she received a visit from Monsieur Lheureux, the dealer in fancy goods. Lheureux was an extremely adroit tradesman.

Gascon by birth but Norman by adoption, he united southern loquacity with Cauchois cunning. His fleshy, flabby, clean-shaven face looked as if it had been stained with pale liquorice extract, and his white hair intensified the fierce glitter of his tiny black eyes. No one knew what his previous occupation had been: a pedlar, some said, while others claimed he had been a banker in Routot. What was indisputable, however, was his ability to carry out, in his head, calculations so complex that even Binet himself found them daunting. Polite to the point of obsequiousness, he always stood leaning forward slightly from the hips, in a posture suggestive of a deferential, or a welcoming, bow.

Depositing his black-banded hat at the door, he placed a green box on the table and began by lamenting, in excessively polite language, the fact that he had not, before this, had the honour of obtaining Madame's patronage. A humble shop such as his was not of a calibre to attract a lady of *fashion*; he emphasized the word. But she had only to make known her requirements and he would undertake to provide whatever she wanted, whether it be haberdashery or lingerie, hosiery or fancy goods, for he went to the city regularly, four times a month. He did business with the best firms. She just need mention his name at the Trois-Frères, the Barbe-d'Or, or the Grand-Sauvage, all those gentlemen knew him like the back of their hand! So today he thought he would take the opportunity to show Madame a few things that, thanks to an exceptional stroke of good fortune, he happened to have obtained. And he drew half a dozen embroidered collars out of the box.

Madame Bovary examined them.

'There's nothing I need,' she said.

So then, with a delicate touch, Monsieur Lheureux laid out before her three Algerian scarves, several packets of English needles, a pair of straw slippers, and, finally, four eggcups carved from coconut shells, in filigree, by convicts. And, leaning with his two hands on the table, his neck stretched, his body bent forward, and his mouth open, he followed Emma's eyes as they wandered indecisively, studying the merchandise. From time to time, as if to remove a speck of dust, he would flick the silk of the scarves as they lay there unfolded to their full length; and they shimmered, rustling very faintly as, in the greenish twilight, the golden spangles of their fabric glittered like tiny stars.

'How much are they?'

'Oh, a mere trifle,' he told her, 'a mere trifle; but there's no rush; whenever it suits you—we're not Jews!'

She thought for a minute or two, and then again said that there was nothing she wanted. Monsieur Lheureux replied imperturbably:

'Oh well! Some other time, I'm sure; I've always got along with the ladies . . . except my own wife, that is!'

Emma smiled.

'What I'm telling you', he went on in a frank and kindly tone, after enjoying his little joke, 'is that I'm not worried about the money . . . I could let you have some, if you needed it.'

She gave a start of surprise.

'Ah!' he said quickly, his voice low, 'and I wouldn't have to go far to find you some, you can be sure of that!'

Then he began asking about old Tellier, the proprietor of the Café Français, who was being attended by Monsieur Bovary.

'So what's the matter with him, old man Tellier? He's got a cough that makes the whole house shake, and I'm very much afraid that he'll soon be needing a wooden overcoat, not a flannel undershirt! He was a great one for going on the spree, when he was young! That sort, Madame, they hadn't a vestige of self-control. He burnt out all his insides with brandy! But even so, it's hard, you know, to see an old acquaintance go.'

And, while he was refastening his box, he went on chatting about the doctor's patients.

'It must be the weather', he said, looking out of the window with a frown, 'that's to blame for these ailments; even I myself don't really feel quite right; in fact one of these days I'll have to come and consult your husband about a pain I have in my back. Well, goodbye for now, Madame Bovary, always delighted to oblige, just say the word!'

And he gently closed the door behind him.

Emma had her dinner served in her room, beside the fire, on a tray; she lingered over her food, enjoying every dish.

'Wasn't I good!' she said to herself, thinking of the scarves.

There were footsteps on the stairs: it was Léon. Getting up, she grabbed off the dresser the top duster from the stack waiting to be hemmed. She appeared very busy when he came in.

The conversation languished. Madame Bovary kept falling silent, and he himself seemed extremely ill at ease. He was sitting on a low chair by the fireside, turning her ivory needle case over and over in his fingers; she kept on sewing or, from time to time, marking a fold in the cloth with her fingernail. She did not speak; he too remained quiet, enthralled by her silence as he would have been by her words.

'Poor fellow!' she said to herself.

'What is it that I've done wrong?' he was wondering.

Eventually Léon remarked that he would be going to Rouen one day soon, to see to some office business.

'Your music subscription has run out, would you like me to renew it?'

'No,' she replied.

'Why not?'

'Because . . .'

Pursing her lips, she slowly drew out a long piece of grey thread.

Léon was finding this work of hers annoying. It seemed to be making Emma's fingertips sore, and a rather bold compliment occurred to him, but he did not dare voice it.

'So, are you giving it up?' he continued.

'What? My music?' she asked quickly. 'Oh, goodness, yes! Haven't I my house to run, my husband to look after, countless things, in fact, to do, lots of more important duties!'

She looked at the clock. Charles was late. She put on a worried air.

'He's so good,' she repeated two or three times.

Although the clerk liked Monsieur Bovary, it came as an unpleasant shock to hear her speak so affectionately of him; nevertheless he went on singing the doctor's praises, saying he heard them on all sides, and particularly from the pharmacist.

'He's a fine man, Monsieur Homais,' said Emma.

'Indeed he is.'

And the clerk began talking about Madame Homais, whose slovenly appearance usually made them laugh.

'What does it matter?' interrupted Emma. 'A good wife and mother doesn't bother about how she looks.'

Then she fell silent again.

It was just the same over the following days; her conversation, her manner, everything changed. People noticed that she devoted herself to her household duties, went back to attending church regularly, and kept a stricter eye on her maid.

She removed Berthe from the wet-nurse. When visitors called, Félicité brought in the baby, and Emma undressed her to show off her limbs. She adored children, she kept declaring; they were her comfort, her delight, her passion, and she accompanied her caresses with a lyrical gushing that, to anyone except an inhabitant of Yonville, would have recalled Sachette, in *Notre-Dame de Paris*.*

When Charles came home, he would find his slippers warming by the fire. His waistcoats, now, never needed a new lining, nor were his shirts ever short of buttons; it was even a pleasure to see all his nightcaps stacked neatly in the cupboard. No longer, now, did she scowl when he proposed a walk in the garden; his wishes were always acceded to, although she never anticipated his desires, to which she submitted without complaint; and when Léon saw him sitting by the fire after dinner, both hands on his stomach, both feet on the fire-dogs, his cheeks flushed with eating, his eyes moist with happiness, the child crawling about on the carpet, and this slender-waisted woman who had just leant over the back of his chair to kiss his forehead—

'I must be out of my mind,' he told himself; 'however could I hope to get near her!'

She seemed so virtuous and inaccessible that all hope, even the most remote, deserted him.

But, by renouncing her in this way, he set her apart, making her into something extraordinary. She became dissociated, for him, from the carnal body that would never be his; and in his heart she soared higher and higher, receding ever further from him as if in some magnificent apotheosis. It was one of those pure emotions that remain quite disconnected from everyday life, that are cherished for their very rarity, and whose loss would bring misery more intense than the happiness inspired by their possession.

Emma grew thinner, her cheeks paler, her face longer. With her black hair, large eyes, straight nose, light step, and her now invariable silence, did it not seem that she went through life barely touching it, and that her forehead bore the faint imprint of some sublime destiny? She was so sad and so calm, so sweet and yet so withdrawn, that in her presence he felt bewitched by an icy charm, just as in church the scent of the flowers blending with the chill of the marble made him shiver. And even other people were not immune to this seduction. As the pharmacist liked to put it:

'She's a remarkably gifted woman! Why, she wouldn't be out of place as the wife of a sub-prefect!'

The local housewives admired her for her thrift, the patients for her politeness, the poor for her charity.

But she was filled with lusts, with rage, with hatred. That neatly pleated dress concealed a tempestuous heart, and those chaste lips uttered no word of her torment. She was in love with Léon, and she sought out solitude the better to luxuriate in his image. The actual physical sight of him distracted her from the voluptuous pleasures of these thoughts. At the sound of his footsteps Emma would tremble; then, in his presence, her agitation evaporated and all she was left with was a feeling of immense astonishment, which gradually turned to sadness.

Léon never suspected that, when he left her house in despair, she immediately rose and went to watch him walk down the street. She wanted to know about everything he did and everywhere he went; surreptitiously she studied his face; she thought up a complicated story as a pretext for seeing his room. Emma considered Homais's wife a most fortunate being, to sleep under the same roof as him, and her thoughts were constantly coming to rest on that house, like the pigeons from the Lion d'Or who alighted there to bathe their rosy feet and white wings in the gutters of its roof. But the more she became aware of her love, the more Emma repressed it, to keep it hidden, and also to weaken its hold. She would have liked Léon to guess her feelings; and she made up fantasies about coincidences and disasters that might precipitate a revelation. Perhaps she was held back by inertia, or terror, as well as by shame. It seemed to her that she had kept him at too great a distance, that the moment had now passed, that now there was no hope. And then the pride, the joy of telling herself: 'I am a virtuous woman,' and of admiring herself, in her mirror, in attitudes of resignation, consoled her somewhat for the sacrifice she believed she was making.

So then her erotic desires, her craving for money, and the depression born of her passion all merged into a single torment; and, rather than striving to turn her thoughts elsewhere, she focused on it more and more, fomenting her pain and seeking out all possible occasions to indulge it. A badly served dish or a door left ajar annoyed her; she mourned for the velvet she did not possess and the happiness that had escaped her, for her dreams that soared too high, for her house that kept her too confined.

What enraged her was that Charles seemed quite unaware of her anguish. His conviction that he was making her happy seemed to her a mindless insult, and his complacent security, ingratitude. So for whose sake, then, did she remain chaste? Was not he himself, in fact, the obstacle to all felicity, the cause of all misery, and as it were the sharp-pointed spike securing the many-stranded girdle that restricted her on every side?

So it was upon him that she focused the multifaceted hatred born of her unhappiness, and every attempt she made to conquer this feeling only served to strengthen it; for the futility of her efforts gave her another reason to despair and intensified her estrangement from Charles. Even her own meekness goaded her to rebel. The mediocrity of her home provoked her to sumptuous fantasies, the caresses of her husband to adulterous desires. She would have liked Charles to beat her, so that she could more justifiably detest him, and seek her revenge. She was sometimes astonished at the appalling possibilities that came into her head; and yet she must go on smiling, go on hearing herself repeat that she was happy, act as if she were, and let everyone believe it!

There were times, however, when she found this hypocrisy repugnant. She would be seized with the temptation to run away with Léon, somewhere, a long way away, and try a new life; but instantly, in her mind, a vague abyss would appear, full of dark shadows.

'Besides, he doesn't love me any more,' she would think. 'What will become of me? What help can I hope for, what comfort, what relief?'

Afterwards, she would be left utterly exhausted, breathless and prostrate, sobbing softly, the tears streaming down her face.

'Why don't you tell Monsieur?' the maid would ask her, when she found her in this state.

'It's nerves,' Emma would reply, 'don't say anything to him, it would upset him.'

'Yes,' Félicité went on, 'you're like old Guérin's daughter, he's that fisherman over at Pollet, well I knew her in Dieppe, before I came here. She was so sad, so awfully sad, that just seeing her standing on the front step made you think of a mourning sheet draped over the door. It seems her trouble was a kind of fog she had in her head, the doctors couldn't do nothing for her, and the curé couldn't neither. When she got it too bad, she'd go all on her own down to the sea, and when he went on his rounds the customs officer'd often find her, stretched right out on her stomach on the pebbles, crying. Then, after she got married, it went away, they say.'

'But with me,' replied Emma, 'it was after I got married that it began.'

CHAPTER VI

One evening, while she was sitting by the open window, after watching Lestiboudois, the sexton, trim the box-hedge, she suddenly heard the angelus ringing.

It was the beginning of April, when the primroses are in bloom; a warm breeze dances over the freshly turned flower beds and the gardens, like women, seem to be adorning themselves for the festivities of summer. Through the trellis of the arbour and beyond in every direction, she could see the meadows, with the river tracing an erratic, sinuous course through the grasses. The evening mist, drifting among the leafless poplars, veiled their silhouettes with a violet film, paler and more translucent than the most diaphanous gauze that might have caught in their branches. Far away, a few cattle were on the move, but no sound of tramping or lowing could be heard; and the bell rang steadily on, filling the air with its gentle lamentation.

Carried back by this repeated ringing, the young woman's thoughts kept straying among old memories of her youth and her years at the convent. She remembered the great candlesticks on the altar, standing taller than the vases of flowers and the tabernacle with its miniature columns. She would have liked, as in the past, to be just one in that long line of white veils, dappled by an occasional patch of black where a nun's stiff cowl bent over a prie-dieu; at mass, on a Sunday, when she raised her head, she would see the sweet face of the Virgin through the rising blue-grey swirls of incense. She was suddenly filled with tenderness; she felt limp and unresisting like a tiny feather tossed in a storm; and it was without conscious thought that she set off for the church, eager for any act of devotion, as long as it would overwhelm her soul and obliterate her entire existence.

In the square she met Lestiboudois, returning from the church; to avoid chipping into his working hours, he preferred to stop what he was doing and then pick it up again, so that he rang the angelus whenever it suited him. Besides, by ringing it early, he reminded the village lads that it was time for catechism.

A few of them were already there, playing marbles on the cemetery flagstones. Others sat astride the wall, swinging their legs, slashing with their clogs at the tall nettles that had pushed up between the low wall and the most recent tombs. This was the only place where anything green grew; all the rest was stone, and, in spite of the sacristan's broom, perpetually covered in a fine dust.

Children in slippers were running about there as if the gravestones were their playground, and she could hear their shrill shrieks above the droning of the bell. The sound gradually died away as the great bell-rope swung more and more slowly. It hung down from the top of the tower, its end trailing on the ground. Swallows flew past giving little chirps, their swift flight slicing through the air as they shot back to their yellow nests beneath the tiles of the eaves. In the depths of the church a lamp was burning, a wick in a hanging glass container. From a distance, its light looked like a whitish blotch that shimmered on the oil. A long shaft of sunlight cut right across the nave, making the shadows in the side-aisles and the corners even blacker.

'Where's the curé?' Madame Bovary asked a young lad who was busy rattling the loose hinge on the turnstile.

'He's coming,' replied the child.

Indeed, just then the presbytery door gave a creak and Abbé Bournisien appeared; the children rushed helter-skelter into the church.

'Those little rascals!' muttered the priest, 'they'll never change!'

And, picking up a tattered catechism on which he had just stumbled:

'They've no respect for anything.'

Then, when he noticed Madame Bovary:

'Please excuse me, I didn't recognize you.'

He stuffed the catechism into his pocket and stood there, still dangling the heavy vestry key between two fingers.

The glow of the setting sun, shining directly onto his face, drained the colour from his heavy black cassock, which was shiny at the elbows and frayed round the hem. Grease and tobacco stains clustered round the line of small buttons running down his broad chest, their number increasing the further away they were from his neckband, on which reposed several folds of his florid skin; this was mottled with yellow blotches that disappeared into the coarse hairs of his greying beard. He had just finished dinner, and was breathing laboriously.

'How are you keeping?' he went on.

'Not well,' replied Emma, 'not at all well.'

'It's just the same with me,' the priest answered. 'These first hot days make you feel ever so weak, don't you find? Well, there we are! We're born to suffer, as St Paul says. But what does Monsieur Bovary think?'

'Oh, him!' she exclaimed, with a scornful gesture.

Very surprised, the simple fellow went on: 'But surely he's prescribed something for you?'

'Ah! It's not earthly remedies I need.'

But the priest kept glancing into the church, where the kneeling boys were shoving each other with their shoulders and falling about like ninepins.

'I wanted to know . . .', she continued.

'Just you wait, Riboudet,' shouted the cleric in a furious voice; 'I'm going to box your ears for you, you little brat!'

Then, turning to Emma: 'He's the son of Boudet the carpenter; his parents are comfortably off and they let him do whatever he wants. Yet he'd learn quickly if he wanted to, he's very bright. So sometimes—well sometimes, as a joke, I call him Riboudet (like that hill on the way to Maronne) and I even say: "mon Riboudet." Ha, ha! Mont-Riboudet, you see. The other day, I told His Grace my little joke, and he laughed at it . . . Yes, he was good enough to laugh at it . . . And so how's Monsieur Bovary?'

She seemed not to hear him, and he went on:

'Busy as ever, I expect? Because he and I, we're certainly the two people in the parish with the most to do. But he looks after the body,' he added with a throaty laugh, 'and I look after the soul!'

She fixed imploring eyes on the priest:

'Yes . . .', she said, 'you bring comfort to all who suffer.'

'Oh, you don't know the half of it, Madame Bovary. Why only this morning, I had to go down to Bas-Diauville for a cow that had "the bloat"; they thought it was bewitched. Every one of their cows, I've no idea why . . . Excuse me! Longuemarre, Boudet! Saints preserve us! Stop it this instant!'

And he dashed into the church.

By this time there were boys swarming round the big lectern, climbing onto the cantor's bench, and opening the missal; some of the bolder lads were even cautiously approaching the confessional. But the curé suddenly swooped down, doling out blows right and left. Grabbing them by the collar, he picked them up bodily and set them on their knees on the stone floor of the choir, pushing them down firmly, as if he would have liked to embed them there.

'Yes indeed!' he said, returning to Emma and unfolding his big calico handkerchief, one corner of which he pushed between his teeth, 'the farmers do have a very hard time!'

'And others, as well,' she replied.

'You're absolutely right! Workers in the city, for instance.'

'I didn't mean . . .'

'Excuse me, but in the city I've known poor mothers of families, virtuous women, I assure you, positive saints, who didn't even have a crust of bread to eat.'

'But what about those,' Emma went on (and the corners of her mouth twisted as she spoke), 'those, Monsieur le Curé, who have bread, but have no . . .'

'Fire in winter,' supplied the priest.

'Oh, what does that matter?'

'What do you mean, what does that matter? As I see it, if you're warm and well fed . . . after all . . .'

'Oh, my God! My God!' she sighed.

'Are you feeling unwell?' he asked, leaning forward anxiously.

'Maybe it's something you ate. You'd better go home, Madame Bovary, and have a cup of tea; that'll pick you up, or perhaps a glass of water with some brown sugar.'

'Why?'

She looked like someone waking from a dream.

'You were putting your hand on your forehead. I thought you might be feeling dizzy.' Then, as an afterthought:

'But weren't you asking me about something? What was it now? I don't remember.'

'Me? No, nothing . . . nothing . . .', said Emma.

And her wandering gaze slowly focused on the old man in his cassock. Face to face, they looked at one another in silence.

'Well then, Madame Bovary,' he said finally, 'you must excuse me, but duty calls, you know. I must see to my young rascals. Not long now till first communion. I'm afraid we won't be ready in time. So, after Ascension Day, I keep them for an extra hour every Wednesday without fail. Poor children! We can't start them too soon on the path of the Lord—as indeed he himself instructs us to do, through the mouth of his divine Son . . . Keep well, Madame; remember me to your good husband.'

And he went into the church, genuflecting at the entrance.

Emma watched him disappear between the double rows of pews, walking heavily, his head bent slightly to one side, his hands half-open, with the palms facing out.

Then, in a single movement, she turned on her heels like a statue on a pivot, and set off for home. But as she walked away she could still hear, behind her, the curé's deep voice, and the clear tones of the children.

'Are you a Christian?'

'Yes, I am a Christian.'

'What is a Christian?'

'One who, being baptized . . . baptized . . . baptized . . .'

She climbed up the stairs holding onto the banister, and once in her room, sank wearily into a chair.

The wavering whitish light from the windows was gradually fading away. The pieces of furniture seemed to have grown more fixed in their places, lost in the shadows as in a darkling sea. The fire was out, the clock ticked on, and Emma felt a vague astonishment at this tranquillity of things, while she herself was full of such turmoil. Between the window and Emma's work table was little Berthe, tottering about in her knitted bootees, and trying to reach her mother and grab hold of the ends of her apron strings.

'Leave me alone,' cried Emma, pushing her away.

The child soon came back, even closer; and, leaning her arms on her mother's knees, gazed up at her with her big blue eyes, while a thread of clear saliva dribbled from her lip onto Emma's silk apron.

'Leave me alone!' she repeated very irritably.

Her expression frightened the child, who began to cry.

'Oh! For heaven's sake leave me alone!' she exclaimed, shoving her away with her elbow.

Berthe fell against the foot of the chest of drawers, cutting her cheek on the brass fitting; the cut began to bleed. Madame Bovary rushed to pick her up, broke the bell pull, shouted for the maid at the top of her voice, and was beginning to reproach herself bitterly, when Charles walked in. It was dinnertime; he had come home.

'Look what's happened, dear,' she said in a calm voice; 'the baby fell while she was playing, she's hurt herself.'

Charles reassured her that it was nothing serious, and went to fetch some diachylon.*

Madame Bovary did not go downstairs for dinner, she insisted on remaining upstairs, alone, to sit with her child. Then, as she watched her sleeping, the last of her anxiety gradually subsided, and she began to think herself very silly and soft-hearted to have become so upset over such a trifle. Berthe, indeed, had stopped sobbing. Her breath now barely lifted the cotton coverlet. Large tears still lay in the corners of her half-closed lids, and through the lashes her pale, sunken pupils were visible; the strip of plaster was pulling the taut skin of her cheek to one side.

'It's really odd,' thought Emma, 'how ugly this child is!'

When Charles came back, at eleven, from the pharmacy, where he had gone to return the remaining diachylon, he found his wife standing beside the cradle.

'Please believe me, it's nothing at all,' he said, kissing her on the forehead, 'do stop worrying, my poor darling, you'll make yourself ill!'

He had stayed quite a time at the apothecary's. Although Charles had not seemed unduly upset, Monsieur Homais had, nevertheless, done his best to help him regain his composure, and 'buck him up'. Then they had talked about all the various hazards children are exposed to, and about the carelessness of servants. *That* was something Madame Homais knew all about, for her chest still bore the scars from a basinful of stew that a cook had once spilt onto her pinafore. Consequently, these careful parents took all kinds of precautions. Knives were never sharpened, nor were floors ever polished. The windows had iron bars and the fireplaces strong fire screens. The Homais young, despite their independence, could not stir from the house without someone to watch them; at the slightest sign of a cold, their father stuffed them with cough syrup, and until well past their fourth birthdays, they were all relentlessly made to wear padded caps. In actual fact this was an obsession of Madame Homais; her husband was secretly unhappy about it, fearing the consequences of such pressure on the organs of the intellect, and sometimes he would go so far as to say to her:

'Are you trying to make them look like little Caribs or Botocudos?'*

Charles, meanwhile, had tried several times to interrupt the conversation.

'There's something I need to talk to you about,' he had whispered softly in the clerk's ear, as Léon set off down the stairs in front of him.

'Might he suspect something?' wondered Léon. His heart was racing and his mind awhirl with conjectures.

Eventually Charles, having shut the door, asked him to enquire, in Rouen, what might be the cost of a good daguerreotype; he wanted to give his wife a sentimental surprise—a portrait of himself in his black tail coat. He felt it would be a really delicate attention. But he wanted to know, beforehand, 'how much it would set him back'; he imagined such an errand would not inconvenience Monsieur Léon, since he went to the city nearly every week.

Why did he go there? Homais suspected 'a romantic intrigue', an affair of some kind. But he was mistaken. Léon was not meeting a sweetheart. He was more depressed than ever, as Madame Lefrançois could easily see from the amount of food that he now left untouched on his plate. Trying to find out more, she questioned the tax collector; Binet replied disdainfully that he 'wasn't in the pay of the police'.

His dinner companion did, however, strike him as extremely strange; for Léon would often fling himself back in his chair, stretch out his arms, and complain vaguely about life.

'It's because you don't have enough diversions,' said the tax collector.

'Such as?'

'If I were you, I'd get a lathe!'

'But I wouldn't know how to use a lathe,' replied the clerk.

'No, of course, you wouldn't,' Binet agreed, stroking his chin with an air of mingled scorn and gratification.

Léon had grown tired of loving to no avail, and was beginning to experience the despondency that comes from leading the same life day in, day out, without any interest to give it purpose or any hope to sustain it. He was so bored by Yonville and the Yonvillians that the sight of certain individuals, or of certain houses, irritated him beyond endurance; and now he was finding the pharmacist, good soul though he was, quite unbearable. Nevertheless, the prospect of a new position seemed as alarming as it was alluring.

This trepidation soon turned into impatience, and then Paris began to sound in his ear its distant fanfare of masked balls and laughing girls. Since he had to go there in any case to complete his law studies, why not leave now?* What was to prevent it? And so he began making imaginary preparations; he planned in advance how he would occupy his time. In his head, he furnished himself an apartment. He'd live the life of an artist there! He'd learn to play the guitar! He'd have a dressing gown, a Basque beret, a pair of blue velvet slippers! And already he was admiring his mental image of the décor over his mantelpiece: a pair of crossed fencing foils, with a skull, and up above this a guitar.

The difficulty was to obtain his mother's consent, although no plan could seem more reasonable. Even his employer kept urging him to spend time in another law practice, where he might develop different skills. As a compromise, Léon looked for a position as second clerk in Rouen, but without success; in the end he wrote his mother a long, detailed letter giving his reasons for going immediately to live in Paris. She consented.

He was in no hurry. Every day for a whole month, Hivert

transported boxes, bags, and parcels for him from Yonville to Rouen and from Rouen to Yonville; and, when Léon had replenished his wardrobe, reupholstered his three armchairs, and bought a supply of silk cravats, when, indeed, he had completed preparations sufficient for a journey round the world, he still delayed his departure from week to week, until a second letter from his mother arrived, urging him to leave immediately, as he hoped to sit for his examination before the holidays.

When the moment came for farewells, Madame Homais wept and Justin sobbed, while Homais manfully concealed his emotion; he insisted on personally carrying his friend's overcoat as far as the notary's gate, for Maître Guillaumin was taking Léon to Rouen in his carriage. The clerk had just enough time to say goodbye to Monsieur Bovary.

At the top of the stairs he paused, he felt so breathless. When he walked into the room, Madame Bovary jumped to her feet.

'It's me again!' said Léon.

'I knew you'd come!'

She bit her lip, and a wave of colour washed over her skin, turning it a deep rose from the roots of her hair to the top of her collar. She remained standing, leaning one shoulder against the panelling.

'Isn't your husband at home?' he continued.

'He's out.'

She said again: 'He's out.'

Then silence fell. They looked at each other, and their thoughts, blending together in mutual anguish, united in a close embrace, like two throbbing hearts.

'I'd love to give Berthe a kiss,' said Léon.

Emma went down a few steps and called Félicité.

Quickly he looked round the room, his sweeping glance taking in the walls, the shelves, the fireplace, as if to absorb it all, carry it all away with him.

But she came back, and the maid brought in Berthe, who was dangling a tiny windmill upside down on a piece of string.

Léon kissed her several times on the neck.

'Goodbye, you sweet little thing! Goodbye, my pet, goodbye!'

And he gave her back to her mother.

'You can take her away,' said Emma.

They were left alone.

Madame Bovary stood with her back turned and her face pressed against a window pane; Léon was holding his cap in his hand, slapping it gently on his thigh.

'It's going to rain,' said Emma.

'I've my coat,' he replied.

'Ah!'

She turned from the window, her chin tucked in and her forehead projecting. The light slid over her brow as if over polished marble, down to the arch of her eyebrows; it was impossible to tell what she was gazing at in the distance, or what her secret thoughts might be.

'Well, goodbye, then!' he sighed.

She raised her head with a sudden movement: 'Yes, goodbye . . . now go!'

They moved towards one another: he held out his hand, she hesitated.

'Yes, English style,* why not,' she said with a forced laugh, giving him her hand.

Léon felt it between his fingers, and the very essence of his entire being seemed to flow into that moist palm.

Then he loosened his grip, their eyes met once more, and he was gone.

When he reached the market he stopped behind a pillar, to gaze one last time at that white house with its four green shutters. He fancied he glimpsed a shadow at the window of her room; but the curtain, freed from its retaining hook as if by magic, slowly stirred its long oblique folds, which then swung out in a single movement, and the curtain hung down as straight and motionless as a plaster wall. Léon began to run.

From a distance, he saw his employer's carriage standing in the road, with a man wearing an apron beside it, holding the horse. Homais and Maître Guillaumin were chatting as they waited for him.

'Give me a hug,' said the apothecary, with tears in his eyes. 'Here's your coat, my dear fellow, wrap up well, it's cold! Take good care of yourself! Don't overdo it!'

'Come on, Léon, get in!' said the notary.

Homais leant over the splashboard and, in a voice shaken by sobs, uttered these two sad words:

'Bon voyage!'

'Goodbye,' replied Maître Guillaumin. 'Off we go!'

They drove away, and Homais returned home.

Madame Bovary had opened her window onto the garden, and was watching the clouds.

They were gathering in the west, towards Rouen, moving rapidly in a black spiralling mass, and behind them long sunbeams radiated out like golden arrows round a display trophy. The rest of the sky was clear, and white as porcelain. But a fierce gust of wind bent the poplars over, and suddenly the rain began to fall, drumming on the green leaves. Then the sun reappeared, the hens cackled; sparrows were flapping their wings in the damp bushes, and the pools of water on the gravel, as they flowed away, carried with them the pink blossoms off an acacia.

'Oh, he must already be so far away!' she thought.

Monsieur Homais, as usual, arrived at half-past six, during dinner.

'Well now!' he remarked as he sat down, 'so we've just seen our young man off!'

'So it appears,' replied the doctor. Then, turning in his chair:

'What's new with you?'

'Nothing special. Except my wife was a bit upset this afternoon. Women, you know, they get upset over nothing! My wife particularly. And we'd be wrong to complain about it, because their nervous system is so very much more sensitive than ours.'

'Poor Léon!' said Charles, 'I wonder how he'll get on in Paris. Do you think he'll settle down there?'

Madame Bovary sighed.

'Oh come on!' rejoined the pharmacist, clicking his tongue, 'nice little suppers in restaurants, masked balls, champagne! He'll have a great time, believe me.'

'I don't think he'll do anything foolish,' objected Bovary.

'Nor do I!' Homais replied promptly, 'but he'll still have to go along with the other fellows, if he doesn't want them to think he's a Jesuit.* And you've no idea of the shenanigans those young devils get up to, in the Latin Quarter, with the actresses! Besides, students are very well thought of, in Paris. If they've just a few social graces they're received in the best circles, and there are even ladies in the Faubourg Saint-Germain who fall in love with them, and that gives them the chance, later on, of making a very good marriage.'

'But,' said the doctor, 'I'm worried that he may . . . in the city . . .'

'You're quite right,' interrupted the apothecary, 'it's the other side of the coin! You've got to keep your hand on your purse every minute. Imagine for example that you're in a public park; someone comes up to you, well dressed, perhaps even a medal, you might take him for a diplomat; he addresses you, you start chatting, he butters you up, offers you a pinch of snuff, say, or picks your hat up for you. Then you get to know each other better; he takes you to a café, invites you down to his country house, and when you've had a few drinks introduces you to all kinds of people; more often than not it's just to get his hands on your purse, or to lead you into wicked ways.'

'That's true,' replied Charles, 'but I was thinking especially of illnesses, typhoid fever, for instance, that students from the provinces seem prone to.'

Emma shivered.

'Because of the change of diet,' continued the pharmacist, 'and the consequent perturbation to the entire system. And then of course there's the Paris water, you know, and restaurant food; in the long run all those spicy dishes overheat the blood; I don't care what people say, they can't hold a candle to a good old-fashioned stew. For my part, I've always preferred plain home cooking; it's healthier! That's why when I was studying pharmacy in Rouen, I had my meals in a boarding house, along with the professors.'

And he went on expounding his general opinions and personal preferences until Justin came to fetch him to prepare an egg-flip for a customer.

'Never a moment's peace!' he exclaimed, 'it's work, work, work! I can't get away for a second! I'm just an old plough horse, sweating blood and water! Nothing but toil and moil!'

Then, as he reached the door:

'By the way, have you heard the news?'

'No, what?'

'It's more than likely', Homais went on, raising his eyebrows and assuming a most solemn expression, 'that this year's Agricultural Show for the Seine-Inférieure will be held here, in Yonville-L'Abbaye. At least that's the rumour going round. There was something about it in the paper this morning. It would be of the utmost importance for our district! But we'll talk about it some other time. I can see my way, thank you; Justin has brought the lantern.'

CHAPTER VII

The next day, for Emma, was funereal. Everything appeared to her shrouded in a black mist that hovered uncertainly over the surface of things, and grief plunged deep into her soul, moaning softly like the winter wind in an abandoned chateau. She sank into that kind of brooding which comes when you lose something forever, that lassitude you feel after every irreversible event, that pain you suffer when a habitual movement is interrupted, when a long-sustained vibration is suddenly broken off.

She felt just the same as after her return from La Vaubyessard with the dance tunes still whirling in her head; she was filled with a bleak melancholy, a numb despair. Léon reappeared before her, taller, handsomer, more polished, less clearly defined; although he was separated from her, he had not left her, he was there, and the walls of the house seemed to shelter his ghostly presence. She could not take her eyes off that rug where he had stepped, or those empty chairs where he had sat. The river still flowed on, its ripples lapping slowly against the slippery bank. There they had so often strolled, listening to that same water murmuring over those same moss-covered stones. How brightly the sun had shone on them! How lovely their afternoons had been, alone in the shade at the bottom of the garden! He, sitting bare-headed on a rustic wooden stool, would read to her, the fresh breeze from the meadows ruffling the pages of his book, and the nasturtiums growing round the arbour . . . Ah! He was gone, the only light of her life, her only possible hope of any happiness! Why had she not grasped that happiness when it lay within her reach? Why had she not held onto him, with both her hands, on her knees, when he tried to leave? And she cursed herself for not having loved Léon; she thirsted for his lips. She was seized with a longing to follow him, to fling herself into his arms, to say to him: 'Here I am, I'm yours!' But the imagined complications of such an enterprise filled Emma with dismay, and her desires, magnified by regret, grew all the more intense.

From that time on, her memory of Léon became the core of her despair; it glittered more brightly than a fire abandoned by travellers on the snows of a Russian steppe. She would rush up to it, huddle over it, delicately stirring the dying embers and searching for anything within reach that might revive it; and the most distant memories as well as the most recent events, her feelings both real and imagined, her now-fading sensual desires, her plans for happiness that snapped in the wind like dead branches, her sterile virtue, her lost hopes, the debris of domestic life—all this she gathered up, all this she took, and used to feed her unhappiness.

But the flames did die down, perhaps from lack, perhaps from excess of fuel. Little by little, love was quenched by absence, and longing smothered by routine; and that fiery glow which tinged her pale sky scarlet grew more clouded, then gradually faded away. Her benumbed consciousness even led her to mistake aversion toward her husband for desire for her lover, the searing touch of hatred for the rekindling of love; but, as the storm still raged on and her passion burnt itself to ashes, no help came and no sun rose, the darkness of night closed in on every side, and she was left to drift in a bitter icy void.

So the bad days of Tostes began again. She believed herself much more unhappy, now, because she had experienced sorrow, and knew for certain that it would never end.

A woman who had exacted such sacrifices of herself might well be permitted a few indulgences. She bought a Gothic prie-dieu, and spent, in one month, fourteen francs on lemons to blanch her fingernails; she wrote to Rouen to order a blue cashmere dress; from Lheureux she chose the finest of his scarves; she would tie it round her waist, over her dressing gown, and, with the shutters closed and a book in her hand, she would lie on her sofa wearing this get-up.

She kept changing the way she arranged her hair. She tried doing it *à la chinoise*, in soft curls, in plaits; she parted it on the side of her head and turned it under, like a man.

She decided to learn Italian: she bought dictionaries, a grammar, and a supply of paper. She embarked on some serious reading, in history, in philosophy. At night, sometimes, Charles would wake with a start, imagining that he was being summoned to a sickbed:

'I'm coming,' he would mumble.

It was the sound of a match Emma had struck, to relight the lamp. But it was the same with these books as with her needlework, pieces of which, half done, cluttered up her wardrobe; she would take them up, put them down, go on to something else.

She had moods when she was easily provoked into outrageous behaviour. One day she insisted, ignoring Charles's objections, that she could easily drink half a large glass of brandy, and, when he was so foolish as to challenge her, downed the spirits to the last drop.

Yet for all her flightiness (as the good ladies of Yonville called it) Emma did not look happy, and the corners of her mouth were usually set in those deep, rigid creases that line the faces of old maids and ambitious failures. She was pale all over, white as a sheet; the skin of her nose was drawn tight round the nostrils, and she had a way of staring at you vacantly. Discovering a few grey hairs at her temples, she began to talk of growing old.

She often suffered from giddy spells, and one day she even spat up some blood. As Charles was fussing over her, obviously worried:

'Bah!' she said; 'Whatever does it matter?'

Charles retreated into his study, where, seated in his office chair under the phrenological head and leaning his elbows on the table, he wept.

Then he wrote begging his mother to come, and they had long discussions together, about Emma.

What ought they to do? What could they do, since she refused any kind of treatment?

'Do you know what your wife really needs?' resumed Madame Bovary senior. 'What she needs is hard work, manual labour. If she was obliged to earn her living like so many have to do, she wouldn't suffer from these vapours, which come from all these ideas she fills her head with, and living such an idle life.'

'Still, she's always busy,' replied Charles.

'Huh! Busy! But doing what? Reading novels, wicked books, books against religion, full of speeches from Voltaire that make fun of priests. This is no laughing matter, my poor boy; someone who has no religion always comes to a bad end.'

So it was decided that Emma was to be prevented from reading novels.* The plan presented certain difficulties. The old lady undertook to carry it out: on her way through Rouen she would call personally at the lending library and tell the proprietor that Emma was cancelling her subscriptions. If, despite this, he persisted in disseminating his poison, would they not be justified in reporting him to the police?

Farewells between mother and daughter-in-law were curt. During the three weeks they had spent together they had barely exchanged four words, other than the customary enquiries and good wishes when they met at table, or were parting for the night.

Madame Bovary senior left on a Wednesday, which was market day in Yonville.

From early morning, the square had been cluttered with a row of carts standing, tipped up on end with their shafts in the air, in front of the houses between the church and the inn. Across from them, canvas booths had been erected, selling cotton goods, woollen blankets and stockings, halters for horses, and bundles of blue ribbons whose ends fluttered in the wind. Big iron pots lay spread out on the ground, between the pyramids of eggs and the baskets of cheese bristling with sticky straw; beside the threshing machines, clucking hens kept poking their necks through the bars of their low squat cages. People were crowding together in one spot, evidently reluctant to move on; at times they looked as if they were about to break down the front of the pharmacy. This was never empty on a Wednesday; people pushed and shoved to get inside, not so much to buy medicine as to consult the pharmacist, so great was Monsieur Homais's reputation in the surrounding villages. His hearty self-confidence had bewitched the country folk. They thought him a greater doctor than any real doctor.

Emma was leaning on her window sill (as she often did: a window, in a country town, is a substitute for the theatre or the park), and she was amusing herself watching the crowd of peasants, when she noticed a gentleman dressed in a green velvet frock coat. He had on yellow gloves, although he also wore heavy gaiters; he was heading for the doctor's house, followed by a peasant with bent head and a pensive air.

'May I see Monsieur?' he asked Justin, who was chatting to Félicité at the door.

And, imagining him to be the Bovarys' servant, he added:

'Tell him Monsieur Rodolphe Boulanger de la Huchette* is here.'

It was not out of a landowner's vanity that the new arrival had added the *de* to his name, but to make it easier to identify him. La Huchette was a property near Yonville; he had just bought the chateau and two adjoining farms that he himself was managing, although not very seriously. He was a bachelor with, rumour had it, 'an income of at least fifteen thousand francs a year!'

Charles appeared. Monsieur Boulanger introduced his servant, who wanted to be bled, because he 'had pins and needles all over'.

'It'll clean me out,' was his response to every objection.

So Bovary began by producing a bandage and a basin, which he asked Justin to hold. Then, turning to the villager, who had already gone very pale:

'It's nothing to be afraid of, lad.'

'No, no, go ahead,' he replied.

And, with an air of bravado, he held out his hefty arm. At the prick of the lancet, the blood spurted out, splashing the mirror.

'Hold the basin closer!' cried Charles.

'Take a look at that!' said the peasant, 'Just like a little fountain! My blood's not half red! That's a good sign, right?'

'Sometimes', remarked the medical officer, 'people feel nothing at first, then they black out, particularly the big strapping ones like this fellow.'

At these words the peasant dropped the lancet case with which he had been fiddling. The chair creaked as his shoulders jerked violently against its back; his hat fell off.

'Just as I thought,' said Bovary, pressing his finger on the vein.

The basin began to shake in Justin's hands; his knees trembled; he turned white.

'Emma! Emma!' shouted Charles.

She was down the stairs in a flash.

'Get the vinegar,' he cried. 'Oh, Lord, two of them at once.'

And, in his excitement, he had trouble applying the compress.

'It's nothing,' said Monsieur Boulanger calmly, as he took Justin in his arms.

He sat him on the table with his back against the wall.

Madame Bovary began undoing his cravat. The strings of his shirt had a knot in them; she spent several minutes working at the young man's neck with her slender fingers; then she poured vinegar onto her batiste handkerchief and kept wetting his temples with quick little dabs, blowing delicately on them.

The carter came to, but Justin's faint persisted, with his pupils disappearing into the white sclera of his eyes like blue flowers into milk.

'Better not let him see this,' said Charles.

Madame Bovary took the basin to put it under the table; the movement of her body as she bent down made her dress (a yellow summer dress with four flounces, long in the bodice and full in the skirt) flare out all round her over the tiled floor of the room; and as she crouched a little unsteadily, spreading out her arms, the ballooning fabric subsided here and there, following the contours of her body. Then she fetched a jug of water and was dissolving some lumps of sugar in it when the pharmacist arrived. The maid had gone to find him in the middle of all the commotion; seeing his pupil with his eyes open, he breathed again. Pacing back and forth in front of Justin, he glared at him scathingly.

'Idiot!' he was saying. 'You're a downright idiot! No other word for it! All because of a simple phlebotomy! And you a fine fellow who's not afraid of anything! Just like a squirrel, he is, he'll climb up as high as you like after nuts. Come on, say something, show off! You'll certainly make a fine pharmacist one day; you could be summoned to appear in court, you know, over some matter of grave importance, to give guidance to the judgement of the magistrates; you'll have to keep your head, and produce reasoned arguments, prove you're a real man, not a halfwit!'

Justin did not answer. The apothecary continued:

'And who asked you to come here anyway? You're always bothering Monsieur and Madame. In any case, on Wednesdays, I need you more than ever. Right now there's twenty people in the shop. I just left everything, because I care about you. Come on! Off with you! Hurry up! Wait for me there, and keep an eye on those jars.'

When Justin, who was retying his cravat, had left, they chatted a little about fainting. Madame Bovary had never fainted.

'That's extraordinary, for a lady!' said Monsieur Boulanger. 'But some people are very sensitive. For example I've seen a witness at a duel pass out simply from the sound of the pistols being loaded.'

'In my case,' said the apothecary, 'the sight of other people's blood doesn't affect me in the least; but just the idea of my own blood flowing would be enough to make me feel faint, if I thought about it too much.'

Monsieur Boulanger, meanwhile, was dismissing his servant, telling him he could rest easy now that he'd got what he wanted.

'This has procured me the privilege of meeting you,' he added.

He gazed at Emma as he said this.

Then he put three francs down on the corner of the table, gave a casual bow, and departed.

He was soon on the other side of the river, on his way back to La Huchette; Emma saw him walking under the poplars in the meadow, and occasionally slowing his pace, like someone deep in thought.

'She's very charming!' he reflected, 'very charming, that wife of the doctor's. Lovely teeth, black eyes, a neat foot, the air of a Parisienne! Where the devil can she be from? Wherever did that great oaf find her?'

Monsieur Rodolphe Boulanger was thirty-four years old, his nature coarse and his intelligence shrewd; he had a broad experience of women and was something of a connoisseur. He considered this one very pretty; so he was thinking about her, and about her husband.

'I'd say he's very stupid. I'd bet she's tired of him. He's got dirty fingernails and a three days' beard. While he toddles off to see his patients, she stays home and darns socks. And everything's so boring! How we'd love to live in the city and dance polkas every night! Poor little thing! Gasping for love like a carp gasping for water on a kitchen table. With just three little words of love, it would worship you, I'd bet on it, it would be so tender and charming! . . . Yes, but how to get rid of it, afterwards?'

And, as he weighed up the possible inconveniences of such an affair, his thought turned, by contrast, to the mistress he kept in Rouen. She was an actress, and, when he had conjured up her image, which, even in retrospect, evoked a certain satiety, he reflected:

'Ah! Madame Bovary is much prettier, and especially much fresher. Virginie is certainly beginning to get too fat. She's so tiresome, with her raptures. And then that mania of hers for prawns!'

The countryside was deserted, and all around him Rodolphe could hear nothing but the regular swishing of the grass against his boots, and the chirping of the crickets sheltering in the distant field of oats; he was seeing Emma again, in that room, dressed as she had just been dressed, and in his mind's eye he was stripping off her clothes.

'Ah, yes, I'll have her!' he exclaimed, breaking up a clod of earth with his stick.

And, immediately, he began considering the strategy of such an enterprise. 'Where could we meet? How?' he wondered. 'There'd always be the brat hanging about, the maid, the neighbours, the husband, all sorts of problems to plague us. No, no, it would all be too much of a waste of time!'

But then he went on:

'Those eyes of hers—they bore right into you. And that pale complexion! . . . I adore pale women!'

When he reached the top of the Côte d'Argueil, he had made up his mind.

'It's just a matter of finding opportunities. All right! I'll drop in from time to time, I'll send them game, poultry; I'll even have myself bled if it comes to that; we'll become friends, I'll invite them over. Of course! dammit,' he added, 'we'll soon be having the Agricultural Show; she'll be there, I'll see her. We'll make a start, a bold start, that's the best way.'

CHAPTER VIII

It was here at last, the day of the great Show!* Early on the morning of that solemn occasion the inhabitants were all at their doors discussing the preparations: the pediment of the Town Hall had been garlanded with ivy; a tent for the banquet had been set up in a field, and in the square, in front of the church, an ancient piece of artillery was to signal the arrival of the Prefect and the announcement of each prizewinner's name. The National Guard from Buchy (Yonville did not have one) had come to swell the ranks of the fire brigade, of which Binet was captain. That day he was wearing an even higher collar than usual; and his upper body, tightly buttoned into his tunic, was so rigid and unmoving that it seemed his vital organs had all descended into his two legs, which rose and fell rhythmically, marking time in a single fluid movement. As the tax collector and the colonel were rivals, each, to demonstrate his talents, drilled his men separately. Turn by turn, red epaulettes and black breastplates marched back and forth. It never ended, but began over and over again! Never, ever, had anyone seen so magnificent a display! The previous day, a number of householders had washed the fronts of their houses; tricolour flags hung down from half-open windows; every bar was full; and the weather was so fine that the starched headdresses, the gold crosses, and the multi-hued kerchiefs shone whiter than snow, glittered in the sunlight, and dappled with bright colour the sombre uniformity of frock coats and blue smocks. As the wives of the local farmers got off their horses they removed the large pins with which they kept their skirts rolled up to the waist, to preserve them from splashes, while their husbands, by contrast, still kept their pocket handkerchiefs over their hats, securing one corner in their teeth.

The crowd was converging on the main street from both ends of the village. They came pouring out of the lanes, the alleys, the houses, and from time to time you could hear a knocker bang against a door as a housewife in cotton gloves emerged to watch the festivities. Particularly admired were two long frames, strung with coloured lights, flanking a platform on which the authorities were to sit; and then there were also, set up against each of the four columns of the Town Hall, four poles, each one displaying a small flag of green cloth, decorated with an inscription in gold letters. One read: 'Commerce', another: 'Agriculture', the third: 'Industry', and the fourth: 'Fine Arts'.

But the jubilation which beamed on every face seemed to fill Madame Lefrançois, the innkeeper, with gloom. Standing on her kitchen steps, she kept muttering under her breath:

'Halfwits! They're halfwits, with their stupid tent! Do they think the Prefect will enjoy having his dinner down there, in a tent, like a circus performer? And they call this kind of carry-on doing the place good! So why bring in some back-street cook from Neufchâtel! And who for? A lot of cowherds! Riff-raff!'

The apothecary walked past. He was wearing a black frock coat, yellow nankeen trousers, beaver-skin shoes, and—amazingly—a hat, a low-crowned hat!

'Good day to you!' he said; 'excuse me, I'm in a hurry.'

And, as the buxom widow enquired where he was going:

'No doubt you're thinking it odd, aren't you? I, who as a rule am more of a prisoner in my laboratory than is the old man's rat in his cheese.'*

'Cheese, what cheese?' asked the innkeeper.

'Never mind, never mind,' replied Homais. 'I was simply attempting to express to you, Madame Lefrançois, the fact that I usually live like a recluse, always at home. Today, however, in view of the special circumstances, I absolutely must . . .'

'Oh, you mean you're going *there*?' she said disdainfully.

'Yes, I am indeed,' replied the apothecary, surprised; 'I'm on the advisory committee, aren't I?'

Madame Lefrançois gazed at him thoughtfully for a few minutes, finally saying with a smile:

'That's a different matter! But what's agriculture got to do with you? So you know about it, do you?'

'Certainly, I know about it, since I'm a pharmacist, that is, a chemist. And since chemistry, Madame Lefrançois, aims at encompassing the science of the reciprocal and molecular behaviour of all natural bodies, it follows, consequently, that agriculture is comprised within its realm! And, indeed, the composition of fertilizers, the fermentation of fluids, the analysis of gases, the influence of noxious effluvia—what are all these, pray tell me, if not chemistry, pure and simple?'

The innkeeper did not reply. Homais went on:

'Do you imagine that, in order to be an agronomist, you have to have tilled the soil or fattened up poultry with your own two hands? No; but you do need to know about the composition of the relevant substances, the geological strata, the effects of atmospheric conditions, the properties of different soils, minerals, types of water, the density of different bodies, and their capillary attraction. And a great deal besides. You have to be thoroughly conversant with the principles of hygiene, if you're going to supervise or evaluate the construction of farm buildings, the feeding of livestock, the dietary requirements of the domestic staff! And furthermore, Madame Lefrançois, you must be well versed in botany and be capable of distinguishing between plants. Do you follow me? Know how to distinguish between the benign and the poisonous; between the unproductive and the nutritious; know if it's advisable to uproot them from one site, and resow them in another, to propagate this kind and eradicate that kind; in a word, you have to keep up to date in scientific matters by reading pamphlets and publications, you must always be on the alert, prepared to suggest improvements . . .'

The innkeeper, meanwhile, had not taken her eyes off the door of the Café Français; the pharmacist continued:

'Would to God that our farmers were chemists, or at least that they were more accepting of scientific advice! Recently I myself wrote a substantial little treatise, a monograph of more than seventy-two pages, entitled: 'Cider: Its Manufacture and its Effects, Followed by a Number of Fresh Observations on the Subject,' which I sent to the Agronomical Society of Rouen,* and which has even procured me the honour of being admitted to membership of that body, Agricultural Section, Subdivision Pomology. Well! If my work had been made available to the public . . .'

But the apothecary stopped talking, for Madame Lefrançois was paying no attention.

'Just look at them!' she was saying; 'would you believe it, patronizing a filthy dive like that!'

And, with shrugs that stretched her knitted sweater tightly across her breasts, she gestured with both hands towards her rival's establishment, from which singing could be heard.

'Anyway, it won't be here for long,' she added; 'less than a week now, then that'll be the end of that.'

In his amazement, Homais took a step back. She came down the three steps and said in his ear:

'Goodness me! You mean you didn't know? The bailiffs are shutting him down this week. It's Lheureux who's forcing the sale. He's done him in with all those bills he got him to sign.'

'What an appalling catastrophe!' exclaimed the apothecary, who could invariably come up with an appropriate expression, whatever the circumstances.

So then the innkeeper began telling him this story, which she had heard from Monsieur Guillaumin's servant Théodore, and, although she detested Tellier, she did not spare Lheureux. He was a bootlicker, a toady.

'Look,' she said, 'he's over there, in the market, bowing to Madame Bovary, who's wearing her green bonnet. *And* she's with Monsieur Boulanger.'

'Madame Bovary! I must go and pay my respects,' exclaimed Homais. 'Perhaps she'd like a seat in the enclosure, under the portico.'

And, paying no attention to Madame Lefrançois, who was calling him back to tell him more, the pharmacist set off at a smart clip, with ready smile and nimble leg, greeting people to right and left, his long black coat tails flying out behind him in the wind, so that he took up a great deal of space.

Rodolphe had noticed him from afar and quickened his pace; but, seeing that Madame Bovary was out of breath, he slowed down and said with a smile:

'I'm trying to avoid that awful fellow, you know, the apothecary.' His tone was savage.

She nudged him with her elbow.

'What does that mean?' he wondered, studying her out of the corner of his eye as they walked on.

Her profile was so composed that it revealed nothing. In the bright daylight it stood out clearly against the oval brim of her bonnet, whose pale ribbons were like strands of river-reed. Her eyes with their long curving lashes gazed straight ahead; although they were wide open, the gently pulsing blood beneath the delicate skin on her cheekbones made them appear half closed. A faint rose-pink tinged the flesh between her nostrils. Her head was bent to one side, and the pearly tips of her white teeth showed between her lips.

'Is she laughing at me?' wondered Rodolphe.

But Emma's gesture had simply been a warning, for Monsieur Lheureux was walking beside them and passing an occasional remark, as if trying to join in their conversation.

'What a magnificent day! Everyone's come out! The wind's from the east.'

Neither Madame Bovary nor Rodolphe uttered a word in reply, but if they made the slightest movement he would edge closer, saying 'I beg your pardon?' and touching the brim of his hat.

When they reached the blacksmith's, instead of following the road up to the gate, Rodolphe turned abruptly onto a footpath, drawing Madame Bovary along with him, and calling out:

'Good day, Monsieur Lheureux, see you soon!'

'You certainly knew how to get rid of him!' she said with a laugh.

'Why let anyone else barge in?' he went on, 'and since, today, I've the great good fortune to be with you . . .'

Emma blushed. He did not complete his sentence. Then he remarked on the fine weather and the pleasure of walking on the grass. A few late daisies were in flower.

'Look at these pretty daisies,' he said, 'there's enough to tell the fortune of every single village girl who's in love.' He added:

'Should I pick a few? What do you think?'

'Are you in love?' she asked, giving a little cough.

'Ah! Who can say!' replied Rodolphe.

The meadow had begun to fill up. Housewives burdened with huge umbrellas, baskets, and babies kept bumping into them, and they often had to step aside to avoid rows of country girls—servants wearing blue stockings, flat shoes, and silver rings, who, from close to, smelled of milk. These young women walked along holding hands in a line that spread right across the meadow, from the row of aspens to the banqueting tent. But it was now time for the judging, and one by one the farmers filed into a kind of arena marked off by a long rope attached to some posts.

The animals were there, muzzles turned towards the rope, rumps of every shape and size forming a straggly line. Drowsy pigs were rooting about in the soil with their snouts, calves were lowing and sheep were bleating, while the cows, with one leg doubled under them, rested their bellies on the grass and, as they slowly chewed their cud, blinked their heavy eyelids at the flies buzzing around them. Bare-armed carters stood holding the halters of the rearing stallions, which were neighing wildly in the direction of the mares. These were standing quietly, their necks stretched forward, their manes hanging down, while their foals lay resting in their shadows, or now and again came up to suck; and, above the long, undulating row of these close-packed bodies, an occasional white mane could be seen, rising in the wind like a wave, or perhaps a pair of sharp horns sticking up, and the heads of some men, running. To one side, about a hundred yards beyond the enclosure, motionless as a statue of bronze, stood a great black bull wearing a muzzle, with an iron ring in its nostril. A child dressed in rags held it by a rope.

Meanwhile, a group of men were ponderously advancing between the two lines, examining each animal, then conferring in low voices. One of them, apparently more important than the rest, was making notes in a book as he walked along. This was the chairman of the panel of judges: Monsieur Derozerays de la Panville. As soon as he recognized Rodolphe he hurried over to him and said with a friendly smile:

'Come now, Monsieur Boulanger, have you deserted us?'

Rodolphe declared that he would be coming in a moment. But, when the chairman had left:

'I'm damned if I will, I much prefer your company.'

And, although he never stopped poking fun at the Show, Rodolphe, in order to circulate more easily, would wave his blue card at the policeman and even occasionally halt in front of some impressive specimen that Madame Bovary barely looked at. Noticing this, he began making jokes about the way the Yonville ladies were dressed; then he apologized for the informality of his own costume. This was an incongruous mixture of the everyday and the sophisticated—the kind of outfit in which the common man sees evidence of an eccentric lifestyle, unbridled passions, the latest artistic edicts, and, invariably, a certain disdain of social conventions—all things that he finds either alluring or exasperating. Accordingly, Rodolphe's cambric shirt with ruffled cuffs ballooned out from the opening of his grey twill waistcoat with every puff of wind, and his broad-striped trousers were cut to reveal his ankles, clad in yellow cloth boots with vamps of patent leather. These were so highly polished that they reflected the grass. He tramped through the horse dung in them, one hand in his jacket pocket, his straw hat tilted over his ear.

'Besides,' he added, 'when you live in the country . . .'

'There's no point in bothering,' said Emma.

'How true!' replied Rodolphe. 'When you think that not one of these good people is even capable of appreciating the cut of a coat!'

So then they talked about provincial mediocrity, of the lives it suffocated, of the dreams that died there.

'That's why I'm becoming more and more depressed,' said Rodolphe.

'You!' She was astonished. 'But I thought you so cheerful always?'

'Oh yes, on the surface; that's because in public I know how to hide my real feelings behind a mask of mockery. Yet how often have I wondered, on seeing a cemetery in the moonlight, whether I wouldn't be better off lying beside those who slumber there . . .'

'Oh! But what about your friends? You're forgetting them.'

'My friends? What friends? Have I any? Who cares about me?'

And he pursed his lips in a kind of whistling sigh as he said these last words.

But they were forced to separate, to make way for a huge stack of chairs carried by someone behind them. The man was so overburdened that no part of him was visible except for the tips of his clogs and the ends of his outstretched arms. It was Lestiboudois, the gravedigger, who was transporting chairs from the church through the crowd. Highly creative where his own interests were concerned, he had hit on this scheme for making a profit from the Show, and so successful was his idea that he had more customers than he could possibly satisfy. Indeed the villagers, who were feeling the heat, kept squabbling over the straw-seated chairs smelling of incense, and they leant with a certain veneration against those solid backs spattered with drips of candle-wax.

Madame Bovary again took Rodolphe's arm; he went on as though talking to himself:

'Yes! I've missed out on so many things! Alone, always alone! Ah, if I'd had a purpose in life, if I'd met someone with true affection, if I'd found someone . . . Oh, how I would have used every last ounce of my strength, overcome every obstacle, crushed every enemy!'

'However,' said Emma, 'I don't see that you're really to be pitied.'

'Ah, you think that, do you?' replied Rodolphe.

'After all . . . you're free.' She hesitated:

'And wealthy.'

'Don't make fun of me,' he answered.

She was solemnly assuring him that this was not the case when a cannon shot rang out, and everyone began to make a wild dash for the village.

It was a false alarm. There was no sign of the Prefect, and the judges found themselves in a quandary, uncertain whether to begin the proceedings or wait a little longer.

Eventually, at the far side of the square, a large hired landau appeared, drawn by two skinny horses that a coachman in a white hat was thrashing ferociously. Binet, and then the colonel also, barely had time to shout 'Fall in!' Everyone hurried to the piled rifles. There was quite a scramble. Some men even forgot to fasten their collars. But the prefectorial equipage seemed to sense the confusion, and the pair of nags, dawdling along in their harness, trotted slowly up to the portico of the Town Hall at the precise moment when the national guard and the firemen were taking up their positions there and marking time, to the beat of the drum.

'Steady!' shouted Binet.

'Halt!' cried the colonel. 'Dressing by the left!'

And, after a 'present arms' where the rattling of the rifle-bands made a racket like a copper pot rolling down stairs, all the rifles were lowered.

They then saw, stepping down from the carriage, a gentleman dressed in a short coat embroidered with silver braid. The front of his head was bald, whereas the back sprouted a thick tuft of hair; he had a pallid complexion and an exceedingly benign air. His eyes were very large with heavy lids, and he screwed them up slightly as he studied the crowd, at the same time raising his sharp-pointed nose and disposing his sunken lips into a smile. Identifying the mayor by his sash, he explained that the Prefect had been unable to come.* He himself was a Councillor at the Prefecture; he then added some apologies. Tuvache produced various compliments in response, and the visitor declared himself quite overwhelmed; and there they stood, face to face, their foreheads almost touching, surrounded by the members of the committee, the municipal councillors, the local dignitaries, the national guard, and the crowd. Clutching his small three-cornered black hat to his breast, the prefectorial Councillor reiterated his salutations while Tuvache, bent like a bow and smiling in response, stammered out some incoherent protestations about his devotion to the monarchy and the honour that was being bestowed on Yonville.

Hippolyte, the ostler at the inn, came up to take the horses' bridles from the coachman; limping on his club foot, he led them over to the entrance of the Lion d'Or, where a number of villagers had gathered to admire the carriage. The drum rolled, the howitzer thundered, and the gentlemen filed up onto the platform and took their seats in the red plush armchairs lent by Madame Tuvache.

All of them looked exactly alike. Their fair-skinned, flabby faces, slightly tanned by the sun, were the colour of sweet cider, and their bushy side-whiskers spilled over high starched collars kept in place by white cravats tied in spreading bows. Every waistcoat was of velvet, and double-breasted; every watch bore, on the end of a long cord, some kind of oval seal made of cornelian; and every man sat with his two hands planted on his two thighs, and his legs carefully parted, the glossy fabric of his trousers shimmering more brilliantly than the leather of his heavy boots.

The ladies of the party were seated in the rear, between the pillars under the portico, while the common folk were all standing or sitting in front of the platform. Lestiboudois had, indeed, fetched over all the chairs from the meadow, and he still kept running back to the church for more, and creating such a bottleneck with his transactions that it was almost impossible to reach the small steps onto the platform.

'In my opinion,' said Monsieur Lheureux (addressing the pharmacist as he headed for his seat) 'I think that they should have set up a pair of Venetian flagstaffs up there: decorated with something dignified but sumptuous, they'd have been a splendid sight.'

'Yes indeed,' replied Homais; 'But what can you expect? The mayor would do everything himself. He hasn't much taste, poor Tuvache, in fact he hasn't a glimmer of what's called artistic sense.'

Meanwhile Rodolphe, with Madame Bovary, had gone up to the first floor of the Town Hall, into the 'council chamber', and, as it was empty, he had declared that it would be just the place for them to enjoy the ceremony in comfort. He took three stools from the oval table, under the bust of the king, and put them near one of the windows, where they sat down side by side.

There was a bit of a commotion on the platform, lengthy whisperings and consultations. Finally the Councillor stood up. It was now known that his name was Lieuvain, and this name was passed on from one to the next in the crowd. When he had satisfactorily arranged several sheets of paper and raised them close to his eyes in order to see them better, he began:

'Gentlemen: May I first be permitted (before addressing you upon the subject of today's gathering, and in so doing, I am confident that I speak for all of you), may I be permitted, I repeat, to pay homage to the national administration, to the government, to the monarch, gentlemen, to our sovereign, to that beloved king for whom no branch of prosperity public or private is a matter of indifference, and who guides the chariot of state with a hand at once so firm and so wise through the unceasing perils of a raging sea, and who, furthermore, knows how to command respect for peace as well as for war, for industry, for commerce, for agriculture, and for the fine arts.'

'Perhaps', said Rodolphe, 'I should move a little further back.'

'Why?' asked Emma.

But at that very moment the Councillor's voice rose to an extraordinary pitch. He was declaiming:

'Gone are the days, gentlemen, when our public squares were

awash in the blood of civil strife, when the landlord, the tradesman, even the labourer himself, as they fell peacefully asleep at night, trembled lest they be rudely awakened by the clamour of an approaching insurgency, when the most subversive principles were brazenly undermining the foundations . . .'

'Because I might be seen from down below,' replied Rodolphe; 'and then I'd be stuck with weeks of apologizing, and, what with my bad reputation . . .'

'Oh, you slander yourself,' said Emma.

'No, it's appalling, I swear,'

'But, gentlemen,' continued the Councillor, 'if, dismissing these sombre images from my memory, I turn my eyes to the present state of our fair homeland, what do I see here? I see commerce and the arts flourishing everywhere; everywhere I see new channels of communication, like so many new arteries that create new relationships within the body politic; our great manufacturing centres are thriving once again; religion, now more securely grounded, smiles in all our hearts; our ports are full, our confidence restored, and France breathes again at last!'

'Besides,' added Rodolphe, 'from the point of view of society, people may possibly be right.'

'How do you mean?' she asked.

'What! Surely you know that some souls suffer relentless torment? Their cravings drive them back and forth between dreams and action, between the most pure passion and the most exorbitant pleasures, so that they hurl themselves into every kind of fantasy, every kind of folly.'

She stared at him as if he were a traveller from some legendary land, and said:

'We poor women are denied even that means of escape!'

'A sad one, since it brings no happiness.'

'But does anything, ever?'

'Oh yes, one day, you find it,' he answered her.

'And that', the Councillor was saying, 'is what you have understood. You, farmers and workers in the fields! You, peace-loving pioneers of a wholly civilized enterprise! You, men of progress and morality! You have understood, I repeat, that political upheavals are indeed more deadly than the raging of the elements . . .'

'One day, you find it,' repeated Rodolphe, 'one day, quite

suddenly, when you've given up hope. Then new horizons stretch before you, and it's like a voice that cries: "Here it is!" You long to tell this person everything that's ever happened to you, to give everything, to sacrifice everything to this person! There's no need for words—you can read each other's thoughts. You've seen each other in your dreams.' (He was staring at her.) 'So, at last, it's here, this treasure you've been so desperately seeking, here, before you, bright and sparkling. But you still feel unsure, you daren't believe in it; you're dazzled, as if you'd come from out of the shadows into the light.'

And, as he completed this speech, Rodolphe added pantomime to words. He passed his hand over his face as if he were feeling faint; then he let his hand drop onto Emma's. She withdrew hers. But the Councillor was still reading:

'And who would find this surprising, gentlemen? Only one so blind, so deeply sunk (let me not shrink from saying it) so deeply sunk in the prejudices of a former age that he could still fail to appreciate the spirit of our agricultural population. Where, indeed, could one find greater patriotism than in the country, greater devotion to the public good, in a word, greater intelligence? And, gentlemen, I am not speaking here of that superficial kind of intelligence, vain ornament of the idle mind, but rather of that wise and temperate intelligence which aims above all at pursuing practical objectives, thereby contributing to the good of every man, to the betterment of society and the preservation of the State, fruit of respect for the law and obedience to duty . . .'

'Oh, no, not again,' said Rodolphe. 'Duty, always duty, I can't stand that word. They're a bunch of old fossils in flannel waistcoats, and sanctimonious old hens with foot-warmers and rosaries, forever droning on at us about "duty, duty!" But, dammit all, our duty is to feel what is sublime and cherish what is beautiful, and not simply to accept all of society's conventions, and all the degradations those conventions inflict on us.'

'Yes . . . but . . .' objected Madame Bovary.

'No, no! Why castigate the passions? Are they not the only beautiful thing on earth, the source of heroism, of enthusiasm, of poetry, music, the arts, in fact of everything?'

'But surely,' said Emma, 'we must, to some extent, pay attention to the opinions of our neighbours, and conform to the accepted standard of morality.'

'Ah! But there's two kinds of morality,' he replied. 'There's the petty, conventional kind, fashioned by men, the kind that keeps changing, that keeps blaring noisily at us and making a great to-do down here among us, like that crowd of idiots you're looking at. But the other, the eternal kind, now that's everywhere about us and above us, like the landscape that surrounds us and the blue sky that gives us light.'

Monsieur Lieuvain had just wiped his mouth with his handkerchief. He went on:

'But what would be the point, gentlemen, of *my* demonstrating to *you* the usefulness of agriculture? For who indeed is it that supplies our needs? Who is it that provides our sustenance? Is it not the farmer? The farmer, gentlemen, who with untiring hand sows the fecund furrows of our countryside with the seeds that bring forth corn, which, once ground, is reduced by means of ingenious machines to powder, emerging as what we call flour and which, once transported to the cities, is then promptly delivered to the baker, who makes it into a food for poor and rich alike. Again, is it not the farmer who raises his teeming flocks in the pastures to give us our clothing? For how would we clothe ourselves, how would we feed ourselves, without the farmer? And indeed, gentlemen, what need is there to look so far afield to find examples? Who has not often reflected on the great benefits we derive from that humble creature, the pride of our farmyards, which supplies both soft pillows for our beds, succulent flesh for our tables, and eggs as well? But I should never finish were I to enumerate one after the other the various products that our well-tilled soil, like a generous mother, lavishes upon her children. Here, we find grapes, there, cider apples, and over beyond, rape; further away, the various cheeses; and flax, gentlemen, do not let us forget flax! Of recent years its production has increased considerably, a fact to which I would most particularly draw your attention.'

There was no necessity for him to do so, for the crowd, openmouthed, was already drinking in his every word. Tuvache, sitting beside him, was listening wide-eyed, Monsieur Derozerays, from time to time, gently blinked his eyelids, while the pharmacist, sitting further away with his son Napoléon between his knees, had cupped his hand round his ear so as not to miss a single syllable. The other members of the committee kept slowly dropping their chins onto their waistcoats to signal their agreement. The firemen, in front of the platform, were leaning on their bayonets, and Binet stood motionless, with his elbow sticking out and his sword pointing up into the air. He might, perhaps, be able to hear, but he surely could not see a thing because the visor on his helmet had fallen down onto his nose. The headgear of his lieutenant, the great Tuvache's youngest son, looked even more extraordinary: for he wore a helmet so enormous that it wobbled about, revealing one end of the cotton scarf tied over his hair. Beneath it, he was smiling a sweet childish smile, and his small white face, dripping with sweat, bore an expression of delight, exhaustion, and sleepiness.

The square was crammed with people right up to the houses. People were leaning on every window sill and standing in every doorway, and Justin, in front of the pharmacy, seemed completely transfixed by the spectacle before him. Despite the silence, Monsieur Lieuvain's voice did not carry at all well in the open air. It reached its audience in disconnected snatches, interrupted now and again by the scraping of the chairs in the crowd; then all of a sudden, coming from somewhere behind, the long-drawn-out lowing of a bullock, or perhaps the sound of lambs bleating to one another would be heard, as they called to each other from street corners. The cowherds and shepherds had actually driven their animals right up to the square, and occasionally a cow would moo as she tore with her tongue at a bit of greenery dangling near her muzzle.

Rodolphe had moved closer to Emma and was speaking rapidly, in a low voice:

'Aren't you disgusted by the way our society conspires together? Is there a single emotion that it doesn't condemn? The noblest of instincts, the purest of affections are persecuted, vilified, and, if two poor souls should finally find one another, everything is so organized that they cannot be united. But they'll still struggle, they'll beat their wings, they'll call out to one another. Ah! But what does it matter? Sooner or later, in six months, in ten years, they'll come together, they'll love one another, because that's what destiny decrees, and they were born for one another.'

Sitting with his arms folded on his knees, he now raised his face to Emma's and stared fixedly at her, from very close. She could see, in his eyes, tiny threads of gold that radiated out all round his black pupils, and she could even smell the perfume of the pomade that made his hair glossy. Then she felt a languor come over her, and she remembered the Vicomte who had waltzed with her at La Vaubyessard, and whose beard gave off the same fragrance of vanilla and lemon as this man's hair; and instinctively she half-closed her eyes so as to breathe it in more deeply. But, drawing herself up on the chair as she did this, she saw in the distance, far off on the horizon, the old Hirondelle, moving slowly down the Côte des Leux, a long plume of dust trailing behind it. It was in that yellow coach that Léon had so often come back to her: and it was along that road that he had left her forever! She fancied she could see him, across the square, there at his window, and then everything became blurred and cloudy; she felt as if she were still waltzing round, under the glowing chandeliers, in the arms of the Vicomte, and that Léon was not far away, that he was coming . . . and yet all this time she could still smell Rodolphe's hair, beside her. The sweetness of this sensation penetrated deep into her desires of long ago, and, like grains of sand blown by a gust of wind, they whirled about in the subtly perfumed air that was mantling her soul. Again and again she opened wide her nostrils to breathe in the freshness of the ivy festooning the tops of the pillars just outside. She took off her gloves, and wiped her hands; then, with her handkerchief, she fanned her face, hearing, above the pulsing in her temples, the noise of the crowd and the voice of the Councillor intoning his phrases.

'Persistence! Perseverance! Heed neither the automatic promptings of routine, nor the ill-considered counsels of reckless empiricism! Direct your efforts above all to the improvement of the soil, to rich fertilizers, to developing the different breeds—equine, bovine, ovine, and porcine. Let this agricultural show be for you like a peaceable arena where the victor, in departing, offers the hand of friendship to the vanquished, fraternizing with him and wishing him better fortune another day! And you, our venerable servants, humblest workers in our households, whose arduous labours no government has, until now, thought worthy of recognition, come forward to receive the reward of your silent virtues, and be assured that henceforth the State will keep watch over you, will encourage and protect you, will see that your just demands are recognized, and will, as far as lies within its powers, ease the burden of your painful sacrifices!'

Monsieur Lieuvain now sat down again, and Monsieur Derozerays rose to his feet and embarked on another speech. His was not, perhaps, quite as flowery as the Councillor's; but it was well received thanks to its more positive style, in that the chairman drew on more specialized knowledge and touched on loftier issues. For example, he devoted less time to praising the government and more to discussing religion and agriculture. He stressed the connection between these, and how they had always worked together for the benefit of civilization. Rodolphe and Madame Bovary, meanwhile, talked of dreams, presentiments, and magnetism.* Going back to the cradle of human society, the orator was describing that primitive age when man lived deep in the forest, subsisting on acorns. Then, casting off his animal skin, he had clad himself in cloth, ploughed the earth, planted the vine. Was this last discovery a blessing, did it not bring with it greater drawbacks than benefits? This was the question Monsieur Derozerays was asking himself. Little by little, Rodolphe had moved from magnetism on to affinities and, while the chairman cited Cincinnatus* at his plough, Diocletian* planting his cabbages, and the emperors of China* celebrating the New Year by sowing seed, the young man was explaining to the young woman that these irresistible attractions originated in some previous existence.

'Take you and me, for example,' he was saying; 'why did we meet? What lucky chance ordained it? It may perhaps be that over the miles dividing us, like two rivers that converge into one, our own particular inclinations have been impelling us towards one another.'

And he seized her hand; she did not withdraw it.

'Prize for all-round excellence in farming!' proclaimed the chairman.

'The other day, for example, when I came to your house . . .'

'To Monsieur Bizet, of Quincampoix:'

'Did I know then that I'd come here with you?'

'Seventy francs!'

'Time and again I've intended to leave, yet I've followed you, I've remained by your side.'

'Manures:'

'Just as I'd remain at your side tonight, tomorrow, day after day, my whole life!'

'To Monsieur Caron of Argueil, a gold medal!'

'For never before have I felt so utterly enchanted by anyone . . .'

'To Monsieur Bain, of Givry-Saint-Martin!'

'So that I'll cherish the memory of you forever.'

'For a merino ram . . .'

'But you'll forget me, I'll have vanished like a shadow.'

'To Monsieur Belot, of Notre-Dame . . .'

'But no, surely not! I'll have a place in your thoughts, shan't I, a place in your life?'

'Porcine breeds: prize shared equally by Messieurs Lehérissé and Cullembourg: sixty francs!'

Rodolphe was squeezing her hand, which felt warm and trembling like a captive dove that is trying to fly away; but then, either in response to his pressure or in attempting to free her fingers, she moved them, and he exclaimed:

'Ah! Thank you! You're not rejecting me! How kind you are! You understand that I belong to you! Let me see you, let me gaze at you!'

A sudden gust, blowing in through the windows, ruffled the cloth on the table, and, in the square below, all the countrywomen's big bonnets fluttered in the wind like the wings of white butterflies.

'Use of oil cakes,' continued the chairman. He was speeding up:

'Flemish fertilizer—cultivation of flax—drainage—long-term leases—domestic service.'

Rodolphe had stopped speaking. They were gazing at each other. Their intense desire made their dry lips tremble, and languorously, effortlessly, their fingers intertwined.

'Catherine-Nicaise-Élisabeth Leroux,* of Sassetot-la-Guerrière, for fifty-four years of service on the same farm, a silver medal—value twenty-five francs!'

'Where is she, where's Catherine Leroux?' repeated the Councillor.

She did not appear, and voices could be heard whispering:

'Go on!'

'No.'

'Over on the left there.'

'Don't be scared!'

'Oh, she's so stupid!'

'Is she here or not?' shouted Tuvache.

'Yes, over there!'

'Well, let's have her up here then!'

They watched as a little old woman made her way apprehensively onto the platform; she seemed to be shrinking away inside her shabby garments. On her feet were thick wooden clogs and from her hips hung a big blue apron. Her skinny face, framed by a very simple cap, was more puckered and wrinkled than a withered russet apple, and from the sleeves of her red blouse two long, gnarled hands stuck out. Decades of dust from barns, bleach from laundry, and grease from wool had left these so encrusted, abraded, and calloused that they looked dirty despite having been washed in clean water; and, from long service, they hung half open, as if offering themselves up as humble witnesses to a lifetime of suffering endured. Something akin to a monastic impassivity added a certain dignity to her expression, but no trace of sadness or tenderness softened that pale stare. Living always with animals, she had taken on their muteness and placidity. This was the first time she had ever found herself in the midst of so large a gathering, and, secretly terrified by the flags and the drums, by the black-coated gentlemen and the Councillor's Legion of Honour medal, she remained rooted to the spot, uncertain whether to step forward or take to her heels, or why the crowd was urging her on or the judges smiling at her. She stood there, before all those beaming bourgeois, the embodiment of half a century of servitude.

'Come along now, venerable Catherine-Nicaise-Élisabeth Leroux!' said the Councillor, who had taken the list of prizewinners from the chairman.

And, looking in turn at the sheet of paper and the old woman, he repeated in a fatherly tone:

'Come along, come along.'

'Are you deaf?' cried Tuvache, jumping up from his chair.

He began shouting in her ear:

'Fifty-four years of service! A silver medal! Twenty-five francs! For you.'

When the medal was in her hand, she gazed at it. Then a blissful smile spread over her face and, as she walked off, she could be heard mumbling:

'I'll give it to our curé, so he'll say some masses for me.'

'What fanaticism!' exclaimed the pharmacist, leaning across to the notary.

The ceremony had ended; the crowd was dispersing, and, now that the speeches had been read, everyone resumed his proper station and everything returned to normal: the masters bullied the servants and the servants beat the animals as, lethargic in their triumph, these made their way back to the stable, a wreath of greenery between their horns.

Meanwhile, the national guard had climbed up to the first floor of the Town Hall, with brioches speared on their bayonets; the regimental drummer was carrying a crate of bottles. Madame Bovary took Rodolphe's arm, and he escorted her home; they parted at her door, then he walked about the meadow alone, waiting for the banquet to begin.

The feast was long, noisy, and badly served; people were so crammed together that they could barely move their elbows, and the narrow planks serving as benches almost gave way under the weight of the guests. They all ate a vast amount. They all made sure they got their money's worth. Sweat poured off every forehead; a whitish mist hovered over the table, between the hanging lamps, like mist over a river on an autumn morning. Rodolphe sat leaning against the canvas of the tent, so absorbed in thoughts of Emma that he heard nothing. Behind him, on the grass, servants were stacking the dirty plates; his neighbours would speak to him, but he did not reply; they kept refilling his glass; a stillness took possession of his mind, despite the growing hubbub. He thought about what she had said and about the shape of her lips; her face shone from the shiny surface of the shakos as though reflected in some magic mirror; the folds of her dress cascaded down the walls and long days of love flowed endlessly across the landscapes of the future.

He saw her again that evening, at the fireworks; but she was with her husband, Madame Homais, and the pharmacist, who was very uneasy about the danger of stray rockets and kept disappearing to give Binet a word of advice.

The over-cautious Tuvache, to whom the fireworks had been delivered, had stored them in his cellar, so that the damp powder was very difficult to light, and the principal piece, which should have depicted a dragon biting its tail, was a complete fiasco. From time to time a miserable little roman candle would go off, and then the gawking crowd would let out a roar, mingled with squeals from the women whose waists were being tickled under cover of the darkness. Emma stood in silence, resting her head lightly on Charles's shoulder; then, lifting up her chin, she would follow the rocket's brilliant track through the night sky. Rodolphe stood watching her by the glow of the lanterns.

One by one, these died out. The stars appeared. A few drops of rain began to fall. She tied her scarf over her bare head.

At that moment, the Councillor's landau emerged from the inn yard. His coachman, who was drunk, suddenly slumped over, and from far away they could see, above the hood and between the two lanterns, his bulky body swaying from side to side with the pitching of the springs.

'Really,' remarked the apothecary, 'severe sanctions should be imposed in cases of drunkenness. I'd like to have posted, weekly, on a special notice board on the door of the Town Hall, a list of the names of all those who, during the preceding week, had been intoxicated by alcohol. Besides, from the statistical point of view, such a list would provide a sort of public record which, should the occasion ever arise . . . Excuse me.'

And once more he dashed over to the captain.

The latter was on his way home. He was going back to his lathe.

'It might be just as well,' Homais told him, 'to send one of your men or to go yourself . . .'

'Leave me alone, will you!' replied the tax collector; 'everything's under control.'

'There's no occasion for anxiety,' the apothecary announced when he rejoined his friends, 'Monsieur Binet assures me that all possible precautions are in place. Not one spark has fallen. The pumps are full. Let us retire to our beds.'

'Goodness me, I'm certainly ready for mine,' said Madame Homais with a tremendous yawn; 'but never mind, we've had a perfectly beautiful day for our Show.'

With a tender glance Rodolphe repeated, his voice low: 'Yes, indeed, perfectly beautiful.'

They said goodnight and went their separate ways.

Two days later a long article about the Agricultural Show appeared in *Le Fanal de Rouen*. Homais had composed it, in a fever of enthusiasm, the very next day:

'Wherefore these festoons, these flowers, these garlands? Whither was this throng rushing, like waves upon a raging sea, beneath a torrential tropical sun that flooded our furrows with its warmth?'

Next, he spoke of the condition of the rural population. Yes, certainly the government was doing a great deal, but not enough! 'Boldness is all!' he admonished the administration. 'A thousand reforms are indispensable, let us carry them out.' Then, turning to the arrival of the Councillor, he did not fail to mention 'the martial air of our militia', nor 'our most captivating village girls', nor the bald-pated elders, 'latter-day patriarchs, a few of them survivors of our immortal phalanxes, whose hearts still beat faster at the virile sound of the drums'. He mentioned his own name near the top of the list of committee members, and even referred, in a note, to the fact that Monsieur Homais, pharmacist, had sent a Memorandum on cider to the Agricultural Society. When he came to the distribution of the prizes, he portrayed the joy of the successful competitors in dithyrambic phrases. 'Father embraced son, brother embraced brother, husband embraced wife. More than one among them proudly showed his neighbours his humble medal, and, once home again with his helpmeet by his side, doubtless hung it, his eyes wet with tears, on the bare wall of his modest cot.

'At about six o'clock, the principal participants in the Show assembled for a banquet served in Monsieur Liégeard's pasture. The occasion was marked throughout by the utmost cordiality. A number of toasts were proposed: Monsieur Lieuvain, 'To the King!' Monsieur Tuvache, 'To the Prefect!' Monsieur Derozerays, 'To Agriculture!' Monsieur Homais, 'To the twin sisters, Industry and the Fine Arts!' Monsieur Leplichey, 'To Progress!' In the evening, a brilliant display of fireworks suddenly illumined the heavens. It was a veritable kaleidoscope, truly a setting from opera, and, for an instant, our humble village imagined itself transported into some dream from the *Arabian Nights*.

'Let us put on record the fact that no untoward incident occurred to mar this family occasion.'

And he added: 'It was noted, however, that no clergy were present. The Church, presumably, entertains a different concept of progress. That is your privilege, apostles of Loyola!'*

CHAPTER IX

Six weeks went by. Rodolphe did not return. Finally, one evening, he appeared.

The morning after the Show, he had told himself:

'Better not go back there too soon, it would be a mistake.'

And, at the week's end, he had left on a hunting trip.

After the trip was over, he wondered if he'd left it too late, then he reflected:

'But if she loved me right from the first, now she'll be desperate to see me again, and she'll love me even more. So, back to the attack!'

And he knew that his reasoning had been correct when, on entering the room, he saw Emma turn white.

She was alone. The light was fading. The little muslin curtains covering the windows deepened the gathering shadows, and the gilding on the barometer, touched by a ray of sunshine, cast fiery reflections, between the branches of the coral, onto the mirror.

Rodolphe remained standing; Emma barely acknowledged his first polite enquiries.

'I've been busy,' he said. 'I've been ill.'

'Anything serious?' she asked.

'Well,' replied Rodolphe, sitting down beside her on a stool, 'No! No, it's . . . it's really that I didn't want to come back.'

'Why?'

'Can't you guess?'

He looked at her again, but with such fierce intensity that she blushed and dropped her gaze. He went on:

'Emma . . .'

'Monsieur!' she exclaimed, moving away a little.

'Oh, it's quite clear', he replied in a melancholy tone, 'that I was right in wanting to keep away; this name, this name which permeates my soul and which I couldn't stop myself saying, you forbid me to use it! Madame Bovary! . . . Everybody calls you that! . . . Besides, it's not your name, it's another's!'

'Another's!' he repeated; and he hid his face in his hands.

'Yes, I think of you constantly . . . the memory of you drives me to despair . . . Oh! Forgive me, I'll leave . . . Goodbye! . . . I'll go far away, so far away that you'll never hear of me again! And yet . . . today . . . some inexplicable force impelled me to come to you once more! You can't fight against fate! You can't resist the smiles of angels! You can't withstand the power of what is beautiful, charming, adorable!'

It was the first time Emma had had such things said to her, and her pride, like someone relaxing in a steam bath, stretched out languorously, surrendering completely to the warmth of this language.

'But', he went on, 'although I didn't visit you, although I couldn't see you, at least I've gazed and gazed at all that surrounds you. In the night, every night, I'd get up and come up here, I'd look at your house, with the roof shining in the moonlight, the trees in the garden swaying across your window, and a little lamp, a tiny glimmer, shining through the window panes, in the dark. Ah! You'd no idea that out there, so near and yet so far, there was a poor wretch . . .'

She turned towards him with a sob.

'Oh! You're so good!' she said.

'No, I love you, that's all! Surely you know that. Tell me you believe it: one word! Just one word!'

Imperceptibly, Rodolphe was sliding off the stool onto the floor; but he heard the sound of clogs from the kitchen, and noticed that the parlour door was standing open.

'You'd be doing me such a favour', he continued, resuming his seat, 'if you were to gratify a fancy of mine.'

He wanted to see round her house; he longed to know what it was like; and as Madame Bovary had no objection, they were both rising, when in walked Charles.

'Good evening, Doctor,' said Rodolphe.

The medical officer, flattered by this unexpected title, was all fawning politeness, and Rodolphe took the opportunity to recover some of his composure.

'Madame was telling me', he said, 'about her health . . .'

Charles interrupted him: it was true, he was extremely worried; his wife's respiratory problems were beginning again. So then Rodolphe enquired whether horseback riding might not be beneficial.

'Yes, indeed! Excellent, perfect . . . What a good suggestion! You ought to follow it.'

And when she objected that she hadn't a horse, Monsieur Rodolphe offered her one; she declined; he did not press the matter; then, to justify his visit, he told them that his carter, the man who had been bled, was still suffering from dizzy spells.

'I'll come and see him,' said Bovary.

'No, no, I'll send him over; we'll come here, that'll be more convenient for you.'

'Very well. Thank you.'

As soon as they were alone:

'Why didn't you accept Monsieur Boulanger's offer? It was so kind.'

Pouting, she made a number of excuses, then finally declared that 'it might look a bit strange'.

'Oh, as if I cared!' said Charles, turning away. 'Your health comes first! You're making a mistake.'

'And how can I go riding when I don't have a riding habit?'

'We must order one for you,' he replied.

The riding habit decided her.

When the habit was ready, Charles wrote to Monsieur Boulanger that his wife was at his disposal, and thanked him for being so obliging.

The next day at noon Rodolphe arrived at Charles's door with two saddle horses. One had pink rosettes decorating its ears and a lady's buckskin saddle.

Rodolphe had put on high, soft boots, telling himself that she'd probably never seen anything of the kind; and Emma was indeed charmed by his outfit, when he appeared at her doorstep in his big velvet coat and white tricot riding breeches. She was ready, and waiting for him.

Justin slipped out of the pharmacy to see her, and the apothecary also abandoned what he was doing. He was full of advice for Monsieur Boulanger.

'An accident can occur so quickly! Be careful! Your horses may be feisty!'

She heard a noise over her head: it was Félicité tapping on the window pane to amuse little Berthe. The child blew her a kiss from up above: her mother waved the handle of her whip in response.

'Have a good ride!' shouted Monsieur Homais. 'Now don't forget, be careful, very careful!'

And, waving his newspaper, he watched them ride away.

As soon as Emma's horse felt earth beneath his hooves, he began to gallop. Rodolphe galloped beside her. Occasionally, they exchanged a few words. With her head slightly bowed, her hand high, and her right arm stretched out, she gave herself up to the rhythmic rocking of the saddle.

At the foot of the hill, Rodolphe loosened his hold on the reins; with a single bound they set off together; then, at the top, suddenly, the horses stopped, and her long blue veil dropped down again.

It was the beginning of October. A mist hung over the fields. A few ribbons of vapour lay along the horizon, following the outline of the hills, while others, separating, drifted higher, and disappeared. When, from time to time, the clouds parted, a ray of sunlight would shine on the distant roofs of Yonville, with its gardens running down to the river, its yards, walls, and church steeple. Emma half closed her eyes as she tried to find her house, and never had this poor village where she lived looked so small to her. From the high ground they had reached, the whole valley resembled a vast, pale lake evaporating into the air. Here and there, clumps of trees stood out like black rocks, and the tall rows of poplars, projecting above the mist, were like the lake's wind-tossed, leafy banks.

Beside them, on the grass, between the fir trees, the light glowed dimly brown in the warm air. The earth, the dusky red of powdered tobacco, deadened the sound of steps, and as they walked the horses kicked fallen pine cones with their metal-shod hooves.

Rodolphe and Emma continued along the edge of the wood. Now and again, to avoid his gaze, she would turn her head away, and then she would see nothing but straight rows of tree trunks in an unending succession that made her feel slightly dizzy. The horses were panting, the saddle-leather creaking.

Just as they entered the forest, the sun came out.

'God's looking after us!' said Rodolphe.

'Do you think so?' she said.

'Come on, let's go on!' he replied.

He clicked his tongue, and both horses began to trot.

Tall bracken growing beside the path kept catching in Emma's stirrup. As he rode along, Rodolphe would bend over and pull it free. At other times, to push a branch out of her way, he would pass close beside her, and Emma would feel his knee brush against her leg. The sky was blue now. Not a leaf was stirring. There were broad clearings full of flowering heather, the stretches of purple alternating with the jumbled piles of leaves beneath the trees, grey, tawny, or gold, depending on the kind of foliage. Often they would hear a tiny flutter of wings quivering out from under a bush, or perhaps the throaty, soft cry of crows as they flew up into the oaks.

They dismounted. Rodolphe tethered the horses. She walked ahead, on the mossy turf between the ruts.

But she found her long skirt awkward to walk in, even though she was holding it up at the back; and Rodolphe, following behind her, gazed at the strip of sheer white stocking showing between the black habit and the black boot, like a foretaste of her nakedness.

She stopped.

'I'm tired,' she said.

'Come on, just a little longer,' he said. 'Don't give up!'

A hundred yards further on she stopped again, and through her veil, which from her man's hat fell at a slant to her hips, you could see her face in a bluish translucence, as though she were swimming under sky-blue water.

'But where are we going?'

He made no reply. She was breathing unevenly. Rodolphe kept looking around him and biting his moustache.

They came to a larger open space, which had been cleared of seedlings. They sat down on a fallen tree trunk, and Rodolphe began telling her of his love.

He was very careful, at first, not to alarm her with compliments. He was calm, serious, melancholy. She sat listening to him with her head bowed, poking at the woodchips on the ground with her toe.

But, at these words:

'Aren't our destinies now bound together?'

'Oh no!' she replied. 'You know that. It's impossible.'

She stood up to go. He grabbed her by the wrist. She stopped, and after gazing at him for a few minutes with loving, tearful eyes, said quickly:

'Oh, please let's not talk about this any more . . . Where are the horses? Let's go back.'

He made an angry, impatient gesture. She said again:

'Where are the horses? Where are the horses?'

Then, with a strange smile, his eyes staring and his teeth clenched, he advanced upon her, arms spread wide. Trembling, she stepped back.

'Oh, you're frightening me!' she stammered, 'you're upsetting me! Let's go.'

'If we really must,' he said, his expression changing.

And abruptly he once again became respectful, tender, diffident. She took his arm and they turned back.

'But what was the matter?' he asked her. 'Why were you frightened? I don't understand. Surely you must have misunderstood. I keep you in a special place in my heart, like a Madonna on a pedestal, sublime, secure, immaculate. But I need you, to continue living. I need your eyes, your voice, your thoughts. Be my friend, my sister, my guardian angel!'

And he reached out his arm and put it round her waist. She tried half-heartedly to free herself. He held her like this as they walked along.

Then they heard the two horses browsing on the greenery.

'Oh, a little longer!' said Rodolphe. 'Don't let's go yet! Please stay!'

He drew her further on, to the edge of a small pond where duck-weed covered the water with green. Shrivelled water lilies floated, motionless, among the reeds. At the sound of their footsteps on the grass, frogs leapt for cover.

'This is wrong, wrong,' she said. 'I'm insane to listen to you.'

'Why? . . . Emma! Emma!'

'Oh, Rodolphe!' said the young woman slowly, leaning against his shoulder.

The cloth of her habit clung to the velvet of his coat; her white throat filled with a sigh as she let it fall back and, half-fainting, weeping, hiding her face, with a deep shudder she gave herself to him.

Evening shadows were falling; the sun, low in the sky, shone through the branches, dazzling her eyes. Here and there, all round her, in the foliage and on the ground, were shimmering patches of light, as if humming birds had scattered their plumage as they flew past. All was silent; a mellow sweetness seemed to be coming from the trees; she could feel her heart beginning to beat again and the blood flowing through her body like a river of milk. Then she heard, in the distance, from the other side of the wood, on those other hills, a vague, long-drawn-out cry, a voice that seemed to linger in the air, and she listened to it in silence, as it blended like a melody with the last vibrations of her tingling nerves. Rodolphe, a cigar stuck between his teeth, was fixing a broken bridle with his knife.

They took the same path to return to Yonville. They saw in the mud, side by side, the tracks left earlier by their horses; they saw the same bushes, the same stones lying on the grass. Nothing around them had changed; yet for her something had happened of greater moment than if the mountains themselves had moved. From time to time Rodolphe would lean over, take her hand, and kiss it.

How charming she looked on horseback! Erect and slender-waisted, her knee bent over the horse's mane and her cheeks faintly flushed from the open air, in the warm glow of the evening light.

As she rode into Yonville her horse pranced on the cobblestones. From behind windows, eyes were watching her.

Her husband, at dinner, thought she looked well; but she seemed not to hear him when he questioned her about her ride; she sat leaning her elbow beside her plate, between the lighted candles.

'Emma!' he said.

'What?'

'Well, this afternoon I went to see Monsieur Alexandre; he has an old mare that's still in fine shape, just a bit broken in the knees, and I'm sure we could get her for about a hundred *écus* or so . . .'

He went on: 'I thought you'd be pleased, so actually I made an offer for her . . . I bought her . . . Did I do right? What d'you think?'

She nodded her assent, then, a quarter of an hour later:

'Are you going out this evening?' she asked.

'Yes, why?'

'Oh, nothing—nothing, dear.'

And, as soon as she was rid of Charles, she went up and shut herself into her room.

At first, it was like a trance: she saw the trees, the paths, the ditches, and Rodolphe; she could still feel his arms around her, with the foliage rustling and the wind whistling in the reeds.

But, on catching sight of herself in the glass, she was astonished at her appearance. Never had her eyes looked so huge, so black, so unfathomable. Some subtle influence had transfigured her whole being.

Again and again she told herself: 'I've a lover! I've a lover!' revelling in the idea as though she were beginning a second puberty. At last she was to experience those joys of love, that delirium of happiness that she had despaired of ever knowing. She was entering a magical realm where life would be all passion, ecstasy, rapture; a bluish immensity surrounded her, lofty heights of emotion glittered brightly in her imagination, while ordinary existence still continued only far, far away, down below, in the shadowy emptiness between those peaks.

Then she recalled the heroines of novels she had read, and that poetic legion of adulteresses began to sing in her memory with sisterly voices that held her spellbound. She herself was actually becoming a living part of her own fantasies, she was fulfilling the long dream of her youth by seeing herself as one of those passionate lovers she had so deeply envied. Besides, Emma felt a satisfying sense of revenge. She had suffered enough, had she not! But now her moment of triumph was here, and love, so long repressed, flowed freely, in joyful effervescence. She gloried in it, feeling no remorse, no anxiety, no disquiet.

The next day brought fresh delights. They exchanged vows. She told him her sorrows. Rodolphe kept interrupting her with kisses, and she, gazing at him through half-closed lids, would beg him to say her name again, and tell her again that he loved her. They were in the forest, as on the previous day, in a hut used by clog-makers. Its walls were of straw, and the roof was so low that they could not stand up. They sat side by side, on a bed of dry leaves.

From then on, they wrote regularly, every night, to one another. Emma took her letter down to the bottom of the garden, and hid it in a crack of the wall by the river. Rodolphe, when he came to fetch it, would replace it with his letter, which she always complained was too short.

One morning, when Charles had left before dawn, she was suddenly seized with the urge to see Rodolphe that very minute. She could get to La Huchette in no time, spend an hour there, and be back in Yonville before anyone had begun to stir. The idea made her ache with desire; very soon she was halfway across the meadow, walking fast, not looking behind her.

Dawn was just breaking. From far away, Emma recognized her lover's house, with its two black, fan-tailed weathervanes standing out sharply in the pale half-light.

Beyond the farmyard rose an important-looking building that must be the chateau. She walked straight in, as if, at her approach, the walls had opened wide of their own accord. A long, single flight of stairs led up to a corridor. Emma lifted the latch of a door and suddenly saw, on the far side of the room, a man asleep. It was Rodolphe. She gave a cry.

'You! You, here!' he kept saying. 'But however did you manage to get here? . . . Oh! Your dress is soaking!'

'I love you', she answered, putting her arms round his neck.

After the success of this first reckless venture, each time Charles left the house early, Emma would quickly dress, then tiptoe down the steps that led to the water's edge.

But, if the plank bridge for the cows had been lifted, she would have to follow the garden walls beside the river; the bank was slippery, and she would grab hold of the clumps of withered wallflowers to avoid falling. Then she would set off through some ploughed fields, where her feet kept sinking deep into the soil as she stumbled about, getting her thin boots heavily caked with mud. The scarf tied round her head kept flapping in the breeze as she crossed the pasture; she was afraid of bulls, and began to run, arriving out of breath, rosy-cheeked, her whole being exuding a fragrance of sap, greenery, and fresh air. At that hour, Rodolphe was still asleep. It was like a spring morning coming into his room.

The yellow curtains over the windows let in a dim, dusky golden light. Emma would grope her way, blinking her eyes, dewdrops clinging to her smoothly parted hair in a topaz halo that framed her face. With a laugh, Rodolphe would pull her close and press her to his heart.

Afterwards, she liked to explore the room, opening the dresser drawers, combing her hair with his comb, and looking at herself in his shaving mirror. Often, she would even put between her teeth the stem of a big pipe that lay among the lemons and lumps of sugar, beside the water jug, on the night table.*

It always took them at least a quarter of an hour to say goodbye. Invariably, Emma wept; she wished she could stay with Rodolphe forever. Something more powerful than herself kept driving her to him, so much so that one day, when she turned up unexpectedly, he frowned, as if annoyed.

'What's the matter?' she asked. 'Are you ill? Tell me!'

Finally, in a serious tone of voice, he declared that her visits were becoming reckless, and she was jeopardizing her reputation.

CHAPTER X

As time passed, she came to share Rodolphe's fears. Love had, at first, intoxicated her; she had had thoughts for nothing else. But, now that she could not live without it, she was afraid of losing any part of it, or even of disturbing it in any way. Coming home from visiting him, she would glance apprehensively about her, scanning every figure on the horizon and every village dormer from which she might be observed. She would listen for footsteps, and voices, and the noise of carts; and she would stop in her tracks, paler and more tremulous than the poplar leaves swaying above her head.

One morning, walking home in this frame of mind, she suddenly thought she could see the long barrel of a gun pointing straight at her. It was poking out at an angle over the rim of a small barrel half buried in the grasses, at the edge of a ditch. Emma, almost fainting with terror, was continuing nevertheless, when a man popped up like a jack-in-the-box out of the barrel. He wore gaiters buckled up to his knees, a cap pulled down over his eyes, his lips were quivering with cold, and his nose was red. It was Captain Binet, out hunting wild duck.

'You ought to have shouted, from far away!' he cried. 'When you see a gun, you should always shout a warning.'

In saying this, the tax collector was trying to cover up the fright Emma had just given him, for an official decree forbade hunting duck except from a boat. Monsieur Binet, in spite of his respect for the law, was in contravention of this edict. Consequently, every other minute, he imagined that he could hear the gamekeeper approaching. But this fear added an edge to his enjoyment, and, all alone in his barrel, he would complacently congratulate himself on being both lucky and cunning.

He seemed immensely relieved at the sight of Emma, and immediately began a conversation: 'Not exactly warm, is it? Quite nippy, in fact!'

Emma made no reply. He went on:

'You're out early, aren't you?'

'Yes,' she stammered, 'I've been visiting the nurse who's taking care of my baby.'

'Ah, yes, indeed! Yes, indeed! I myself have been right here where you see me now since dawn, but it's such a foul day that unless a bird lands right on . . .'

'Goodbye, Monsieur Binet,' she interrupted, turning on her heel.

'Your servant, Madame,' he replied curtly.

And he retreated once more into his barrel.

Emma regretted having left the tax collector so abruptly. No doubt he'd jump to some undesirable conclusions. The story about the nurse was the worst possible excuse, since everybody in Yonville knew perfectly well that the Bovarys' child had been back with her parents for a year. Besides, there was nobody living round there; that path led only to La Huchette; so Binet must have guessed where she'd been, and he wouldn't keep quiet about it, he'd be sure to spread it about! She spent the entire day racking her brains, thinking up every conceivable kind of lie, unable to rid herself of the mental image of that nitwit with his game-bag.

After dinner Charles, seeing that she was fretting over something, decided to take her to visit the pharmacist as a distraction, and of course the first person she saw in the pharmacy had to be him, the tax collector! He was standing at the counter, in the glow from the big red jar, saying:

'I'd like half an ounce of vitriol, please.'

'Justin,' shouted the pharmacist, 'fetch the sulphuric acid.'

Then, to Emma who was starting up the stairs to see Madame Homais:

'No, stay here, it's not worth bothering, she's on her way down. Get warm by the stove while you're waiting . . . Excuse me . . . Good evening, Doctor . . .' (for the pharmacist took great pleasure in enunciating the word 'doctor', as though, in using it to address another, some of the status he attached to it would reflect on himself) 'Justin, take care not to knock over the mortars! No, no, fetch some chairs from the small parlour, you know we never move the chairs in the drawing room.'

And Homais was hurrying out from behind the counter to put his armchair back in its place, when Binet asked him for half an ounce of sugar acid.

'Sugar acid?' repeated the pharmacist disdainfully. 'Never heard of it! Perhaps you mean oxalic acid? Oxalic acid, isn't that right?'

Binet explained that he needed a corrosive; he was making up a metal solvent to clean the rust off some of his hunting gear. Emma gave a start. The pharmacist said:

'Indeed, this weather's far from ideal, because of the humidity.'

'Nevertheless,' remarked the tax collector slyly, 'some people don't seem to find it a problem.'

Her heart was in her mouth.

'And I'll also need . . .'

'Isn't he ever going to leave!' she was thinking.

'A half-ounce of rosin and of turpentine, four ounces of yellow wax, and an ounce and a half of bone black, please, for cleaning the patent leather parts of my gear.'

The apothecary was starting to cut the wax when Madame Homais appeared with Irma in her arms, Napoléon at her side, and Athalie trailing behind. She sat down on the velvet-covered bench by the window, and the little boy squatted on a stool while his elder sister hung about the jujube box,* close to her dear papa. The latter was filling bottles with a funnel, then corking them, gluing on labels, and doing up packets. No one spoke; the only sound was the occasional clink of the weights on the scales, and the murmured remarks of the pharmacist as he instructed his pupil.

'How's your little girl?' Madame Homais suddenly enquired.

'Silence!' exclaimed her husband, who was entering some figures in a rough notebook.

'Why didn't you bring her with you?' she went on in a low voice.

'Hush!' said Emma, indicating the pharmacist.

But Binet, wholly intent on checking the bill, had probably not heard. At last, he left. Emma heaved a great sigh of relief on being rid of him.

'Aren't you breathing heavily!' observed Madame Homais.

'Oh, it's very warm in here,' she answered.

So, the next day, they talked about how best to arrange their meetings. Emma wanted to bribe her maid with a present, but a better plan was to find some safe, discreet house in Yonville. Rodolphe promised to look for one.

All through the winter, three or four times a week, he came to the garden at dead of night. Emma had deliberately removed the key to the gate, letting Charles believe that it was lost.

To alert her, Rodolphe threw a handful of gravel at the shutters. Emma would start up; but occasionally she had to wait, for Charles loved to sit by the fire and chat, and he talked on and on.

She would grow frantic with impatience; if she could have done it with a look, she would have hurled him out of the window. In the end she would begin preparing for bed; then open a book and calmly start to read, as though she found it very interesting. But Charles, already in bed, kept calling her to join him.

'Come on, Emma, it's late,' he said.

'Yes, yes, I'm coming!'

But the light from the candles dazzled him, so he turned to the wall and fell asleep. She made her escape, holding her breath, smiling, trembling, half-undressed.

Rodolphe had an enormous cloak; he would envelop her completely in it, and, putting his arm round her waist, take her down, without a word, to the end of the garden. It was to the arbour that they went, to that same dilapidated wooden bench where Léon had once sat and gazed at her so adoringly on summer evenings. Now she scarcely gave him a thought.

The stars shone through the bare branches of the jasmin. Behind them they could hear the river flowing, and occasionally the crackle of dried-up reeds on the banks. Here and there, in the darkness, immense shadows loomed, which would sometimes, quivering in unison, surge up and then arch over, like huge black waves that had moved closer to give them shelter. The chill of the night spurred them to more passionate embraces; the sighs on their lips seemed to them more ardent; their eyes, dimly seen, seemed to them larger, and, in the silence, low-spoken words dropped into their hearts with a crystalline ring, echoing there with an ever-growing resonance.

Whenever the night was wet, they took refuge in the consulting room, between the shed and the stable. She used to light one of the kitchen candles, which she kept hidden behind the books. Rodolphe made himself completely at home there. The sight of the bookshelves and the desk, indeed of the whole room, filled him with glee, and he could not resist making lots of jokes at Charles's expense that Emma found embarrassing. She would have liked to see him be more serious, and even, occasionally, more dramatic, as when she thought she heard steps approaching in the alley.

'Someone's coming!' she said.

He blew out the candle.

'Have you your pistols?'

'What for?'

'Why . . . to defend yourself,' Emma replied.

'D'you mean against your husband? Huh . . . him . . .!'

And Rodolphe completed his remark with a gesture that implied 'I'd squash him like a fly . . .'

She marvelled at his bravery, even though she sensed in it a kind of coarseness and naive vulgarity that shocked her.

Rodolphe thought hard about this business of the pistols. If she'd been in earnest, then it was utterly ridiculous, he considered, in fact rather horrible, since he himself had no reason to hate good old Charles, not being, as the expression went, 'devoured by jealousy'. In this regard, Emma had made him a solemn vow that he did not think in the best of taste.

Besides, she was becoming dreadfully sentimental. They had to exchange miniatures, they had cut locks of each other's hair, and now she was asking for a ring, an actual wedding ring, as a symbol of everlasting union. She often spoke to him of the 'bells of evening' and of the 'voices of nature'; and then she would carry on about her own mother, and about his. It was twenty years since Rodolphe had lost his mother, but Emma, nevertheless, consoled him in affected language more appropriate for comforting a little waif. Sometimes, gazing at the moon, she would even say to him:

'I'm sure that they're up there together, giving their blessing to our love!'

But she was so pretty! So few of his mistresses had been so free of guile! This love without debauchery was for him a new experience, which, in making him depart from his casual habits, pandered both to his pride and to his sensuality. Emma's raptures, although they excited his down-to-earth bourgeois scorn, actually, in his heart of hearts, delighted him, because it was he who inspired them. So then, certain of being loved, he stopped taking pains to please her, and imperceptibly his manner changed.

No longer were there any of those sweet words which, in the early days, had made her weep, nor any of those frenzied caresses which had driven her wild; so that their great love, in which she was totally immersed, seemed to be diminishing before her very eyes, like the waters of a river seeping away through its own bed, and letting her glimpse the mud on the bottom. She tried not to believe it; she redoubled her ardour; Rodolphe concealed his indifference less and less.

She did not know whether she regretted having yielded to him or whether, on the contrary, she wanted to cherish him all the more. The humiliation of acknowledging her own weakness fed a rancour that was soothed by caresses. No longer was it love; it was more like a perpetual seduction. He was subjugating her. It almost frightened her.

Nevertheless, on the surface, their relationship seemed more harmonious than ever, since Rodolphe was now able to conduct the affair entirely to suit himself; and, at the end of six months, when spring came, they were treating one another like a married couple who are calmly tending a domestic flame.

It was now the time when, every year, old Monsieur Rouault sent his turkey in remembrance of his mended leg. The present always came accompanied by a letter. Emma cut the string tying it to the hamper, and read the following:

My dear children,

I hope these lines find you in good health and that this bird's as good as the others; I think it's a bit tenderer, if I may say it as shouldn't, and heavier. But next time, by way of a change, I'll make it a cock, unless you'd rather stick to "gobblers", and please send me back the hamper, if you don't mind, along with the other two. I've had a bit of bad luck with my cart-shed, one night when it was blowing hard the roof flew off into the trees. My harvest wasn't all that special either. So, I don't know when I'll be getting over to see you. I find it very difficult to leave the house now, since there's nobody but me, my poor Emma!

Here there was a space between the lines, as if the old man had put down his pen for a minute or two and let his thoughts wander.

As for me, I'm very well, except for a cold I caught the other day at the Yvetot fair, where I'd gone to hire a shepherd, having sacked the one I used to have due to him being altogether too fussy about his food. Really we have a hard time of it, dealing with all these rascals. And this one was dishonest as well.

I heard from a pedlar who was over your way during the winter and had a tooth pulled, that Bovary is still busy as ever. Not that I'm surprised! And he showed me his tooth; we had some coffee together. I asked him if he'd seen you, and he said no, but he'd seen two horses in the stables, so I suppose things must be going nicely for you. I'm so glad, my dear children, and may the good Lord send you all possible happiness.

It grieves me that I haven't seen my darling granddaughter Berthe Bovary yet. I've planted a special plum tree for her under your window, and I don't want them touched, unless it's to make preserves, later, that I'll keep stored in the cupboard for her to have when she visits me.

Goodbye, my dear children; I kiss you on both cheeks, daughter, and you, son-in-law, and the little girl too.

I am,
With my very best wishes,
Your loving father,
Théodore Rouault

She sat for a while with the sheet of coarse paper in her hand. The spelling mistakes came thick and fast one upon another, and Emma pondered over the affectionate thoughts that clucked their way through the letter like a hen half hidden in a thorn hedge. The ink had been dried with ash from the fireplace, for a trickle of grey powder fell from the paper onto her dress; she could almost see her father leaning down to pick up the tongs from the hearth. How long it was since she'd sat on the stool by the fire, at his side, burning the end of a stick in the big flames from the blazing furze! She remembered summer evenings bright with sunshine. The foals would whinny when you came near, and break into such a gallop! There was a beehive under her window, and sometimes the bees, whirling about in the light, would strike the panes like bouncing golden balls. How happy those days had been! How free! How full of hope, how fertile in illusions! Now, she had no illusions left. She'd used up a few of them at each new venture of her spirit, at each successive stage of her experience—in virginity, in marriage, and in love—losing them continually, one by one, throughout the course of her life, like a traveller who leaves behind some part of his wealth at every inn on the road.

But who then was making her so unhappy? What extraordinary disaster had befallen her? She raised her head and looked all round, as if searching for the cause of her suffering.

A ray of April sunshine shimmered on the porcelain on the dresser; the fire was burning brightly; she could feel, through her slippers, the softness of the carpet; the day was clear, the air mild, and she could hear her child shrieking with laughter.

The little girl was rolling about on the lawn, in the cut grass that had been spread out to dry. She lay on her stomach on top of one of the piles. The maid had hold of her by the skirt. Lestiboudois was raking close by, and every time he approached she would lean right down, flapping her arms about in the air.

'Bring her to me!' her mother cried, rushing out to give her a kiss. 'Oh, how I love you, my poor baby! How I love you!'

Then, noticing that the tips of her ears were slightly dirty, she quickly rang for warm water, washed her, changed her underclothes, her stockings, and her shoes, asked endless questions about her health as if she had just returned from a journey, and finally, with more kisses and a few tears, handed her back to the maid, who stood there gaping in astonishment at this excessive display of affection.

That night Rodolphe found her more serious than usual.

'It won't last,' he thought, 'it's just a whim.'

And he missed three consecutive meetings. When he finally did come, she behaved coldly, almost disdainfully.

'Oh, this won't get you anywhere, my dear . . .' And he pretended not to notice her melancholy sighs, and the handkerchief she kept producing.

Then Emma did indeed repent.

She even wondered why it was that she loathed Charles, and whether it would not have been better to be able to love him. But so devoid was he of qualities to justify this renewal of affection that she was in a quandary as to how to satisfy her urge for self-sacrifice, when the apothecary conveniently provided her with an opportunity.

CHAPTER XI

Homais had recently read an article praising a new method for curing club foot; and, as he was a believer in progress, he came up with a patriotic scheme: Yonville, to 'keep up with the times', should have an operation for talipes.

'Because,' as he kept telling Emma, 'what do you risk? Think about it:' (and here, counting on his fingers, he enumerated the advantages of the undertaking) 'almost certain success, relief of discomfort and improvement in appearance for the patient, instant renown for the surgeon. Now why shouldn't your husband, for example, patch up our poor Hippolyte, at the Lion d'Or? You can be certain he'd tell every traveller about his cure, and then' (lowering his voice and glancing cautiously round) 'what's to prevent my sending a short paragraph about it to the newspaper? And—Lord knows—a newspaper item circulates . . . it gets talked about . . . who can say what it might lead to! Who can say!'

In point of fact, Bovary might well be successful; Emma had no reason to think him incompetent at his job, and how satisfying she would find it, to encourage him in a step that would promote his fame and fortune! All she wanted was to have something more solid than love to depend on.

Swayed by the joint appeals of the apothecary and Emma, Charles let himself be persuaded. He ordered Doctor Duval's treatise* from Rouen, and, with his head in his hands, buried himself in its perusal every evening.

While he was studying the equinus, varus, and valgus forms* of talipes, that is to say strephocatopodia, strephendopodia, and strephexopodia (or, in layman's terms, the different malformations of the foot downwards, inwards, and outwards) along with strephy-popodia and strephanopodia (downward torsion and upward stretching), Monsieur Homais, mustering every possible argument, kept exhorting the stable boy to undergo the operation.

'At most you may perhaps feel a little discomfort; it's just a pin-prick, like being lightly bled, not even as bad as having some types of corns excised.'

Hippolyte thought about it, rolling his ox-like eyes.

'In any case,' said the pharmacist, 'it's all the same to me! What I'm saying is entirely for your sake! Out of pure compassion! I'd like to see you, my boy, freed from your hideous claudification, and from that rocking movement of the lumbar region that must seriously hamper you in performing your duties, whatever you may claim.'

Homais went on to describe how much sprier and more vigorous he would feel, even hinting that he would be all the better placed to please the ladies, and the stable boy began to grin sheepishly. Then the pharmacist started working on his vanity:

'Call yourself a man, do you? Merciful heavens, what would you have done if you'd been called up, had to fight for your country? Oh, Hippolyte! . . .'

And Homais would turn away, declaring himself mystified by such stubbornness, such blind rejection of the blessings of science.

Finally, in the face of what was almost a conspiracy, the wretched fellow consented. Binet, who never meddled in other people's business, Madame Lefrançois, Artémise, the neighbours, and even

Monsieur Tuvache, the mayor, everybody advised him and lectured him and shamed him; but what finally decided him was that 'it wouldn't set him back a penny'. Bovary was even prepared to provide the apparatus required after the operation. This generous offer had been Emma's idea, and Bovary agreed, thinking in his heart that his wife was an angel.

So, guided by the pharmacist's advice, he managed, on the third attempt, to have a sort of box constructed by the cabinetmaker, aided by the locksmith. It weighed about eight pounds, and required a vast quantity of iron, wood, sheet-metal, leather, nuts, and screws.

However, in order to know which of Hippolyte's tendons should be cut, it was necessary to determine first which type of club foot he had.

His foot made almost a straight line with his leg, but that did not prevent it from being twisted inwards, which made it an equinus tending towards a varus, or else, perhaps, a slight varus with pronounced equinus characteristics. Still, even with this equinus, which was indeed as big as a horse's hoof, and had rough skin, stringy tendons, very large toes, and black nails resembling horseshoe nails, the strephopod bounded about like a deer from dawn to dusk. He was constantly to be seen in the market place, hopping round the carts, swinging his bad leg forward first. In fact he seemed stronger in that leg than in the other one. Long years of service had, as it were, endowed it with moral attributes—qualities of patience and energy—and whenever he was given some really heavy jobs to carry out, Hippolyte preferred to rely on his bad leg for support.

Now, since it was an equinus, his Achilles tendon would have to be cut, even if it meant dealing later with the anterior tibial muscle, to cure the varus; for the medical officer did not dare risk two operations at once, and indeed already felt very apprehensive lest he cut into some vital part of the foot that he knew nothing about.

Most certainly, neither Ambroise Paré, applying, for the first time since Celsus had done it fifteen centuries earlier, a ligature directly to an artery, nor Dupuytren preparing to lance an abscess through a thick layer of encephalic matter, nor Gensoul,* performing the first ablation of the upper maxillary, could have approached their patients with a heart beating so fast, a hand trembling so violently, and a mind as keyed up as were Monsieur Bovary's when, *tenotome** in hand, he approached Hippolyte. And, just like a real hospital, you could see, lying on an adjacent table, a pile of lint, some waxed thread, and a lot of bandages, a veritable pyramid of bandages, the entire stock of bandages from the pharmacy. It was Monsieur Homais who had been busy since early morning with all these preparations, as much to dazzle the multitude as to delude himself. Charles pierced the skin; a sharp snap was heard. The tendon had been cut, the operation completed. Hippolyte could not get over his astonishment; he seized Bovary's hands and covered them with kisses.

'Now, now, calm down,' said the apothecary; 'there'll be plenty of time later on to show your gratitude to your benefactor.'

And he went out to report the result to five or six bystanders waiting in the yard, who imagined that Hippolyte would reappear walking upright. Then Charles, having buckled his patient into the contraption, returned home, where Emma was anxiously awaiting him at the door. She flung her arms round his neck; they sat down at the table; he ate a great deal and even, at dessert, fancied a cup of coffee, although normally he only indulged in such debauchery on Sundays when they had guests.

They spent a delightful evening talking over their dreams. They talked about their future wealth and about the improvements they would make to their home; he pictured his reputation growing, his prosperity increasing, his wife loving him forever, while she was happy to find herself refreshed by an unfamiliar sensation, one that was more wholesome, more acceptable, a feeling, in fact, of affection for that poor Charles who loved her so. The thought of Rodolphe crossed her mind for an instant, but then her eyes turned to Charles; she even noticed, with some surprise, that his teeth were not at all unsightly.

They were in bed when Homais, ignoring the protests of the cook, burst into their room, holding in his hand a page he had just finished composing. It was the announcement he had written for the *Fanal de Rouen*. He had brought it for them to read.

'You read it to us,' said Bovary.

He read:

' "In spite of the web of prejudices still veiling part of the face of Europe, light is, nevertheless, beginning to penetrate into our countryside. This very Tuesday, indeed, our little town of Yonville furnished the setting for a surgical experiment that was also an act of pure philanthropy. Monsieur Bovary, one of our most distinguished practitioners . . ." '

'Oh, that's too much! Too much!' said Charles, almost speechless with emotion.

'No, not at all! What nonsense! ". . . performed an operation for club foot. . ." I didn't use the scientific term because, as you know, in a newspaper . . . perhaps not everyone would understand; the masses will have to be . . .'

'Exactly,' said Bovary. 'Go on.'

'To resume . . .' said the pharmacist. ' "Monsieur Bovary, one of our most distinguished practitioners, performed an operation for club foot. The patient, one Hippolyte Tautain, has served as stable boy for the past twenty-five years at a hostelry in the Place d'Armes, the Lion d'Or, run by Madame Lefrançois. The innovative nature of the enterprise and the interest taken in the patient drew a crowd of our townspeople so large as literally to obstruct access to the inn. The operation, moreover, was carried out as if by magic; barely a drop or two of blood appearing on the skin, as though to declare that the mutinous tendon had finally yielded to the surgeon's art. The patient, strange to say (and we testify to this fact *de visu*), experienced no pain. At the time of writing, his condition leaves nothing to be desired. Everything points to a rapid convalescence, and who can say that, at our next village festival, we shall not see our good Hippolyte dancing to our merry measures in the midst of a cheerful throng, and thereby demonstrating to every onlooker, with his spirited leaps and bounds, the completeness of his cure? All honour, therefore, to our philanthropic men of science! All honour to those indefatigable spirits who sacrifice their nights to the betterment or to the relief of their fellow men! All honour to them! And again, all honour! Are we not entitled to declare that the blind will see, the deaf will hear, and the lame will walk? But that which, in ages past, fanaticism promised to its chosen few, science is now achieving for all mankind! We shall keep our readers informed of the successive stages of this remarkable cure." '

But Homais's eloquence had no effect on what happened next. Five days later, Madame Lefrançois rushed over in a terrible panic, screaming:

'Help! He's dying! I don't know which way to turn!'

Charles dashed into the Lion d'Or, and the pharmacist, seeing him cross the square without his hat, abandoned the pharmacy. He arrived out of breath, red-faced and anxious, asking everyone he met on the stairs: 'Whatever can be the matter with our fascir/ting strephopod?'

The strephopod was writhing about in appalling convulsions, convulsions of such violence that the mechanical contraption clamped round his leg kept striking the wall hard enough to knock it down.

So, with many precautions to avoid disturbing the position of the leg, they removed the box, and revealed a horrifying sight. The shape of the foot had completely disappeared beneath a swelling of such severity that the skin seemed on the point of bursting, and it was covered with ecchymoses* inflicted by the famous contraption. Hippolyte had already complained of pain, but no one had paid any attention; but now they were obliged to admit his complaints were not unjustified, and to leave his foot free for a few hours. But barely had the oedema subsided somewhat, than the two experts deemed it appropriate to replace the foot in the apparatus, screwing it in more tightly to hurry things along. Eventually, after another three days, as Hippolyte could not stand it any longer, they removed their contraption again, and were quite amazed at the result they observed. A livid tumefaction was spreading right up the leg, which was mottled with phlyctenae from which oozed a black liquid. Things seemed to be taking a turn for the worse. Hippolyte was beginning to lose patience, and Madame Lefrançois moved him to the small parlour near the kitchen, where at least he would have some distraction.

But the tax collector, who had dinner there every day, complained bitterly of this unwanted company, so Hippolyte was carried into the billiard room. There he lay, whimpering under his coarse blankets, pale, unshaven, and hollow-eyed, occasionally turning his sweaty head on the dirty, fly-ridden pillow. Madame Bovary often came to see him. She brought cloths for his poultices, comforted him, and reassured him. Besides, he did not lack for company, particularly on market days, when the country folk would gather there, playing billiards, duelling with the cues, smoking, drinking, singing, and brawling.

'How's it going?' they would ask, slapping him on the shoulder.

'You don't look up to much, do you. Only yourself to blame, you know. Why ever didn't you. . .' And they would tell him stories of people cured by methods quite different from this one, then, to console him, they would add:

'Fact is, you're coddling yourself too much! Get up! You're cosseting yourself like royalty! All right, old chap, all right—but my! you don't half stink!'

The gangrene was indeed moving higher and higher. Bovary himself found it hard to stomach. He came by every hour, every other minute. Hippolyte would gaze at him with eyes full of terror and mumble between sobs:

'When will I be better? Oh, please save me! I feel terrible, terrible!'

On leaving, the doctor always advised him to eat sparingly.

'Don't you listen to him, my lad,' Madame Lefrançois would say, 'they've tormented you enough already. You'll get even weaker. Here, swallow this down!'

And she brought him bowls of rich broth, slices of mutton, chunks of bacon, and, occasionally, tots of brandy, which he could barely raise to his lips.

The Abbé Bournisien, hearing that he was getting worse, asked to see him. He began by commiserating with him in his suffering, at the same time declaring that he should see it as a cause for rejoicing, since it was the Lord's will, and quickly take the opportunity to reconcile himself with heaven.

'For', the priest went on in a fatherly tone, 'you've been neglecting your religious duties a bit, you know. We've hardly ever seen you at mass, and how many years is it since you last took communion? It's quite understandable that with your job, and all the distractions around you, you've given little thought to your eternal salvation, but now the time has come to reflect upon it. But you've no cause to despair; I've known some great sinners who, realizing they'd soon have to appear before God (of course I know you're not at that stage yet), implored him for mercy, and most assuredly they died in a state of grace. Let's hope that, like them, you'll be an example for us all! So, just to be on the safe side, what's to stop you reciting a "Hail, Mary, full of grace" and an "Our Father which art in heaven" every morning and evening? Yes, do that, as a favour to me! It's not much to ask . . . Will you make me that promise?'

The poor devil promised. The curé returned every day. He always had a chat with the innkeeper and even told her stories full of jokes and puns that Hippolyte could not understand. Then, at the appropriate juncture, he would return to matters religious, his features assuming a suitable expression.

His zeal appeared to bear fruit: for soon the strephopod began to talk of making a pilgrimage to Bon-Secours* if he was cured; to which Monsieur Bournisien replied that he saw nothing against it; two precautions were better than one. 'What had he got to lose?'

The apothecary was furious about what he called the 'priest's machinations'; he claimed that they were hindering Hippolyte's convalescence, and kept admonishing Madame Lefrançois:

'Leave him alone! Leave him alone! You're undermining his morale with this mysticism of yours!'

But the good woman refused to listen to another word. It was 'all his fault'. And, in a spirit of contrariness, she even hung a stoup of holy water and a branch of boxwood* at the head of the patient's bed.

However, religion did not appear to help him any more than had surgery, and the relentless putrefaction continued its ascent from the extremities towards the abdomen. In vain did they vary the medicines and change the poultices; every day the muscles rotted more, and eventually Charles responded with an affirmative nod when Madame Lefrançois asked him whether she might not, as a last resort, send for the celebrated Monsieur Canivet, of Neufchâtel.

A medical doctor of fifty, well established in his practice and full of self-assurance, this fellow practitioner made no effort to suppress a contemptuous laugh as he uncovered the leg, now gangrenous right up to the knee. Then, having declared flatly that it would have to be amputated, he took himself off to the pharmacy where he railed against the idiots who had reduced this poor fellow to such a state. Grabbing hold of Monsieur Homais by a coat button and shaking him, he stood there in the pharmacy, shouting.

'This is damn-fool nonsense from Paris! Just the kind of notion those gentlemen in our capital go in for! It's like strabismus, chloroform, and lithotrity,* a load of monstrous claptrap that the government ought to forbid! But no, people want to show off, they stuff you full of remedies without giving a thought to the consequences. Out here we don't see ourselves as prodigies; we're not know-it-alls, we don't dress up to the nines, we're not ladies' men; we're practitioners, healers, it wouldn't enter our heads to operate on someone who's perfectly well! Straighten a club foot, indeed! However can you straighten a club foot! It would be like trying to straighten a hunchback!'

This diatribe was agony for Homais, but he concealed his

suffering with an obsequious smile, knowing he must humour Monsieur Canivet, whose prescriptions occasionally penetrated as far as Yonville; he therefore made no attempt to defend Bovary or to say anything himself, and, abandoning his principles, sacrificed his dignity to the more urgent priorities of his business.

For the village, this mid-thigh amputation performed by Doctor Canivet was a real event! On the day in question, all the inhabitants were up earlier than usual, and the Grande-Rue, although thronged with people, had a funereal air about it, as if an execution were about to take place. At the grocer's, everyone was discussing Hippolyte's illness; the shops did no business, and Madame Tuvache, the mayor's wife, never stirred from her window, so eager was she to watch the arrival of the surgeon.

He came in his gig, driving himself. Over the years, the right-hand springs had sagged under the burden of his corpulence, so the vehicle listed slightly to that side as it rolled along, permitting a clear view, on the cushion beside him, of a colossal case bound in red leather and secured by three brass clasps that glittered magisterially.

The doctor drove like a whirlwind into the yard of the Lion d'Or, bellowed for someone to unharness his mare, then went into the stable to make sure that the animal was being properly fed with oats; when he visited a patient he always first made sure that his horse and his gig were looked after. In this connection people would say: 'That Monsieur Canivet's quite a character!' They respected him all the more for this imperturbable coolness. The universe and everyone in it could have kicked the bucket and he would not have changed his habits one iota.

Homais appeared.

'I'm relying on you,' said the doctor. 'Are we ready? Let's go!'

But, with a blush, the apothecary confessed that he was too impressionable to watch an operation of that nature.

'When you're just a bystander,' he said, 'it can be really overpowering, you know, to the imagination. And I'm so highly strung . . .'

'Nonsense!' interrupted Canivet. 'On the contrary, you strike me as an apoplectic type. And I can't say it surprises me, because all you pharmacists are stuck in your kitchens day after day, and in the long run that must affect your constitutions. Now just look at me: I'm up at four every morning, shave in cold water (I'm never cold), don't ever wear flannel, and never catch a cold—sound as a bell. Sometimes I eat well, sometimes badly, whatever comes my way; it's all the same to me. That's why I'm not thin-skinned, like you; it makes no difference to me whether I carve up a Christian or some chicken I've been served. Just a question of habit, no doubt—just a question of habit!'

Then, with no consideration whatsoever for Hippolyte, who was sweating in anguish under his bedding, the gentlemen embarked on a conversation in which Homais likened the sang-froid of a surgeon to that of a general; this comparison appealed to Canivet, who expatiated at length on the demands of his art. He saw it as a sacred office, for all that nowadays it had been tarnished by the *officiers de santé*. Finally, coming back to the subject of Hippolyte, he examined the bandages Homais had provided—the same that had appeared for the operation on the club foot, and asked for someone to hold the limb for him. They sent for Lestiboudois, and Monsieur Canivet, having rolled up his sleeves, went into the billiard room, while the apothecary remained behind with Artémise and the innkeeper, who, their faces whiter than their aprons, were standing with their ears pressed to the door.

All this time, Bovary had not dared set foot outside his house. He was sitting downstairs in the parlour, beside the empty grate, his chin slumped on his chest, his hands clasped together and his eyes blankly staring. What dreadful luck! he was thinking, what a disappointment! And yet he had taken every possible precaution. Destiny must have had a hand in it. But it made no difference—if Hippolyte were to die, later, it would be he who had murdered him. And then, when he visited patients, what explanation could he give, when people asked him about it? Perhaps he'd made a mistake of some kind? He tried to think what this might be, but could find nothing. The most celebrated surgeons, however, certainly made mistakes. But who in the world was ever going to believe that? On the contrary, people would laugh at him, repeat spiteful gossip about him. It would spread as far as Forges! Neufchâtel! Rouen! Everywhere! Who could say—perhaps colleagues would write letters denouncing him? A controversy would ensue, he'd have to defend himself in the newspapers. Hippolyte might even sue him. He saw himself dishonoured, ruined, lost! And his imagination, beset by a host of possibilities, was tossed from one to another like an empty barrel that is floating on the sea and being tossed from wave to wave.

Opposite him, Emma sat staring at him; she did not share in his humiliation, her humiliation was of a different order: that she could ever have imagined such a man might be worth something, as if she had not, twenty times over, already seen sufficient proof of his mediocrity.

Charles began pacing up and down the room. His boots squeaked on the parquet.

'Sit down,' she said, 'you're getting on my nerves.'

He sat down again.

How then had it come about that she (she who was so clever!) had made yet another mistake? And what disastrous compulsion drove her to wreck her life by perpetual self-sacrifice? She thought of all her yearning for luxury, all the privations her soul had endured, the degradations of marriage and of housekeeping, her dreams falling in the mud like wounded swallows, everything she had longed for, everything she had denied herself, everything that she might have had! And for what, for what?

In the silence that hung over the village, a terrible scream rent the air. Bovary turned deathly pale. Her brow contracted in a nervous frown, then she resumed her brooding. Yet it was for his sake, for this creature, for this man who understood nothing, who felt nothing. There he sat, perfectly serene, quite oblivious to the fact that henceforth the ridicule inspired by his name would dishonour her as well. She had tried hard to love him, and had wept tears of repentance for giving herself to another.

'But perhaps it was a valgus?' abruptly exclaimed Bovary, breaking his meditative silence.

The sudden impact of these words, as they clattered into her consciousness like a leaden bullet onto a silver platter, made Emma shudder, and she looked up, wondering what he meant; they stared at one another, not speaking, almost stunned at seeing one another, so widely separated were they by their thoughts. Charles was gazing at her with the bleary eyes of a drunken man while he listened, motionless, to the patient's final screams issuing from the inn; these followed one upon the other, trailing off into long-drawn-out modulations, punctuated by staccato shrieks, like the distant howling of some beast being slaughtered. Emma kept biting her bloodless lips as, rolling between her fingers a sliver she had broken off the polyp-ary, she fixed Charles with a fierce glare from eyes like burning arrows ready to fly. Everything about him exasperated her now, his face, his clothes, what he did not say, his entire being, his very existence. She repented, as if for a crime, her past virtue, and what yet remained of it now crumbled away beneath the enraged onslaughts of her pride. All the sordid ironies of adultery triumph-ant filled her with exultation. The memory of her lover made her dizzy with desire, and she abandoned her soul to it, drawn to this image by a new-found ardour; Charles seemed to her as discon-nected from her life, as eternally absent, as impossible, as nullified, as if he were lying at the point of death before her very eyes.

They heard footsteps on the pavement. Charles looked through the lowered blind and saw Doctor Canivet out in the sunlight, at the corner of the market place, mopping his forehead with his hand-kerchief. Behind him came Homais with a large red box in his hand; they were both making for the pharmacy.

Suddenly overwhelmed by tenderness and despair, Charles turned to his wife, saying:

'Kiss me, darling!'

'Leave me alone!' she replied, scarlet with rage.

'What's wrong? What's wrong?' he kept repeating, dumbfounded. 'Calm down, you're not yourself; you know how much I love you! . . . Come to me, please!'

'Stop it!' she screamed in a terrible voice.

And, rushing out of the room, Emma banged the door so hard that the barometer fell off the wall and shattered on the floor.

Bewildered, Charles slumped down in his armchair and wept, trying to think what could be the matter with her, imagining it must be a nervous complaint, vaguely conscious that round him the air was heavy with a sense of something deadly and incomprehensible.

When Rodolphe arrived in the garden that night, he found his mistress waiting for him at the bottom of the river steps. They fell into each other's arms, and all their rancour melted away like snow in the warmth of their embrace.

CHAPTER XII

Their love affair began again. Often, even in the middle of the day, Emma would suddenly decide to write to him. From her window she would signal to Justin, who whipped off his apron and raced to La Huchette. When Rodolphe arrived, it was to be told that she was miserable, that her husband was unbearable and her life horrible!

'But what can I do about it?' he exclaimed impatiently one day.

'Oh, if you only would . . .'

She was sitting on the floor between his knees, her hair flowing loosely, her gaze unfocused.

·'Would what?' asked Rodolphe.

She sighed.

'We'd go and live far away . . . somewhere . . .'

'You're mad, you really are!' he said with a laugh. 'How could we do that?'

She mentioned it again; he pretended not to understand and changed the subject. What he really could not understand was the reason for all this to-do about something as simple as love. But Emma had a reason, a motive, for her feelings, an additional stimulus, as it were, to passion.

This passion, in fact, was every day growing fiercer, fuelled by her loathing of her husband. The more she surrendered to the one, the more she detested the other; never did Charles repel her more, never did she think his fingers stubbier, his wits slower, his habits coarser than when she was with him after being with Rodolphe. Then, even as she played the role of virtuous wife, she would be on fire with the memory of that head with its black hair curling down over the bronzed forehead, that body at once so powerful and so elegant, of that man, in fact, who was so cool in his judgement and yet so passionate in his desire. It was for him that she filed her fingernails with the precision of an artist, for him that there was never enough cold cream on her skin, nor enough patchouli scenting her handkerchiefs. She adorned herself with bracelets, rings, necklaces. Whenever she expected him, she filled her two big blue glass vases with roses, and arranged her room and her person like a courtesan awaiting a prince. All day long the maid was kept busy washing her linen; Félicité never stirred from the kitchen, where young Justin, who often kept her company, watched her as she worked.

Leaning his elbow on the long board she used for ironing, he would stare hungrily at all those feminine garments spread around him: crisp cotton petticoats, fichus, collars, and drawstring pantalets, very wide in the hips, then narrow, lower down.

'What's this for?' the lad would ask, running his hand over the crinoline, or down the panel of hooks and eyes.

'Don't tell me you've never seen 'em before!' laughed Félicité; 'as if your mistress, Madame Homais, don't wear just the same.'

'Oh, well, yes, Madame Homais!' And he went on, his tone meditative:

'Is she a lady, though, like Madame?'

But it got on Félicité's nerves to have him hanging around her all the time. She was six years his senior, and Théodore, Monsieur Guillaumin's servant, had started courting her.

'Get along with you!' she would say, moving her pot of starch. 'Why don't you go and pound the almonds; you're forever meddling about with women's things; you're a bad lad, time enough for that when you've got a beard on your chin.'

'Come on, don't be cross, I'm going to "do her boots" for you.'

And he would quickly reach up to the shelf above the fire for Emma's boots, which were all caked with mud—the mud from the rendezvous. The dirt crumbled into dust beneath his fingers, and he watched the dust motes as, caught in a ray of sunlight, they gently floated upwards.

'You aren't half particular about them boots!' said the servant, who never took that much trouble with them herself, because as soon as the fabric looked in the least bit shabby, Madame passed them on to her.

Emma had several pairs in her cupboard, and wore them out at a great rate, without Charles ever uttering a word of complaint. Nor did he balk at spending three hundred francs on a wooden leg that she thought should be presented to Hippolyte. The leg was cushioned with cork, and had spring joints; it was a complicated contrivance covered in a black trouser leg, with a polished boot on the end. But Hippolyte, not daring to use such a handsome leg every day, begged Madame Bovary to get him a more ordinary one. Of course the doctor paid for that as well.

So, little by little, the stable boy took up his work again. Once again he was to be seen all over the village, and when, from far away, Charles heard the sharp tap of his wooden leg on the cobbles, he would quickly take another path.

It was Monsieur Lheureux, the draper, who had dealt with the commission; this gave him the opportunity to pay Emma several visits. He would chat to her about the merchandise newly arrived from Paris, and all the latest fads in ladies' fashions; he could not have been more obliging, and never mentioned money. Emma surrendered to this effortless way of satisfying her every whim. For instance, she wanted to give Rodolphe a very handsome riding whip she had seen in an umbrella shop in Rouen. The following week Monsieur Lheureux placed it on her table.

But, the next day, he turned up at her house with a bill for two hundred and seventy francs, not counting the centimes. Emma could not think what to do; all the drawers in the desk were empty; they owed more than two weeks' pay to Lestiboudois, two trimesters' wages to the maid, as well as a number of other debts, and Bovary was waiting impatiently for Monsieur Derozerays's account to be settled; as a rule he paid it, every year, about the end of June.

For a while she managed to put Lheureux off, but eventually he lost patience: he himself was being pressed, his capital was tied up and if he didn't recover some of his outlay, he'd be obliged to take back all the goods she'd bought.

'Oh, take them!' said Emma.

'Oh, I was only joking,' he replied. 'Except for the riding crop; I am rather concerned about that: yes, indeed, I'll ask Monsieur to return it!'

'No, no!' she said.

'Ha! Got you!' thought Lheureux.

And, certain of having found her out, he left, repeating, in his usual sibilant murmur: 'Well, we'll see, we'll see!'

Emma was wondering how to resolve her predicament when the servant came in, and placed on the mantelpiece a small cylindrical packet, wrapped in blue paper, 'from Monsieur Derozerays'. Seizing it, she tore it open. The packet contained three hundred francs in gold napoleons*—the payment for the account. Hearing Charles on the stairs, she flung the coins into the back of her drawer and removed the key.

Three days later, Lheureux came back.

'I have a proposition to put to you,' he began. 'If, instead of paying the sum in question, you would prefer to take . . .'

'Here you are!' she said, handing him fourteen napoleons.

The draper was dumbfounded. To conceal his disappointment, he launched into endless apologies and offers of service, all of which Emma refused; then she stood for a few minutes fingering, in her apron pocket, the two five franc pieces he had given her in change. She kept telling herself she was going to economize, so that later she could repay . . .

'Bah!' she thought; 'he'll forget all about it.'

In addition to the riding crop with the silver-gilt knob, she had given Rodolphe a seal bearing the motto *Amor nel cor*,* also a big warm scarf, and lastly a cigar-case just like the Vicomte's—the case Charles had found on the road years ago, and Emma still treasured. But Rodolphe felt mortified by these gifts. He refused several of them, but eventually, in the face of her insistence, gave in, thinking her dictatorial and interfering.

And then she had some bizarre ideas:

'When it strikes midnight, you must think of me!' she would say.

And, if he confessed that he had forgotten, a flood of reproaches always followed, culminating in the eternal question:

'Do you love me?'

'Yes, of course I love you!'

'Very much?'

'Yes of course, very much.'

'You've never loved anyone else?'

'Do you imagine I was a virgin?' he exclaimed, laughing.

Seeing Emma in tears, he did his best to comfort her, enlivening his protestations with little jokes.

'It's that I love you,' she kept repeating, 'I love you so much I can't do without you, do you understand? Sometimes I long so desperately to see you again that I feel torn to pieces by a rage of love. I wonder: "Where is he? With other women, perhaps? They're smiling at him, he's going up to them . . ." Oh, tell me it's not so, there's no other woman for you, is there? There are some more beautiful, but I know better how to love! I'm your servant, your concubine! You're my king, my idol! You're good! You're handsome! You're intelligent! You're strong!'

He had heard these things said to him so many times, that they no longer held any surprises for him. Emma was just like all his mistresses, and the charm of novelty, gradually falling away like a garment, laid bare the eternal monotony of passion, which never varies in its forms and its expression. He could not see—this man of such broad experience—the difference of feeling, beneath the similarity of expression. Because wanton or venal lips had murmured the same words to him, he only half believed in the sincerity of those he was hearing now; to a large extent they should be disregarded, he believed, because such exaggerated language must surely mask commonplace feelings: as if the soul in its fullness did not sometimes overflow into the most barren metaphors, since no one can ever tell the precise measure of his own needs, of his own ideas, of his own pain, and human language is like a cracked kettle on which we beat out tunes for bears to dance to, when what we long to do is make music that will move the stars to pity.

But, with the heightened percipience of someone who, whatever the relationship, never wholly surrenders himself to it, Rodolphe saw a way of extracting further sensual gratification from the love affair. He deemed modesty in all its forms an inconvenience. He abandoned every semblance of respect and consideration. He made of her something pliant, something corrupt. Hers was a mindless infatuation, a blissful, numbing torpor, compounded of adoration of him and of indulgence in her own sexual pleasure; her soul sank into this besottedness, drowning in it, shrivelling up like the Duke of Clarence in his butt of malmsey.

As a direct consequence of her amorous habits, Madame Bovary's appearance and manner changed. Her glance grew bolder, her speech freer; she was even so indiscreet as to be seen walking with Monsieur Rodolphe with a cigarette between her lips, 'as if to thumb her nose at all the neighbours'. In the end, those who were still wondering about her wondered no longer when she was seen, one day, emerging from the Hirondelle wearing a close-fitting waistcoat like a man's; and Madame Bovary senior, who, following a dreadful scene with her husband, had taken refuge with her son, was not the least scandalized of the good ladies of Yonville. A great many other things displeased her; Charles had ignored her advice about proscribing novels; and then, she didn't care for 'the goings on in the household'; she took the liberty of passing some remarks that gave offence, especially on one occasion, concerning Félicité.

Passing along the corridor on the preceding evening, Madame Bovary senior had caught Félicité talking to a man, a man of about forty with a small brown beard,* who, at the sound of footsteps, had quickly vanished from the kitchen. Emma had laughed when she heard about it, and her mother-in-law, enraged, declared that unless one cared nothing for standards of morality, it was essential to keep a close eye on the morals of the servants.

'Where've you been all your life?' asked her daughter-in-law, with such an impertinent look that Madame Bovary asked her whether she might not be defending her own cause.

'Get out!' cried the young woman, springing to her feet.

'Emma! . . . Mother! . . .' exclaimed Charles, trying to smooth it over.

But both of them had walked out in a fury. Emma kept stamping her foot angrily and saying:

'What manners! What a peasant!'

He rushed to his mother's side; she, beside herself with rage, was stammering:

'She's so insolent! So flighty! Worse, perhaps!'

She declared she would leave there and then, unless she received an apology. Charles went back to his wife and begged her, on his knees, to give in; finally she agreed:

'Very well! I'll do it.'

She offered her hand to her mother-in-law with the dignity of a marquise, and said: 'My apologies, Madame.'

Then, back in her own room, Emma threw herself face down on the bed and, burying her head in her pillow, sobbed her heart out like a child.

She and Rodolphe had agreed that, in the event of some kind of emergency, she would fasten a strip of white paper to the shutter, so that, should he happen to be in Yonville, he could hurry over to the lane behind the house. Emma set up the signal, and had been waiting for three-quarters of an hour, when she suddenly caught sight of Rodolphe at the corner of the market place. She was tempted to open the window and call him, but he had already vanished, and she sank back on the bed in despair.

Soon, however, she fancied she heard footsteps in the lane; it could only be him. She went down the stairs and through the yard: he was there, outside. She flung herself into his arms.

'Do be careful,' he said.

'Oh, if you only knew!' she replied.

So then she told him the whole story, rapidly and incoherently, exaggerating some facts and inventing others, and including so many parenthetical irrelevancies that he was unable to make head or tail of it all.

'Cheer up, my poor angel, don't take it so hard! Be patient!'

'But for four years now I've been patient, I've been suffering! A love like ours ought to be proclaimed openly, before heaven! They're torturing me. I can't bear it a moment longer. Save me!'

She was clinging to Rodolphe. Her eyes, brimming with tears, glittered like flames seen through water; her breast rose and fell rapidly; never had he felt such love for her, so that he lost his head and asked:

'What must I do? What do you want?'

'Take me away!' she cried. 'Oh, I beg you, take me away from here!'

And she fell upon his mouth, as if to snatch from it the unexpected consent he murmured through his kisses.

'But . . .' Rodolphe went on.

'But what?'

'And your little girl?'

She pondered for a minute or two, then replied:

'We'll take her—there's nothing else to be done.'

'What a woman!' he thought as he watched her go. She had slipped into the garden; someone was calling her.

Over the next few days Charles's mother was quite amazed at the transformation in her daughter-in-law. Emma did indeed seem more submissive, even carrying deference to the extreme of asking her for a recipe for pickling gherkins.

Was this simply the better to delude them? Or was she trying, with a kind of voluptuous stoicism, to experience more intensely the bitterness of the life she was about to abandon? But just the opposite was the case; she paid no attention to what was happening around her, but was totally absorbed in the anticipated delights of her approaching happiness. With Rodolphe, this provided an inexhaustible topic of conversation. Leaning on his shoulder, she would whisper:

'Just think what it'll be like, in the stagecoach! ... Can you imagine it? Is it really possible? I believe that when I feel the coach begin to move, it'll be as if we were flying up in a balloon, as if we were setting off into the clouds. I'm counting the days. Aren't you?'

Never had Madame Bovary been as beautiful as she was at this time; hers was that indefinable beauty born of joy, of ardour, of success, a beauty that is simply a harmony of temperament and circumstances. Her desires, her sorrows, her experience of sensual pleasure, and her still-unspoiled illusions had, by slow degrees, brought her on, the way a flower is brought on by fertilizer, by rain, by wind, and by sun, and now, at last, she was blossoming in the fullness of her nature. Her eyelids seemed expressly fashioned for those long amorous gazes in which her pupils seemed to melt away, and each time she gave a deep sigh her slender nostrils dilated, lifting the fleshy corners of her lips, which were shadowed, in the daylight, by a trace of dark down. Some artist skilled in depravity might have devised the way her hair coiled at the nape of her neck; it wound about in a heavy mass, its careless twists determined by the caprices of adultery, which loosened it every day. Her voice, now, held more languorous inflections, as did her body; something subtle and piercing seemed to emanate from the very folds of her dress and arch of her foot. As in the early days of their marriage, Charles found her enchanting, utterly irresistible.

When he came home in the middle of the night, he did not dare waken her. A round shimmering glow from the porcelain nightlight played on the ceiling, and the drawn curtains of the small crib made it look like a white hut curving out from the shadows at the side of the bed. Charles stood there, watching them sleep. He fancied he could hear the light breathing of his child. She'd grow bigger every day now; soon every season would bring a change, he could already visualize her coming home from school in the evening, laughing, her sleeves ink-stained, her basket on her arm; then they'd have to send her away to boarding school, and that would cost a great deal, however would they manage? He thought about it. He might lease a small farm in the neighbourhood, one he himself could oversee, on his way to visit his patients every morning. He'd save the income from it, and put it into a savings account; then he'd buy some shares, any shares, it didn't matter what sort; in any case his practice would grow, he was relying on that, he wanted Berthe to be well educated, to be accomplished, to play the piano. Oh! How pretty she'd be, later on, at fifteen, when she'd look just like her mother, and wear, in summer, a large straw hat like hers! From a distance people would take them for sisters. He pictured her sitting beside them in the evening, in the lamplight, busy with her work; she'd embroider slippers for him; she'd help with running the house; she'd fill their home with her sweetness and her laughter. Eventually they'd think about getting her settled; they'd find her some fine young man with good prospects; he'd make her happy; it would last forever.

Emma was not asleep, she was pretending to be asleep; and, while he was dozing off at her side, she lay awake, dreaming other dreams.

For a week now, four galloping horses had been speeding her towards a new land, from which they'd never return. On and on they went, sitting with their arms entwined, not speaking. Often, from a mountaintop, they'd catch a sudden glimpse of a magnificent city with domes, and bridges, and ships, and forests of lemon trees and cathedrals of white marble, whose slender steeples were capped by storks' nests. Their carriage had slowed to walking pace because of the enormous flagstones; the ground was strewn with bouquets of flowers that women in red bodices held up to you as you passed by. You could hear the ringing of bells and the whinnying of mules, blending with the murmur of guitars and the sound of fountains, the moisture from which, carried on the breeze, was cooling pyramids of fruit heaped below pale statues that smiled through the flying spray. And then, one evening, they'd come to a fishing village, where brown nets lay drying in the wind along the cliff and in front of the cottages. This was where they'd stop and make their home: they'd live in a low, flat-roofed house shaded by a palm tree, in the shelter of a bay, by the sea. They'd ride in gondolas, they'd laze in swaying hammocks, and their life would be free and flowing like their silken garments, warm and star-studded like the soft night skies they'd gaze at. Yet in this limitless future she pictured to herself, nothing specific ever stood out: the days, each one magnificent, were as alike as the waves of the sea; everything hovered in a harmonious, sun-drenched, bluish haze along the boundless horizon. But then the child in her crib would cough, or else Bovary would give a louder snore, and Emma would not fall asleep till morning, when dawn was whitening the window panes and young Justin, out in the square, was already opening the pharmacy shutters.

She had sent for Monsieur Lheureux and told him:

'I shall need a cloak, a big one with a good high collar, and lined.'

'You're going on a trip?' he enquired.

'No! . . . but . . . Anyway, I can leave it to you, can't I? Soon!'

He bowed.

'And I'll also need,' she went on, 'a trunk, not too heavy . . . but a good size.'

'Yes, yes, I know what you want, about three feet by one-and-a-half, that's what they're making these days.'

'And an overnight bag.'

'No doubt about it,' thought Lheureux, 'something funny's going on.'

'And here,' said Madame Bovary, unpinning her watch from her belt, 'take this: you can use it to pay for everything.'

But the shopkeeper protested: there was no need for that, they knew one another, he trusted her, didn't he? What nonsense! But she insisted that he take the chain, at least, and Lheureux had already pocketed it and was about to leave when she called him back.

'Keep everything in your shop. And as for the cloak'—she pretended to think it over—'don't bring that either; just give me the address of the tailor and tell them to have it ready for me.'

They were to elope the following month. She would set off from Yonville as if for a day's shopping in Rouen. Rodolphe would have booked seats, obtained passports, and even written to Paris to reserve a private coach as far as Marseilles, where they would buy a barouche and continue, without stopping, on the road to Genoa.* She would have taken the precaution of sending her luggage to Lheureux, to be put directly onto the Hirondelle; no one, consequently, would suspect anything. In all of this nothing was ever said about her child. Rodolphe was careful not to mention her; perhaps Emma had forgotten about her.

He wanted two more weeks to complete some arrangements; then, after a week, he asked for two more, then he said he was ill; then he left on a trip; August came and went; then, after all these delays, they settled definitely on the fourth of September, a Monday.*

The last Saturday, the Saturday before the Monday, finally arrived. Rodolphe came that evening, earlier than usual.

'Everything's ready?' she asked him.

'Yes.'

They wandered round a flower bed and went to sit by the river bank, on the wall.

'You're sad,' said Emma.

'No, why?'

And yet, he kept looking at her strangely, his expression tender.

'Is it because you're going away?' she went on, 'leaving things you're fond of, leaving your whole life behind? Oh! I can understand that . . . But as for me, I've nothing, nothing in the whole world! For me you're everything. And I'll be everything for you, I'll be your family, your homeland; I'll take care of you, I'll love you.'

'You're so enchanting!' he said, seizing her in his arms.

'Am I?' she murmured, with a luxurious laugh. 'Do you love me? Swear you love me!'

'Do I love you! Do I love you? But I worship you, my darling!'

The moon, a crimson disc, was rising straight up from the earth at the far end of the meadow. It climbed rapidly up between the branches of the poplars, which, like a tattered black curtain, screened it in places from their view. Next it showed itself, brilliantly white, in the empty sky, filling it with light, and then, moving more slowly now, it cast upon the river a great patch of brightness that shivered into a multitude of stars; this silvery radiance seemed to be spiralling down through the depths like a headless snake covered in luminous scales. It looked, also, like some enormous candelabra with droplets of molten diamond streaming from its arms. The gentle night lay spread out around them; the foliage was webbed with shadows. Emma kept sighing deeply as, her eyes half closed, she breathed in the cooling breeze. Wholly absorbed in their reverie, they were no longer speaking. The lovingness of their early days revisited their hearts, as rich and silent as the river flowing beside them, as sweetly soft as the scent of the syringas, and projected across their memories shadows vaster and more melancholy than those cast across the grass by the motionless willows. Often some nocturnal creature, a hedgehog or a weasel, would rustle through the leaves, or they would hear the sound of a single ripe peach dropping off the espalier.

'Ah! What a lovely night!' said Rodolphe.

'We'll have others!' Emma replied.

And, as though talking to herself:

'Yes, it'll be good to travel . . . So why do I feel sad? Is it fear of the unknown . . . the thought of leaving everything familiar behind me . . . or is it . . .? No, it's because I'm too happy! How weak I am, aren't I? Forgive me!'

'There's still time!' he exclaimed. 'Think carefully, you might be sorry later.'

'Never!' she cried impetuously.

And, drawing closer to him:

'What harm could possibly befall me? There isn't a desert or a precipice or an ocean that I wouldn't cross with you. When we're living together, every passing day will be like an embrace uniting us more closely, more completely! There'll be nothing to disturb us, no cares, no obstacles! We'll be alone, just you and me, forever! Say something, answer me, Rodolphe.'

He answered 'yes . . . yes' at regular intervals. She kept running her fingers through his hair, and, despite the big tears coursing down her cheeks, murmured his name again and again in a childish voice: 'Rodolphe! Rodolphe! Ah! My own sweetest Rodolphe!'

Midnight struck.

'Midnight! Now it's tomorrow!' she said. 'One more day!'

He stood up to leave; and as if his movement were the signal for their departure, Emma suddenly brightened:

'You have the passports?'

'Yes.'

'There's nothing you've forgotten?'

'Nothing.'

'You're sure?'

'Yes, I'm sure.'

'And you'll be there waiting for me at the Hôtel de Provence, won't you? . . . at noon?'

He nodded.

'Till tomorrow, then,' said Emma, giving him one final caress.

And she watched him as he walked away.

He did not look back. She ran after him and, leaning over the bushes at the water's edge, called: 'Till tomorrow!'

He was already on the other side of the river, walking rapidly across the meadow.

After a few minutes Rodolphe stopped, and, when he saw her

white dress gradually disappearing into the shadows like a ghost, his heart began beating so violently that he had to lean against a tree to keep from falling.

'What an idiot I am!' he muttered, with a fierce oath. 'Oh, well, she was certainly a delightful mistress!'

And immediately Emma's beauty, and all the pleasures this affair had brought him, came flooding back into his mind. At first he was touched, but then resentment seized him.

'After all,' he exclaimed, gesticulating, 'I can't exile myself from my country, saddle myself with a child.'

He was telling himself these things to strengthen his resolve.

'And anyway there's all those problems, all that expense, as well. Oh, no! No way! It would have been too stupid!'

CHAPTER XIII

The very instant he reached home, Rodolphe sat down at his desk, under the mounted stag's head displayed on the wall. But once he had his pen in his hand he could not think what to say, so, leaning on his elbows, he began to reflect. Emma seemed to him to have receded into the distant past, as if the decision he had taken had suddenly interposed an immense distance between them.

In an effort to recapture some sense of her, he fetched from the cupboard at the head of his bed an old Rheims biscuit tin where he always stowed away his letters from women. From it arose a smell of damp dust and withered roses. The first thing he found was a handkerchief spotted with faint stains. It was hers; she had had a nosebleed one day when they were out walking—he could not remember exactly. Beside it, all its corners bent from contact with the tin, was the miniature Emma had given him; her dress struck him as pretentious and her sidelong gaze dreadfully affected; then, by dint of gazing at this picture and recalling the appearance of the original, very gradually Emma's features became blurred in his memory, as if the real face and the painted face had, by rubbing one against the other, worn each other away. Then he read some of her letters; they were full of details about their journey, as brief, practical, and peremptory as any business letter. He decided to reread the longer ones, written in the early days; to find them at the bottom of the box, he had to disarrange all the others, and automatically he began to sift through this pile of papers and objects, haphazardly coming upon several bouquets, a garter, a black mask, pins, locks of hair—so many locks of hair! Dark hair, fair hair; some had even caught in the hinges of the tin, and broke off when he opened the lid.

Roaming idly among his souvenirs, he studied the various hand-writings and styles of the letters, which were as diverse as their spelling. They were tender or lively, funny or sad; some begged for love, others for money. A word might summon up the memory of a face, a particular gesture, a tone of voice; sometimes, however, he could remember nothing at all.

Indeed, as they all came flocking simultaneously into his thoughts, these women kept pushing each other out of the way and growing smaller, as if rendered indistinguishable by the reductive sameness of his love. He picked up a miscellaneous pile of letters and amused himself for a few minutes letting them cascade from hand to hand. Eventually, bored and sleepy, Rodolphe put the box back in the cupboard, saying to himself as he did so:

'Such a load of trash!'

Which summed up what he thought; for his pleasures, like boys playing in a school yard, had so thoroughly trampled on his heart that nothing green would grow there, and whatever passed through it, more heedless than the children, did not even leave behind, as they did, a name scratched into the wall.

'Come on,' he told himself, 'get a move on.'

He wrote:

Courage, Emma, courage! I can't let myself ruin your life . . .

'After all, that's quite true,' thought Rodolphe; 'I'm doing it for her sake, I'm being quite honest.'

Have you thoroughly weighed your decision? Have you any idea of the abyss into which I was enticing you, my poor angel? You haven't, have you? You were going ahead in your trusting, reckless way, believing in happiness, believing in the future . . . Ah! How wretched, how insane we mortals are!

Here Rodolphe paused, searching for some good excuse. 'Suppose I told her I've lost all my money? No . . . In any case, that wouldn't put a stop to things. It would all begin again later. How can you make women like that see sense?'

He pondered, then went on:

I shall never forget you, I beg you to believe this, and I shall always remain deeply devoted to you; but one day, sooner or later, this passion of ours would inevitably have begun to cool, for such is the fate of all things human. We would have known periods of weary apathy, and who can say that I would not have experienced the dreadful anguish of witnessing your remorse and of sharing in it myself, since I would have been its cause.

The mere thought of your being unhappy is torture to me, Emma! Forget me! Why did I have to meet you? Why were you so beautiful? Am I to blame for that? No, dear God, no; let us blame Fate, only Fate.

'Now there's a word that always makes an impression,' he said to himself.

Had you been a shallow frivolous creature like so many women, I could indeed have selfishly pursued this plan without putting you at risk. But that entrancing intensity of feeling, which is at once your charm and your cross, has blinded you—adorable angel that you are—to the falsity of our future position. I, too, had given it no thought at first, and was relaxing in the shade of our ideal of happiness as though beneath a poisonous manchineel tree,* without foreseeing the consequences.

'Perhaps she'll think I'm backing out because I'm stingy. Oh, well, who cares! Too bad, I must get this finished!'

The world is cruel, Emma. Wherever we had gone, it would have hounded us. You'd have had to endure prying questions, calumny, contempt, perhaps even insults. You, insulted! Oh! . . . When what I would wish is to seat you upon a throne! I shall carry the thought of you away with me like a talisman. Exile is to be my punishment for all the harm I have done you. I'm leaving. Where am I going? Who knows, I'm half out of my mind. Farewell! Be good, always. Cherish the memory of the wretched man who led you astray. Teach your child my name, so that she may repeat it in her prayers.

The two candles were flickering. Rodolphe stood up to close the window, and, when he had sat down again: 'That's all, I think. Oh, yes, and this, just in case she "pesters me"':

I shall be far away when you read these sad lines, for I decided to depart immediately, to avoid the temptation of seeing you once more. I must be resolute! I shall return, and some day, perhaps, we may reminisce quite calmly about our love of long ago. Adieu!

He added a final 'adieu', separated into two words: 'A Dieu!' which he thought in excellent taste.

'Now how to sign it?' he wondered. 'Your most devoted? . . . No. Your friend? . . . Yes, that's it.'

'Your friend.'

He reread his letter. He decided it sounded fine.

'Poor little woman!' he thought tenderly. 'She'll think I've a heart of stone; a few tears on it would have been just the thing; but I'm no good at crying, I can't help it.' So Rodolphe filled a glass with water, dipped his finger in it and, holding it over the page, let fall a large drop, which made a pale blot on the ink; then he searched about for a seal for the letter, and came across the signet ring with the words *Amor nel Cor*.

'That's hardly appropriate . . . Oh, who cares!'

Whereupon he smoked three pipes, and took himself off to bed.

Next morning, when he was up (at about two, for he slept late) Rodolphe had a basket of apricots picked. He put the letter at the bottom, under some vine leaves, and instructed Girard, his plough-boy, to carry it carefully to Madame Bovary. This was how he always communicated with her, sending her game or fruit, depending on the season.

'If she asks about me,' he said, 'tell her I've left on a trip. You must give the basket to her personally—put it into her very own hands. Off you go, and be careful!'

Girard put on his new smock, tied his kerchief round the apricots, and, plodding along in his great iron-tipped clogs, calmly set off on the path to Yonville.

When he reached her house, Madame Bovary was helping Félicité sort a stack of linen on the kitchen table.

'Here,' said the lad, 'this is for you, from my master.'

She was filled with foreboding and, while searching for some coins in her pocket, gazed at the farm lad with panic-stricken eyes, while he stared at her in bewilderment, unable to understand why such a gift should upset anyone so much. Finally, he left. Félicité was still in the kitchen. Emma could bear it no longer; she rushed into the parlour as if intending to put the apricots there, tipped the basket up, tore away the leaves, found the letter and opened it; then, as though fleeing from some raging fire, she raced, terrified, up the stairs to her room.

Charles was there, she realized; he spoke to her but she, hearing nothing, dashed further on up the stairs, out of breath, desperate, reeling, still clutching that horrible piece of paper, which rattled in her hand like a sheet of tin. On the second landing, she stopped outside the attic door, which was shut.

Then she attempted to calm herself; she remembered the letter; she must finish it, but she did not dare. In any case, where? How? She would be seen.

'Oh, no, here, I'll be all right here,' she thought.

Emma pushed the door open and went in.

Suffocatingly hot air pulsated directly down from the slate roof, pressing on her temples and stifling her; she dragged herself over to the shuttered dormer window and slid back the bolt; the room was suddenly filled with dazzling light.

Opposite, above the rooftops, the open country stretched on and on, as far as the eye could see. Down below, beneath her, the village square lay empty; the stones of the pavement glittered, the weather-vanes on the houses stood motionless; at the street corner, a kind of buzzing sound, rising now and then to a screech, came from a lower storey. It was Binet at his lathe.

Leaning on the window frame, she reread the letter, occasionally giving vent to an angry, derisive laugh. But the more she concentrated on it, the more confused her ideas became. She could see him, she could hear him, she was holding him in her arms; and her heart began to thump, pounding her chest with great hammer-blows, faster and faster, in an irregular rhythm. She gazed all round her, longing for the earth to open. Why not end it all? What was stopping her? She could do whatever she liked. She moved forward, staring at the pavingstones and telling herself:

'Go on! Go on!'

The ray of bright light reflected from directly below was pulling the weight of her body down into the abyss. The ground of the square seemed to be swaying and tilting, climbing up the sides of the houses, and the attic floor was sloping down at one end, like a pitching ship. She stood on the very edge, almost hanging there, surrounded by a vast space. The blue of the sky was invading her, the air around her was flowing through her empty skull, she had only to give way, to let herself be gathered up; and the buzzing of the lathe kept on and on, like an angry voice summoning her.

'Emma! Emma!' cried Charles.

She stopped.

'Where are you? Come down!'

The thought that she had so closely escaped death made her almost pass out from terror; she shut her eyes; then, feeling a hand on her sleeve, she shuddered: it was Félicité.

'Monsieur is waiting for you, Madame; the soup's on the table.'

She had to go down! Had to sit through the meal!

She tried to eat. The food choked her. So she unfolded her napkin as if to examine the places where it had been darned, and she tried to concentrate on this project, to count the threads in the fabric. Suddenly, she remembered the letter. Had she lost it? Where might it be? But so exhausted was she in her mind that she could think of no excuse for leaving the table. Besides, she was afraid to: she was afraid of Charles, he knew everything, surely he must! And strangely enough he actually declared:

'Apparently we won't be seeing Monsieur Rodolphe for some time.'

She gave a start: 'Who told you that?'

'Who told me?' he repeated, somewhat taken aback by her brusqueness, 'It was Girard, I met him just now outside the Café Français. He's left on a trip, or he's leaving today.'

She gave a sob.

'What's so surprising about that? He goes off like this from time to time to enjoy himself, and, goodness me, why not! When you've plenty of money and you're unmarried! . . . Anyway, our friend certainly knows how to have a good time! He's quite a lad, Monsieur Langlois was telling me . . .'

He broke off, discreetly, as the maid came in.

Félicité replaced in the basket the apricots that lay scattered over the sideboard; Charles, not noticing his wife's scarlet face, had the fruit brought over, took an apricot, and bit into it.

'It's perfect!' he said. 'Here, try one.'

He offered her the basket, but she pushed it gently aside.

'Do smell them; what an aroma!' He kept waving the basket back and forth under her nose.

'I can't breathe!' she cried, jumping up.

But then, with a determined effort, she controlled herself, saying:

'It's nothing! Nothing! Just nerves! Sit down, eat your fruit.'

She was afraid she might be questioned, fussed over, never left alone.

Obediently, Charles had sat down again, and kept spitting the apricot pits into his hand, then putting them on his plate.

Suddenly, a blue tilbury crossed the square at a rapid trot. Emma gave a cry, and fell onto her back, in a dead faint,* on the floor.

And indeed Rodolphe, after careful thought, had decided to leave for Rouen. There being no road between La Huchette and Buchy other than the one via Yonville, he had been obliged to cross through the village, and Emma had recognized him by the glow of the carriage lanterns that flashed through the gloaming like a streak of lightning.

The pharmacist, hearing the commotion at the Bovarys', rushed to the house. The table, with all its plates, had been knocked over; the sauce, the meat, the knives, the salt, the oil and vinegar, lay scattered round the room; Charles kept shouting for help; Berthe was crying from fright, while Félicité, with trembling hands, was unlacing Madame, whose entire body shook convulsively.

'I'll run and get some aromatic vinegar from my laboratory,' suggested the apothecary.

Then, when Emma, breathing the fumes, opened her eyes: 'I knew it; this stuff would revive a corpse.'

'Speak to us! Speak to us!' Charles kept saying. 'Come on! It's me, it's your Charles, who loves you! D'you recognize me? Look, here's your little girl: give her a kiss!'

The child reached out to put her arms round her mother's neck. But, turning her head away, Emma gasped:

'No . . . no . . . nobody!'

She fainted again. They carried her to her bed.

She lay stretched out on it, mouth open, eyes closed, hands flat at her sides, as motionless and white as a wax statue. Two streams of tears coursed slowly from her eyes onto the pillow. Charles stood at the foot of the bed; beside him, the pharmacist kept thoughtfully silent, as befits the solemn moments of this life.

'Don't worry,' he said, nudging his elbow; 'I think the paroxysm has passed.'

'Yes, she's resting a little now!' Charles replied, watching her sleep. 'Poor woman! Poor woman! It's the old trouble again!'

So then Homais enquired into the circumstances of the attack, and Charles told him that it had come upon her suddenly, while she was eating apricots.

'Extraordinary! . . .' remarked the pharmacist. 'But it's perfectly possible that the apricots could have triggered the syncope! Some natures are extremely sensitive to certain odours. Indeed that would make a fascinating subject of study, both in its pathological and its physiological implications. Priests are well aware of its importance, for they've always included aromatic substances in their ceremonial. They employ them to deaden the understanding and induce a state of ecstasy, which is easy to do in those of the fair sex, who are so much more highly strung than other people. Cases have been documented of females fainting at the smell of burnt horn, of fresh bread . . .'

'Be careful not to wake her! . . .' said Bovary softly.

'And it's not only humans who are subject to these anomalies,' continued the apothecary; 'animals are as well. You are surely not unacquainted with the highly aphrodisiac effect of the *Nepeta cataria*, commonly known as catnip, on the feline species; or again— to mention an example whose authenticity I can personally vouch for—Bridoux (a former schoolmate of mine, now established in the Rue Malpalu) owns a dog that has convulsions the minute it's shown a snuff-box. He often demonstrates this to his friends, out at his summer place in Bois Guillaume. Who would ever have thought that a simple sternutator* could play such havoc with the constitution of a quadruped? It's quite remarkable, wouldn't you say?'

'Yes,' said Charles, who was not listening.

'Here we find further proof,' said the pharmacist, smiling with an air of benign complacency, 'of the innumerable irregularities of the nervous system. As far as Madame is concerned, she had always impressed me, I tell you frankly, as possessing a highly sensitive nervous system. Consequently, my dear Bovary, I would certainly not recommend any of those so-called remedies that, under the guise of attacking the symptoms, actually attack the constitution. No—no unnecessary medication! A careful diet, nothing else! Sedatives, lenitives, dulcifiers. And then, don't you agree that it might be wise to stimulate the imagination?'

'What with? How?' asked Bovary.

'Ah! That is the problem. Yes, indeed, that is precisely the problem. And, to quote something I saw in the paper recently, "*That is the question*"'* he concluded in English.

But Emma, waking up, exclaimed:

'Where's the letter? The letter!'

They thought she must be delirious, which, about midnight, she in fact became: brain fever had set in.

For forty-three days Charles never left her bedside. He abandoned all his patients; he no longer went to bed; he was constantly taking her pulse, applying mustard poultices, and cold-water compresses. He sent Justin to Neufchâtel for ice; the ice melted on the way; he sent him back again. He called in Monsieur Canivet for consultation and summoned from Rouen Doctor Larivière, his former teacher; he was in despair. What frightened him most was Emma's state of utter prostration; for she never spoke, seemed not to hear anything, and even seemed not to be in pain—as though her body and her soul had together sought repose after all the turmoil they had known.

Towards the middle of October, she could sit up in bed, supported by pillows. Charles wept when he saw her eat her first slice of bread and jam. Her strength was returning; she was able to get up for a few hours in the afternoon and, one day when she was feeling better, he tried taking her out, leaning on his arm, for a walk in the garden. Dead leaves covered the gravel of the paths; she took one step at a time, trailing her slippers and leaning against Charles's shoulder, a fixed smile on her face.

They went like this down to the bottom of the garden, near the terrace. She drew herself up slowly, and shielded her eyes with her hand, to look: she gazed far, far away, into the distance, but there was nothing on the horizon except some big grass-fires, smoking on the hills.

'You'll tire yourself, sweetheart,' said Bovary. And, gently urging her into the arbour:

'Sit down on this bench; you'll be all right here.'

'No, no, not there, not there!' she cried in a faltering voice.

She was overcome by dizziness, and that evening her illness returned, although this time its nature seemed less clearly defined, with more complex symptoms. Now it was her heart that hurt, now her chest, now her head, now her limbs; she began vomiting, which made Charles think he recognized the first symptoms of cancer.

And, on top of all that, the poor man had money worries!

CHAPTER XIV

In the first place, he could not see how to reimburse Monsieur Homais for all the medicines his pharmacy had provided; although, as a doctor, he was not required to pay for them, he found such an obligation rather demeaning. Then the household expenses, now that the cook was in charge, were rising alarmingly; bills were pouring in, the tradesmen were grumbling; Monsieur Lheureux, in particular, kept harassing him. In fact, at the height of Emma's illness, Lheureux, taking advantage of the crisis to pad his bill, had lost no time in delivering the cloak, the travelling bag, two trunks instead of one, and several other items as well. In vain did Charles tell him that he didn't need them, the merchant arrogantly retorted that all these things had been ordered, and he wasn't about to take them back; in any case, doing so might upset Madame in her convalescence; Monsieur should think it over carefully; in a word, he was determined to take him to court rather than relinquish his rights, or repossess his goods. A few days later, Charles gave instructions that everything be returned; Félicité forgot; he had other things on his mind and thought no more about it; Monsieur Lheureux renewed his demands, and, alternately menacing and whining, contrived to get Bovary to sign his name to a six-month promissory note. Hardly had he signed it than Charles was struck by a daring idea: to borrow a thousand francs from Monsieur Lheureux. He therefore enquired, in considerable embarrassment, whether this could somehow be arranged, adding that he needed the loan for one year, at whatever rate Lheureux required. Lheureux raced back to his shop, returned with the money and dictated another promissory note, in which Bovary undertook to pay to his order, on 1 September of the following year, the sum of 1,070 francs; which, added to the 180 already stipulated, came to 1,250. In this way, lending at a rate of 6 per cent, plus his quarter commission and at least 33 per cent profit on the goods, he would make 130 francs* in twelve months; and he hoped that that wouldn't be the end of the matter, that it would be impossible to discharge the debt, that the notes would be renewed and that his skinny little capital, nourished under the doctor's care like a patient in a sanatorium, would return to him one day considerably fattened up, stout enough to split the seams of the bag.

Indeed, all his affairs were doing nicely. He had secured the contract for supplying cider to the hospital in Neufchâtel; Monsieur Guillaumin had promised him some shares in the peatbogs at Grumesnil, and he was hoping to set up a new coach service between Arcueil and Rouen, which would quickly and surely spell the end of that old boneshaker at the Lion d'Or, and which, being faster, cheaper, and capable of transporting larger loads, would give him control over all the trade in Yonville.

Charles often wondered how, by next year, he would ever be able to repay so large a sum; he racked his brains, imagining various expedients, such as asking his father for help, or selling something. But his father would turn a deaf ear, and he himself owned nothing worth selling. And he would come up against so many daunting obstacles that he quickly banished such unpleasant reflections from his consciousness. He reproached himself for allowing them to distract him from Emma—as if all his thoughts belonged to her, and he was in a sense cheating her if he failed to think about her all the time.

It was a hard winter. Madame's convalescence was a long one. On fine days they pushed her in her chair up to the window, the window that looked over the square, for she disliked the garden now, and the shutters on that side were kept permanently closed. She wanted her horse sold; things that she had enjoyed in the past she now found disagreeable. She seemed to take no interest in anything beyond her own health. She spent her days in bed, eating her light meals there, ringing for her maid to enquire about her herb tea, or just to chat. During this time, the snow on the market roof filled her bedroom with a white, still glare; then, later in the winter, it rained. And every day Emma awaited, with a kind of anxiety, the unvarying recurrence of the same trivial events, little though they mattered to her. The most important of these was the arrival, every evening, of the Hirondelle. The innkeeper would give a shout and other voices would reply, while Hippolyte's lantern, as he reached for the boxes and packages on the roof, shone like a star in the darkness. At midday, Charles came in; then he went out; then she drank a cup of broth; then, about five, at the end of the day, the schoolchildren, trailing home in their wooden clogs, would, one after the other, rap the hooks on the window shutters with their rulers as they went past along the pavement.

This was the time of day when Monsieur Bournisien usually paid a call. He would enquire after her health, pass on the latest news, and exhort her to piety in a coaxing little chat that was not without charm. The mere sight of his cassock comforted her.

One day, at the height of her illness, when she believed she was dying, she had asked for communion; and while her room was being prepared for the sacrament, while her dresser with all its medicine bottles was being transformed into an altar and Félicité was strewing the floor with dahlia blossoms, Emma felt something powerful pass over her that relieved her of all her suffering, of all perception, of all feeling. Her body, freed from its burdens, had become weightless, a new life was beginning; she felt that her being, rising up towards God, would dissolve into his love the way burning incense dissolves into vapour. The sheets of her bed were sprinkled with holy water; the priest took the white host from the holy ciborium, and, almost fainting with celestial bliss, she thrust forward her lips to receive the body of her Saviour. The curtains of her bed, like clouds, billowed gently out around her, and the rays from the two tapers burning on the dresser looked to her like dazzling haloes. She let her head fall back, fancying that she could hear, coming through the ether, the music of seraphic harps, and that she could see, in a sky of azure, on a throne of gold, surrounded by saints holding branches of green palm, God the Father in all his majesty, gesturing to angels with wings of flame to descend to earth and carry her in their arms up to heaven.

This glorious vision remained in her memory as the most beautiful of all possible dreams, so that she kept striving, now, to recapture the sensation, which did still linger on, but in a form that was less predominant, though fully as piercingly sweet. Her soul, worn out by pride, was finally finding repose in Christian humility; and, luxuriating in her own frailty, Emma watched the annihilation of her own will, which would leave the path wide open to the irresistible forces of grace. There existed, therefore, greater joys beyond mere happiness, a different love transcending all others, a love without interruption or end, which would grow greater throughout eternity! Among the illusions bred by her hopes she glimpsed a realm of purity floating high above the earth, merging with heaven: that was where she yearned to be. She aspired to become a saint. She bought rosaries, she wore amulets; she longed to have a reliquary, studded with emeralds, placed at the head of her bed, so that she could kiss it every night.

The curé marvelled at these predilections, although he did feel that Emma's religion might, by its very fervour, develop into something that verged on heresy and even extravagance. But, being somewhat inexperienced in these matters, as soon as they went beyond a certain point, he wrote to Monsieur Boulard, the archbishop's bookseller, asking him to send 'something first-rate suitable for a very clever member of the fair sex'. Giving the matter as little thought as if he were sending off baubles to Negroes, the bookseller indiscriminately bundled together every work of piety then current—small manuals composed of questions and answers, pamphlets in the condescending style popularized by Monsieur de Maistre* and sentimental, sugary-sweet novelettes churned out by seminary poetasters or repentant blue-stockings.* There were such titles as: *Weigh It Well*; *The Man of the World at the Feet of Mary*, by Monsieur de***, Knight of***, Honorand of***; *The Errors of Voltaire, Designed for the Edification of Youth*; etc.

Madame Bovary's mind was not yet sufficiently clear for serious application of any kind; besides, she plunged into this reading far too impetuously. The regulations governing the ritual irritated her; the arrogance of the polemical tracts annoyed her with their relentless attacks on people she had never heard of; and the secular stories embellished by religion seemed to her to be written in such complete ignorance of the world that, by imperceptible degrees, they discouraged her from believing the very truths she longed to see proven. She persisted nevertheless; and, when the book fell from her hands, she believed herself possessed by the purest Catholic melancholy ever experienced by an ethereal soul.

As for the memory of Rodolphe, she had buried it deep down in her heart; there it remained, more solemn and motionless than a royal mummy in a subterranean vault. A fragrance emanated from this great, embalmed love, penetrating everywhere, scenting with tenderness the atmosphere of undefiled purity in which she longed to live. When she knelt at her Gothic prie-dieu, she would address her Lord with the same caressing words that, in the rapturous transports of adultery, she had murmured to her lover. She did this to summon up her faith; but heaven never touched her soul with bliss, and she would rise to her feet, her limbs weary, feeling that somehow she was the victim of an immense hoax. Her quest would thereby, she believed, be all the more to her credit, and, proud in her piety, Emma compared herself to those great ladies of past ages over whose glory she had daydreamed as she gazed at a portrait of La Vallière,* and who, so majestically trailing their long bejewelled trains, retired into seclusion to shed at the feet of Christ the tears that life's cruel barbs wrung from their hearts.

Next she became excessively charitable. She sewed garments for the poor, she sent firewood to women in childbirth; and Charles, on returning home one day, found three tramps sitting at the kitchen table eating soup. She arranged for her little girl, whom Charles, during her illness, had sent away to the wet-nurse, to be brought home. She tried to teach her to read; despite all Berthe's tears, Emma, now, never lost her temper. She had adopted a conscious attitude of resignation, of indulgence towards all. She constantly used high-flown language. She would say to her child:

'Is your stomach-ache better, my angel?'

Madame Bovary senior found nothing to criticize, except perhaps her passion for knitting camisoles for orphans instead of mending her dusters. But the good woman, tormented by discord in her own home, enjoyed living in this peaceful household, and even stayed until after Easter, in order to avoid the sarcastic tongue of Charles's father, who never failed, on Good Friday, to order a dish of sausages for dinner.

Besides the company of her mother-in-law, who steadied her somewhat by her rectitude of mind and gravity of manner, Emma received other visitors almost every day. These were Madame Langlois, Madame Caron, Madame Dubreuil, Madame Tuvache, and, regularly from two to five, the excellent Madame Homais. *She* had never believed a word of any of the gossip circulating about her neighbour. The Homais children also came to visit her, escorted by Justin. He would accompany them upstairs to her room, and remain standing in the doorway, never stirring, never speaking. Often, indeed, Madame Bovary, forgetting he was there, would sit down at her dressing table to complete her toilette. She began by removing her comb, and giving her head a brisk shake; the first time he saw this head of hair with its black ringlets falling freely down to her knees, he felt, poor lad, as if he had suddenly been initiated into something new and extraordinary whose splendour frightened him.

In all likelihood Emma never noticed his silent devotion, nor his timidity. She never suspected that love, which had vanished from her life, was pulsating there close beside her, beneath that coarse cloth shirt, in that adolescent heart that was awakening to the emanations of her beauty. Moreover she now approached everything with such utter detachment, with words so amiable yet a gaze so haughty, with manners so unpredictable, that you could no longer distinguish egotism from charity, depravity from virtue. One evening, for example, she flew into a temper with the maid, who wanted to go out and was mumbling some pretext or other, then quite suddenly:

'So you love him?' she said.

And, without waiting for the blushing Félicité to reply, she added rather sadly:

'Oh, off you go! Enjoy yourself!'

In early spring she had the garden completely redone from end to end, despite Bovary's objections; he was, however, pleased to see her at long last taking an interest in something. As her health improved, her decisiveness returned. First she managed to get rid of Mère Rollet, the wet-nurse, who had, during Emma's convalescence, taken to dropping in to the kitchen far too often, bringing with her the two infants she was nursing, as well as her little boarder, who ate like a horse. Then she distanced herself from the Homais family and successively discouraged all her other visitors; she even began to attend church less regularly, much to the delight of the apothecary, who remarked amicably:

'You were getting rather too cosy with the black coats, weren't you?'

Monsieur Bournisien still continued with his daily visits after catechism. He preferred sitting outside in the open air, 'ensconced in the boscage', as he liked to call the arbour. This was the time of day when Charles came home. They were hot; sweet cider would be brought out to them; they both drank to Madame's complete recovery.

Binet was often there—a little further down, that is, alongside the terrace wall, fishing for crayfish. Bovary would offer him a drink; he was a real expert at uncorking the cider jugs.

'The trick is', Binet would say, gazing smugly about him at his companions and then at the distant landscape, 'to hold the bottle upright on the table and, when the strings have been cut, prise the cork up just a fraction at a time, very, very gently, the way they open seltzer water in restaurants.'

But frequently, during his demonstration, the cider would spurt out, splashing their faces, and then the curé, with a throaty laugh, never failed to trot out his joke:

'Its quality certainly springs to the eye!'

He was really very good-natured, even raising no objection one day when the pharmacist advised Charles to take Emma, for a change, to the theatre in Rouen, to see the famous tenor Lagardy. When Homais, amazed at this restraint, asked for his opinion, the priest declared that he considered music less dangerous to morality than literature.

But the pharmacist leapt to the defence of letters. The theatre, he claimed, helped attack prejudices, and, under the guise of pleasure, inculcated virtue.

'Castigat ridendo mores,* Monsieur Bournisien! Take, for example, the majority of Voltaire's tragedies;* they're very cleverly sprinkled with philosophical reflections, which make them an invaluable resource for instructing the common people in morality and diplomacy.'

'Well,' said Binet, 'I once saw a play called *Le Gamin de Paris*,* where there's this character—an old general—that's absolutely tip-top! He really gets the better of a rich young fellow who's seduced a working girl, and in the end . . .'

'Of course!' went on Homais, 'there's bad literature just as there's bad pharmacy; but to condemn in its totality the most important of the fine arts is in my opinion a dreadful blunder, a barbarous idea, worthy of that infamous age that imprisoned Galileo.'

'I quite agree', rejoined the priest, 'that there are some good writers who produce good works; nevertheless, simply the fact that people of opposite sex are gathered together in a charming audi-torium that's ostentatiously decorated with worldly luxuries—and then there's the heathenish costumes, the greasepaint, the footlights, the effeminate voices—all these things cannot fail in the end to engender a certain degree of free-thinking, and encourage licentious ideas and impure desires. Such, at any rate, is the opinion of the Church Fathers.* After all,' he added, his voice suddenly assuming an exalted tone, as he rolled himself a pinch of snuff, 'if the Church condemned the theatre, it was for good reason; we must submit to her decrees.'

'But why', enquired the pharmacist, 'does she excommunicate actors? In the past, surely, they took part openly in religious ceremonies. Yes, they used to put on kinds of farces right there in the choir; those mysteries, as they were called, often offended against the laws of decency.'

The priest merely groaned by way of comment, as the pharmacist pressed on:

'It's the same with the Bible, there's . . . well . . . quite a few details . . . juicy details, and some bits . . . that are really and truly you-know-what!'

And, seeing Monsieur Bournisien's gesture of annoyance: 'You must surely agree that it's not a book to put into the hands of a young person, and I'd be sorry to see Athalie . . .'

'But it's the Protestants, not us, who advocate reading the Bible!' the priest exclaimed impatiently.

'That's not the point,' said Homais; 'it amazes me that these days, in this enlightened age, anyone should still persist in banning an intellectual diversion that's harmless, morally uplifting, and even, upon occasion, healthy—as I'm sure, Doctor, you'll agree?'

'Yes, I dare say,' the doctor replied noncommittally, perhaps because, though agreeing with Homais, he wished to avoid giving offence, or perhaps because he had no opinion.

The topic seemed to have been exhausted, when the pharmacist saw fit to try a final thrust.

'I've known priests who put on ordinary clothes to go and watch dancing girls showing off their legs!'

'Oh, come on!' said the priest.

'Yes, I have indeed!'

And, dragging out each syllable separately, Homais repeated:

'Yes . . . I . . . have!'

'Well, so they did wrong,' said Bournisien, resigning himself to hearing everything.

'And Lord knows, that's not all they did, either,' exclaimed the apothecary.

'Monsieur!' replied the priest, the look in his eyes fierce enough to intimidate Homais.

'I'm only trying to say', he then added in a less aggressive tone, 'that tolerance is the surest means of drawing souls to religion.'

'Very true! Very true!' the curé conceded, sitting down again.

But he only stayed for a couple of minutes. When he had gone, Monsieur Homais remarked to the doctor:

'Now that was quite a run-in, wasn't it! I had the better of him all the time, didn't I? . . . Anyway, do as I advise and take Madame to the theatre, even if it's simply, dammit, for once in your life, to annoy one of those Holy Joes! If there were anyone to replace me, I'd go with you. Don't delay! Lagardy's only giving one performance; he's booked in England for colossal fees. People say he's quite a Casanova! Rolling in money! Travels with three mistresses, as well as his cook! All these great artists burn the candle at both ends; they have to lead a wild kind of life, to spark their imagination a bit. But they die in the poorhouse, because they didn't have the sense, while they were young, to put something by. Well, enjoy your dinner, see you tomorrow!'

This idea of the theatre rapidly took root in Bovary's mind. He immediately suggested it to his wife, but at first she refused, on the grounds of fatigue, trouble, and expense; quite exceptionally for him, however, Charles did not give way, he was so convinced that this diversion would do her good. He could see no objection to it; his mother had sent them three hundred francs that he no longer expected, their current debts were nothing out of the ordinary, and the due date on the debts to Lheureux was so far away that there was no point in worrying about that. Besides, imagining that Emma was just being tactful, Charles kept insisting so that eventually, weary of being pressed, she agreed to go. And at eight o'clock the next morning they set off in the Hirondelle.

The apothecary, who had nothing to keep him in Yonville, but who was convinced he could never stir from his pharmacy, sighed as he saw them off.

'Have a good journey, you lucky people!' he told them.

Then, turning to Emma, who was wearing a blue silk dress with four flounces:

'You look as pretty as a picture! You'll be "the belle of the ball", in Rouen.'

The coach set them down at the Hôtel de la Croix Rouge, in the Place Beauvoisine. It was one of those inns you find on the outskirts of every provincial city, with big stables and tiny bedrooms, where chickens scratch for grain in the middle of the courtyard, under the mud-spattered gigs of the travelling salesmen—good old-style hostelries whose worm-eaten wooden balconies creak in the wind on winter nights, perpetually full of people, hubbub, and food, their blackened tables sticky with spilt coffee-and-brandy, their thick window panes yellowed by flies, their damp napkins stained by red wine; hostelries that still somehow declare their country origin, like farmhands dressed in their best town clothes, with a café giving onto the street in front, and a vegetable garden facing onto fields at the back. Charles immediately set off on his errands. He confused the orchestra stalls with the gallery, the pit with the boxes, asked for explanations that he misunderstood, was referred by the box-office assistant to the general manager, came back to the inn, returned to the box office, and, in this manner, crossed and recrossed the whole town from the theatre to the boulevard several times.

Madame bought herself a hat, a pair of gloves, and a bouquet. Monsieur was very nervous lest they miss the curtain and, without allowing themselves time even for a bowl of soup, they arrived at the entrance to the theatre* before the doors had been opened.

CHAPTER XV

The crowd was neatly lined up between railings, along the wall on either side of the theatre entrance. At the adjoining street corners, huge posters announced in baroque lettering: '*Lucie de Lammermoor** . . . Lagardy . . . Opéra etc.' It was a fine evening; everyone was feeling the heat; ringlets were running with sweat and handkerchiefs mopping flushed brows; now and again a tepid breeze, blowing off the river, languidly stirred the edges of the canvas awning that hung outside a tavern door. But just a little further away, refreshing gusts of chilly air smelling of tallow, leather, and oil could be felt. This was coming from the Rue des Charettes, a street filled with vast murky warehouses into which casks were rolled for storage.

Afraid of looking ridiculous, Emma decided they would stroll round the port before going into the theatre, and Bovary prudently kept hold of the tickets inside his trouser pocket, pressing his hand against his stomach.

Once they were inside the foyer her heart began to pound. She gave an involuntary little smile of self-satisfaction as she watched the crowd rushing down the corridor to the right, whereas she was climbing the staircase to the dress circle. She took a childish pleasure in pushing the big padded doors open with her finger; she filled her lungs with the dusty smell of the corridors and, when she was seated in her box, she drew herself up with the haughty ease of a duchess.

The theatre was filling up, people began taking opera glasses out of cases, and the regular subscribers, recognizing one another from afar, were exchanging bows. They had come to restore themselves in the arms of the Muses from the pressures of commerce, but, never forgetting their own 'business affairs', they talked still of cotton, liquor, or indigo. There were old men with inscrutable, tranquil faces; their grey-white hair and grey-white skin gave them the look of silver medals tarnished by lead fumes. The young bucks were strutting about in the stalls, displaying, in the openings of their waistcoats, cravats of rose-pink or apple-green; and Madame Bovary gazed admiringly at them from above as they rested their palms, tightly gloved in yellow, on the golden knobs of their canes.

Meanwhile the orchestra candles had been lit; the chandelier came down from the ceiling, its sparkling crystals filling the hall with sudden brightness; then the musicians entered one behind the other, producing, at first, an endless cacophony of growling double basses, screeching violins, trumpeting horns, and whining flutes and flageolets. Then came three sharp raps on the stage floor; there was a rolling of the drums and a striking of chords from the brass, and the curtain rose on a country scene.

It was a clearing in a wood, with, on the left, a spring, shaded by an oak. A group of peasants and nobles, their tartans on their shoulders, were singing a hunting song in chorus; next entered a captain who, raising both arms to heaven, called upon the Spirit of Evil; another captain then joined him, they left together and the hunters took up their song again.

She found herself back in the familiar books of her youth,* deep in Walter Scott. She fancied she could hear, through the mist, the sound of bagpipes echoing across the heather. Her recollections of the novel helped her to grasp the story, so that she followed the libretto line by line, while fleeting memories kept straying into her mind, only to vanish instantly under the impetus of the music. She let herself be lulled by the melodies, feeling her whole being vibrate, as if the bows of the violins were playing on her own taut nerves. Her avid gaze took in every detail of the costumes, the set, the characters, the painted trees that quivered when anyone walked past, the velvet caps, the cloaks, the swords, all that imagined reality which the music, like the atmosphere of some other world, quickened into life. But now a young woman was approaching, and tossing a purse to a squire dressed in green. She was left alone on the stage, and a flute was heard, sounding like a murmuring spring or a warbling bird. Lucie gravely began her cavatina in G major; she lamented over her love, she longed for wings. Emma, also, yearned to escape from life, to fly off in an embrace. Suddenly, Edgar Lagardy appeared.*

His skin had that magnificent pallor which bestows something of the majesty of marble upon the passionate races of the south. His powerful body was clad in a brown doublet; a small chased dagger swung against his left thigh, and he cast languorous glances about him, displaying gleaming white teeth. Rumour had it that a Polish princess, hearing him sing one evening on a beach at Biarritz, where he was repairing boats, had fallen in love with him. She had ruined herself for his sake. He had abandoned her for other women, and this notoriety as a lover had done no disservice to his reputation as an artist. The artful histrion even made sure that a few poetic words describing his personal fascination and his sensitivity of soul were always slipped into the playbills. A beautiful voice, imperturbable poise, more personality than intelligence, and more grandiloquence than lyricism, all these combined to create this glorious specimen of the charlatan, with its touches of the hairdresser and the toreador.

He had the audience in raptures from his very first scene. He kept clasping Lucie in his arms, then walking away, only to return, seemingly in despair; he would storm with fury then break into mournful cadences of infinite sweetness, the notes, as they throbbed from his bare throat, fraught with sobs and kisses. Emma's nails clawed at the plush lining of their box, as she leaned over to watch him. She was filling her heart with those melodious lamentations that lingered on to the accompaniment of the double basses, like cries of the drowning while a tempest rages. She recognized that same rapture, that same anguish that had brought her so close to death. The voice of the soprano seemed simply an echo of Emma's own heart, and the illusion that held her spellbound a part of Emma's very own life. But no one in the wide world had loved *her* like this! *He* had not wept, as Edgar was weeping, that last evening in the moonlight, as they were saying to one another: 'till tomorrow, till tomorrow!' The house was reverberating with shouts of 'bravo'; the entire stretto was repeated; the lovers spoke of the flowers on their graves, of vows and exile, of fate and hope, and when their voices joined in their final farewell, Emma gave a shrill cry which merged with the vibrations of the concluding chords.

'But why,' asked Bovary, 'does that lord keep on tormenting her like that?'

'No, no,' she replied; 'he's her lover.'

'But he's been swearing vengeance on her family, whereas the other one, the one who was here a minute ago, said: "I love Lucie and believe she loves me." Besides, he went off arm in arm with her father. That's her father, isn't it, the ugly little fellow with a cock-feather in his cap?'

In spite of Emma's explanations, when they reached the recitative in which Gilbert describes his appalling machinations to his master, Ashton, Charles, on seeing the false engagement ring that was intended to deceive Lucie, believed it to be a love token sent by Edgar. He admitted, however, that he couldn't keep the story straight, because of the music, which really spoiled the words.

'What does it matter?' said Emma. 'Oh, do be quiet!'

'But I really like to understand what's going on,' he replied, leaning over her shoulder; 'you know I do.'

'Be quiet! Oh please be quiet!' cried Emma impatiently.

Lucie, half supported by her women, was advancing across the stage, a wreath of orange blossom in her hair, her face paler than the white satin of her dress. Emma was remembering her own wedding day; in memory she saw herself over there, walking through the wheat fields on the narrow path that led to the church. So why had she not, like Lucie, resisted and pleaded? But no, quite the contrary, she had been full of joy, unaware of the abyss towards which she was rushing . . . Ah! If only, in the full bloom of her loveliness, before the defilement of marriage and the disillusion of adultery, she had been able to root her life in the firmness of some noble heart, then virtue, tenderness, sensual pleasure, and wifely duty would all have fused into one, and never would she have fallen from so lofty a pinnacle of happiness. But that happiness must surely be a fraud, devised for the despair of all desire. Now she knew how paltry were those passions that art portrays with such hyperbole. So, forcing her thoughts onto a different path, she tried to see this image of her own suffering merely as an artistic fantasy intended to delight the eye, and she was even smiling to herself in scornful pity when there emerged, from the velvet curtains at the back of the stage, a man in a black cloak.

With a gesture he flung aside his big Spanish hat, and orchestra and singers immediately began the sextet. Edgar's pure tenor, flashing with fury, dominated all the other voices; Ashton, in his deep bass, kept menacing Edgar with mortal threats; Lucie repeated her shrill lament; Arthur sang his asides in the middle register and the minister's bass-baritone resonated like an organ, with the voices of the women echoing him in an enchanting chorus. They stood side by side across the stage, gesticulating, expressions of rage, vengeance, jealousy, terror, pity, and amazement issuing simultaneously from their half-open mouths. The outraged lover was brandishing his naked sword; his lace collar rose with a jerk each time he took a breath, and his silver-gilt spurs jangled on the boards as he strode up and down in his soft flaring boots. His love, Emma felt, must be infinite, if he could pour it forth so lavishly over the audience. Every denigrating impulse evaporated as the poetic power of the role gripped her and, drawn to the real man by the mirage of the fictional character, she tried to imagine his life, that dazzling, extraordinary, sumptuous life, a life she too might have lived had fate so decreed. They might have met, they might have loved one another! With him she would have travelled from capital to capital through all the kingdoms of Europe, sharing in his tribulations and in his triumphs, gathering up the flowers cast at his feet, embroidering his costumes with her own hand; then, each evening, behind the gilded screen of her box, she would have greedily drunk in the effusions of that soul that sang for her alone; from the stage, as he played his part, he would have gazed up at her! A mad idea took hold of her: he was looking at her, she knew he was! She longed to fly into his arms and take shelter in his strength, as if he were the very embodiment of love, and say to him, cry out to him: 'Take me away, carry me off! I am yours, yours! All my love and all my dreams are yours!'

The curtain fell.

The smell of the gaslights mingled with stale breath; the

movement of air from the ladies' fans made the atmosphere even more stifling. Emma tried to go outside, but the corridor was crammed with people and she fell back into her seat, overcome by palpitations. Charles, afraid she might faint, hurried to the bar to fetch her a glass of barley-water.

He had great difficulty returning to his place, for he was holding the glass with both hands and people kept jogging his elbows; indeed he actually spilt most of its contents down the shoulders of a Rouen lady in a short-sleeved gown, who, feeling the cold liquid trickle down her spine, began to screech like a peacock, as if she were being murdered. Her husband, a mill owner, flew into a rage at Charles's clumsiness, and while with her handkerchief she mopped the stains on her handsome dress of cherry-red taffeta, he kept muttering in surly tones about compensation, cost, and reimbursement. At last, gasping for breath, Charles reached his wife:

'My goodness, I thought I'd never get back here again! There's such a crowd! Such a crowd!'

Then he added:

'Guess who I ran into* up there? Monsieur Léon!'

'Léon?'

'Indeed yes. He's coming over to say hallo.'

And hardly had Charles finished telling her this, when the former Yonville clerk entered the box.

He held out his hand with the easy assurance of a gentleman, and Madame Bovary automatically offered him hers, yielding no doubt to the force of a stronger will. She had not felt its power since that spring evening when rain was falling on the early greenery, and they had said goodbye, standing at the window. But, quickly reminding herself of the demands of convention, she made an effort to shake off the languor of these memories, and began stammering a few hasty remarks.

'Good evening! . . . Well, what a surprise; it's really you!'

'Quiet!' cried a voice from the pit, for the third act was beginning.

'So—you're in Rouen now?'

'Yes.'

'Since when?'

'Out! Out! Out!'

People were turning round to look at them; they fell silent.

But, from that moment on, she listened no more; and the chorus of the wedding guests, the scene between Ashton and his servant, the great duet in D major, to her it all seemed to be happening far away, as if the instruments had become less sonorous and the characters more distant; she remembered the card games at the pharmacist's and the walk to the wet-nurse's, the reading in the arbour, the tête-à-têtes by the fireside, all the details of that pathetic little love affair which had been so tranquil and so enduring, so discreet and so tender, and which she had nevertheless forgotten. So why was he here again? What conjunction of chance events was bringing him back into her life? He was standing behind her, leaning his shoulder against the partition of the box, and from time to time, as she sensed his warm breath on her hair, she felt herself shiver.

'Are you enjoying this?' he asked, bending over so close to her that the tip of his moustache brushed against her cheek.

She replied nonchalantly:

'Oh dear me, no! Not really.'

So then he suggested that they leave the theatre and go somewhere for an ice.

'No, not just yet! Let's stay,' said Bovary. 'Her hair's all coming down,* I think it's going to turn tragic.'

But Emma did not find the mad scene interesting, and she thought the heroine's acting overdone.

'Her shrieks are too loud,' she said, turning to Charles, who was listening to the opera.

'Well . . . yes . . . perhaps a little,' he answered, torn between his own genuine enjoyment, and his respect for his wife's opinion.

'It's awfully hot,' sighed Léon.

'It's unbearable! You're quite right.'

'Is it too much for you?' asked Bovary.

'Yes, I can't breathe; let's go.'

Monsieur Léon carefully draped her long lace shawl round her shoulders, and the three of them went down to the port where they sat in the open air outside a café. They talked first about her illness, although Emma interrupted Charles now and again, for fear, she said, of boring Monsieur Léon; then Léon told them that he had come to Rouen to spend two years with an important law firm, so as to learn the way business was conducted in Normandy, which was different from what went on in Paris. Then he enquired after Berthe, and the Homais family, and old Madame Lefrançois; and since, in the presence of her husband, they had nothing more to say to one another, the conversation soon petered out.

People emerging from the theatre walked past them on the pavement, humming or loudly bellowing 'O bel ange, ma Lucie!'* So then Léon, to show off his expertise, began to talk about music. He had heard Tamburini, Rubini, Persiani, Grisi;* compared to them, Lagardy, for all his brilliant reputation, really didn't count.

'Still,' interrupted Charles, who was consuming his rum sorbet in tiny spoonfuls, 'people say that in the last act he's absolutely wonderful; I'm sorry we left before the end, because I was beginning to enjoy it.'

'In any case,' the clerk went on, 'he'll soon be giving another performance.'

But Charles replied that they were leaving the next morning.

'Unless', he added, turning to his wife, 'you'd like to stay on by yourself, sweetheart?'

And, changing his tactic at this unexpected opportunity to pursue his hopes, the young man began extolling Lagardy's performance in the final scene. It was superb, sublime! So then Charles insisted:

'You can come home on Sunday . . . Come on, make your mind up! You shouldn't hesitate if you feel it would do you even just a bit of good.'

Meanwhile the nearby tables were emptying. A waiter discreetly stationed himself close by; Charles took the hint and produced his purse, but the clerk stopped him with a restraining hand, and even remembered the tip for the waiter, flinging two coins noisily onto the marble.

'I don't like to see you spending your money on us . . .' murmured Bovary.

With a deprecating, friendly shrug, Léon picked up his hat, saying:

'So it's agreed, isn't it, tomorrow at six?'

Charles protested again that he couldn't be away any longer, but there was nothing to stop Emma . . .

'It's just that . . .' she stammered, smiling in an odd way, 'I'm not sure . . .'

'All right! You think it over, and sleep on it; we'll decide in the morning.'

Then he said to Léon, who was walking along beside them: 'Now you're back in our part of the world I hope you'll drop in for dinner now and again?'

The clerk assured him that he'd certainly do so, as he had to visit Yonville in any case, on a legal matter. They separated by the Passage Saint-Herbland,* just as half past eleven was striking from the cathedral.

PART THREE

CHAPTER I

Monsieur Léon, while pursuing his legal studies, had become almost a regular at the dance hall La Chaumière,* where he made quite a hit with the grisettes,* who pronounced him 'very distinguished'. He was a model student; he wore his hair neither too long nor too short, never spent his entire quarter's allowance at the beginning of the month, and kept on good terms with his professors. Excesses he had always avoided, as much from timidity as from fastidiousness.

Often, when reading in his room, or sitting in the evening under the limes of the Luxembourg Gardens, he would let his copy of the Code* slip to the ground and give himself up to the memory of Emma. But, very gradually, this longing had faded, overlaid by different cravings, although it did linger on in spite of these, for Léon had not lost all hope: it was as if the future held out a vague promise for him, like a golden fruit dangling from some fantastic greenery.

Then, on seeing her again after a three-year separation, he felt his passion reawaken. This time, he thought, he really must make up his mind to have her. Besides, his former diffidence had worn thin in the frivolous circles he had frequented, and he now returned to the provinces full of disdain for anyone who had never sauntered along the boulevards shod in patent leather. On meeting an elaborately dressed *Parisienne* in the salon of a celebrated physician with a ribbon in his lapel and his own carriage, the poor clerk would doubtless have trembled like a child; but here, in Rouen, down by the quay, with the wife of this little country doctor, he felt at ease, confident that he would dazzle her. Self-assurance depends upon surroundings: you speak a different language in the salon and the garret, and a rich woman's wealth seems to protect her virtue like a cuirass, as if all her banknotes were stitched into her corset lining.

After saying goodnight to Monsieur and Madame Bovary the previous evening, Léon had followed them, at a distance, down the street, until he saw them enter the Croix Rouge; then he had turned back and spent the rest of the night mulling over his plan.

At about five the next afternoon, therefore, his throat tight with anxiety, his face white, and his heart filled with the blind resolution of the coward, Léon walked into the kitchen at the inn.

'Monsieur's not here,' said a servant.

This struck him as a good omen. He went up.

She did not seem disconcerted by his arrival; on the contrary, she apologized for having forgotten to tell him where they were staying.

'Oh! I guessed,' said Léon.

'How?'

He claimed that a kind of instinct had led him to her, purely by chance. She began to smile, so, to remedy his blunder, he quickly told her that he had spent his morning searching for her in one hotel after another, throughout the city.

'You've decided to stay, then?' he went on.

'Yes,' she replied, 'and I was wrong. One should not indulge in such impossible pleasures when one has a thousand responsibilities . . .'

'Oh, yes, I can imagine . . .'

'No, you can't, because you're not a woman.'

But men also had their troubles, and the conversation took a philosophical turn. Emma dwelt at length on the worthlessness of earthly attachments and the eternal isolation in which the human heart is entombed.

Either out of a wish to impress her, or because, inspired by Emma's example, he felt a naive impulse to echo her melancholy, the young man declared himself to have been monumentally bored during the entire period of his studies. Legal procedures exasperated him, he felt drawn to other professions, and his mother nagged him in every letter she wrote. For, carried away by these progressive revelations, they both, as they continued to talk, grew more explicit about why they were unhappy. But, occasionally, they would shrink from giving full expression to a thought, and search then for some phrase to convey the general idea. She did not confess her passion for another; he did not admit to having forgotten her.

Perhaps he no longer remembered those suppers following the costume balls, with girls in stevedore outfits; and she had probably forgotten her assignations of long ago, when, in the early morning, she used to race through the long grasses towards her lover's chateau. The sounds of the city barely reached them; the room seemed tiny, the better to confine them closely in their solitude. Emma, wearing a cotton dressing gown, sat resting her chignon against the back of an old armchair; the yellow wallpaper made a ground of gold behind her, while the mirror repeated the image of her bare head with its gleaming centre parting and the tips of her earlobes peeping out from beneath the smooth bands of her hair.

'But please forgive me!' she said; 'I really shouldn't bore you with my everlasting complaints!'

'No, never, never!'

'If you only knew,' she continued, raising her lovely tear-filled eyes to the ceiling; 'all the dreams I've dreamed!'

'It's the same with me! Oh, how I've suffered! So often I've just left, walked out, and trudged all along the quays, trying to numb my brain with the noise of the crowd, without being able to rid myself of the obsession hounding me. In a print shop on the boulevard there's an Italian engraving of one of the Muses. She's swathed in a tunic and gazing at the moon; her hair is loose, with forget-me-nots in it. Something drew me to that place over and over again; I've spent hours there.'

Then, his voice shaking: 'She looked rather like you.'

Madame Bovary turned away her head, to conceal the smile she was unable to suppress.

'Often, I would write you a letter, then tear it up.'

She made no reply. He went on:

'Sometimes I'd imagine that we'd meet accidentally. I'd believe I'd recognized you on a street corner; and if, through a cab window, I caught a glimpse of a veil or a shawl like yours, I'd chase after it . . .'

She seemed determined to let him talk without interrupting him. She sat with her arms crossed, looking down at the rosettes on her slippers, occasionally wriggling her toes slightly inside the satin.

Eventually, she gave a sigh. 'Surely the very worst thing is to lead a useless life, like me. If our suffering were of use to someone, the notion of sacrifice would be a consolation!'

He began singing the praises of virtue, duty, and silent self-sacrifice; he himself was driven by an extraordinary urge for selfless devotion that nothing could satisfy.

'I would dearly love', she said, 'to belong to an order of Nursing Sisters.'

'We men, alas, are denied such sacred opportunities of service, and I can think of no vocation . . . unless perhaps that of doctor . . .'

With a slight shrug, Emma interrupted him to lament the fact that her illness hadn't been fatal: such a pity! She would no longer be suffering now. Léon immediately joined her in yearning for 'the stillness of the tomb'; one night, he said, he'd even made out his will, asking to be buried in the handsome velvet-banded coverlet she'd given him; for that was how they wished to see themselves. They were both imagining an ideal self, and refashioning the past to fit it. Besides, speech, like a rolling press, invariably enlarges and extends the emotions.

But, on hearing this tale about the rug, Emma asked:

'But why?'

'Why?' He hesitated. 'Because I loved you so very much!'

And, congratulating himself on having cleared that hurdle, Léon, out of the corner of his eye, studied her expression.

It was like the sky when a gust of wind clears away the clouds. The mass of sombre thoughts that had shadowed her blue eyes seemed to vanish: her whole face radiated joy.

He waited. Finally she replied: 'I always thought so.'

So then they went over, together, all the trifling events of those far-off days, whose pleasures and pains they had just evoked with that single word. He recalled the clematis-covered arbour, the dresses she had worn, the furniture in her room, her entire house.

'And our poor cactuses, what became of them?'

'They were killed by the cold this winter.'

'You know, I've thought of them so often! I've so often pictured them as they looked in those days, with the sun shining on the shutters on a summer morning . . . and I would see your two bare arms moving about among the flowers.'

'You poor man!' she said, giving him her hand.

Hastily, Léon pressed it to his lips. Then, after taking a deep breath:

'You seemed, at that time, to exercise a kind of incomprehensible power over me that held me captive. For example, there was one time when I came to see you—but you probably don't remember?'

'Yes, yes, I do. Go on.'

'You were downstairs, in the hall, standing on the bottom stair, ready to go out—you were wearing a hat with tiny blue flowers—and, without any sort of invitation, in spite of myself, I went along as well. But I was more and more conscious, every moment, of how stupid of me this was, and I just went on walking near you, not actually daring to walk beside you, but not wanting to leave you. When you went into a shop I'd stay outside, and watch you through the window unbuttoning your gloves and putting the money down on the counter. Then you rang Madame Tuvache's bell, and they opened the door, and I just stood there like an idiot in front of that great big door, which shut with a bang behind you.'

Listening to him, Madame Bovary was astounded at how old she felt; all these things that were re-emerging from the past seemed to be extending her existence, creating vast emotional distances on which she could look back; and from time to time she murmured, her eyes half closed:

'Oh yes, yes . . . that's true . . . that's true . . .'

They heard eight o'clock strike on the countless clocks of the Beauvoisine district, an area of Rouen packed with boarding houses, churches, and old, abandoned mansions. They had stopped talking; but as they stared at one another they were conscious of a resonance in their heads, as if their steady gazing had released from their pupils some audible vibration. They had just clasped hands; past and future, memories and dreams, all merged together in this sweet rapture. Night was thickening along the walls, where they could still make out, half lost in shadow, bright glints of garish colour from four prints representing four scenes out of *La Tour de Nesle*,* with captions below in Spanish and French. Through the sash window they could see, between peaked roofs, a patch of black sky.

She rose to light two candles on the dresser, then sat down again.

'Well?' said Léon.

'Well?' she replied.

He was wondering how to resume their interrupted conversation, when she asked him:

'How has it come about that no one, until now, has ever said these things to me?'

The clerk declared that idealistic natures were difficult to understand. He himself had loved her from the very first moment; and he was filled with despair at the thought of the happiness they might have known, had fortune blessed them by bringing them together sooner, and allowing them to be united by an indissoluble bond.

'I've sometimes had those same thoughts,' she said.

'Ah, what a dream!' murmured Léon.

And, delicately fondling the blue border of her long white sash, he added:

'But what's to prevent us beginning again?'

'No, my dear,' she replied. 'I'm too old . . . you're too young . . . you must forget me! Others will love you . . . and you'll love them.'

'Not as I love you!' he protested.

'What a child you are! Come now, we must be sensible. I mean it!'

She elaborated on the impossibility of a love affair between them. They should continue to be just friends, brother and sister, as in the past.

Did she really mean what she was saying? Perhaps Emma herself had no idea, absorbed as she was by the charm of the seduction and the need to resist it; and, gazing tenderly at the young man, she gently fended off the timid caresses of his trembling hands.

'Oh, forgive me,' he said, moving away.

And, in the face of this timidity, Emma was filled with vague disquiet; it was more dangerous to her than Rodolphe's audacity when he had advanced upon her with open arms. Never had she thought any man so handsome. His whole bearing expressed an exquisite innocence. He had lowered his long, delicate, curly eyelashes. The velvety skin of his cheek was tinged with pink—out of desire for her, Emma supposed, and she felt an irresistible urge to press her lips to it. So then, leaning towards the clock as though to see the time:

'My goodness, it's so late!' she said; 'how we've talked!'

He took the hint and picked up his hat.

'I even forgot all about the opera! And poor Bovary left me here just because of that! Monsieur Lormaux, in the Rue Grand-Pont, was going to escort me, with his wife.'

And now it was too late, because she was leaving the next day.

'You really are?' he asked.

'Yes.'

'But I must see you again,' he went on, 'I had something to tell you . . .'

'What?'

'Something serious . . . important. Oh, no, you can't leave, no, it's quite impossible! If you only knew! Listen . . . Do you still not understand? Do you mean you haven't guessed?'

'But actually you're very good at expressing yourself,' said Emma.

'Oh, don't joke! Please don't! Take pity on me, let me see you again . . . just once . . . only once.'

'Well . . .' She paused; then, as if changing her mind:

'But not here!'

'Wherever you like.'

'Would you . . .'

She seemed to be thinking, then said tersely:

'Tomorrow, at eleven, in the cathedral.'

'I'll be there!' he exclaimed, seizing her hands; she pulled them away.

And, as they were both now standing, he behind her and Emma with bowed head, he leant down and kissed her lingeringly on the nape of her neck.

'Oh, you're crazy, absolutely crazy!' she kept saying between little peals of laughter, as the kisses multiplied.

Then, leaning forward over her shoulder, he seemed to be searching her eyes for consent, but the gaze she turned upon him was icy and majestic.

Léon stepped back, towards the door. On the threshold he paused, and in a tremulous voice whispered:

'Till tomorrow.'

With a nod, she vanished like a bird into the adjoining room.

That evening, Emma wrote the clerk an interminable letter cancelling their rendezvous: it was all over, and, for the sake of their own happiness, they must never meet again. But, when the letter was written, she could not think what to do, as she had no idea where Léon lived.

'I'll give it to him myself,' she decided, 'he's sure to come.'

Next morning, Léon opened his window wide and went onto his balcony, where, humming softly, he polished his dress shoes himself, using several layers of polish. He put on white trousers, thin socks, a green coat, doused his handkerchief with every perfume he possessed, and then, having had his hair curled, combed it out again, to give it a more natural elegance.

'It's still too early!' he thought, studying the barber's cuckoo clock, which showed that it was only nine.

He read an old fashion magazine, went outside, smoked a cigar, walked along three streets, decided it was now time, and set off at a brisk pace for the parvis of Notre-Dame.

It was a fine summer morning. Silver trinkets glittered from the jewellers' shop windows, and, in the slanting rays of the sun, the cracks in the grey stones of the cathedral sparkled; above, in the blue sky, a flock of birds kept swirling round the trefoiled turrets. The square, echoing with cries, was scented by the banks of flowers bordering its flagstones: roses, jasmine, carnations, narcissus, and polyanthus, irregularly interspersed with dewy, green clusters of catnip, and chickweed for the birds; in the centre the fountain gurgled on, and, beneath large umbrellas, among tall pyramids of cantaloupes, bareheaded flower-sellers sat wrapping paper round bunches of violets.

The young man chose one. This was the first time he had bought flowers for a woman; and, when he inhaled their perfume, his breast swelled with pride, as if this tribute intended for another had redounded upon him.

But, afraid of being seen, he walked resolutely into the church.

Just then the verger was standing at the entrance, in the middle of the left portal beneath the figure of the dancing Salome,* his plumed hat upon his head, his rapier against his calf, and his staff in his fist, more majestic than a cardinal and shining like a sacred ciborium.

He advanced upon Léon and, with that coaxingly benign smile that ecclesiastics adopt when questioning the very young:

'I imagine Monsieur must be a stranger here? Would Monsieur care to be shown round the church?'

'No,' was the reply.

First he explored the side-aisles. Then he went and inspected the square. No Emma. He walked up as far as the choir.

The nave, the base of the vaulting, and some sections of stained glass were mirrored in the brimming stoups of holy water.* But the reflected images broke off at the marble rims of the stoups, continuing beyond, across the flagstones, where they spread out like a multi-coloured carpet. The bright day outside came streaming into the church in three immense shafts of light, through the three open portals. Occasionally, in the distance, a sacristan would hurry across the nave, genuflecting before the altar with that slanting movement the devout resort to when pressed for time. The crystal chandeliers hung motionless. In the choir, a silver lamp was burning; and, from the side chapels and the shadowy recesses of the church, came occasional sounds like long-drawn-out sighs, then the slam of a grille closing, its echo reverberating beneath the lofty arches of the roof.

Léon walked solemnly round, keeping close to the walls. Never had life seemed so good to him. Any moment now she would be here, charming, flustered, glancing behind her to see if anyone was watching her; in her flounced dress, her gold lorgnette, and her delicate little boots, she would be adorned by all manner of feminine refinements he had never until then experienced, and radiating the ineffable allure of virtue on the point of surrender. Like a gigantic boudoir, the church was preparing to receive her; the vaulting was bending forward to welcome within its shadows the confession of her love; the windows were radiant with colour to illuminate her face, and the incense would be burning so that she might, like an angel, appear before him in a cloud of scented vapour.

But still she did not come. He took a chair and found himself gazing at a blue stained glass window depicting boatmen carrying baskets.* He concentrated on it for a long time, counting the scales on the fish and the buttonholes on the doublets, while his thoughts roved about in search of Emma.

The verger was standing to one side, inwardly raging at this person who dared to admire the cathedral all on his own. This behaviour struck him as shocking, a kind of theft, almost like a sacrilege.

There came the frou-frou of silk on the flagstones, the brim of a hat under a black hood . . . It was she! Léon rose and hurried over to meet her.

Emma looked pale. She was walking fast.

'Read this!' she said, handing him a sheet of paper . . . 'Oh no! Don't!'

And, quickly snatching away her hand, she slipped into the Lady Chapel,* knelt down against a chair, and began to pray.

At first the young man felt irritated by this overly pious whim, but then he found a certain charm in seeing her, in the middle of an assignation, lose herself in prayer like some Andalucian noblewoman; then, very soon, he began to be bored, for she went on and on praying.

Emma was praying, or rather trying to pray, in the hope that heaven would suddenly bestow upon her the decisiveness she lacked; and, the better to attract this divine assistance, she feasted her eyes on the splendours of the cathedral,* breathed in the scent of the flowering white stocks in the tall vases, and listened to the silence of the church, which only intensified the tumult of her heart.

She was on her feet and they were about to leave, when the verger hurried over, saying:

'I imagine Madame is a stranger here? Would Madame care to be shown round the church?'

'Oh, no!' exclaimed the clerk.

'Why not?' she replied.

For her wavering virtue was grasping at everything: at the Virgin, at the sculptures, at the tombs, at whatever came to hand.

Then, in order to proceed 'systematically' with the tour, the verger conducted them to the entrance near the square, where with his staff he pointed out a large circle of black stones without any kind of inscription or engraving:*

'Here,' he announced majestically, 'we see the circumference of the great bell* of Amboise. It weighed forty thousand pounds. There was not its equal in all of Europe. The craftsman who cast it died of joy . . .'

'Let's go,' said Léon.

The verger set off again; then, returning to the Lady Chapel, he spread out his arms in a gesture of all-embracing showmanship, and, prouder than a country landowner showing off his espaliers: 'Beneath this simple stone lies Pierre de Brézé,* Lord of Varenne and Brissac, Grand Marshal of Poitou and Governor of Normandy, who died at the battle of Montlhéry,* 16 July 1465.'

Léon kept biting his lip, and impatiently tapping his foot.

'And, to our right, this gentleman in full armour on a rearing steed is his grandson Louis de Brézé, Lord of Breval and Montchauvet, Count of Maulevrier, Baron of Mauny, Chamberlain to the King, Knight of the Order and likewise Governor of Normandy, who died 23 July 1531, a Sunday, as the inscription tells us, and below, this figure about to descend into the grave portrays the same individual. It is impossible to imagine, I am sure you will agree, a more perfect representation of the nothingness of death?'

Madame Bovary raised her lorgnette. Léon stood motionless, gazing at her, no longer even attempting to utter a single word, or make a single gesture, so discouraged did he feel in the face of this stubborn partnership of loquacity and indifference.

The inexhaustible guide was still holding forth:

'The weeping lady kneeling at his side is his wife, Diane de Poitiers,* Countess of Brézé, Duchess of Valentinois, born in 1499 and deceased in 1566; to our left, with a babe in her arms, we see the Holy Virgin. Now, turning to this side: we have here the Amboise tombs.* They were both cardinals and archbishops of Rouen. That one was minister to King Louis XII.* He was a great benefactor of the cathedral. His will included a legacy of thirty thousand gold crowns to the poor.'

And, still without pausing in his monologue, he urged them into a chapel that was cluttered with railings,* some of which he moved aside, to reveal a sort of stump that could well have been a crudely made statue.

'At one time,' he said, with a long-drawn-out sigh, 'this adorned the tomb of Richard Cœur de Lion, King of England and Duke of Normandy. It was the Calvinists, Monsieur, who reduced it to its present condition.* They had buried it in the ground, out of spite, beneath His Grace's episcopal throne. Look, this is the door that he uses to gain access to his residence—His Grace, that is. Now let us proceed to view the Gargoyle Window.'*

But, grabbing Emma by the arm, Léon hastily pulled a coin out of his pocket. The verger stood there perplexed, astounded by this visitor's premature liberality when there yet remained so many sights to enjoy. So he called after him: 'Monsieur! The steeple! The steeple!'

'No, thank you,' said Léon.

'Monsieur is making a bad mistake! You'll find it measures four hundred and forty feet, nine less than the great pyramid of Egypt. It's made entirely of cast iron, it . . .'

Léon fled; he felt that his love, which for nearly the past two hours had, like the stones of the church, been frozen in immobility, was now about to evaporate like steam through that kind of truncated pipe or elongated casing or pierced chimney which rises so grotesquely high above the cathedral, like the preposterous experiment of some fantastical metalworker.*

'But where are we going?' she asked.

He walked rapidly on without replying, and Madame Bovary was already dipping her finger in the holy water, when they heard behind them the sound of loud panting, punctuated by the tapping of a cane. Léon turned round.

'Monsieur!'

'What?'

He recognized the verger, who was carrying, tucked under his arm and balanced against his stomach, a score or so of thick paperbound tomes. These were works 'that dealt with the cathedral'.

'Idiot!' muttered Léon, as he dashed out of the church.

A lad was idling about on the parvis.

'Fetch me a cab!'

The boy set off like a shot down the Rue des Quatre-Vents; they were left alone for a few minutes, face to face, faintly embarrassed.

'Oh, Léon, really . . . I don't know . . . if I ought to . . .'

She was simpering. Then, very seriously: 'It's highly improper, you know.'

'In what way?' replied the clerk. 'Everyone does it in Paris!'

This remark, like a conclusive argument, settled the matter.

Meanwhile there was no sign of the cab. Léon was afraid that she might go back into the cathedral. At last, the cab appeared.

'But do at least leave by way of the north door!'* shouted the verger, who still stood waiting at the entrance. 'So you can take a look at the Resurrection, the Last Judgement, Paradise, King David, and the Souls of the Damned, burning in hell fire.'

'Where to, Monsieur?' asked the cab driver.

'Wherever you like!' said Léon, pushing Emma into the cab.

And the heavy vehicle rumbled off.

It drove down the Rue Grand-Pont, through the Place des Arts, along the Quai Napoléon, over the Pont Neuf, and stopped dead in front of the statue of Pierre Corneille.*

'Keep going!' called a voice from inside.

The cab moved off again, and, speeding up as it raced down the slope from the La Fayette crossroads, it drove into the railway station at a full gallop.

'No, straight on!' cried the same voice.

The carriage emerged from the gates, and turning before long onto the promenade, trotted quietly down it between the rows of tall elms. The driver wiped his forehead, stuck his leather hat between his legs and steered the cab off beyond the side-lanes to the water's edge, close to the grass.

For a long time it kept to the pebbled towpath beside the river, going beyond the islands, in the direction of Oyssel.

But then, quite suddenly, it darted off through Quatremares, Sotteville, the Grande-Chaussée, the Rue d'Elbeuf, coming to its third halt outside the Jardin des Plantes.

'Keep going!' shouted the voice, even more furiously.

It promptly began to move again, passing through Saint-Sever, along the Quai des Curandiers and the Quai aux Meules, over the bridge once more, through the Place du Champ-de-Mars and behind the gardens of the Home for the Elderly, where, in the sunshine, old men clad in black jackets stroll up and down a terrace green with ivy. It climbed up the Boulevard Bouvreuil, travelled along the Boulevard Cauchoise, then right over Mont-Riboudet as far as the hill at Deville.

It returned; and then, without plan or purpose, it wandered about at random. It was spotted at Saint-Pol, at Lescure, at Mont Gargan, at Rouge-Mare, and the Place du Gaillardbois; in the Rue Maladrerie, Rue Dinanderie, in front of Saint-Romain, Saint-Vivien, Saint-Maclou, Saint-Nicaise—in front of the Customs Hall—at the Basse-Vieille-Tour, the Trois-Pipes, and at the Cimetière Monumental. From time to time the driver, from his box, cast a despairing glance at a tavern. He could not understand what rage for locomotion could be compelling this pair never to stop. Occasionally he would attempt to do so, but immediately would hear angry cries coming from behind his back. Then he would whip up his two sweating nags all the harder, paying no attention to the potholes, bumping into things right and left, unheeding, demoralized, and almost weeping from thirst, fatigue, and misery.

And the local folk down by the harbour, among the wagons and the big barrels, or walking along the streets or standing at the corners, all stared wide-eyed in astonishment at this spectacle unheard of outside the capital: a cab with drawn blinds that constantly reappeared, sealed up tighter than a tomb and tossing like a ship.

Once, in the middle of the day,* deep in the countryside, when the sun's rays were beating down most fiercely on the old plated carriage-lanterns, a bare hand emerged from between the tiny yellow cloth curtains and flung out some torn scraps of paper, which scattered in the breeze and landed a little way off, like white butterflies, in a field of flowering red clover.

Then, about six o'clock, the cab drew up* in an alley in the

Beauvoisine district, and a woman stepped out, walking off with her veil lowered, never looking back.

CHAPTER II

When she reached the inn, Madame Bovary was astounded not to find the stagecoach there. Hivert had waited fifty-three minutes for her, but had finally left.

Actually there was nothing that compelled her to return, but she had promised to be back that evening. Besides, Charles was expecting her, and her heart was already harbouring that craven docility which is, with so many women, at once the penalty for their adultery and the price they pay to atone for it.

Quickly she packed her bags, paid the bill, hired a gig in the yard, and, by dint of alternately exhorting and encouraging the driver, and repeatedly asking him what the time was and how far they had travelled, managed to catch up with the Hirondelle on the outskirts of Quincampoix.

Hardly had she settled in a corner seat than she closed her eyes, not reopening them until they reached the foot of the hill, where, from far away, she recognized Félicité standing on the watch for her in front of the blacksmith's. Hivert halted the horses, and the cook, stretching up to speak to her through the window, said mysteriously:

'Please, Madame, you're to go straight away to Monsieur Homais's. It's really urgent.'

As usual, silence reigned in the village. At every street corner a little rose-pink mound lay steaming into the air, for this was jam-making time, and everyone in Yonville had chosen the same day to make their supply of jam. But a much larger mound in front of the pharmacy was attracting general admiration, its greater volume a sign of the necessary superiority of a dispensary over an ordinary kitchen stove, of universal demand over personal whim.

She went in. The big armchair had been knocked over, and even the *Fanal de Rouen* lay strewn on the floor, between two pestles. She pushed open the corridor door: there in the middle of the kitchen, surrounded by the earthenware crocks full of stemmed currants, the grated sugar, the lump sugar, the scales on the table, the jam-pans on the stove, she saw all the Homais, large and small, swathed up to the chin in aprons, with forks in their hands. Justin was standing with bent head, while the pharmacist kept shouting:

'Whoever told you to go to the capharnaum* for it?'

'What's going on?' asked Emma. 'What's happened?'

'What's happened?' replied the apothecary. 'We're making jam, it's on the boil, but it's going to boil over because it's boiling too fast, so I send him for another jam-pan. And he, out of sheer sloppiness or laziness, goes and gets, from my laboratory, where it's hanging on its nail, the key to the capharnaum!'

This was the apothecary's name for a small storeroom under the eaves that was crammed with the tools and supplies required in his profession. He had the habit of spending many hours there by himself, labelling, decanting, repackaging; and he thought of it not simply as a storeroom but as a veritable sanctuary, from which there later emerged, fashioned by his own hands, all manner of pills, boluses, infusions, lotions, and potions, destined to spread his fame far and wide. Not a soul was permitted to enter it; and he treated it with such profound respect that he always swept it out himself. In fact, while the pharmacy, open to all comers, was the theatre where he gloried in displaying his talents, the capharnaum was, for Homais, the refuge where he could selfishly luxuriate in the pleasures of his chosen calling. He therefore saw Justin's blunder as a piece of shocking irreverence; and, his face redder than the berries, he kept repeating:

'Yes, to the capharnaum! The key that locks up the acids and the caustic alkalis! Imagine taking one of my special pans! One with a lid! One that I may never have reason to use! Everything has its function in the delicate operations of our art! It's essential to distinguish, for God's sake, between quasi-domestic and pharmaceutical uses! It's as if you were to carve up a chicken with a scalpel, or a magistrate were to . . .'

'Do please calm down!' Madame Homais kept saying.

Athalie was tugging at his frock coat:

'Papa! Papa!'

'Leave me alone!' continued the apothecary, 'leave me alone! Hell! I might just as well be a grocer, yes, damn it all, a grocer! Come on! No respect, that's what it is, smash everything, break everything, let the leeches out, burn the marshmallow, use the medicine jars for pickling, tear up the bandages!'

'I believe there was something. . .' said Emma.

'In a moment, Madame! Do you know the risk you were running? Didn't you see anything, in the corner, over on the left, on the third shelf? Come on, speak, answer me, say something!'

'I . . . I dunno,' stammered the lad.

'Ah! You don't know! Well, I do know, yes, *I* do. You saw a bottle, a blue glass bottle, sealed with yellow wax, full of a white powder, on which I'd even written: "Danger!" And do you know what was in it? Arsenic! And then you go messing around near *that*! Taking a pan that's standing beside *that*!'

'Beside it!' cried Madame Homais, clasping her hands. 'Arsenic? You might have poisoned every one of us!'

And the children began wailing, as if their bowels were already gripped by excruciating pains.

'Or poisoned a patient!' continued the apothecary. 'Do you want to see me standing in the dock, at the Assizes? Do you want to see me dragged to the scaffold? Don't you know how meticulously careful I am in handling my materials, even though I've been doing it forever? I often frighten myself, when I think of my responsibilities! The government's constantly on our backs, and the idiotic legislation that regulates us is literally a sword of Damocles hanging over our heads!'

Emma had given up trying to find out why she was wanted, as the breathless spate of words rushed on:

'So this is how you show your appreciation of our kindness to you! This is how you repay me for the truly paternal care I've showered on you! Because, if it weren't for me, where would you be? What would you be doing? Who feeds you, educates you, clothes you, provides you with all the means to achieve an honourable position in society one day? But, in order to do that, you have to work like a galley slave, sweat blood, as the saying goes. *Fabricando fit faber, age quod agis.*'*

He was so enraged that he was quoting Latin. He would have quoted Chinese or Greenlandic, had he known them; for he was in the grip of one of those crises where the soul indiscriminately reveals everything within it, just as the ocean at the height of a storm shows us glimpses of everything within it, from the sea wrack of its shores to the sand of its deeps.

He continued: 'I'm beginning bitterly to rue the day I ever took you on! I'd certainly have done a lot better just to leave you where you were, rotting in the poverty and squalor you were born in! You'll never be fit for anything more than tending cows! You've no aptitude whatever for the sciences! You can hardly manage to stick on a label! And yet here you are living a life of ease under *my* roof, and gorging on the fat of the land at *my* expense!'

But Emma, turning to Madame Homais, said: 'I was told to come here . . .'

'Oh, merciful heaven!' the good lady interrupted in a mournful tone, 'how can I possibly break it to you? It's so dreadful!'

She never finished. The apothecary was bellowing:

'Empty it out! Scour it out! Put it back! Get a move on!' And, grabbing Justin by the collar of his smock, he shook him. A book fell out of his pocket.

The lad bent down. Homais was faster, and, picking up the volume, gazed at it open-mouthed, his eyes starting from his head.

'*Conjugal . . . Love!*'* he said slowly, separating the two words. 'Oh! Very nice! Very nice indeed, lovely! Illustrated, what's more. Oh, this is too much!'

Madame Homais stepped forward.

'No! Don't touch it!'

The children begged to see the pictures.

'Out!' he shouted imperiously.

And out they went.

At first he strode vigorously back and forth across the room, holding the book open between his fingers, choking, wild-eyed, swollen-cheeked, apoplectic. Then he walked up to his pupil and stood before him with his arms crossed:

'So you've all the vices, have you, you miserable little wretch! . . . I warn you, you've set your foot on a slippery slope! I suppose it never occurred to you, did it, that this filthy book might have fallen into my children's hands, that it might have been just enough to set them off, to sully the purity of Athalie and corrupt Napoléon! He's already a man, physically! Can you at the very least give me your word that they've not read it? Can you guarantee . . .?'

'Excuse me, Monsieur, but didn't you have something to tell me . . .?'

'Yes, Madame, I did; your father-in-law's dead!'

And indeed Monsieur Bovary senior had died very suddenly two days earlier, of an apoplectic stroke, on leaving the dinner table; and

Charles, full of solicitude for Emma's sensibilities, had asked Homais to break this horrible news to her with the utmost circumspection.

He had pondered over what to say, making his phraseology more orotund, more polished, and more harmonious; it was a masterpiece of prudence, judicious transitions, subtle wording, and delicacy; but rage had sent rhetoric flying.

Emma, realizing she was not going to hear any details, immediately left the pharmacy, for Homais had resumed his vituperations. But he had calmed down, and was now grumbling in a fatherly way as he fanned himself with his cap:

'It's not that I entirely disapprove of the work. The author was a doctor. Certain scientific matters are discussed in it about which a man perhaps ought to know, indeed I think I can go so far as to say about which a man definitely *should* know. But all in good time, all in good time! At least wait until you yourself are a grown man, and your character is formed.'

When Emma knocked at the door, Charles, who had been waiting for her, met her with a warm embrace and said, his voice full of tears:

'Oh, my dearest love . . .'

And he bent down to kiss her gently. But at the touch of his lips she was filled with memories of the other man, and she passed her hand over her face, shivering.

But she did, nevertheless, reply:

'Yes, I know . . . I know.'

He showed her the letter in which his mother, without a trace of sentimental hypocrisy, described what had happened. The only thing she regretted was that her husband had died without the ministrations of religion, for he had breathed his last in a street in Doudeville* outside a café, following a patriotic banquet he had attended with some former fellow officers.

Emma handed back the letter; then, at dinner, out of politeness, she pretended she was not hungry. But when Charles urged her, she did make a good meal, while he, opposite her, sat motionless, sunk in depression.

He raised his head from time to time, giving her a long, sad look. Once he sighed:

'I'd have liked to see him again!'

She said nothing. Eventually, realizing that she ought to say something:

'How old was he, your father?'

'Fifty-eight!'

'Ah!'

And that was all.

A quarter of an hour later he added:

'My poor mother! What's to become of her, now?'

She shrugged. Seeing her so taciturn, Charles supposed she must be deeply upset, and he kept silent so as not to increase her pain. But then, shaking off his own grief, he asked her:

'Did you enjoy yourself, yesterday?'

'Yes.'

When the tablecloth had been removed, Bovary did not stir.

Nor did Emma; and, little by little, as she gazed at his face, the dullness of this sight banished all compassion from her heart. He seemed paltry, impotent, non-existent, in fact a pathetically poor specimen, in every sense. How was she to rid herself of him? What an interminable evening! She felt stupefied, as if drugged by the fumes of some substance like opium.

They heard, coming from the hall, the tap-tap-tap of a stick on the floorboards. It was Hippolyte, delivering Madame's luggage. In order to set the bags down, he had to execute an awkward manœuvre with his wooden leg.

'He never even spares him a thought any more!' she said to herself, as she watched the poor devil, whose thick red hair was dripping with sweat.

Bovary was fishing in his purse for a coin; and, without seeming to grasp how personally humiliating was the presence there, before him, of this man, this living reproach to his own irremediable ineptitude: 'Oh look! You've a pretty bunch of flowers!' he exclaimed, noticing Léon's violets on the mantelpiece.

'Yes,' she replied casually, 'I bought them earlier . . . from a beggar-woman.'

Charles picked up the violets, and, cooling his tear-reddened eyes with them, delicately breathed in their scent. Quickly she took them from his hand, and went to put them in water.

Madame Bovary senior arrived next day. She and her son wept a lot. Emma discovered she had some household orders to give, and disappeared.

The following day, the ladies had to see about their mourning clothes, and they took their workbaskets down to the arbour, by the river.

Charles was thinking of his father, and was astonished by the affection he felt for this man to whom, until then, he had believed himself only slightly attached. His mother was also thinking of her husband. The worst days of the past now seemed desirable. The slate was wiped clean by the instinctive regret born of such a long-enduring habit; and from time to time, as she plied her needle, a big tear slid down her nose and remained there for an instant, hanging. Emma was thinking that it was barely forty-eight hours since they had been together, far from the world, intoxicated by one another, unable to take their eyes off one another. She tried hard to recapture the minutest details of that vanished day. But the presence of her mother-in-law and her husband obtruded. She would have liked to hear nothing, to see nothing, so as not to disturb the rapture of her recollections, which were gradually being dissipated, no matter what she did, by the pressure of external sensations.

Surrounded by scraps of fabric, she was busy unpicking the seams of a dress; the older Madame Bovary, never raising her eyes from her task, was wielding a pair of squeaky scissors, while Charles, wearing cloth slippers and his ancient brown coat that served him as a dressing gown, sat with his hands in his pockets, equally silent; near them, Berthe, in a little white apron, scraped the sand off the paths with her spade.

Suddenly, they saw Monsieur Lheureux, the draper, approaching through the garden gate. He had come to offer his services, 'with regard to the melancholy event'. Emma replied that she believed they did not require anything. But the merchant was not about to give up so easily.

'A thousand pardons,' he said, 'but I would greatly appreciate a private word with you.'

Then, in a low voice:

'It's about what we were discussing . . . you remember?' Charles turned scarlet to the tips of his ears.

'Oh yes . . . of course.'

Embarrassed, he turned to his wife:

'I wonder, my dear, would you mind . . .?'

She seemed to understand him, for she rose, and Charles said to his mother:

'It's nothing! Just some trivial domestic matter, I imagine.'

He did not want her to know about the promissory note, for fear of what she would say.

As soon as he was alone with Emma, Monsieur Lheureux, without further ado, began to congratulate her on the inheritance; then he rambled on about this and that, about the fruit trees, and the harvest, and his own health, which was just 'so-so, neither one thing nor the other.' In fact, although he slaved away like the devil, he barely managed to scrape a decent living, whatever people might say.

Emma let him talk. Life had been so boring these past two days!

'So you're quite recovered now, are you?' he went on. 'My goodness, what a state your poor husband was in! He's a good chap, for all we've had our differences.'

She pressed him for details; Charles had never told her about the disagreement over Lheureux's account.

'But you know all about that!' said Lheureux. 'It was those things you fancied, those pieces of luggage.'

He had pulled his hat down low over his eyes, and stood with his hands behind his back, smiling and whistling softly, staring straight at her in an insufferable manner. Did he suspect something? She was filled with a host of misgivings. Eventually, however, he continued:

'We've made it up now, and I've come today with another proposal.'

It was to renew the note Bovary had signed. Of course, Monsieur could do whatever he thought best; he shouldn't let it worry him, especially now when there would be so much for him to deal with.

'Actually, he'd do well to hand some of it over to another person, to you, for example; it would be perfectly simple, with a power of attorney,* and then you and I could see to these little matters ourselves . . .'

She did not understand. He dropped the subject. Then, reverting to his own business concerns, Lheureux declared that surely Madame intended to order *something* from his store. He'd send her a dozen metres of black *barège*, enough to make a dress.

'The one you're wearing is good enough for the house. You need another for going out. I noticed the instant I saw you. I've an eye like a hawk!'

Instead of sending the material, he brought it himself. He came back to take the measurements; then he found other pretexts for returning again and again, taking pains each time to be agreeable and helpful, becoming her liege man, as Homais might have put it, and invariably slipping in a few words of advice about the power of attorney. He never mentioned the promissory note. The subject never entered Emma's head: Charles had, indeed, told her something of the matter in the early part of her convalescence, but her state of mind at the time had been so unsettled that she had forgotten all about it. Besides, she scrupulously avoided any discussion of money matters; this surprised Charles's mother, who attributed her changed disposition to the religious sentiments she had developed during her illness.

But the very moment her mother-in-law had left, Emma amazed Bovary with her practical common sense. They were going to have to make enquiries, verify the terms of mortgages, find out whether they needed to sell at auction, or liquidate. She paraded technical terms at random, mouthing fine-sounding words like 'order', 'the future', 'foresight', and constantly magnifying the complications of the inheritance; then, one day, she showed him the draft of a general authorization to 'manage and administer his affairs, negotiate all loans, sign and endorse all promissory notes, pay out all moneys, etc.' She had profited from Lheureux's teaching.

Charles enquired naively where this document had come from.

'From Monsieur Guillaumin.'

And, as cool as a cucumber, she added:

'I don't altogether trust him. Notaries have such an appalling reputation! We ought perhaps to consult someone . . . But we only know . . . Oh, there's no one, really . . .'

'Unless perhaps Léon?' replied Charles, who was thinking.

But it was not an easy matter to explain by letter. She was prepared to make the trip in person. He thanked her but demurred. She insisted. A contest in mutual consideration ensued. Eventually, putting on an archly defiant tone, she exclaimed:

'No, please, I *am* going!'

'You're so good!' he said, kissing her on the forehead.

The very next morning she set off in the Hirondelle for Rouen, to consult Monsieur Léon; she remained there for three days.

CHAPTER III

They had three intense, exquisite, glorious days, a real honeymoon.

They stayed at the Hôtel de Boulogne, down on the quay. They spent their time in their room, with their shutters latched and their doors closed, their floor strewn with flowers, drinking chilled fruit cordials that were brought to their room all day long.

In the late afternoon, they would hire a small boat and go to an island for dinner. At that time of day, the docks echoed with the thump of caulking mallets against the hulls of vessels. Smoke from the tar drifted up between the trees, and on the river floated large oily patches, like Florentine bronze plaques, that danced irregularly about in the purplish glow of the sun.

They made their way downstream among moored craft whose long, slanting cables gently caressed the awning of their boat.

Imperceptibly, the noises of the city grew fainter, the rumbling of carts, the hubbub of voices, the yapping of dogs from the decks of boats. She untied the ribbons of her hat and they stepped ashore onto their island.

They would sit in the low-ceilinged room of a tavern that had black fishing-nets hanging over its door. They ate fried smelt, and cream, and cherries. They lay down in the grass; they kissed in unfrequented spots beneath the poplars; they would have loved to live forever, like a pair of Robinson Crusoes, in this tiny place, which seemed to them, in their beatitude, the most splendid place on earth. This was not the first time they had seen trees, or blue sky, or grass, nor the first time they had heard water flowing or the breeze rustling the leaves of the trees, but certainly these things had never before filled them with such wonder. It was as if nature had never existed before, or as if she had only become beautiful with the fulfilment of their desires.

At night, they returned. The boat hugged the shoreline of the islands. Together they sat in the stern, hidden by the shadows, not speaking. The square-cut oars creaked in the metal rowlocks; the sound punctuated the silence like the beat of a metronome, while a tiny, soft lapping sound came continually from the painter trailing behind them in the water.

One evening, the moon appeared; then, inevitably, they trotted out all the florid phrases, calling the planet melancholy, deeply poetic. She even began singing:

> 'Un soir, t'en souvient-il? nous voguions,* etc.'

Her slight, melodious voice died away over the water, as the breeze dispersed the tremolos; Léon listened to them float past him like a fluttering of wings.

She sat opposite him, leaning against the bulkhead, with the moonlight shining through one of the open shutters. The folds of her black dress fanned out all round her, making her seem more slender, and taller. Her head was tilted up, her hands clasped, and her eyes gazing heavenwards. Sometimes, the shadow of the willows hid her completely, then, suddenly, like a vision, she would reappear in the light from the moon.

Léon, sitting close to her at her feet, found a piece of ribbon, a flame-coloured silk ribbon, under his hand.

The boatman examined it and eventually declared:

'Ah! It probably belongs to some folks I took on the river the other day. There was a whole lot of 'em, out for a good time they were, fellows an' their girls, they'd brought cakes an' champagne an' trumpets, the whole caboodle. One in particular, a tall good-looking chap, with a little moustache, he had 'em in stitches! They kept saying: "Come on, tell us another . . . Adolphe, . . . Dodolphe . . . something like that." '

She shivered.

'What's the matter?' asked Léon, moving closer to her.

'It's nothing. Probably just the cool night air.'

'And I'll bet he don't lack for lady friends, neither,' the old boatman added softly, as a tribute to his present passenger.

Then, spitting on his hands, he took up the oars again.

But in the end they had to part! The farewells were sad. He was to write to her in care of Mère Rollet; and she gave him such precise instructions about the double envelope that he was overwhelmed with admiration for her cunning in love.

'So, you're quite certain that it's all in order?' she said as they kissed for the last time.

'Oh yes, absolutely!' But why in the world, he wondered later, as he made his way back along the streets alone, why is she so dead set on this power of attorney?

CHAPTER IV

Very soon, Léon began putting on airs in front of his fellow clerks, avoiding their company, and completely neglecting his paperwork.

He lived for her letters; he read and reread them. He wrote to her constantly. He would conjure up her image with all the power of his desire and of his memories. Instead of being lessened by absence, this craving to see her again grew more intense, so much so that one Saturday morning he slipped away from the office.

When he gazed down upon the valley from the top of the hill and saw the church steeple with its tin flag turning in the breeze, he was filled with that exquisite blend of triumphant complacency and egotistical sentimentality, that millionaires must experience when they return to their native village.

He went and hung about outside her house. A light was burning in the kitchen. He watched for her shadow behind the curtains. There was no sign of her.

Old Madame Lefrançois exclaimed loudly over his appearance, declaring him 'taller and thinner', whereas Artémise, by contrast, thought he had 'filled out, and looked more bronzed'.

He dined as of old in the small dining room, but by himself, without the tax collector; for Binet, 'fed up' with waiting for the Hirondelle, had definitively advanced his dinner time by one hour and now had his meal at five on the dot, although, more often than not, he would grumble that 'that old wreck of a clock's slow'.

Eventually Léon did summon up his courage and knocked on the doctor's door. Madame was in her room, and did not emerge till a quarter of an hour had passed. Monsieur seemed delighted to see him again, but he never budged from the house all evening, nor during the whole of the following day.

He saw her alone very late on the Sunday night, behind the garden, in the lane—in the lane, like the other one! There was a thunderstorm, and they stood under an umbrella to talk, with the lightning flashing around them.

Separation was becoming unbearable.

'I'd rather die!' said Emma.

She was twisting about in his arms, and weeping.

'Goodbye! . . . Goodbye! Oh, when shall I see you again?'

They turned back again for one last kiss; it was then she promised him that she would, without delay, she didn't exactly know how, find the means for them to meet freely and regularly at least once a week. She was certain this would be possible. Indeed, she felt very confident; she'd be receiving some money shortly.

Consequently she bought herself, for her room, a pair of yellow curtains with broad stripes that Monsieur Lheureux had assured her were an excellent buy. She longed for a carpet, and Lheureux, declaring that 'nothing could be simpler', politely undertook to obtain one for her. She could no longer manage without his services. She would send for him twenty times a day, and immediately, without a murmur, he would drop whatever he was doing, and come. Another mystery was why Mère Rollet lunched every day in Emma's kitchen, and even saw her privately.

It was about this time, when winter was approaching, that she suddenly seemed filled with an intense passion for music.

One evening when Charles was listening to her play, she started the same piece over again four times, always breaking off and declaring herself dissatisfied, while he, hearing nothing wrong, kept exclaiming:

'Bravo! . . . very good! . . . no, you're quite mistaken, it's lovely!'

'Oh no! It's atrocious! My fingers are all thumbs.'

Next day he begged her to 'play something for him again'.

'Yes, all right, if you want.'

And Charles did admit that she'd lost her touch a bit. She confused the staves, she bungled the notes; then, stopping abruptly:

'Oh, I give up! I really need some lessons, but . . .' Biting her lip, she added: 'twenty francs a time, it's too expensive!'

'Well, yes, a bit . . .' said Charles with a vacuous laugh. 'Still, I'd have thought you might find someone for less; musicians who aren't so well known are often better than the celebrities.'

'Well, you find them,' said Emma.

When he came home the next day he glanced at her knowingly, and in the end could not resist saying:

'You're so stubborn sometimes! I've been to Barfeuchères today. Well! Madame Liégeard assures me that her three daughters, pupils at the Miséricorde convent, are having lessons for two francs fifty a time, and from a first-rate piano teacher!'

She shrugged, and did not touch her instrument again.

But, whenever she walked past it (if Bovary was in the room) she would sigh:

'Oh, my poor piano!'

And if visitors came to see her, she never failed to inform them that she'd given up her music and was unable, for compelling reasons, to take it up again. Everyone felt sorry for her. What a pity! She had such a wonderful gift! Some people even spoke reproachfully to Bovary about it, the pharmacist in particular.

'What a mistake you're making! One ought never to leave natural talents uncultivated. Besides, my dear fellow, just reflect: if you encourage Madame to study now, you'll save money later, on your child's musical training! I am of the opinion that mothers should teach their children themselves. It's an idea of Rousseau's,* a trifle innovative, perhaps, but which I'm convinced will eventually carry the day, just like the idea of the mother nursing her own child,* and vaccination.'*

So Charles returned to the question of the piano. Emma replied tartly that they'd better sell it. Her poor old piano had been for Bovary the source of so much prideful gratification that to see it disappear would somehow be like watching Emma kill a part of herself.

'If you'd like . . .' he said, 'now and again, to have the odd lesson, I don't suppose it'd be the ruin of us, would it?'

'But lessons aren't any good,' she replied, 'unless they're regular.'

And that is how she succeeded in obtaining her husband's consent to a weekly visit to the city, to meet her lover. It was even observed, after only a month, that she had made considerable progress.

CHAPTER V

It was Thursday. She always slipped out of bed and dressed without a sound so as not to disturb Charles, who would have pointed out that she was getting ready far too soon. Then she would pace up and down, or stand by the window gazing at the square. Early morning light was filtering through the pillars of the market place, and on the pharmacist's house, where the shutters remained closed, the capital letters of his sign glinted in the pale rays of dawn.

When the clock said a quarter past seven she would cross over to the Lion d'Or, where Artémise, yawning, had just opened the door for her. From beneath the ashes in the grate, the servant dug out the still-smouldering coals for Emma's comfort, then left her by herself in the kitchen. Now and again Emma would venture outside. Hivert was taking his time harnessing the horses, listening as he did so to old Madame Lefrançois, who, sticking her head, encased in a cotton nightcap, through a small upper window, used to bombard him with such a load of errands and instructions as would have bewildered any other man. Emma kept stamping the soles of her boots on the courtyard flagstones.

Finally, when he had drunk his soup, put on his heavy cloak, lit his pipe, and picked up his whip, he settled himself unhurriedly on his box.

The Hirondelle always set off at an easy trot, and for the first mile or two drew up at various stops to pick up passengers, who stood watching for it at the side of the road, in front of their farmyard gates. Those who had reserved their places the previous day kept the coach waiting; some were even still in their beds; Hivert called, shouted, cursed, then got down from his box and pounded loudly on the door. The wind whistled through the cracks in the coach windows.

Meanwhile the four benches were filling up, and the coach lumbered along, passing endless rows of apple trees; the road ahead, between its two ditches filled with yellow water, stretched on and on, gradually narrowing as it neared the horizon. Emma knew it from end to end; she knew that after a pasture came a signpost, then an elm, a barn, or a road-mender's hut; sometimes, in order to surprise herself, she shut her eyes. But she never lost her acute awareness of how far they still had to travel.

At long last there were brick houses built closer together, the road resounded under their wheels, and the Hirondelle was rolling along between gardens, where Emma might catch a glimpse, through a fence, of statues, a landscaped mound crowned by a trellised arbour, clipped yew trees, or a swing. Then, suddenly, the town lay spread out before her eyes.

Sloping down like an amphitheatre, drowned in mist, it sprawled untidily out on the farther side of the bridges.* Beyond, open country sloped steadily up with monotonous uniformity until it met the indeterminate line where the pale sky began. Seen like this from above, the whole landscape had the stillness of a painting: the ships at anchor huddling together in one corner, the river curving round the foot of green, wooded hills, the oblong-shaped islands lying in the water like great, black, motionless fish. The factory chimneys were belching out immense dark plumes of smoke that kept dissolving along their apexes into the atmosphere. She could hear the rumbling of the foundries and the clear chimes from the church steeples that loomed up through the mist. The trees in the boulevards, bare of leaves, looked like violet-hued bushes scattered about among the houses, whose roofs gleamed wetly from the rain, their brilliance greater in the higher neighbourhoods. Sometimes, a gust of wind would sweep the clouds up against the Côte Sainte-Catherine, like waves of air silently breaking against a cliff.

She felt a kind of dizzying energy rising up from this crowded mass of lives, and her heart swelled luxuriantly, as if all of the hundred and twenty thousand souls throbbing down there had collectively sent up to her exhalations of those passions she imagined theirs. Her love grew vaster in the presence of this vastness, and was filled with turmoil as it absorbed the vague hum rising from below. She, then, returned this love, pouring it forth into the air beneath her, showering it upon the squares, the avenues, the streets; to her eyes the ancient Norman city was like a gigantic metropolis, like a Babylon into which she was about to enter. She bent forward through the window, leaning on her two hands, smelling the breeze; the three horses galloped on. The coach wheels screeched on the stones in the muddy road, the vehicle lurched, Hivert, from far off, shouted warnings to the carts he was passing on the way, while the local worthies who had spent the night at home in Bois-Guillaume drove sedately down the hill in their modest family carriages.

They stopped at the city gate; Emma would unbuckle her overshoes, change her gloves, adjust her shawl, and, about twenty paces further on, step out of the Hirondelle.

The town was just coming to life. Clerks in caps were busy polishing shopfronts, and women stood at the street corners, resting their basket on one hip and advertising their wares with intermittent, resounding cries. She walked along with her eyes on the ground, keeping close to the walls, and smiling with pleasure under her lowered black veil.

Afraid of being seen, she did not, as a rule, take the shortest route.

She would plunge down sunless alleys, emerging, drenched in sweat, at the bottom of the Rue Nationale, near its fountain. This is the area of theatres, bars, and whores. Often, a cart passed close beside her, laden with a wobbling piece of theatrical décor. Youths in aprons were spreading sand on the paving stones, between the tubs of green shrubbery. There was a smell of absinthe, cigars, and oysters.*

Turning a corner, she would recognize him by his curly hair, which invariably escaped from beneath his hat. Léon continued along the pavement. She followed him to the hotel; he climbed the stairs, opened the door, entered the room . . . Then, what an embrace!

After the kisses, came the rush of words. They told one another all the vexations the week had brought, all their forebodings, all their fears about their letters; but now, everything was forgotten, and they gazed at one another, laughing with delight as they exchanged murmured endearments.

The mahogany bed was large, and shaped like a boat. The crimson silk curtains, suspended from the ceiling, were looped back rather low down, close to the flaring headboard, and nothing in the whole world could have been lovelier than her dark head and white skin seen against this rich red, when, in a gesture of modesty, she crossed her bare arms and hid her face in her hands.

The warm room, with its quiet carpet, its playful ornaments, and its tranquil light, seemed perfectly designed for the intimacies of passion. The arrow-tipped canopy rods, the brass curtain hooks, and the great knobs on the andirons would suddenly glow brightly when the sun shone in. Standing on the mantelpiece, between the candelabra, were two of those large rose-pink shells which, when you hold them to your ear, sound like the sea.

How they loved that dear room that was so bright and cheerful, despite its air of slightly faded glory! They always found the furniture arranged exactly as it had been before, and sometimes even the hairpins that she had left behind, under the clock-stand, the previous Thursday. They always lunched by the side of the fire, on a small pedestal table inlaid with rosewood. Emma did the carving, piling the slices on his plate while keeping up a flow of loving nonsense, and she would laugh a deep, shameless laugh when the froth of the champagne overflowed the rim of the delicate glass and ran down her beringed fingers. They were so utterly lost in the possession of one another that they believed they were in their own private home, where they were destined to live together until death, like an eternally youthful married couple. They spoke of 'our room', 'our carpet', 'our armchairs'; she even said 'our slippers': these were a gift from Léon, prompted by a whim of hers. Made of pink satin, they were edged in swansdown. When she was sitting on his knee, her legs, now too short to reach the floor, would swing in the air, with the dainty slippers, which had no heel, dangling from her bare toes.

Now, for the first time in his life, he was savouring the inexpressible subtleties of feminine refinement. Never before had he encountered this grace of language, this elegant restraint in dress, these postures reminiscent of a sleeping dove. He was filled with wonder by the sublimity of her soul and by the lace of her petticoat. Besides, she was 'a woman of the world', was she not, a married woman? A real mistress, in fact!

Her mercurial temperament, by turns mystical and joyful, loquacious and taciturn, passionate and cool, constantly stirred a thousand desires in him, awakening different instincts or memories. She was the beloved of every novel, the heroine of every drama, the vague *she* of every volume of poetry. The skin of her shoulders reminded him of the amber-gold tones of the Bathing Odalisque* of popular painting; she was as long-waisted as any feudal chatelaine; and she looked, too, like Musset's 'pale beauty of Barcelona',* but she was, above all else, an Angel!

Often, as he gazed at her, he felt as if his soul, escaping in search of her, spread out like a wave over the contours of her head, and was then drawn down into the whiteness of her breast.

He used to kneel down before her, raising his face, resting his elbows on her knees, and staring up at her with a smile. She, bending towards him, almost overcome with ecstasy, would whisper:

'Oh, don't move! No, don't say a word! Look at me! I'm drinking in something so sweet from your eyes, something that's doing me so much good!'

She called him 'child':

'Child, do you love me?'

And she would barely hear the reply, so avidly did his lips reach for hers.

On top of the clock stood a tiny, simpering bronze Cupid supporting a gilded wreath on his rounded arms. They often laughed over it together; but, when the moment of parting came, everything, to them, became serious.

Motionless, gazing at one another, they kept repeating:

'Till Thursday! Till Thursday!'

Then, without warning, she would grasp his head in her hands, quickly kiss his forehead, cry 'goodbye,' and fly down the stairs.

She always visited a hairdresser's in the Rue de la Comédie, to have her hair arranged. Night was falling, and in the shop the gas-lights were being lit. She could hear the bell of the theatre ringing to summon the players to the performance, and would watch the white-faced men and shabbily dressed women walking past along the pavement opposite, then entering through the stage door.

It was hot in that small low-ceilinged room, with the stove hum-ming away among the wigs and pomades. The smell of the curling irons, and the feel of plump fingers working on her scalp, soon made her head swim, and she would doze a little, sitting there under the protective gown. Often, the assistant, as he did her hair, offered her tickets for the masked ball.

Then she would set off! She trudged back up the streets to the Croix Rouge, retrieved her overshoes from beneath the bench where she had concealed them that morning, and squeezed into her place among the impatient passengers. Some of them got out at the foot of the hill to walk up, and she would be left alone in the coach.

At each turning in the road, she could see more and more of the lights of the town; they gave off a luminous haze that hovered above the jumbled mass of houses. Kneeling on the cushions, Emma let her gaze wander over this dazzling spectacle. She kept sobbing, calling Léon's name, and sending him tender messages with kisses that were scattered by the wind.

A poor devil of a tramp with a stick wandered about on this hillside, right in among the vehicles. His clothes were layers of rags and a battered old beaver-skin hat, turned down all round like a basin, hid his face; but, when he removed his hat, he revealed, where his eyelids should have been, two gaping, bloodstained sockets. The flesh was constantly flaking away in bloody shreds, and from it oozed liquid that formed into green viridescent scabs right down to his nose, where his black nostrils kept sniffling convulsively. When he was about to speak to you, he would fling back his head with a halfwitted laugh—and then his bluish eyeballs, rolling incessantly round in the sockets, would, near the temples, come right up against the edges of the open sores.

He often sang a little ditty as he followed the carriages:

> Souvent la chaleur d'un beau jour
> Fait rêver fillette à l'amour.*

The rest of it was all about birds, sunlight, and greenery.

Sometimes, he suddenly loomed up behind Emma, his head bare. She would recoil, with a cry. Hivert liked to tease him, suggesting that he get a stall at the Saint-Romain fair, or enquiring, with a laugh, whether his sweetheart was keeping well.

Often, as they lumbered up the hill, he pushed his head with a sudden thrust through the window into the coach, clinging on with his free arm and perching on the running board between the mud-splashed wheels. His voice, at first just a feeble keening, would grow shrill. It lingered in the night air, like an indistinct, plaintive wail of distress; and, heard through the jangling of the harness bells, the murmur of the trees, and the dull rumbling of the half-empty coach, it had about it a quality of remoteness that Emma found profoundly disturbing. It spiralled down into the very depths of her soul like a whirlwind into an abyss, and then swept her out into the reaches of an infinite melancholy. But Hivert, noticing the difference in the balance of his coach, used to strike out fiercely with his whip at the blind man. The lash would land on the raw ulcerated flesh, and he would fall into the mud, howling.

Eventually, the other passengers in the Hirondelle all nodded off, some with their mouths hanging open, others with their chins on their chests; they slept leaning on a neighbour's shoulder or else hanging onto a strap and swaying in time with the coach; the light reflected from the lantern outside as it swung back and forth over the rumps of the shaft horses shone in through the curtains of chocolate-coloured calico, clothing these motionless travellers in blood-red shadows. Emma, drunk with misery, kept shivering under her cloak, her feet chilled to the bone, despair reigning in her heart.

At the house, Charles was waiting for her; the Hirondelle was always late on Thursdays. But, at long last, Madame was home! She would hardly even bother to give her child a kiss. The dinner wasn't ready, but she didn't care! She found excuses for the cook. The girl seemed to get away with anything, now.

Frequently her husband, noticing her pallor, enquired if she were unwell.

'No,' Emma replied.

'But,' he would persist, 'you seem so strange, this evening?'

'Oh, it's nothing! Nothing!'

There were even some Thursdays when she disappeared into her room almost as soon as she returned. Justin would be up there; he would move noiselessly about, more adroit at looking after her than the most experienced lady's maid. He used to place the matches, the candlestick, and a book ready to hand, lay out her nightgown, and turn down the bed.

'Fine,' she would say, 'that'll do! Now off you go!'

For he still stood there, his hands hanging at his sides, his eyes staring, as if wrapped in the myriad strands of a fleeting dream.

The next day was terrible, and the following days even more intolerable because of Emma's impatience to repossess her happiness. Hers was a raw craving, inflamed to fever pitch by familiar images, and to which, on the seventh day, she could surrender without restraint in Léon's caressing hands. *His* raptures were cloaked in effusions of amazement and gratitude. Emma took a judicious, concentrated delight in this love of his, nurturing it with every amorous resource at her disposal, always a little fearful that, in time, it might die away.

Often she said to him, in a gentle, melancholy tone:

'Ah! One day you'll leave me . . . You'll get married . . . You'll be like the others . . .'

'What others?' he asked.

'Oh . . . just men, I mean.' Then, languorously pushing him away, she said:

'You're all vile!'

One day when they were chatting in a philosophical vein about life's disillusionments, she actually told him (testing his jealousy or perhaps yielding to an irresistible urge to speak freely) that in the past, before she knew him, she had loved someone, hastily adding 'not the way I love you', and swearing on the life of her child that 'nothing had happened'.

The young man believed her, but nevertheless wanted to know what the profession of the 'other' had been.

'He was a ship's captain.'

In saying this did she not forestall further questions, and at the same time exalt herself, by this supposed fascination exerted over a man who was by nature bellicose, and accustomed to deferential admiration?

Then the clerk felt all the lowliness of his own position; he longed for epaulettes, decorations, a title. These things must surely please her greatly; her spendthrift ways seemed to suggest as much.

Even so, Emma kept quiet about a number of her extravagant fancies, about how, for example, she yearned to possess, for her trips to Rouen, a blue tilbury drawn by an English horse, and driven by a groom wearing top-boots. It was Justin who had inspired this fantasy, by begging her to take him on as footman; and although this privation did not attenuate the joy she experienced on her arrival every Thursday, it undoubtedly intensified the bitterness of her return.

Often, when they were talking about Paris, she would murmur: 'Oh, how happy we'd be, living there!'

'But we are happy, aren't we?' the young man would reply, gently stroking her hair.

'Yes, yes of course we are; I'm being silly. Kiss me!'

She was more charming than ever to her husband, making him pistachio creams and playing him waltzes after dinner. He therefore believed himself the luckiest man in the world, and Emma was living without a cloud on her horizon when quite suddenly, one evening:

'It's Mademoiselle Lempereur, isn't it, who's giving you your piano lessons?'

'Yes.'

'Well! I've just met her,' continued Charles, 'at Madame Liégeard's. I mentioned you to her; she doesn't know who you are.'

It was like a bolt from the blue. She managed, however, to reply quite naturally:

'She must have forgotten my name.'

'But perhaps,' said the doctor, 'there's several Mademoiselle Lempereurs in Rouen, who teach piano?'

'Possibly.' Then, quickly, she added:

'But I've got her receipts. Here! Look!'

And she went to the desk, rummaged in all the drawers, mixed up all the papers and worked herself up into such a state that Charles implored her not to go to so much trouble for the sake of some wretched receipts.

'Oh, I'll find them,' she said.

And indeed, the following Friday, when Charles was pulling on one of his boots in the dark little closet where his clothes were kept, he felt a piece of paper between the leather and his sock, took it out and read:

> Received, for one quarter's lessons, plus various supplies, the sum of 65 francs.
>
> Félicie Lempereur, Music Instructor.

'How the devil did that get into my boot?'

'It must have fallen out of that old box of bills on the edge of the shelf.'

From that moment on, her life was nothing but a tissue of lies with which she enveloped her love, to veil it from the world.

Lying became, for her, a necessity, an obsession, a pleasure, to the point where, if she remarked that she had walked down the street, the previous day, on the right side, you could be certain that she had actually walked down on the left.

One morning when she had set out, as usual, rather lightly clad, it suddenly began to snow; and while Charles was staring out of the window at the weather, he caught sight of Monsieur Bournisien in Monsieur Tuvache's gig; they were driving to Rouen. So he hurried down and handed the priest a heavy shawl to give to Madame as soon as he arrived at the Croix Rouge. On reaching the inn, Bournisien immediately enquired for the wife of the Yonville doctor. The landlady replied that Madame almost never patronized her establishment. That evening, therefore, when the priest recognized Madame Bovary in the Hirondelle, he told her of his dilemma, although without appearing to attribute any great importance to it; for then he launched into praises of a preacher currently attached to the cathedral, a prodigy of eloquence, to whose sermons all the ladies were flocking in droves.

Still, although he had not demanded an explanation of her, others, in the future, might not be so tactful. It therefore seemed prudent to leave the Hirondelle, each Thursday, at the Croix Rouge and take a room, with the result that those good neighbours of hers from the village who saw her there on the stairs never suspected a thing.

One day, however, Monsieur Lheureux ran into her as she was emerging from the Hôtel de Boulogne on Léon's arm; and she was filled with alarm, imagining he would talk. He was not such a fool. Three days later, however, he came to see her, closed the door, and said:

'I would like some money.'

She declared she had none to give him. Lheureux began whining, reminding her of the many occasions when he had helped her out. Indeed, of the two promissory notes Charles had signed, Emma had thus far paid off only one. As for the second, Lheureux, at her request, had agreed to replace it with two others, which had in their turn been renewed, for an extremely long term. The merchant then fished out of his pocket a list of goods that had not been paid for: the curtains, the carpet, the material to cover the armchairs, a number of dresses, and various toiletries, the total cost of which was about two thousand francs.

She hung her head. He continued:

'Well, even if you've no cash, you do own "property".'

And he mentioned a tumbledown shack in Barneville, near Aumale, which brought in little revenue. It had once belonged to a small farm that Monsieur Bovary senior had sold, for Lheureux knew everything, down to the acreage, and the names of the neighbours.

'Now if I were in your shoes,' he said, 'I'd get rid of it, and I'd still have a nice little sum left over.'

She objected that finding a buyer would be hard; he thought he might be able to help solve that difficulty; then she enquired how to go about selling it, legally.

'You've power of attorney, haven't you?'

His words were like a breath of fresh air to her.

'Leave your bill with me,' said Emma.

'Oh, no, don't give it a second thought,' replied Lheureux.

He returned the following week, boasting that, after many enquiries, he had managed to discover a certain Langlois, who had evidently been eyeing the property covetously for quite some time, although without ever naming the price he would pay.

'Oh, the price doesn't matter!' she exclaimed.

On the contrary, he insisted, it would be best to move slowly, and sound this character out. It was worthwhile going in person, and since she was not free to do so, he offered to make the trip on her behalf and negotiate directly with Langlois. On his return, he announced that the purchaser had made an offer of four thousand francs.

Emma beamed with delight on hearing this.

'Frankly,' he said, 'it's a good offer.'

She received half the money immediately; but when she tried to settle her account, Lheureux told her: 'To be perfectly honest with you, it really upsets me to see you part with so "substantial" a sum all at one go.'

At this she stared at the two thousand francs, as a vision came into her head of the endless meetings with her lover that they represented: 'What? How do you mean?' she stammered.

'Oh, come on!' he went on with a genial laugh; 'you can put anything you like on a bill. Do you suppose I don't know about married couples' little arrangements?'

And he gazed at her fixedly, running his nails up and down two long strips of paper he was holding. Finally, opening his billfold, he spread out on the table four promissory notes, each for a thousand francs.

'Sign these, and keep it all,' he said.

Shocked, Emma exclaimed in protest.

'But if I give you the surplus,' he answered brazenly, 'I'm doing you a service, aren't I?'

And, picking up a pen, he wrote across the bottom of the bill: 'Received from Madame Bovary, four thousand francs.'

'What's to worry about, since in six months you'll get the balance on your shack, and I've made the final one of these notes due after that date?'

Emma found these calculations somewhat confusing,* and her ears kept ringing as if from the noise of gold coins bursting out of their bags and clattering onto the wooden floor all around her. Lheureux went on to explain that he had a friend named Vinçart, a banker in Rouen, who would discount the four notes, after which he himself would return to Madame anything over and above the amount actually owing him.

However, instead of two thousand francs, he brought only eighteen hundred, declaring that his friend Vinçart (as was only 'fair') had kept two hundred francs for commission and discount.

Then, casually, he asked her for a receipt.

'You understand . . . there are times, in business . . . Oh, and date it, please, date it.'

A host of realizable fantasies now paraded through Emma's imagination. She was sufficiently prudent to set aside three thousand francs, with which she paid off the first three notes when they fell due; but the fourth happened to arrive at the house on a Thursday, and Charles, quite distraught, waited patiently for his wife to come home and explain it to him.

If she had said nothing to him about this loan, it was in order to spare him worry over domestic problems; she sat herself down on his knee, stroked his cheeks, crooned soothingly, and embarked on an endless enumeration of all the indispensable items she had acquired on credit.

'So you really have to agree that, considering what a lot of things we bought, it's not all that expensive.'

At his wits' end, Charles soon turned to the inevitable Lheureux, who promised to calm things down if Monsieur would sign two promissory notes for him, one of which, for seven hundred francs, would fall due in three months' time. To ensure that he would be able to meet this, Charles wrote a pathetic letter to his mother. Instead of sending an answer, she came in person, and when Emma asked whether he had got anything out of her, he replied: 'Yes, but she insists on seeing the bill.'

At dawn the following morning Emma flew to Monsieur Lheureux's, and begged him to make out another bill totalling less than a thousand francs; for, if she were to show the one for four thousand, she would have had to admit to paying off two-thirds of it, and, in consequence, to selling off the cottage; this affair had been handled very discreetly by Lheureux, and indeed did not become known until later.

Despite the very low price of each article, the elder Madame Bovary naturally thought the expense excessive.

'Couldn't you have managed without a carpet? Why had you to re-cover the armchairs? In my day, there was only one armchair in a house, for anyone elderly—at any rate, that was the case in my mother's home, and she was a most respectable woman, I assure you. Not everyone can be rich! There's no such thing as a fortune that can't be frittered away! I'd be ashamed to pamper myself the way you do! Yet I'm an old woman, and I need my comforts. Just look at this! And this! Nothing but finery and frippery! My goodness! Why get silk at two francs for the lining when there's perfectly adequate cotton jaconet to be had at half a franc, or perhaps even less?'

Emma, lounging on the sofa, answered with complete calm: 'Yes, Madame, you've made your point.'

The older woman kept on expostulating, predicting that they'd end their days in the poorhouse. Anyway, it was really Bovary's fault. What a blessing he'd promised to cancel this power of attorney . . .

'What?'

'Yes, I have his word,' replied the good lady.

Opening the window, Emma summoned Charles, and the poor man was forced to admit that, in the face of his mother's persistence, he had indeed given his word.

Emma vanished and, returning almost immediately, majestically handed her mother-in-law a large sheet of paper.

'Thank you,' said the old lady. And she flung the power of attorney into the fire.

Emma burst out into loud, strident laughter, which went on and on: it was an attack of hysterics.

'Oh! My God!' exclaimed Charles. 'You're in the wrong too— carrying on and upsetting her like this!'

With a shrug, his mother declared that 'it was all just put on'.

But Charles, turning against her for the first time, took his wife's side, with the result that Madame Bovary senior declared she was going home. She left the very next day; and when he attempted, on the doorstep, to persuade her to stay, she replied:

'No, no! You love her more than me, and that's right, that's as it should be. Well, there's nothing to be done, but you'll see, you'll see! . . . Good luck with it! Because I won't be back here again any time soon, "carrying on and upsetting her", as you put it.'

Even so, Charles felt very abashed in the presence of his wife, who made no effort to hide how bitterly she resented his lack of trust; it took a lot of coaxing before she would agree to renew the power of attorney, and he even accompanied her to Monsieur Guillaumin's to have a second, precisely similar, document drawn up.

'I fully understand your decision,' said the notary, 'a man of science cannot concern himself with all the practical minutiae of daily life.'

Charles took comfort in this sycophantic remark, which recast his cowardice in the flattering light of a preoccupation with higher things.

What an overflowing of joy, the following Thursday, in their room at the hotel, with Léon! She laughed, wept, sang, danced, had sorbets brought up, and demanded cigarettes; he thought her wildly excessive, but adorable, magnificent.

He had no notion of what fundamental urge was impelling her to hurl herself ever more recklessly into the pleasures of the flesh. Increasingly irritable, greedy, and sensual, she would walk beside him in the street with her head held high, unafraid, she claimed, of being compromised. Nevertheless, there were times when Emma trembled at the unbidden thought of encountering Rodolphe; for she sensed that, although they had parted for ever, she was not wholly free of him.

One evening, she did not return to Yonville. Charles grew frantic with anxiety, while little Berthe, who refused to go to bed without seeing her mother, cried and sobbed as if her heart would break. Justin had set out on a haphazard search along the road, and Monsieur Homais had actually abandoned his pharmacy.

Finally, at eleven, Charles could bear it no longer. He harnessed his trap, jumped in, and whipped up his nag, reaching the Croix Rouge at two in the morning. No Emma. Might Léon perhaps have seen her? But where did he live? Luckily, he managed to remember the address of the clerk's employer. He hurried there.

Dawn was breaking. He could just make out a nameplate above an entrance: he knocked. Someone, without opening the door, bellowed the required information through it, along with a string of invective directed at those who disturbed decent folk in the middle of the night.

The building where the clerk lived boasted neither bell, nor knocker, nor porter. He thundered on the shutters with his fists, but then, seeing a policeman approach, crept away in alarm.

'What an idiot I am,' he thought; 'they must have kept her for dinner at Monsieur Lormeaux's.'

The Lormeaux family no longer lived in Rouen.

'She'll have stayed behind to look after Madame Dubreuil. Oh, no! Madame Dubreuil's been dead ten months! . . . But where in the world can she be?'

He had a brainwave. In a café he asked for a directory, and rapidly searched for the name of Mademoiselle Lempereur, who lived at No. 74, Rue de la Renelle-des-Moraquiniers.

Just as he turned into this street, Emma herself appeared at the far end of it; he did not so much embrace her as fling himself upon her, crying:

'Whatever kept you, yesterday?'

'I was taken ill.'

'What was the matter? . . . Where? . . . What happened?'

Passing her hand over her forehead, she replied:

'At Mademoiselle Lempereur's.'

'Oh, I was sure of it! I was on my way there.'

'There's no point,' said Emma. 'She's just gone out. But, another time, you mustn't get so worked up. I won't feel I can do anything, you see, if I know that the smallest delay in my return gets you in a state like this.'

Thus she gave herself a kind of licence to consider nothing, in her escapades, but her own desires. And she certainly took full and unconstrained advantage of this dispensation. Whenever she felt the urge to see Léon, she set off for Rouen on the slightest pretext, and, as he did not expect to see her that day, she had to fetch him from his office.

On the first few occasions, his delight was intense; but, before long, he no longer tried to hide the truth: that his employer kept complaining vociferously about these interruptions.

'Oh, who cares! Come on,' she would say.

And he would slip out.

She wanted him to dress entirely in black and grow a tiny pointed beard, after the style of Louis XIII portraits. She demanded to see his rooms, and pronounced them dull; this comment made him blush, but she paid no attention, advising him to buy curtains like her own; when he objected because of the expense:

'Aha! You do like to watch your pennies, don't you?' she said, laughing.

At each meeting, Léon had to tell her exactly what he had done since the last time. She demanded poetry, poetry composed for her, a 'love poem' written in her honour; he could never come up with rhymes for the second stanza, and was reduced to copying a sonnet in a keepsake album.

He did this less from vanity than from a simple desire to please her. He never disagreed with any of her ideas; he acquiesced in all her tastes; he was becoming her mistress, rather than she his. Her sweet murmurs and her kisses ravished his soul. Where could she have learnt this corruptness, so deep-seated and so dissembling as to seem almost intangible?

CHAPTER VI

On those occasions when he travelled to Yonville to see Emma, Léon had often dined at the pharmacist's; he therefore felt obliged, out of politeness, to return his hospitality.

'Delighted!' Homais had replied; 'it's high time, in any case, that I got back into the swing of things; I'm getting set in my ways here. We'll go to a show, have dinner in a restaurant, paint the town red!'

'Oh, my dear!' murmured Madame Homais tenderly, alarmed by these unspecified perils her husband would be facing.

'Well, what's wrong now? Don't you think I'm already wrecking my health thoroughly enough, perpetually breathing those chemical fumes! That's women for you, isn't it: they're jealous of Science, but they object if you indulge in some perfectly innocent diversion! Never mind, you can count on me, I'll come to Rouen one of these days and we'll really have some high jinks.'

In the past, the apothecary would never have permitted such an expression to cross his lips, but he had recently adopted a playful, Parisian style that he believed the height of good taste. Like his neighbour Madame Bovary, he would eagerly cross-examine Léon about the manners of the capital, and he even used slang to impress his worthy fellow citizens, affecting expressions like 'hole', 'digs', 'dandy', 'dandier', 'Breda Street' (in English), and saying 'I must push off' for: I must go.*

So, one Thursday, Emma was surprised to find Monsieur Homais in the kitchen of the Lion d'Or, dressed in his travel clothes, that is, enveloped in an ancient cloak that no one knew he possessed, holding a small case in one hand and in the other the footmuff from the pharmacy. He had not breathed a word about his plan to anyone, fearful lest his absence alarm the public.

The prospect of revisiting the haunts of his youth must have excited him, for he never stopped talking the whole way to Rouen, and the coach had barely drawn to a halt when he leapt out and set off to find Léon; in vain did the clerk protest, Monsieur Homais dragged him off with him to the vast Café de Normandie, where the pharmacist made a majestic entrance with his hat still on his head, believing it dreadfully provincial to remove one's hat in a public place.

Emma waited for Léon for three-quarters of an hour. Finally she hurried to his office, and then, lost in conjectures of every kind, heaping reproaches upon him for his heartlessness and upon herself for her weakness, she spent the afternoon with her face glued to the window of their room.

At two o'clock, the men were still sitting opposite one another at table. The big dining room was emptying; the stove chimney, made in the shape of a palm tree, spread out in a golden fan against the white ceiling; and close to their table, inside the window, in full sunlight, a tiny jet of water gurgled away into a marble pool where, amid watercress and asparagus, floated three sluggish lobsters that kept lunging at a nearby pile of recumbent quail.

Homais was revelling in it all. Although he was intoxicated by the luxurious surroundings rather than by the fine fare, the bottle of Pomard had stirred his faculties somewhat, and when the rum omelette appeared, he began to expound various immoral theories about women. What he found particularly seductive was the quality of 'chic'. He adored an elegantly turned-out woman in a beautifully furnished setting, and, as for physical attributes, well, he was not averse to 'a nice bit of stuff'.

Léon gazed in despair at the clock. The apothecary went on drinking, eating, talking.

'You must be feeling really deprived, here in Rouen,' he suddenly remarked. 'But, of course, she's not *that* far away.'

And, when the clerk blushed:

'Oh, come on, be honest! You're not going to deny, are you, that in Yonville . . .?'

The young man began stammering something.

'At Madame Bovary's, weren't you courting . . .?'

'Who do you mean?'

'Why, the maid!'

Homais was perfectly serious; however Léon, his vanity rather than his prudence carrying the day, protested indignantly. In any case, he only fancied brunettes.

'I agree with you,' said the pharmacist, 'they have a more amorous temperament.'

And, leaning forward to whisper in his friend's ear, he enumerated the signs by which one could recognize a woman of amorous temperament. He even launched into an ethnographic digression: German women were dreamy, French women licentious, Italian women passionate.

'What about black women?' enquired the clerk.

'Artists go for them,'* said Homais. 'Waiter, two coffees!'

'Shall we go?' Léon finally asked impatiently.

'Yes.' Homais replied in English.

But, before leaving, he insisted on seeing the proprietor, to convey his compliments. Then, to get rid of him, the young man claimed he had some business to attend to.

'I'll come with you!' declared Homais.

And, walking along the streets at Léon's side, he held forth about his wife, his children, their future, and his pharmacy, describing the neglected state it had once been in, and the degree of perfection it had now attained, under his care.

When they reached the Hôtel de Boulogne, Léon abruptly abandoned him and raced up the stairs. He found his mistress in a state of extreme agitation.

At the mention of the pharmacist, she flew into a rage. However, he had plenty of reasonable excuses: it wasn't his fault, she knew what Monsieur Homais was like, didn't she? Could she possibly believe that he, Léon, preferred his company to hers? But she went on turning her head away; he did not let her go, but fell on his knees, encircling her waist with his arms, in a languorous pose full of desire and entreaty.

She was still standing; her huge, blazing eyes were fixed on him, with a grave, almost terrible gaze. Then tears dimmed her eyes, her rosy eyelids closed, she gave him her hands, and Léon was showering them with kisses when a servant knocked on the door, saying that someone was enquiring for Monsieur.

'You'll come back?' she said.

'Yes.'

'But when?'

'Right away.'

'It's just a "ploy",' said the pharmacist on seeing Léon. 'I thought I'd interrupt this interview that you didn't seem too pleased about. Let's go to Bridoux's for a cordial.'

Léon swore that he must return to the office. At this, the pharmacist started cracking jokes about legal red tape, and bureaucracy.

'Come on, for heaven's sake just dump Cujas and Barthole* for a bit. What's to stop you? Be a pal! Let's go to Bridoux's; you'll see his dog. It's quite fascinating!'

And as the clerk obstinately refused to change his mind:

'Then I'm coming too. I'll read the paper while I wait for you, or glance through a law book.'

Dazed by Emma's anger, Homais's chatter, and also, perhaps, by his heavy lunch, Léon stood there indecisively, as if bewitched by the pharmacist, who kept repeating:

'Come to Bridoux's! It's just round the corner, in Rue Malpalu.'

So then, out of cowardice, or stupidity, or one of those elusive impulses that entice us into acts we really deplore, he allowed himself be taken to Bridoux's. They found him in his tiny courtyard, supervising three waiters who were panting and heaving at the huge wheel of a machine for making seltzer water.* Homais offered them some advice; he embraced Bridoux; they drank their cordial. Again and again Léon tried to get away, but each time his companion grabbed his arm, saying:

'Hold on! I'm just leaving. We'll go to the *Fanal de Rouen*, and see everybody there. I'll introduce you to Tomassin.'

Managing at last to shake him off, Léon raced to the hotel. Emma was no longer there.

She had just left, in a rage. She loathed him now. She saw this failure to keep his word as an insult, and cast about for further reasons to break with him: he was incapable of heroism, weak, trite, more spineless than a woman, miserly as well, and a coward.

Then, when she calmed down, she began to see that she had probably been unjust. But to speak ill of those we love always requires of us a certain degree of detachment. We should never maltreat our idols: the gilding rubs off on our fingers.

Increasingly, they were reduced to talking about matters extraneous to their love; and the letters that Emma wrote to him were full of flowers and poetry, the moon and the stars—naive stimulants for a flagging passion that sought nourishment from any and every external source. She continually promised herself that her next trip would bring her profound bliss; then, afterwards, she had to admit that she had felt nothing extraordinary. This disappointment would rapidly be expunged by a fresh surge of hope, and Emma would return to him more ardent, more voracious, than before. She would strip off her clothes with savage hands, tearing at the delicate laces of her corset, which slithered down over her hips with a serpentine hiss. Barefoot, she would tiptoe over to check again that the door was bolted, then, in a single movement, would let fall all her garments at once—and, pale and silent, grave of face, cast herself into his arms with a long, shuddering sigh.

And yet, in that brow pearled with cold sweat, in those stammering lips and unfocused eyes, in those gripping arms, there seemed to Léon to be something excessive, shadowy, and ominous, something that kept slipping between them, subtly, to separate them.

He did not dare question her; but, realizing how experienced she was, he told himself that she must have sampled every extreme of pain and of pleasure. What had charmed him at first now rather frightened him. Besides, he rebelled against the way, with each passing week, his personality was becoming increasingly dominated by hers. He resented Emma for this ongoing victory. He even struggled to stop himself loving her, but, at the sound of her boots on the parquet, he would feel his will-power draining away, like a drunkard at the sight of strong liquor.

True, she never failed to shower him with attentions of every kind, from delicacies for the palate to seductive garments and languorous glances. She brought roses from Yonville in her bosom and threw them in his face; she enquired anxiously about his health, gave him advice on how to behave, and, to bind him closer, perhaps in the hope of securing divine assistance, she placed round his neck a medal of the Blessed Virgin. Like a virtuous mother, she questioned him about his friends. She used to say to him:

'Don't see them, don't go out with them, think of nothing but us, love me!'

She would have liked to be able to watch his every move, and even toyed with the idea of having him followed. There was a sort of tramp who used to hang about near the hotel and accost travellers; he would be glad to . . . But her pride rebelled.

'Oh! Why bother! Let him cheat on me, what do I care! Does it matter?'

One day when they had parted early, and she was returning alone along the boulevard, she caught sight of the walls of her convent; she sank down onto a bench, in the shade of the elms. How tranquil those days had been! How she used to thirst for that indescribable emotion of love that she'd tried so hard to imagine, from her reading!

The early months of her marriage, her rides in the forest, the Vicomte waltzing, Lagardy singing—all this she saw again in her mind's eye . . . And, suddenly, Léon appeared, looking just as remote as the others.

'But I do love him!' she told herself.

What difference did it make; she wasn't happy, she'd never been happy! Why did life fall so far short of her expectations, why did whatever she depended on turn instantly to dust beneath her hand? But if somewhere there existed a strong, handsome being, a heroic spirit full of both passion and delicacy, a poet's heart in an angel's body, a lyre with strings of steel, sounding elegiac epithalamia to the heavens, then why mightn't *she* meet such a person? What an impossible dream! Nothing, in any case, was worth the effort of searching. Everything was a lie! Every smile concealed a yawn of boredom, every joy a curse, every pleasure brought revulsion, and the sweetest kisses left upon your lips only a vain craving for a still more sublime delight.

A long-drawn-out metallic wheezing filled the air, and four chimes sounded from the convent bell. Four o'clock! It seemed to her that she had been sitting there, on that bench, since the birth of time. But an infinity of passion can be compressed into a single minute, like a crowd into a small space.

Emma's days continued to revolve solely round her passion: she gave no more thought to money than would an archduchess.

One day, however, a puny little man, red-faced and bald, arrived at the house, saying he had come on behalf of Monsieur Vinçart, of Rouen. He removed the pins securing the side pocket of his long green coat, stuck them in his sleeve and politely handed her a document.

It was a note for seven hundred francs, bearing her signature, which Lheureux, despite his assurances, had signed over to Vinçart.

She dispatched her servant to fetch Lheureux. He was unable to come.

Then the stranger, who still stood there, casting curious glances round the room from under the cover of his pale bushy eyebrows, innocently enquired:

'What reply should I give Monsieur Vinçart?'

'Well!' said Emma; 'well, tell him . . . that at the moment I can't . . . It'll have to be next week, he must wait . . . Yes, next week.'

And the little man departed without a word.

But the following day, at noon, she received a writ; and the sight of the legal stamped document, on which there appeared several times, in large letters, the words 'Maître Hareng, court officer in Buchy', frightened her so badly that she flew round to the merchant's shop.

She found him there, tying up a parcel.

'At your service, Madame,' he said. 'What can I do for you?'

Lheureux nevertheless continued with his task, helped by his thirteen-year-old clerk; she had a slight hunchback, and served as both his assistant and his cook.

Then, his clogs clattering on the wooden floor of his shop, he preceded Madame up to the first floor, and ushered her into a tiny office, where a large pine desk supported a number of ledgers secured by a padlocked iron bar lying across them. Against the wall, under some lengths of calico, Emma caught a glimpse of a safe, of a size that suggested it held something other than merely banknotes and coins. Monsieur Lheureux, in fact, was a pawnbroker, and the safe was where he had stored away Madame Bovary's gold chain, as well as the earrings he had acquired from poor Tellier. Forced in the end to sell his café, Tellier had bought a sorry little grocery business in Quincampoix, where he was slowly dying of his asthma, surrounded by a stock of candles less yellow than his face.

Settling himself in his big wicker armchair, Lheureux said:

'So, what's new?'

'Look.' And she showed him the paper.

'Well, what can I do about it?'

At this she lost her temper, reminding him that he had sworn not to circulate her promissory notes; he admitted as much.

'But I myself was forced into it; I had a knife at my throat.'

'What will happen now?' she asked.

'Oh, it's perfectly simple; a court order, then the bailiffs . . . Nothing to be done!'

It was all Emma could do not to hit him. She quietly enquired whether there might not be some way of calming down Monsieur Vinçart.

'Huh! Calm down Vinçart—not very likely. You don't know him, he's more ferocious than an Arab.'

But, she insisted, Monsieur Lheureux absolutely *must* help her out.

'Now just you listen to me. Up till now, I believe, I've been pretty good to you.'

He opened one of his ledgers.

'Look!' He ran his finger up the page:

'Let's see ... let's see ... Third of August, two hundred francs ... Seventeenth of June, a hundred and fifty ... Twenty-third of March, forty-six ... And in April ...'

He stopped, as if afraid of saying the wrong thing.

'And I'm not even mentioning the notes signed by Monsieur, one for seven hundred francs, the other for three hundred! As for those little instalments of yours, and the interest, there's no end to it, it's all a hopeless muddle. I wash my hands of it!'

Emma was weeping, even calling him her 'dear Monsieur Lheureux'. But he kept laying all the blame at the door of 'that shark Vinçart'. Besides, he himself was on his uppers, no one was paying their bills at the moment, his creditors were trying to get the very clothes off his back, a poor shopkeeper like himself couldn't advance money.

She said nothing more, and Monsieur Lheureux, who was chewing the end of his quill pen, perhaps found her silence disquieting, for he went on:

'Unless, of course, something were to come in one of these days ... in that case I could ...'

'Anyway,' she said, 'as soon as the balance on the Barneville property ...'

'What?'

On hearing that Langlois had not yet paid up, he seemed very surprised. Then, in mellifluous tones:

'So, we understand one another, do we, as to terms ...'

'Oh yes, whatever you think proper.'

So then, after closing his eyes in concentration, he scribbled a few figures, and, declaring that it would be a real struggle for him, that he was taking a risk and 'bleeding himself white', he dictated four notes for two hundred and fifty francs apiece, payable consecutively at monthly intervals.

'Let's hope Vinçart is prepared to listen to me! Anyway, we're agreed. I'm not one to shilly-shally, I believe in plain dealing.'

Then he casually showed her some new items he had in stock, not one of which, in his opinion, was good enough for Madame.

'When I think that this is a dress material that sells at seven sous a metre, and it's guaranteed colour-fast! But believe me, they all fall for it, and naturally no one tells them anything different.' He hoped, by admitting that he swindled other people, to convince her that he was perfectly straight with her.

Then he called her back, to show her three lengths of guipure lace that he had come across recently at a 'bankruptcy auction'.

'Isn't it beautiful!' Lheureux kept saying: 'it's very much in demand just now, for antimacassars, it's the latest thing.'

And, quicker than any conjuror, he wrapped up the lace in blue paper and put it into Emma's hand.

'But at least tell me what . . .'

'Oh, later,' he replied, turning away.

That same evening, she urged Bovary to write to his mother, and ask her to send, without delay, the residue of his inheritance. Her mother-in-law replied that there was nothing left. The estate had been wound up; apart from the Barneville property, they could still count on an annual sum of six hundred francs, which she would faithfully send on to them.

So then Madame posted off accounts to two or three patients, and, before long, she was using this resource regularly, for it produced results. She always made a point of adding, as a postscript: 'Please don't mention this to my husband, you know how proud he is . . . Forgive me . . . Your obedient servant . . .' There were a handful of complaints, but she intercepted them.

To raise money, she began to sell her old gloves, her old hats, bits and pieces of old metalware; true to her peasant's rapacious instincts, she always drove a hard bargain. Then, on her trips to Rouen, she picked up second-hand oddments that Monsieur Lheureux would certainly buy if no one else wanted them. She bought herself ostrich plumes and Chinese porcelain and travelling chests; she borrowed money from Félicité, from Madame Lefrançois, from the proprietress of the Croix Rouge, from anybody, anywhere. With the money that she finally received from the Barneville sale, she paid off two bills; the other fifteen hundred francs just melted away. She took out fresh loans, and so it went on!

Sometimes, it is true, she did actually try to work out her finances, but she would come up with such outrageous totals that she found them impossible to credit. Then she would begin afresh, soon grow confused, drop the whole enterprise, and think no more about it.

The house was such a dismal place, now! Tradesmen were seen to emerge from it in a fury. Scarves lay around forgotten on top of stoves, and little Berthe, to the shocked disapproval of Madame Homais, went about with holes in her stockings. If Charles dared to risk a comment, she would retort savagely that it wasn't her fault!

Why did she fly into these tempers? He blamed everything on her old nervous complaint; and, reproaching himself for confusing physical illness with defects of character, he accused himself of selfishness, and longed to go and take her in his arms.

'Oh, no,' he reflected, 'I'd only irritate her!'

And he would stay where he was.

After dinner, he used to walk about the garden on his own, or, taking his small daughter on his knee, pick up his medical journal and try to teach her to read. The child, who had never been made to study, would soon open wide her large sad eyes and burst into tears. To console her, he fetched water in the watering can for her to make rivers in the sand, or snapped off branches of privet so that she could plant trees in the flower beds; this could hardly spoil the garden, which was overgrown with tall weeds; they owed Lestiboudois for so many days' wages! The child would complain of feeling cold, and ask for her mother.

'Better call Félicité,' said Charles. 'You know, sweetheart, that mama doesn't like to be disturbed.'

Autumn was approaching and the leaves were already starting to fall, just like two years ago, when she was ill! When, oh when would this come to an end? He went on pacing up and down, his hands clasped behind his back.

Madame was in her room. No one went up there. She stayed in it all day, sunk in lethargy, only half dressed, occasionally burning exotically scented pellets she had bought in Rouen, in a shop belonging to an Algerian. At night, to escape the sleeping presence of that man stretched out at her side, she had finally, by dint of nasty looks, exiled him to the attic; and, till dawn came, she lay awake, reading sensational novels full of orgies and bloody violence. Often, gripped by sudden terror, she screamed aloud. Charles came running.

'Oh, do go away!' she would say to him.

At other times, when the secret fire fed by her adultery tormented her more sharply, gasping, frantic, burning with desire, she flung open her window and breathed in the cold air, letting her thick hair fan out in the wind as she gazed up at the stars, dreaming of princely loves. Her thoughts were of him, of Léon. At that moment she would have given anything for a single one of those encounters that sated her craving.

Those were her gala days. She wanted them to be magnificent! When he was unable to meet the expense, she freely contributed the rest; this happened almost every time. He tried to make her see that they would be just as happy somewhere else, in some more modest hotel; but she always objected.

One day, she pulled out of her purse six tiny silver-gilt spoons (their wedding present from old man Rouault), and asked Léon to take them for her, immediately, to the pawnbroker; Léon obeyed, although the errand was not to his liking. He was afraid of being compromised.

Thinking about this afterwards, he decided that his mistress was beginning to act very strangely; perhaps people had a point, in urging him to break with her.

In fact, someone had sent his mother a long anonymous letter, warning her that 'he was ruining himself with a married woman'; whereupon the good lady, her head filled with visions of that eternal menace to family life, that nebulous, baleful creature, that siren or fantastical monster who lurks in the deepest reaches of love, wrote to Maître Dubocage, his boss, who handled the matter with perfect tact. He lectured Léon for three-quarters of an hour, doing his best to open his eyes, and warn him of the quicksands lying ahead. An affair of this sort would, later on, damage his career. He implored him to break it off, and if he could not make this sacrifice for his own sake, then to make it for him, Dubocage!

In the end Léon had promised not to see Emma again; and he reproached himself for not keeping his word, when he considered the power this woman possessed to embroil him in dubious situations, or inspire gossip, quite apart from the jokes that circulated among his fellow clerks every morning, when they gathered round the stove. Besides, he was about to be promoted to head clerk; the time had come to be serious. So he gave up the flute, and transports of emotion, and flights of imagination—for every respectable middle-class man, in the ferment of his youth, has seen himself, if only for one day, or one hour, as capable of grand emotions and lofty enterprises! The most half-hearted libertine has fantasized about Oriental queens; and every notary carries within himself the vestigial traces of a poet.

He felt bored, now, when Emma, without warning, burst into sobs in his arms; and, like a listener who can only endure a certain dose of music and no more, his heart was growing torpid with indifference towards this clamorous love, whose delicate nuances he could no longer distinguish.

They knew one another too well to experience that wonderment in mutual possession that increases its joy a hundredfold. She was as sick of him as he was weary of her. Emma was rediscovering, in adultery, all the banality of marriage.*

But how to rid herself of him? And then, despite the humiliation of craving such base pleasures, she had come, either out of habit or depravity, to depend on them, and each day she pursued them with a greater frenzy, exhausting every possibility of happiness by the excess of her demands. She blamed Léon for her disappointed hopes, as if he had betrayed her; and she even longed for some disaster that would occasion their separation, since she herself lacked the courage to bring this about.

But in spite of this she did continue to write him love letters, faithful to the idea that a woman should always write to her lover. But, as she wrote, she saw a different man, created from her most passionate memories, her most beautiful passages of fiction, and her most intense yearnings; and in the end he became so real and tangible that her heart would throb in amazement, but without her being able to conjure him up in precise detail, for, like some god, his outline would be blurred by the very multiplicity of his attributes. He inhabited that hazy blue region where silken ladders sway from balconies, and the bright moonlight is heavy with the scent of flowers. She could feel him close to her, he was approaching, he would ravish her with a kiss and carry her off with him. Then, afterwards, she would come back to earth utterly spent and broken—

for those vague amorous raptures left her more exhausted than the most extreme debauchery.

Emma lived, now, in a state of total, unremitting weariness. Often, she would even receive a summons, an official, stamped document, and barely give it a glance. She would have liked to stop living, or stay asleep forever.

On the day of the mid-Lent festivities she did not return to Yonville, but stayed on for the masked ball. She wore velvet breeches with red stockings, a wig with a queue and a cocked hat tilted over one ear. All night long she leapt about to the frenzied notes of the trombones; people circled round, watching her; and in the morning she found herself on the portico of the theatre, with five or six revellers disguised as stevedores or sailors, Léon's friends, who were discussing where to go for supper.

The nearby cafés were all full. Down by the harbour they discovered a dubious-looking restaurant whose proprietor opened up a small room for them, on the fourth floor.

The men gathered in a corner, whispering; probably they were consulting about the cost. There was a clerk, two medical students, and a shop assistant: what company for her! As for the women, Emma soon realized, from their accents, that almost all of them must be of the very lowest class. She felt a thrill of fear, pushed back her chair and stared at the floor.

The others began to eat. She ate nothing; her forehead was burning, her eyelids were smarting, and her skin felt icy cold. In her head she could still feel the ballroom floor rebounding to the rhythmic thump of a thousand dancing feet. The smell of punch and cigar smoke made her dizzy. She fainted; they carried her to the window.

Dawn was just breaking; a great splash of crimson was slowly spreading over the pale sky near the Côte Sainte-Catherine. The wind kept rippling the leaden surface of the river; the bridges were deserted; the street lamps were going out.

Soon, however, she began to feel better, and her thoughts turned to Berthe, fast asleep over there in Yonville, in the servant's room. But a cart laden with long strips of iron drove past, raising a deafening clatter as the vibrating metal echoed off the walls of the houses.

She quickly slipped out of the room, changed from her costume, told Léon she must go home, and finally found herself alone at the Hôtel de Boulogne. Everything—including herself—had become unendurable. She longed to escape like a bird, to fly somewhere where she could recapture her youth, far, far away, out in immaculate space.

Leaving the hotel, she crossed the boulevard and the Place Cauchoise, then walked through a residential area till she reached an open street overlooking some gardens.* She walked fast; the fresh air soothed her; little by little the faces in the crowd, the masks, the quadrilles, the chandeliers, the supper, those women, everything began to vanish like mist before the wind. Then, back at the Croix Rouge, she threw herself down on her bed, in the tiny second-floor room with the prints of the *Tour de Nesle*. At four o'clock, Hivert woke her up.

When she walked into her house, Félicité showed her a piece of grey paper tucked behind the clock. She read:

'By virtue of the order, and in execution of the judgement of the court . . .'

What judgement? And indeed, the preceding day, another document had been delivered that she had not seen; so she was astounded by these words:

'To Madame Bovary: By order of the King, and in the name of the law . . .'

Skipping a few lines, her eye was caught by the words:

'Within twenty-four hours without fail . . .' What? 'Pay the total sum of eight thousand francs.' And it even said, lower down: 'She will be constrained thereto by all due processes of law, and in particular by the seizure of her furniture and effects.'

What was she to do? In twenty-four hours: tomorrow! Lheureux, she thought, must intend to frighten her again; for she suddenly guessed how he had manipulated her, and why he had always been so very obliging. But she was reassured by the exaggeration of the sum specified.

Still, by dint of buying on credit and never paying, by borrowing, signing bills and then renewing them, so that they grew larger with every due date, she had eventually amassed a nice capital sum for the esteemed Lheureux, which he was eager to get his hands on and use for his speculations.

She walked into his shop with a casual air.

'Do you know what's happened to me? I suppose it must be a joke!'

'No!'

'What do you mean?'

He turned away slowly and said, crossing his arms:

'My dear lady, did you imagine that I was going to supply you for ever and ever with goods and money, just out of Christian charity? Let's be fair, I have the right to recover my outlay, do I not?'

She protested at the amount of the debt.

'Too bad! The court upheld it, judgement has been passed, you have been notified. In any case, it's not me, it's Vinçart.'

'But couldn't you . . .?'

'No, I can do nothing.'

'But . . . surely . . . can't we talk it over . . .'

And she started casting about for excuses: she'd known nothing about it . . . it was a dreadful shock. . . .

'Whose fault is that?' asked Lheureux with an ironic bow. 'While I'm spending my days here working like a black, you're out having yourself a good time.'

'Oh, spare me the moralizing!'

'It never does any harm,' he retorted.

Losing her nerve, she pleaded with him; she even pressed her lovely long, slender hand on the shopkeeper's knee.

'Don't touch me! Anyone would think you're trying to seduce me!'

'You're despicable!' she exclaimed.

'My, you're quite a firebrand, aren't you!' replied Lheureux with a laugh.

'I'll tell everyone what you are. I'll tell my husband . . .'

'Ah yes, well, *I* have a little something to show your husband!'

And Lheureux took out of his safe a receipt for eighteen hundred francs, which she had given him for the note discounted by Vinçart.

'Do you imagine', he added, 'that the poor dear man won't understand about your little bit of double-dealing?'

At this she collapsed, more stunned than if she had been hit with a club. He was pacing between the window and the desk, repeating:

'Oh! I'll certainly show it to him . . . I'll certainly show it to him.'

Then he went right up to her and murmured softly: 'I know this isn't pleasant; but after all, nobody's died of it, and, since it's the only way you have left of repaying my money . . .'

'But where am I to get it?' said Emma, wringing her hands.

'Oh! Come on! Somebody like you, with so many good friends!'

And he stared at her with such a knowing, terrifying look that a deep shudder of fear ran through her.

'I promise you, I'll sign . . .' she said.

'I've had enough of your signatures!'

'I can still sell . . .'

'Don't pretend! You've nothing left to sell,' he replied with a shrug.

And he shouted through the tiny window that opened into the shop: 'Annette! Don't forget the three remnants of n.14.'

The servant appeared; Emma understood, and enquired 'how much money was needed to put a stop to the proceedings'.

'It's too late!'

'But if I brought you several thousand francs, a quarter of the sum, a third, nearly all of it?'

'No, no, it's useless!'

And he was urging her gently towards the stairs.

'I beseech you, Monsieur Lheureux, just a few more days!' She was sobbing.

'Oh, lovely! So now it's tears!'

'You're pushing me to the edge!'

'I couldn't care less!' he said, shutting the door.

CHAPTER VII

She was stoical, the next morning, when the bailiff, Maître Hareng, with two witnesses, appeared at her house to draw up the inventory for the seizure.

They began with Bovary's consulting room, and did not list the phrenological head, which was considered an 'instrument of his profession'; but in the kitchen they counted the plates, the pots and pans, the chairs, the candlesticks, and, in the bedroom, all the knick-knacks on the dresser. They inspected her dresses, the linen, the contents of her dressing room; and her existence, down to its most intimate details, was laid out like a cadaver at an autopsy, wholly exposed to the scrutiny of those three men.

Maître Hareng, buttoned into a close-fitting black coat, with a white cravat and tautly stretched gaiters, enquired from time to time:

'If I may be permitted, Madame? If I may be permitted?'

Frequently he would exclaim:

'Charming! . . . Quite delightful!'

Then he would continue making his list, dipping his quill in the inkhorn he held in his left hand.

When they had completed the rooms, they climbed up to the attic.

She kept a desk up there in which Rodolphe's letters were locked away. She had to open it.

'Ah! A correspondence!' remarked Maître Hareng with a knowing smile. 'But, if I may be permitted . . . For I must ascertain that the box contains nothing else.'

And he gently tipped up the letters, as if to dislodge any gold coins they concealed. She was filled with indignation, watching that coarse red hand, with its flaccid, slug-like fingers, touch those pages that had made her heart throb with love.

At long last they left! Félicité came back. Emma had sent her to watch out for Bovary and keep him away from the house; and they quickly settled the bailiff's agent up in the attic, where he promised to remain.

During the evening, she thought Charles seemed worried. Emma studied him with agonized eyes, imagining that every line of his face was an accusation. Then, when her gaze strayed to the mantelpiece adorned with Chinese screens, to the generous folds of the curtains, to the armchairs, to all those things which had palliated the bitterness of her life, she was filled with remorse, or rather with a vast regret, which, far from subduing her passion, served only to exacerbate it. Charles sat placidly stirring the fire, his feet propped up on the fender.

At one point the bailiff's man, perhaps feeling bored in his hiding place, made a noise.

'Is there somebody walking about in the attic?' asked Charles.

'No!' she replied, 'a skylight's been left open, it's banging in the wind.'

The next day, Sunday, she left for Rouen, intending to see every single banker whose name she knew. They were all in their country houses, or away. She did not give up; those that she was able to find, she asked for money, protesting that she needed it, that she would pay it back. Some of them laughed in her face; they all refused.

At two, she hurried to Léon's place, and knocked at the door. Nobody answered. Eventually, he appeared.

'Why've you come?'

'Do you mind?'

'No . . . but . . .'

And he admitted that the landlord disliked his tenants receiving 'women' in their rooms.

'I have to talk to you,' she said.

So then he reached for his key. She stopped him.

'No, over at our place.'

And they went to their room, at the Hôtel de Boulogne.

The first thing she did was to drink a large glass of water. She was very pale. She said to him:

'Léon, there's something you must do for me.'

Clutching both his hands tightly, she kept shaking him as she added:

'Listen, I need eight thousand francs!'

'You must be crazy!'

'No, not yet.'

Then she told him about the attachment of the property, pouring out every detail of her predicament: Charles knew nothing about it; her mother-in-law loathed her, and her father couldn't help: but he, Léon, was going to set about obtaining this vital sum . . .

'But how in the world do you expect? . . .'

'You've no guts!' she cried.

Then he said, stupidly, 'You're exaggerating the problem. Perhaps just two or three thousand would keep this character quiet.'

All the more reason to try to do something; how could it be impossible to come up with three thousand francs? Anyway, Léon could sign for it, instead of her.

'Go on! Try, you must try! Hurry! . . . Oh do try! I'll love you . . . oh, how I'll love you!'

He left, and was back again within an hour. He said, his expression solemn:

'I've been to three people . . . nothing doing!'

Then they remained sitting opposite one another, on either side of the fireplace, motionless, not speaking. Emma kept shrugging and tapping her foot. He heard her mutter:

'If I were in your shoes, *I'd* certainly know where to find it!'

'Where?'

'At your office!'

And she stared at him.

Her eyes were blazing with diabolic recklessness, and she slowly lowered her eyelids in voluptuous invitation, so that Léon sensed his resolution waver before the silent determination of this woman who was willing him to commit a crime. He was filled with fear, and, so as to avoid any kind of confrontation, suddenly struck himself on the forehead, exclaiming:

'Morel's coming home tonight! He won't refuse me, I hope.' (Morel was a friend of his, the son of a very wealthy merchant.) He added: 'I'll bring you the money tomorrow.'

Emma did not seem to welcome this hopeful proposal as joyfully as he had expected. Did she suspect a lie? Turning red, he went on:

'But if I'm not there by three, don't expect me, darling. I'll have to go now, please forgive me . . . Goodbye!'

He pressed her hand, but it lay lifelessly in his. Emma was incapable of feeling anything more.

Four o'clock struck, and she rose to return to Yonville, responding like an automaton to the prompting of habit.

It was a fine day, one of those bright, sharp March days when the sun shines from a pale, unclouded sky. Dressed in their Sunday best, the Rouennais were contentedly strolling about. She reached the square in front of the cathedral. Vespers had just ended; the crowd was streaming out through the three portals, like a river through the three arches of a bridge, and, in the centre, immovable as a rock, stood the beadle.

Then she remembered the day when, full of trepidation and hope, she had entered that vast nave which, though it stretched endlessly before her, was not as boundless as her love; and she walked on, weeping under her veil, dizzy, unsteady, almost fainting.

'Clear the way!' came a shout from a courtyard entrance as the doors opened.

Emma stopped to let a black horse pass in front of her; it pranced between the shafts of a tilbury driven by a gentleman wearing sable. Who was it? . . . She knew him. The carriage leapt forward and disappeared.

Of course, it was he, the Vicomte! She turned; the street was empty. She felt so defeated, so miserable, that she leaned against a wall to keep from falling.

Then she thought that she must have been mistaken. Anyway, she really had no idea. Everything within her, and outside, was abandoning her. She felt she was lost, roaming haphazardly about in some unfathomable abyss; and it was almost with joy that she saw, when she reached the Croix Rouge, her good neighbour Homais; he was supervising the loading onto the Hirondelle of a huge box of pharmaceutical supplies; in his hand he held six *cheminots** enveloped in a cloth, for his wife.

Madame Homais was very fond of these small, heavy bread rolls, shaped like a turban, that are eaten with salted butter, during Lent— the last surviving relics of Gothic fare, dating back, perhaps, to the Crusades, and upon which, in past ages, the lusty Normans used to gorge themselves, imagining that before them on the table, lit by the yellow glow of torches and flanked by flagons of hippocras and giant slabs of salted pork, lay the heads of Saracens served up for them to devour. Like the Normans, the pharmacist's wife, despite her terrible teeth, valiantly gnawed her way through them; and whenever Monsieur Homais made a journey to the city he never failed to bring her some, which he always bought from the best bakery for them, in the Rue Massacre.

'Delighted to see you!' he declared, offering Emma his hand to help her into the Hirondelle.

Then, placing the *cheminots* in the overhead net, he settled himself down, his head bare and his arms folded, in a meditative, Napoleonic pose.

But, when the blind beggar made his customary appearance at the foot of the hill, he exclaimed:

'I fail to understand why the authorities still tolerate such antisocial activities! These unfortunate people should be locked away, and obliged to perform some kind of labour. I must say that Progress advances at a snail's pace. We are still mired in Dark Age barbarism!'

The blind man held out his hat, which swung to and fro outside the window like a loose piece of upholstery.

'What we have here,' pronounced the pharmacist, 'is a scrofulous affection!'

And, although he knew the poor devil, he pretended to be seeing him for the first time, murmuring terms such as *cornea*, *sclera*, *sclerotic*, *facies** and then asking him in a paternal tone:

'How long, my good man, have you been suffering from this

appalling affliction? Instead of imbibing in bars, you'd be better off following a careful regimen.'

He advised him to drink good wine and good beer, and eat good roast meat.* The blind man went on with his song; he seemed, in fact, almost halfwitted. Finally, Monsieiur Homais opened his purse.

'Here's a *sou* for you: you must make change, and give me back half. Now be sure to follow my advice, it will benefit you.'

Hivert was bold enough to express doubts as to its efficacy. But the apothecary vowed he could cure the man himself, with an antiphlogistic salve of his own making, and he gave his address:

'Monsieur Homais, near the market: you can't miss it.'

'All right!' said Hivert. 'Now you've got your *sou*, you must "do your thing" for us.'

The blind man squatted on his haunches, threw back his head and, rolling his greenish eyes and sticking out his tongue, rubbed his belly with both hands while emitting a kind of rumbling howl, like a famished dog. Filled with disgust, Emma, over her shoulder, flung him a five-franc piece. It was all she had left in the world. To cast it away like that was, she thought, beautiful.

The carriage had already moved off again, when Monsieur Homais suddenly leant out of the tiny window and shouted:

'Nothing farinaceous, no dairy products! Wear wool next to the skin and expose the diseased parts to the smoke of juniper berries!'

Little by little, the sight of the familiar scenes through which they were speeding distracted Emma from her present anguish. Her whole being was engulfed in intolerable weariness, and she was in a state of dazed and drowsy misery by the time she reached her house.

'What will be, will be!' she thought.

And anyway, who could say? Why should not something extraordinary happen, at any moment? Lheureux might even die!

At nine the next morning she was awakened by the sound of voices in the square. People in the market place were crowding round one of the pillars, reading a large poster that was displayed on it, and she watched as Justin climbed onto a boundary stone to tear it down. But at that instant the village policeman seized him by the collar. Monsieur Homais had emerged from the pharmacy, and she could see old Madame Lefrançois, apparently holding forth, in the middle of the crowd.

'Madame! Madame!' cried Félicité, coming into the room, 'it's abominable!'

And the poor girl, very upset, handed her a yellow poster she had just pulled off the door. A single glance showed Emma that all the contents of her house were for sale.

They stared at one another in silence. The two of them, mistress and servant, had no secrets from each other. Eventually Félicité sighed:

'If I were you, Madame, I'd go and see Maître Guillaumin.'

'You really think so?'

This question meant: You know what goes on there from his servant. Does the master ever mention me?

'Yes, do go, it's the best thing.'

She dressed in her black dress and jet-beaded bonnet; and, so as not to be seen (the square was still full of people), she took the path by the river, skirting the village.

She was out of breath by the time she reached the notary's gate; the sky was overcast, and a few flakes of snow were falling.

At the sound of the bell, Théodore, in his red waistcoat, appeared on the doorstep; he came down to open the gate, his manner almost familiar, as if she were an old friend, and showed her into the dining room.

A large porcelain stove was humming away beneath a cactus plant that filled the whole alcove, and hanging against the oak-grained wallpaper, framed in black wood, were Steuben's *Esméralda** and Schopin's *Putiphar*.* The table laid ready for breakfast, the pair of silver dish-warmers, the crystal door knobs, the parquet, and the furniture, everything gleamed with immaculate, English cleanliness; the windows, at each corner, were decorated with panes of coloured glass.

'Now this,' thought Emma, 'is how I'd like my dining room to look.'

The notary came in, his left arm holding his dressing gown, patterned with palm trees, close to his body, while with his other hand he rapidly raised and replaced his maroon velvet skull cap. This he wore modishly tilted to the right, and from beneath it emerged the ends of three locks of fair hair which, starting at the back of his head, had been carefully combed round his bald cranium.

After offering Emma a chair, he sat down to his breakfast, apologizing repeatedly for his impoliteness.

'Monsieur,' she said, 'I would like to ask you . . .'

'Yes, Madame, pray continue . . .'

She began to explain her predicament.

Maître Guillaumin knew all about it, for he was secretly in league with the merchant, on whom he relied to provide the financing required for the mortgage loans his clients asked him to arrange. He therefore knew (better than she did) the long story of those loans, made out initially for paltry sums, endorsed by a variety of names, payable at distant dates, and continually renewed, until the day came when, gathering together all the writs for non-payment, Lheureux, wishing not to appear bloodthirsty in the eyes of his neighbours, had called upon his friend Vinçart to initiate the necessary proceedings in his own name.

She interspersed her account with recriminations against Lheureux, to which the notary occasionally responded with a meaningless word or two. He sat eating his cutlet and drinking his tea, his chin half-hidden in a sky-blue cravat pierced by a pair of diamond tiepins secured with a tiny gold chain; and he kept smiling a strange, equivocal smile, cloyingly sweet. Then, noticing that her feet were damp:

'Do move nearer to the stove . . . Rest them on it . . . higher . . . against the porcelain.'

She was afraid of making it dirty. The notary replied in a gallant tone:

'Pretty things can never do any harm.'

So then she tried to soften him, and, growing emotional herself, began telling him about having to run her house on almost nothing, about her personal conflicts, and her needs. He understood perfectly: a lady of her distinction! Without interrupting his breakfast, he had turned right round towards her, so that his knee kept grazing her boot, whose sole was curling up a little as it steamed in the heat of the stove.

But, when she asked him for three thousand francs, he pursed his lips, saying how very sorry he was not to have had the management of her money in the past, for there were countless easy ways—even for a lady—to turn her money to good account. They could have invested it, say, in the Grumesnil peatbogs or the building land at Le Havre, both excellent, almost risk-free speculations; and he let her work herself into a rage, imagining the fantastic sums she would certainly have made.

'How did it happen,' he went on, 'that you didn't come to me?'

'I really don't know,' she said.

'Why was it, eh? Did you find me so very frightening? I'm the one who should be complaining! We scarcely know one another! But even so I'm deeply devoted to you, as I hope you now appreciate?'

Stretching out his hand, he grasped hold of hers, planting a voracious kiss on it, then held it on his knee; and he toyed gently with her fingers while mouthing an endless succession of sweet nothings.

His toneless voice babbled on like a flowing stream; his eyes sparkled behind his glinting spectacles, and his hands were creeping up inside Emma's sleeve, stroking her arm. She could feel his urgent breath against her cheek. What a horrible man!

She sprang from her chair, saying:

'Monsieur, I'm waiting!'

'What for?' asked the notary, suddenly turning chalk-white.

'The money . . .'

'But . . .'

Then, yielding to an overwhelming surge of desire: 'Well, yes, yes! . . .'

He was shuffling towards her on his knees, with no thought for his dressing gown.

'I beg you, don't go! I love you!' And he seized her round the waist.

Instantly, a wave of crimson flooded Madame Bovary's face. She pulled away from him, a terrible look on her face, and cried:

'You are shamelessly taking advantage of my distress, Monsieur! I am to be pitied, but I am not for sale!'

And she walked out.

Stunned, the notary sat staring at his handsome embroidered slippers. They were an offering of love. Gradually the sight of them brought consolation. Besides, he reflected, an amorous intrigue of that kind would have led him into uncharted waters.

'What an infamous creature! What a cad! How despicable!' she said to herself as she fled, trembling, down the aspen-lined road. The disappointment of having failed exacerbated her indignation over the insult to her honour; Providence, she thought, was intent on hounding her, and, drawing strength from pride in her own conduct, she was, more than ever before in her life, filled with a sense of her own worth and of her contempt for others. She felt ready to take on the whole world. She wanted to lash out at men, to spit in their faces, to crush them, every one; and she strode rapidly on, pale, quivering, enraged, searching the empty horizon with tearful eyes, and almost relishing the hatred that was stifling her.

When she caught sight of her own house a kind of paralysis stopped her in her tracks. She could go no further, but she had no choice; and in any case, where else was there?

Félicité stood at the door, waiting for her.

'Well?'

'No!' said Emma.

And, for a quarter of an hour, the two of them went through all the individuals in Yonville who might conceivably be willing to help her. But, each time Félicité named someone, Emma replied:

'Oh no, no, impossible! They'd never be willing to do it.'

'Monsieur will be back soon!'

'I'm well aware of that . . . Leave me by myself.'

She'd tried everything. There was nothing left now; and when Charles arrived, she'd have to say to him:

'Go away. This carpet you're stepping on doesn't belong to us any more. You haven't anything left of your home, not a stick of furniture, not a pin, nothing, nothing at all, and I'm the one who's ruined you, you poor man!'

Then he'd give a great sob, and weep copiously, and eventually, when the shock had passed, he'd forgive her.

'Yes,' she kept muttering through clenched teeth, 'he'll forgive me, he whom I'd never forgive for choosing *me*, even if he cast a fortune at my feet . . . Never, never!'

This idea of Bovary's moral superiority over her enraged her. And in any event, whether or not she told him everything, he'd very shortly, or in a few hours, or tomorrow, learn of the catastrophe; so she must prepare to endure this dreadful scene and bear the burden of his magnanimity. She thought of returning to see Lheureux: but what would be the point? She could write to her father: no, it was too late for that; and perhaps she was beginning to regret not having submitted to the other man, when she heard the sound of a horse trotting down the alley. It was Charles; he opened the gate; his face was whiter than the plaster wall. Racing down the stairs, she escaped into the square; and the mayor's wife, as she stood chatting to

Lestiboudois in front of the church, saw her enter the tax collector's house.

Madame Tuvache hurried over to tell Madame Caron. The two ladies climbed up to the garret where, concealed by the washing laid out on racks to dry, they took up posts that commanded an excellent view into Binet's home.

He was alone, in his garret, intent on copying, in wood, one of those incredible ivory artefacts composed of crescents and hollowed-out spheres nestled one inside the other, the whole affair as upright as an obelisk and entirely useless; he was just embarking on the final piece—could he really be about to complete it? In the chiaroscuro of the workshop, the yellow sawdust showered out from his lathe like a spray of sparks from beneath the hooves of a galloping horse; the two wheels kept turning, kept whirring; Binet, smiling, his chin hanging slackly and his nostrils flaring, seemed sunk in one of those states of perfect bliss which can probably only be induced by mediocre pursuits, occupations which challenge the intelligence with superficial difficulties, and satisfy it with a sense of achievement greater than which cannot even be imagined.

'Ah! There she is!' said Madame Tuvache.

But it was almost impossible, because of the lathe, to hear what she was saying.

Eventually, the two ladies thought they made out the word 'francs', and Madame Tuvache whispered softly: 'She's begging for a postponement of her taxes.'

'That's what it looks like!' replied the other.

They could see her pacing up and down, examining the serviette rings, candlesticks, and banister knobs displayed round the walls, while Binet sat complacently stroking his chin.

'Perhaps she's come to order something?' suggested Madame Tuvache.

'But he never sells anything!' objected her neighbour.

The tax collector seemed to be listening, staring wide-eyed, as if he did not understand. She went on speaking with an air of tender entreaty. She moved closer to him, her breast heaving; they had stopped conversing.

'Is she making up to him?' said Madame Tuvache.

Binet was blushing to the roots of his hair. She took hold of his hands.

'Oh, this beats all!'

And she must surely be proposing something infamous, for the tax collector—and he a man of valour, who had fought at Bautzen and Lutzen,* gone through the French campaign,* and even been 'recommended for a decoration'—suddenly, as if he had seen a snake, sprang well away from her, shouting:

'Madame, whatever can you mean? . . .'

'Women like that should be whipped,' said Madame Tuvache.

'But where's she gone?' replied Madame Caron.

For she had vanished during this exchange; then, catching sight of her as she darted down the Grande-Rue and turned to the right as if heading for the cemetery, the two ladies were soon deep in speculation.

'Mère Rollet' gasped Emma as she reached the nurse's house, 'I can't breathe! Undo my laces.'

She sank onto the bed; she was sobbing. Mère Rollet covered her with a petticoat and stood beside her. Then, as Emma made no reply to her questions, the good woman moved away, took up her wheel and began to spin flax.

'Oh, do stop that!' murmured Emma, imagining she could hear Binet's lathe.

'What's bothering her?' the nurse was wondering. 'Why's she come here?'

She had raced there, propelled by a kind of terror that forced her to flee her own home.

As she lay on her back, motionless, staring vacantly around, she saw objects only as a vague blur, although she focused her attention on them with a mindless persistence. She studied the peeling plaster on the walls, the two logs smouldering end to end in the fireplace, and a large spider that was crawling along the crack in the beam above her head. Finally, she collected her thoughts. She could remember . . . one day, with Léon . . . Oh! how long ago that was . . . the sun shining on the river and the air heavy with the fragrance of clematis . . . Then, swept along by her memories as if by a raging torrent, she suddenly recollected the events of the previous day.

'What time is it?' she asked.

Mère Rollet went outside, held up the fingers of her right hand towards the brightest part of the sky, and, coming slowly in again, said:

'Nearly three o'clock.'

'Ah! Thank you, thank you.'

For he would come, she felt certain of it! He'd have got the money. But perhaps he'd go to the house; it wouldn't occur to him that she was here; and she told the nurse to run to the village and fetch him.

'Hurry! Hurry!'

'I'm going, Madame, I'm going!'

She felt amazed, now, that she hadn't thought of him in the first place; he'd promised, yesterday, and he wouldn't break his word; and she could already visualize herself at Lheureux's, laying down the three banknotes on his desk. Then she'd have to dream up some story to satisfy Bovary. What?

The nurse, however, was taking her time coming back. But as the cottage had no clock, Emma thought uneasily that perhaps she was exaggerating how long she had been gone. She began taking little turns round the garden, walking slowly. She went along the path beside the hedge, returning very fast, hoping to find the nurse had come home by some other route. Eventually, exhausted with waiting, beset by doubts that she tried to suppress, no longer knowing whether she'd been in that cottage a minute or an eternity, she sank down in a corner, closed her eyes, and blocked her ears. The gate squeaked, she leapt to her feet; before she could say a word, Mère Rollet announced:

'There's nobody at your house!'

'What?'

'Nobody! Only Monsieur, and he's crying. He keeps calling for you. They're looking for you.'

Emma did not reply. She was gasping for breath and staring wildly all around, while the nurse, frightened by her expression, instinctively stepped back, thinking she must be mad. Suddenly, with a cry, she struck herself on the brow, as the memory of Rodolphe, like a bolt of lightning across a dark night sky, flashed into her mind. He was so good, so sensitive, so generous! And, in any case, if he seemed reluctant to help her, she'd know how to persuade him, by reminding him, with a single glance, of their lost love. So she set off for La Huchette, quite unaware that she was now eager to strike the very bargain that had so enraged her only hours before, and never for a moment suspecting that she was about to prostitute herself.

CHAPTER VIII

She wondered, while she walked along, what she would say, where she would begin. As she drew nearer, she began to recognize bushes and trees, the furze growing on the hill, then the chateau, beyond. She found herself reliving the emotions of her first love affair, and her poor tormented heart swelled with tenderness. A mild breeze fanned her cheeks; the melting snow was slowly dripping off the budding leaves, onto the grass.

She entered, as she had always done, through the small gate in the park wall, and reached the main courtyard, which was bordered by a double row of bushy lime trees. Their long branches swayed and rustled. All the dogs in the kennels began to bark, and their yapping raised the echoes without bringing anyone to the door.

She climbed the straight, broad staircase, which had banisters of wood, and led to the corridor paved in dusty tiles off which opened a row of rooms, in the style of a monastery, or an inn. His was at the end, right at the back, on the left. When she felt the latch under her fingers, her strength suddenly abandoned her. She was afraid that he wouldn't be there, she almost hoped he wouldn't, and yet, he was her only hope, the sole recourse remaining to her. She paused for an instant, composing herself, and then, drawing courage from the urgency of her plight, walked in.

He was sitting by the fire, his feet propped up on the moulding round the fireplace, smoking his pipe.

'Good Lord! It's you!' he said, jumping up.

'Yes, it's me! Rodolphe, I . . . I want to ask your advice.'

But, try as she might, she found it impossible to say another word.

'You haven't changed, you're as charming as ever!'

'Oh!' she replied bitterly, 'my charms! They can't be worth much, since you spurned them.'

He began to explain his behaviour, justifying himself in the vaguest terms, unable to think up anything better.

She let herself be swayed by his words, and still more by the sound of his voice and the sight of his person; so that she pretended to believe, or perhaps actually did believe, the excuse he gave for breaking with her: it was a secret, upon which depended the honour, and possibly even the life, of a third person.

'What does it matter?' she said, gazing at him sadly, 'I've suffered so much!'

He replied philosophically:

'That's life!'

'Has life at least treated you well, since our separation?' continued Emma.

'Oh! neither well . . . nor badly.'

'It might perhaps have been better never to part.'

'Yes . . . perhaps!'

'Do you really think so?' She moved closer, and with a sigh, continued:

'Oh, Rodolphe, if you only knew! . . . I loved you so much!'

She took his hand, and for a while their fingers remained inter-locked—like the first time, at the Show! Pride made him struggle against his feelings. But she leaned her head against his breast, saying:

'How did you ever imagine I could live without you? Happiness isn't a garment you can suddenly cast off! I was in despair! I thought I'd die! I'll tell you about it, and you'll understand. But you, you've been avoiding me!'

Indeed, for the last three years, he had scrupulously avoided her, out of that natural cowardice peculiar to the stronger sex; and Emma, with appealing, tiny movements of her head, more coaxing than an amorous she-cat, went on:

'You've loved other women, admit it! Oh! I can understand them, of course I can! I forgive them; you'll have seduced them, just as you seduced me. You're a real man, you're everything a woman wants in the man she loves. But we can start again, can't we? We'll love one another! Look at me, I'm laughing, I'm happy! . . . Oh, say something, please!'

She was an enchanting sight, with a tear trembling in her eye like a raindrop in the blue calyx of a flower.

He drew her onto his knee, caressing, with the back of his hand, the smooth bands of her hair where a last ray of sunshine sparkled, in the half-light of dusk, like an arrow of gold. She bent her head; soon he was kissing her on the eyelids, very delicately, barely brushing them with his lips.

'But you've been crying!' he said. 'Why?'

She broke into sobs. Rodolphe, imagining them prompted by the intensity of her passion, interpreted her continuing silence as the final refuge of modesty. He exclaimed:

'Oh, forgive me! You're the only woman for me. I've been stupid and vile! I love you! I'll always love you! What's the matter? Please tell me!'

He was on his knees.

'Well, then! . . . Rodolphe, I'm ruined! You must lend me three thousand francs!'

'But . . . but . . .,' he said, slowly standing up, a serious expression coming over his face.

'You see,' she went on rapidly, 'my husband had entrusted his entire fortune to a notary; well, he absconded. We've borrowed; the patients weren't paying their bills. In any case the liquidation isn't yet complete and we'll have some money, later. But, today, because we can't come up with three thousand francs, we're going under the hammer; now, I mean, this very moment; so, relying on your friendship, I've come to you.'

'Ah!' thought Rodolphe, suddenly turning extremely pale: 'so that's why she's here!'

Finally he said, without a trace of emotion:

'I haven't got three thousand francs, dear lady.'

He was not lying. Had he had them, he would probably have given her them, although such generous gestures are almost invariably unpleasant: of all the icy blasts that can lay waste to love, a financial demand is the coldest and most devastating.

She stood there for a few moments, staring at him.

'You haven't got them!'

Several times she repeated:

'You haven't got them! . . . I should have spared myself this final humiliation. You've never loved me! You're no better than the others!'

She was giving herself away, courting disaster.

Interrupting, Rodolphe declared that he himself was 'feeling the pinch'.

'Oh! I feel so sorry for you!' Emma said, 'yes, very, very sorry!'

And, gazing at a gleaming damascened rifle displayed as a trophy on the wall:

'But, when you're so poor, you don't have chased silver on the stock of your rifle. You don't buy things inlaid with tortoiseshell!' she went on, pointing to the buhl clock; 'nor silver-gilt whistles for your whips'—she touched them—'nor charms for your watch! Oh! He doesn't deny himself a thing! There's even a liqueur-tray in his room. You love yourself first and best, you live like a king, you've a chateau, farms, woods, you hunt, you take trips to Paris . . . Huh! Even just with these,' she cried, picking up his cuff links from the mantelpiece, 'or with any of these stupid knick-knacks, you could raise some money! . . . Not that *I* want them! You can keep them.'

And she flung the cuff links clear across the room. Their gold chain broke as it hit the wall.

'But I'd have given everything, sold everything, worked with my hands, begged on the streets, just for a smile, just for a glance, just to hear you say "thank you"! And there you are, still calmly sitting in your armchair, as if you hadn't already made me suffer enough! You know very well, don't you, that if it hadn't been for you, my life would have been happy! What made you do it? Was it for a bet? And yet you did love me, you said you did . . . And even just now . . . Ah! You'd have done better to throw me out! My hands are still warm from your kisses, and here's the place, here on the carpet, where you swore on your knees that you'd love me forever. You made me believe in it: for two whole years you led me on with the most magnificent, the most entrancing of dreams. Do you remember our plans for our journey, do you remember? Ah! That letter of yours, that letter . . . it broke my heart. And then, when I come to him again, come to him, a wealthy, happy, free man, to beg him for help that anyone would gladly give, when I come, full of love, and beseech him, he turns his back on me, because it would cost him three thousand francs!'

'I haven't got them!' repeated Rodolphe, with that perfect calm which serves to shield resigned anger.

She left. The walls were shaking, the ceiling about to crush her. Once more she went down the long avenue, stumbling over the piles of dead leaves that the wind kept blowing about. At last she reached the boundary ditch, and the gate; she broke her nails on the latch, so frantic was she to open it. Then, a short distance further on, breathless, almost fainting, she stopped. Turning, she saw again the impassive chateau, with its park, its gardens, its three courtyards, and its rows of windows along the façade.

She stood there utterly stupefied, aware of her own existence only by the throbbing of her arteries, which she thought she could hear outside herself, resonating through the countryside with a deafening music. The ground beneath her feet felt more unresisting than water, the furrows looked to her like vast, dark breakers, unfurling. Everything in her consciousness—every memory, every idea, was bursting forth at the same instant, in a single spurt, like the thousand flashes of a firework. She saw her father, Lheureux's office, *their* room, another, different, landscape. She sensed madness taking hold of her and felt afraid, but then managed to pull herself together, although she was still confused, for she had no recollection of the reason for her horrible state, the problem of the money. She was suffering purely through her love, and at the thought of it she felt her soul slipping out from her body—just as the wounded, in dying, feel their life slipping away through their bleeding wounds.

Night was falling, rooks were circling in the sky.

Suddenly, her vision was filled with fiery-red spheres exploding in the air like balls of flame that flattened out; then, spinning, ever spinning, they fell among the branches of trees,* where they melted in the snow. In the centre of each one appeared an image of Rodolphe's face. The spheres were multiplying, coalescing, penetrating her: then everything vanished. She recognized the lights of houses, far away, gleaming through the mist.

Immediately, like an abyss, her situation lay clearly before her. She was panting, her lungs on the point of bursting. In a transport of heroism that filled her almost with joy, she raced down the hillside, over the plank bridge, along the path and alley, through the market place, to the pharmacy.

It was empty. She was about to enter, but the sound of the bell might alert someone; instead she slipped through the gate, holding her breath, feeling her way along the walls, until she came to the door of the kitchen, where a lighted candle shone on the stove. Justin, in his shirtsleeves, was carrying out a dish.

'Ah! They're at dinner. I'll wait.'

He returned. She tapped on the glass. He came out.

'The key! The one for upstairs, where he keeps the . . .'

'What!'

And he stared at her, astonished by the pallor of her face, which stood out dead-white against the blackness of the night. She seemed to him extraordinarily beautiful, phantom-like in her majesty; without understanding what she wanted, he sensed it was something terrible.

But she said again, rapidly and quietly, her voice sweet, melting:

'I want it! Give me it.'

The wall was thin, and they could hear, from the dining room, the clinking of forks on plates.

She claimed that she had to kill some rats that were keeping her awake.

'I'll have to tell Monsieur.'

'No! Stay here!'

Then, casually:

'Oh, it's not worth bothering him. I'll tell him myself, later. Come on, give me some light.'

She went into the corridor that led to the laboratory door. A key labelled *Capharnaum* was hanging on the wall.

'Justin!' shouted the apothecary, growing impatient.

'Let's go up!'

And he followed her.

The key turned in the lock, and she went directly to the third shelf, so faithfully did her memory serve her, seized the blue jar, pulled out the cork, thrust in her hand, and drew it out full of a white powder, which she began to cram straight into her mouth.

'Stop!' he screamed, flinging himself upon her.

'Quiet! Someone might come . . .'

Desperate, Justin wanted to call for help.

'Don't say a word about it, it would all be blamed on your master!'

Then she went home, suddenly at peace, almost serene, as though filled with the consciousness of a duty done.

When Charles, utterly distraught at the news of the seizure, returned home, Emma had just left. He shouted for her, he wept, he fainted, but she did not come. Wherever could she be? He sent Félicité to the pharmacy, to Monsieur Tuvache's, to Lheureux's, to the Lion d'Or, everywhere; and, whenever his anguish over her faded a little, he pictured his reputation destroyed, their money all lost, Berthe's future ruined! But why? . . . Not one single word! He waited for her until six that evening. Finally, unable to bear it another moment, and supposing that she must have gone to Rouen, he went out onto the highway, walked a couple of miles without seeing a soul, waited a bit longer, and then came back.

She was home.

'What happened? . . . Why? . . . You must tell me!'

She sat down at her desk, wrote a letter, sealed it slowly, and added the date and time. Then she said in a solemn tone:

'You can read it tomorrow; between now and then, don't ask me a single question, I beg you! No, not a single one!'

'But . . .'

'Oh, leave me alone!'

And she stretched out on her bed.

A bitter taste in her mouth woke her up. Catching sight of Charles, she shut her eyes again.

She was observing herself intently, to see if she felt any pain. No! Nothing, not yet. She could hear the ticking of the clock, the crackling of the fire, and Charles's breathing, as he stood beside her bed.

'Ah! Death's nothing much, really!' she thought; 'I'll sleep, then it'll all be over!'

She drank a mouthful of water and turned to face the wall.

That horrible taste of ink persisted.

'I'm thirsty! Oh, I'm so thirsty!' she sighed.

'But what's wrong with you?' asked Charles, handing her a glass.

'It's nothing! . . . Open the window! . . . I can't breathe!'

She was overcome by such a sudden wave of nausea* that she barely had time to grab her handkerchief from under the pillow.

'Take it away!' she said sharply, 'Get rid of it!'

He questioned her; she made no reply. She was lying absolutely still, afraid that the tiniest movement would make her vomit. But she could feel an icy chill spreading from her feet up to her heart.

'Oh, now it's beginning!' she whispered.

'What's that you said?'

She kept gently rolling her head from side to side in a movement that suggested extreme pain, while repeatedly stretching wide her jaws as if she had something very heavy on her tongue. At eight o'clock, the vomiting began again.

Charles noticed in the bottom of the bowl, clinging to the porcelain sides, a kind of white gravel.

'How extraordinary!' he kept repeating, 'How peculiar!'

But she said loudly:

'No, you're wrong!'

So then, his touch delicate, almost caressing, he passed his hand over her stomach. She gave a shrill scream. He drew back, greatly alarmed.

Next she began to moan, feebly at first. A violent attack of shivering made her shoulders shake, and she had turned whiter than the sheet at which her rigid fingers kept clawing. Her erratic pulse was now almost imperceptible.

Sweat was dripping from her blue-tinged face, which looked as if it had been glazed in the fumes of some metallic vapour. Her teeth were chattering, her dilated eyes stared vaguely round her, and her sole reply to every question was a mere nod; she even smiled a few times. Gradually, her moaning grew louder. A muffled howl broke from her: then she declared she was feeling better and would soon get up. But she was seized with convulsions, and cried out, 'Oh God, what agony!'

He flung himself down on his knees by the side of her bed.

'Tell me! What have you been eating? Tell me, for God's sake!'

He gazed at her with an intensity of love in his eyes that she had never seen before.

'All right . . . there . . . over there . . .' she murmured in a faltering voice.

He flew to the desk, broke the seal and read aloud: 'Let no one be blamed . . .' He stopped, passed his hand over his eyes, and read on.

'What! Help! Oh, help!'

He could do nothing but say the word over and over again: 'Poisoned! Poisoned!' Félicité rushed to find Homais, who shouted it loudly into the square; Madame Lefrançois heard it in the Lion d'Or; some people got out of bed to go and tell their neighbours, and all through the night the village never slept a wink.

Desperate, incoherent, on the verge of collapse, Charles paced round the room. He kept lurching into the furniture and tearing at his hair, and the pharmacist would not have believed that his eyes could ever behold so shocking a spectacle.

Homais returned home to write to Monsieur Canivet and Doctor Larivière. He lost his head: he wrote more than fifteen rough drafts. Hippolyte set off for Neufchâtel, and Justin spurred Bovary's horse so mercilessly that he had to abandon it on the hill at Bois-Guillaume, done in and almost done for.

Charles tried to leaf through his medical dictionary, but could make nothing of it; the lines kept dancing about.

'Calm down!' said the apothecary. 'It's simply a matter of administering a powerful antidote. What is the poison?'

Charles showed him the letter. It was arsenic.

'Very well,' continued Homais. 'We'll have to analyse it.'

For he knew that, in all cases of poisoning, an analysis must be carried out; and Charles, without understanding, replied:

'Yes, do it, do it, save her . . .'

Then, returning to her, he sank down onto the carpet, and remained with his head resting against the edge of her bed, sobbing.

'Don't cry!' she said to him. 'Soon I won't be tormenting you any more!'

'Why? What made you?'

'I had to do it, my dear,' she replied.

'Weren't you happy? Is it my fault? Although I did all I could!'

'Yes . . . it's true, you did . . . you're a good man!'

And, slowly, she ran her fingers through his hair. The sweetness of this sensation intensified his misery; he felt his whole being collapse in despair at the thought of losing her, just now when she was being more loving to him than ever before; yet he could think of nothing he might do—there was nothing he knew, nothing he dared try, the urgent need for immediate action having robbed him of his last vestiges of presence of mind.

They were behind her forever, thought Emma, all the betrayals, the infamies, and the myriad cravings that had tormented her. She did not hate anyone, now; a twilight confusion was settling over her thoughts, and, of all the world's sounds, Emma heard only the intermittent sobbing of that poor man, soft and faint, like the fading echo of an ever-more distant symphony.

'Bring me the child,' she said, raising herself up on her elbow.

'You're not feeling worse, are you?' asked Charles.

'No! No!'

The child arrived in the nurse's arms, her bare feet peeping out from beneath her long nightgown, her expression serious, only half awake. She stared in astonishment at the disordered room, screwing up her eyes, dazzled by the candles burning on the various pieces of furniture. They probably reminded her of the mornings of New Year's Day or the mid-Lent Festival, when, awakened early like this by candlelight, she would be brought to her mother's bed to receive her slipper full of presents, for she asked:

'Where is it, mama?' And, as no one said anything: 'I can't see my little slipper.'

Félicité was leaning over the bed with her, but she kept glancing towards the fireplace.

'Did nurse take it?' she asked.

And, at that word, which carried her back in memory to her adulteries and calamities, Madame Bovary turned away her head, as if in disgust at the taste of a different, harsher poison in her mouth. Berthe, meanwhile, was still on the bed.

'Oh! How big your eyes are, mama! You're so pale! And so sweaty!' Her mother gazed at her.

'I'm scared!' cried the child, shrinking back.

Emma grasped Berthe's hand to kiss it, but she kept struggling.

'That's enough! Take her away!' said Charles, who was standing near the bed, sobbing.

The symptoms abated for a few moments; she seemed calmer; and, with each insignificant remark, with each easier breath, his hopes revived. At last, when Canivet walked in, he threw himself into his arms, weeping.

'Ah! You've come, thank you! How good of you! But things are going better. Here, see for yourself . . .'

His colleague was of a quite different opinion; and, not believing, as he himself put it, in 'beating about the bush'; he prescribed an emetic, to void the stomach completely.

Soon she began to vomit blood. Her lips pressed more tightly together. Her limbs were contorted, her body covered with brown blotches, and her pulse quivered under the doctor's fingers like a taut wire, like the string of a harp just before it breaks.

Then she began to scream, horribly. She cursed the poison, railed at it, begged it to hurry, and pushed away with rigid arms everything that Charles, his own agony more dreadful than hers, tried to make her drink. He stood with his handkerchief to his lips, gasping hoarsely, weeping, choking with sobs that shook him from head to foot; Félicité was darting busily round the room; Homais, motionless, kept sighing deeply; and Monsieur Canivet, still apparently perfectly composed, was beginning to feel disquieted.

'What the devil! But . . . she's been purged, and, as soon as the cause disappears . . .'

'The effect should disappear,' said Homais. 'That's obvious.'

'Oh, save her!' Bovary kept exclaiming.

So, without paying any attention to the pharmacist, who was venturing yet another hypothesis: 'this paroxysm may perhaps be a sign of recovery,' Canivet was on the point of administering theriac, when they heard the cracking of a whip; all the window panes rattled, and a post-chaise, drawn at lightning speed by three mud-encrusted horses, suddenly shot into sight round the corner of the market place. It was Doctor Larivière.*

The appearance of a god could not have occasioned greater excitement. Bovary raised his hands, Canivet stopped what he was doing, and Homais doffed his cap well before the doctor walked in.

He belonged to that great school of surgery established by Bichat,* to that generation, now long gone, of philosopher-practitioners who cherished their art with fanatical devotion, and exercised it with fervour and sagacity. The entire hospital trembled when his anger was aroused, and his students regarded him with such intense veneration that they began imitating him as best they could almost before they had put up their plate, so that you could often see, in one of the neighbouring towns, someone dressed like him with a long woollen cloak over an ample black frock coat; he wore *his* with its unbuttoned cuffs partly covering his well-muscled hands, very beautiful hands, invariably gloveless, as if to be all the readier to minister to human suffering. Disdainful of decorations, titles, and academic distinctions, hospitable, generous, fatherly towards the poor, practising virtue without believing in it, he would almost have passed for a saint had not his razor-sharp intellect made him feared like a devil. His gaze, more piercing than his scalpel, penetrated straight into your soul, and prised out, from beneath all the allegations and evasions, every lie. And so he went through life, radiating a majestic benevolence which sprang from a consciousness of his exceptional gifts, of his wealth, and of the forty years he had dedicated to a hard-working, irreproachable existence.

At the threshold he frowned, catching sight of Emma's cadaverous face as she lay flat on her back, with her mouth open. Then, while apparently listening to Canivet, he kept rubbing his upper lip with his index finger as he repeated: 'Yes, yes.'

But now he gave a slow shrug. Bovary saw it: they stared at one another: and that man, inured as he was to the sight of suffering, could not stop a tear dropping onto the ruffle of his shirt.

He called Canivet out into the adjoining room. Charles followed them.

'She's very bad, isn't she? What about trying a mustard poultice? Oh, anything! Surely *you* can think of something, you who've saved so many lives!'

Charles had embraced Larivière round the waist, and was gazing at him with eyes full of fear and entreaty, almost collapsing against his chest.

'Come on, my poor fellow, you must be brave! There's nothing more we can do.'

And the doctor turned away.

'Are you leaving?'

'I'll be back.'

He went out, as if to give an order to the postilion, with Canivet, who likewise had no desire to see Emma die under his hands.

The pharmacist caught up with them in the square. He was temperamentally incapable of keeping away from celebrities. He therefore begged Monsieur Larivière to do him the signal honour of accepting his hospitality at breakfast.

They immediately sent to the Lion d'Or for pigeons, to the butcher for every cutlet in the shop, to Tuvache's for cream, to Lestiboudois for eggs, and the apothecary himself was lending a hand with the preparations, while Madame Homais, plucking at the laces of her bodice, kept repeating:

'You must excuse us, Monsieur; out here in this dead-end spot, unless we know ahead of time . . .'

'The stemmed glasses!' hissed Homais.

'At least, if we lived in town, we'd know we could always get stuffed pigs' trotters . . .'

'Be quiet! . . . Please come to the table, Doctor!'

He deemed it appropriate, after the first few bites, to provide some details about the calamitous event:

'First we noted a sensation of siccity in the pharynx, then intolerable pain in the epigastrium, followed by superpurgation, and coma.'

'But how did she poison herself?'

'I do not know, Doctor, nor I do I have any idea where she managed to procure the arsenious acid.'

Justin, who was carrying in a pile of plates, began to tremble, violently.

'Whatever's the matter with you?' said the pharmacist.

At this question, the young man dropped the entire pile, with a resounding crash, on the floor.

'Idiot!' shouted Homais, 'clumsy oaf! damned fool!'

Then, instantly controlling himself:

'I decided, Doctor, to try an analysis, and, *primo*, carefully inserted into a tube . . .'

'It would have been more useful,' observed the surgeon, 'to insert your fingers into her throat.'

His colleague kept quiet, having just received, in private, a stern rebuke on the subject of his emetic. As a result the worthy Canivet, so arrogant and loquacious at the time of the operation on Hippolyte, today was modesty personified; his face bore a permanent smile of approbation.

Beaming with pride, Homais was revelling in his role of host; and, in some vague way, the thought of Bovary's distress enhanced his pleasure, when he selfishly compared their situations. Moreover, he was exhilarated by the presence of the doctor. He paraded his erudition, indiscriminately dropping references to cantharides, upas, manchineel,* and the viper.

'And I've even read, Doctor, of cases where people have been poisoned, completely prostrated, after eating blood sausages that had undergone an excessively powerful fumigation! At least, that is what is reported in a very fine article composed by one of our pharmaceutical luminaries, one of our masters, the celebrated Cadet de Gassicourt!'*

Madame Homais reappeared, bearing one of those wobbly contraptions which are heated up over spirits of alcohol; for Homais preferred to make his own coffee at the table, having, moreover, first roasted, ground, and blended it himself.

'*Saccharum*, Doctor,' he said, offering the sugar.

Then he summoned down all his children, curious to hear what the surgeon might say about their constitution.

Monsieur Larivière was at last preparing to leave, when Madame Homais asked for advice about her husband. His habit of nodding off every evening after supper was making his blood dense.

'Oh, you don't have to worry about his *blood* being dense.'

And, smiling slightly over this sally, which was entirely lost on his audience, the doctor opened the door. But the pharmacy was bursting with people, and he had the greatest difficulty getting away from Monsieur Tuvache, who worried that his wife might develop inflammation of the lungs from habitually spitting into the embers, and Monsieur Binet, who was occasionally tormented by sudden cravings,* and Madame Caron, who had tingling skin, and Lheureux, who had dizzy spells, and Lestiboudois, who had rheumatism, and Madame Lefrançois, who had heartburn. Finally the three horses set off, and it was generally felt that he had not behaved very graciously.

The attention of the group was then distracted by the sight of Monsieur Bournisien, crossing the market place with the viaticum in his hands.

True to his principles, Homais likened priests to crows that are drawn to the smell of death; he himself found the sight of an ecclesiastic repellent, for a cassock made him think of a shroud, and he loathed the one partly out of dread of the other.

Nevertheless, not flinching from what he termed 'his mission', he went back to Bovary, together with Canivet, whom Monsieur Larivière, before leaving, had strongly urged to return; indeed, had his wife not objected, Homais would have taken with him his two sons, in order to accustom them to the dire experiences of life, that it might serve as a lesson, an example, an awe-inspiring spectacle that they would retain forever in their memory.

Upon entering, they found the bedroom full of an atmosphere of mournful solemnity. A white napkin had been spread over the sewing table, and on it stood a silver platter holding five or six tiny balls of cotton wool. Nearby was a large crucifix, flanked by a pair of lighted candelabra. Emma lay with her chin sunk down on her breast and her eyes abnormally wide open; her poor hands were plucking at the sheets with that ghastly, feeble gesture of the dying, who already seem anxious to cover themselves with their shroud. Pale as a statue, his eyes red as burning coals, Charles, no longer weeping, kept vigil opposite her at the foot of the bed, while the priest, on one knee, was mumbling some inaudible prayers.

She slowly turned her head, and seemed overjoyed on suddenly catching sight of the purple stole, perhaps experiencing afresh, in that extraordinary moment of tranquillity, the forgotten rapture of her first mystical yearnings, together with a vision of the eternal bliss to come.

The priest rose to take the crucifix, she thrust her neck forward like someone parched with thirst, and, fastening her lips to the body of the Man-God, she bestowed upon it with every ounce of her dying strength the most passionate kiss of love that she had ever given. Then he recited the *Misereatur* and the *Indulgentiam*, dipped his right thumb into the oil, and began administering extreme unction: first upon the eyes, which had so fiercely craved every earthly luxury, then upon the nostrils, so greedy for caressing breezes and erotic scents, then upon the mouth, which had opened to lie, to bemoan her wounded pride, and to cry out in lustful pleasure, then upon the hands, so avid for pleasurable sensations; and lastly upon the soles of the feet, once so swift in speeding her to satisfy her desire, and which now would never walk again.

The curé wiped his fingers, tossed the oily balls of cotton wool in the fire, and came back to sit beside the dying woman, to tell her that she should now join her suffering with the suffering of Jesus Christ, and surrender herself to the mercy of the Almighty.*

As he finished his exhortations, he attempted to put into her hand a consecrated taper, symbol of the celestial glory in which she would soon be enfolded. But Emma was too weak to grasp it with her fingers, and, had it not been for Monsieur Bournisien, the taper would have fallen on the floor.

However, she no longer looked so pale, and her face bore an expression of serenity, as if the sacrament had healed her.

The priest did not fail to remark on this; he even explained to Bovary that, occasionally, the Lord would prolong a life where he deemed such a delay appropriate for the individual's salvation; and Charles remembered another similar occasion when, close to death, she had received communion.

'Perhaps there's still some hope,' he thought.

And, indeed, she did gaze slowly round, like someone waking from a dream; then, in a clear voice, she asked for her mirror, and stared at herself for some considerable time, until her eyes brimmed over with large tears. Then, with a sigh, she let her head drop back onto the pillow.

Immediately, her breast began rising and falling in rapid gasps. Her entire tongue protruded from her mouth; her rolling eyes dimmed like lamp globes as they fade into darkness, so that she might have been dead already, had it not been for the terrifying movements of her ribs, faster and faster, driven by her desperate breathing, as if the soul were struggling violently to break free. Félicité knelt before the crucifix, and even the pharmacist seemed to be bending very slightly at the knee, while Monsieur Canivet stood staring vacantly into the square. Bournisien was praying again, his face bowed over the edge of the bed, his long black cassock trailing out into the room behind him. Charles, on his knees at the opposite side, kept his arms stretched out towards Emma. He had taken her hands in his own and was grasping them tightly, starting at every beat of her heart as if at every tremor of a collapsing building. As the death rattle grew more pronounced, the priest's prayers grew more urgent, mingling with Bovary's muffled sobs; at times, every sound seemed to be overlaid by the muted drone of the Latin syllables, which resonated like a tolling bell.

Suddenly, they heard the sound of heavy clogs on the pavement, and the soft rapping of a stick; then a voice rose from below, a raucous voice, singing:

> Souvent la chaleur d'un beau jour,
> Fait rêver fillette à l'amour.

Emma reared up like a galvanized corpse, her hair hanging down her back, her wide-open eyes staring fixedly.

> Pour amasser diligemment
> Les épis que la faux moissonne,
> Ma Nanette va s'inclinant
> Vers le sillon qui nous les donne.

'The blind man!' she cried.

And Emma began to laugh, a ghastly, frenzied, despairing laugh, believing she could see the wretch's hideous face, like a symbol of ultimate terror, looming through the dark shadows of eternity.

> Il souffla bien fort ce jour-là,
> Et le jupon court s'envola!

A spasm cast her back onto the mattress. They all drew close. She no longer existed.

CHAPTER IX

Always, after someone's death, a feeling akin to stupefaction sets in, so impossible is it to grasp the reality of this nothingness, to resign oneself to believing in it. But when Charles noticed her immobility, he flung himself upon her, crying:

'Goodbye, goodbye!'

Homais and Canivet managed to get him out of the room.

'You must calm down!'

'Yes,' he replied, struggling, 'I'll be calm, I'm not going to do anything desperate. But let me go! I have to see her! She's my wife!'

He was weeping.

'Go on, weep,' said the pharmacist; 'let nature have its course, it'll do you good!'

Feebler than a baby, Charles allowed himself to be led downstairs to the parlour, and shortly thereafter Monsieur Homais returned home.

Crossing the square, Homais was accosted by the blind beggar, who had dragged himself all the way to Yonville in the hope of obtaining the antiphlogistic ointment. He had been enquiring of every passer-by where the apothecary lived.

'Oh, for God's sake! As if I hadn't enough to deal with already! Too bad, you'll just have to come another time!'

And he hurried into the pharmacy.

He had to write two letters, prepare a sedative for Bovary, fabricate some story that would cover up the poisoning for his report to the *Fanal*, and for the ears of all the people waiting to hear the latest; and when the Yonvillians had all listened to his tale of how she had mistaken arsenic for sugar while making a vanilla custard, Homais went back to Bovary's house.

As Canivet had just departed, he found Charles by himself, sitting in his armchair by the window, staring vacantly at the tiles of the parlour floor.

'Now,' said the pharmacist, 'you'll have to decide on the time of the ceremony.'

'Why? What ceremony?'

Then, in a faltering, frightened voice: 'No! No, do you understand? I want to keep her.'

Disconcerted, Homais picked up a carafe from one of the shelves and set about watering the geraniums.

'Oh, thank you!' said Charles. 'You're so good!' He broke off, overcome by the profusion of memories evoked by this action of the pharmacist's.

So then, in an effort to distract him, Homais embarked on a brief horticultural disquisition: plants needed moisture. Charles nodded in agreement.

'Anyway, we'll soon be having nice weather again.'

'Ah!' said Bovary.

Running out of ideas, the apothecary gently pulled aside the curtain over the window pane.

'Goodness, there's Monsieur Tuvache going by.'

Charles repeated mechanically: 'Monsieur Tuvache going by.'

Homais dared not mention the funeral arrangements again; it was the priest who eventually persuaded him.

He shut himself into his study, took his pen, and, after shedding many tears, wrote:

'I want her to be buried in her wedding dress, with white shoes, and a wreath. Her hair is to be spread out over her shoulders. Three coffins: one oak, one mahogany, one lead. No one is to say anything to me, I shall have the strength to endure. Cover the coffin with a large piece of green velvet. I want this done. Do it.'

The others were astounded by these romantic ideas of Bovary's, and the pharmacist immediately said to him: 'The velvet strikes me as supererogatory. Besides, the expense . . .'

'Is that any of your business?' cried Charles. 'Leave me alone! You didn't love her! Go away!'

Taking him by the arm, the priest suggested that they stroll round the garden. He expatiated on the vanity of all earthly things. God was great, God was good; one should submit to his decrees without a murmur, one should even thank him.

Charles burst into a stream of profanity.

'As for your God, I abominate him!'

'You are still imbued with the spirit of rebellion!' sighed the ecclesiastic.

Bovary had walked away. He was striding up and down beside the wall where the fruit trees grew, grinding his teeth, his furious gaze addressing curses to the heavens; but not so much as a leaf quivered.

A fine drizzle was falling. After a while Charles, whose neck was bare, began to shiver; he went back into the house and sat in the kitchen.

At six o'clock, a rattling sound came from the square; it was the Hirondelle arriving; and he stayed at the window with his forehead pressed against the pane, watching the passengers emerge one after the other from the coach. Félicité put a mattress for him on the parlour floor: he flung himself down on it and fell asleep.

For all his rationalism, Homais respected the dead. So, without bearing poor Charles any ill will, he returned that evening to keep watch beside the body, armed with three books and a writing case so that he could take notes.

Monsieur Bournisien was already there. Two tall candles were burning at the head of the bed, which had been pulled out into the room.

The apothecary, who found silence a burden, soon began to lament the fate of this 'unfortunate young woman', and the priest replied that all they could do now was pray for her.

'Nevertheless,' retorted Homais, 'one of the following must be true: either she died in a state of grace (as the Church puts it), in which case she has no need of our prayers; or she died unrepentant (I think that's the correct ecclesiastical term), and in that event . . .'

Bournisien interrupted him, declaring truculently that prayer was necessary whatever the case.

'But,' objected the pharmacist, 'since God knows all our needs, what can be the point of prayer?'

'Whatever do you mean? Prayer!' exclaimed the priest. 'Aren't you a Christian?'

'I beg your pardon!' said Homais. 'I admire Christianity. In the first place it freed the slaves, and gave the world a moral code . . .'

'That's not what it's about! All the texts . . .'

'Oh! Well, as for the texts, just take a look at history; everyone knows the texts were falsified by the Jesuits.'

Charles walked in and, going up to the bed, slowly opened the curtains.

Emma lay with her head resting on her right shoulder. The corner of her mouth, which was open, made a black hole in the lower part of her face, and both thumbs lay rigidly across her palms; a kind of white dust powdered her eyelashes, and her eyes seemed to be disappearing behind a pale, viscous film, a diaphanous veil, as if spiders had been weaving webs there. The sheet sagged hollowly from her breast to her knees, rising, further down, over her toes; and to Charles it seemed that an infinite mass, a colossal weight, was pressing down upon her.

The church clock chimed two. They could hear the deep murmur of the river, flowing through the dark shadows below the terrace. From time to time Monsieur Bournisien would noisily blow his nose; Homais's pen scratched on the paper.

'My good friend, go downstairs,' he said; 'don't linger here; this sight is too painful!'

With Charles gone, the pharmacist and the priest returned to their discussion.

'Read Voltaire!' one kept saying; 'read d'Holbach, read the *Encyclopédie*.'*

'Read *Les Lettres de quelques juifs portugais*!'* retorted the other; 'read *La Raison du christianisme*, by Nicolas,* the former magistrate!'

They were arguing heatedly, red in the face, talking at the same time, neither listening to the other; Bournisien felt outraged by Homais's audacity, while the pharmacist marvelled at the priest's stupidity; they were almost at the point of exchanging insults when, quite suddenly, Charles reappeared. He was drawn there by some kind of fascination. He kept coming back up the stairs.

He positioned himself opposite Emma in order to see her better, and became so intensely absorbed in gazing at her that he was no longer conscious of his pain.

He was remembering stories about catalepsy, and tales of miracles wrought by magnetism; he told himself that by sheer force of will he might perhaps succeed in resuscitating her. Once he even leaned over towards her, and softly cried: 'Emma! Emma!' So powerful was his breath that it blew the flickering candle flames against the wall.

At dawn, Madame Bovary senior arrived; when he kissed her, Charles's tears began flowing again. She, like the pharmacist, made an attempt to discuss the expense of the funeral. He grew so enraged that she desisted, and he even sent her off, there and then, to buy what was needed in Rouen.

Charles spent the entire afternoon alone; Berthe had been taken over to Madame Homais; Félicité remained upstairs, in the bedroom, with old Madame Lefrançois.

In the evening, he received callers. He would get to his feet and shake hands, but could not say a word; the visitor would take his place beside the others in a wide semicircle round the fire. They sat gazing at the floor, crossing their knees and swinging one leg, sighing deeply at regular intervals; everyone was bored stiff, but no one felt it proper to be the first to leave.

When he came back again at nine, Homais—who for the last two days had seemed to be continually crossing the square—brought a supply of camphor, benzoin, and aromatic herbs. He also carried over a container full of chlorine, to dispel any 'noxious effluvia'. At that very moment the maid, Madame Lefrançois, and Madame Bovary were busy with Emma, finishing dressing her; they lowered the long, stiff veil, which covered her completely, down to her satin slippers.

Félicité was sobbing:

'Oh, my poor mistress! My poor mistress!'

'Just look at her,' sighed the innkeeper, 'how pretty she still looks! Wouldn't you swear she's going to get up any minute now?'

They bent over her to put on her bridal wreath.

They had to lift her head slightly, and as they did so a stream of black liquid, like vomit, flowed from her mouth.

'Oh, God! Her dress, be careful of her dress!' exclaimed Madame Lefrançois. 'Come on, give us a hand!' she urged the pharmacist. 'Perhaps you're scared to?'

'Me, scared?' he replied with a shrug. 'Not likely! I saw plenty of these at the hospital, when I was studying pharmacy! We used to make punch in the theatre, while we were doing dissections. A philosopher does not fear death. As I've repeatedly declared, I even intend to bequeath my body to the hospitals, so that it may, one day, be of some utility to Science.'

The priest, when he arrived, enquired how Bovary was holding up. On hearing the pharmacist's reply, he remarked:

'The shock, you understand, it's still too recent!'

Then Homais congratulated him on not being subject, as most people were, to losing a dear companion; this developed into a discussion about the celibacy of priests.

'For,' remarked the pharmacist, 'it isn't natural for a man to do without women! There've been crimes committed . . .'

'But, my goodness,' exclaimed the priest, 'how could you expect a person who was married to respect the secrets of the confessional?'

Then Homais attacked confession. Bournisien defended it; he dwelt on the acts of reparation it prompted, and cited various instances of thieves suddenly converted to a virtuous lifestyle. There were soldiers who, upon entering the confessional, felt the scales fall from their eyes. A minister in Fribourg . . .

His companion was fast asleep. Oppressed by the stifling air in the room, the priest opened the window, and this woke up the pharmacist.

'Here, take a pinch of snuff, it'll clear your head,' he said to him.

A sound of continuous barking came from somewhere in the far distance.

'Can you hear that dog howling?' asked the pharmacist.

'People do say that they can smell death,' replied the priest. 'It's the same with bees; they leave the hive when someone dies.' Homais did not challenge these superstitions; he had fallen asleep again.

Monsieur Bournisien, who was hardier, continued for some time silently moving his lips; then, little by little, his chin dropped lower and lower, he let his heavy book slip from his fingers, and he began to snore.

They sat opposite one another, their stomachs thrust forward, their faces puffy and their expressions scowling, finally, after so much discord, united in the same human frailty; and they stirred no more than did the corpse by their side, which might have been sleeping.

When Charles came in he did not waken them. This was the last time. He had come to bid her farewell.

The aromatic herbs were still smouldering, and swirls of bluish vapour mingled, on the window sill, with the mist that was blowing in. A few stars gleamed in the mild night.

Big drops of wax kept falling off the candles onto the bed sheets. Charles watched the candles burning, their dazzling yellow light wearying his eyes.

The watered satin of her dress, pale as a moonbeam, glinted and shimmered. He felt as if Emma was disappearing under it, spreading out beyond herself, mingling, somehow, into the surroundings of things, into the silence, into the night, into the passing breeze, into the damp scents that rose from the earth.

Then suddenly, he could see her in the garden at Tostes, on the bench, beside the thorn hedge, in the streets of Rouen, standing on the threshold of their house, in the farmyard at Les Bertaux. He heard again the high-spirited laughter of the youths dancing under the apple trees; the room was full of the perfume of her hair, and her dress rustled and crackled in his arms. It was that same dress, that very one!

He spent a long time like this, remembering every vanished joy, her way of standing, of sitting, her gestures, the tone of her voice. After each wave of despair another followed; on and on they came, unending, like the overflowing waters of a floodtide.

A terrible curiosity gripped him: slowly, with the tips of his fingers, his heart beating violently, he raised her veil. His horrified scream woke the other two. They helped him downstairs, to the parlour.

Then Félicité came up to say that he was asking for some of her hair.

'Cut some!' the pharmacist replied.

But, as she was afraid, he himself took the scissors and leaned over to do it. He was trembling so violently that he nicked the skin of the temples in several places. Eventually, however, getting a hold of himself, Homais hacked off two or three thick locks at random, leaving white gaps in that beautiful head of black hair.

The pharmacist and the priest settled down again to their respective occupations, not without nodding off occasionally, a fact they never failed to point out to one another each time they woke up. Monsieur Bournisien would then sprinkle some holy water round the room and Homais would spread a little chlorine over the floor.

Félicité had thoughtfully set out a bottle of brandy, a cheese, and a big brioche for them on the chest of drawers. Towards four in the morning the apothecary, who could resist no longer, announced with a deep sigh:

'I have to admit that a little sustenance would be most welcome!'

The priest readily agreed; he went out to say mass and returned, then they ate and clinked their glasses, chuckling a bit, without knowing why, prompted by that vague elation that we experience after a period of grieving; raising his final tot of brandy, the priest slapped the pharmacist on the back, declaring:

'We'll be good friends yet!'

Downstairs, in the hall, they found the workmen arriving, and for two hours Charles had to endure the torture of listening to hammers resounding on wooden planks. Then they put her into her oak coffin, which they then nested inside the two others; however, as the outer coffin was too wide, the spaces had to be stuffed with wool taken from a mattress. At last, when the three lids had been planed, nailed down and soldered, the bier was exposed outside the entrance; the doors were thrown open, and the people of Yonville began to crowd into the house.

Old man Rouault arrived. On catching sight of the black pall, he fell in a dead faint, in the square.

CHAPTER X

The pharmacist's letter had not reached him until thirty-six hours after the event. Homais, out of consideration for his feelings, had worded it in such a way that it was impossible to know what to think.

On first reading it, the old man collapsed, as though stricken by apoplexy. But then he grasped the fact that she was not actually dead ... not yet, although she might be dying ... In the end he had slipped on his smock, picked up his hat, stuck spurs onto his boots, and set off at top speed; racked with anguish, he gasped for breath as he galloped along the road to Yonville. Once he even had to dismount from his horse. His eyes had fogged over, he could hear voices all around him, he felt he must be going mad.

Dawn was breaking; he saw three black hens asleep in a tree, and, terrified by the omen, shuddered violently. So then he promised the Holy Virgin three chasubles for the church, and that he'd walk, barefoot, all the way from the Bertaux cemetery to the chapel at Vassonville.

He rode into Maronne already shouting for the servants at the inn; he broke open the stable door with his shoulder, grabbed a sack of oats, poured a bottle of sweet cider into the manger, leapt back into the saddle, and galloped off, his nag's hooves raising a shower of sparks.

He kept telling himself that they'd certainly save her; the doctors would find a cure, of course they would. He recalled all the miraculous cures he had heard about.

Then he had a vision of her, dead. There she was, lying on her back in the middle of the road, in front of him. He pulled up on the reins and the hallucination vanished.

In Quincampoix, to get his courage up, he tossed back three cups of coffee in rapid succession.

Perhaps they'd put the wrong name on the letter? He felt for it in his pocket and fingered it, but did not dare open it.

He even began wondering if it might be a 'hoax', somebody's way of getting their own back, or a perhaps a prank born of too much cider? Besides, if she were dead, he would surely know it! But no, there was nothing extraordinary about the landscape: the sky was blue, the trees swayed in the breeze; a flock of sheep crossed the road. The village came into view; villagers along the way watched him come racing towards them, hunched over his horse, beating it fiercely; the saddle girths were dripping blood.

When he regained consciousness, he fell, weeping, into Bovary's arms:

'My daughter! Emma! My child! Please, tell me . . .'

His son-in-law sobbed his reply:

'I don't know, I don't know! It's a curse . . .'

The apothecary separated them.

'There's no point in going into all the terrible details. I'll tell Monsieur later. Look, people are arriving. Show some dignity, for heaven's sake, some fortitude!'

Determined to appear strong, Charles kept repeating:

'Yes . . . courage, courage.'

'You're right!' exclaimed the old man. 'I'll show 'em, God damn it! I'll stick by her to the last.'

The bell was tolling. Everything was ready. It was time to start.*

And, seated next to each other in a choir stall, they watched as the three cantors moved back and forth in front of them, intoning. The serpent player* was blowing with all his might. Monsieur Bournisien, ceremonially robed, was intoning in a high voice; he repeatedly bowed low before the tabernacle, raised his hands, spread his arms wide. Lestiboudois, his verger's staff in his hand, paced about the church; the bier lay beside the lectern, between four rows of candles. Charles felt an urge to get up and extinguish them.

Nevertheless he tried to work himself up into a devout frame of mind, to grasp at the hope of a future life where he would see her again. He thought of her as having left on a journey to a distant place, a long time ago. But then, when he reflected that she was down there in her coffin, and that it was all over, that she was to be buried in the earth, he was filled with a terrible, savage, desperate rage. Sometimes, he thought he wasn't feeling anything any more; and he took pleasure in this alleviation of his pain, even while reproaching himself for being so contemptible.

They heard a regular tapping sound, like the noise of a metal-tipped stick striking the flagstones. It came from the back of the church, stopping abruptly in a side-aisle; a man in a coarse brown jacket lowered himself painfully to his knees. It was Hippolyte, the ostler from the Lion d'Or. He had put on his new leg.

One of the cantors walked round the nave taking up the collection, and the heavy coins fell with a clatter, one after another, onto the silver plate.

'Get on with it! It's more than I can bear!' cried Bovary, angrily tossing in a five-franc piece; the cantor made him a stately bow in thanks.

People were singing, and kneeling down, and standing up, again and again. Would it never end? He remembered that once, in the early days, they had gone to mass together, and had stood side by side, over on the right, by the wall. The bell resumed its tolling. There was a shifting and scraping of chairs. The pallbearers slipped their three poles under the bier, and they all left the church.

Justin appeared at the pharmacy door, but then, white-faced and trembling, suddenly vanished inside again.

People stood at their windows to watch the procession pass. Charles, at the head of it, held himself very erect. He put on a bold front, giving tiny nods of recognition to people as they emerged from doorways and alleyways to join the throng. The six men, three on either side, were panting slightly as they marched at a slow pace. The priests, the cantors, and the two little choristers were reciting the *De Profundis*, their voices rising and falling in waves that faded away over the fields. Sometimes, at a turning in the path, they would disappear from sight, but the great silver cross always remained visible through the tops of the trees.

At the rear came the women, wearing black cloaks with turned-down hoods; they were all carrying large lighted candles. Dizzied by the endless succession of prayers and lights, and by the cloying aromas of candles and cassocks, Charles began to feel faint. A fresh breeze was blowing, the fields of rye and rape were turning green, and tiny drops of dew trembled on the thorn hedges bordering the road. All manner of cheerful noises filled the air around them: the distant sound of a cart rattling over ruts; the recurrent crowing of a cock, the hoof-beats of a foal cantering off into the apple trees. Pink clouds dappled the clear sky; bluish smoke swirled round thatched roofs thick with wild flowers; Charles recognized farmyards as he went along. He remembered mornings like this one, when, after visiting a patient, he would leave the cottage and set off home, to her.

Occasionally the black pall, embroidered with white teardrops, would billow up, revealing the coffin. The weary pallbearers were slowing their pace, and the bier kept advancing in fits and starts, like a boat pitching forward with every wave.

They arrived.

The men walked on to the far end, to a place in the grass where the grave had been dug.

They all took their places round it; and while the priest was speaking, the red earth, piled up on the edges, trickled in at each corner, silently, continuously.

Then, when the four ropes had been positioned, the coffin was pushed onto them. He watched it go down. Further and further down.

Finally, they heard a thud; the ropes creaked as they were brought back up. Then Bournisien took the spade from Lestiboudois, and with his left hand, while he sprinkled holy water with his right, he vigorously heaved a large spadeful of earth into the grave; the pebbles, as they rained down on the wood of the coffin, made that terrifying drumming that resounds in our ears like the voice of eternity.

The priest passed the aspergill to the person nearest to him. It was Monsieur Homais. He shook it solemnly, then gave it to Charles, who flung himself onto his knees on the ground, casting in great handfuls of earth as he cried: 'Goodbye!' He kept sending her kisses and dragging himself ever closer to the edge of the grave, as if wanting to be buried in it with her.

They led him away; he quickly regained his composure, aware, perhaps, like everyone else, of a vague sense of relief that it was all over.

On the way back, old Rouault calmly lit his pipe, an act which

Homais, deep down, deemed rather improper.* He also noted that Monsieur Binet had not been present, that Tuvache had 'slipped away' right after the mass, and that Théodore, the notary's man-servant, had worn a blue coat, 'as if he couldn't find a black coat; after all, devil take it, it's the done thing to wear black!' He moved about among the groups of mourners, passing on these comments. People were lamenting Emma's death, especially Lheureux, who had not failed to attend the obsequies.

'That poor sweet lady! What a dreadful thing for her husband!'

The apothecary replied:

'Actually, had it not been for me, he would have done something desperate!'

'Such a fine person! And to think that I saw her in my shop only last Saturday!'

'I just didn't have the time', explained Homais, 'to prepare a brief tribute to deliver at the graveside.'

When they reached home, Charles changed out of his funeral clothes, and Père Rouault put his blue smock back on. It was brand new and, as he had kept wiping his eyes on the sleeve during the ride to Yonville, the dye had come off on his face, and his tears had left streaks in the dust that coated his features.

The older Madame Bovary was with them. All three sat in silence. Eventually, the old man sighed:

'D'you remember, my boy, when I came to Tostes, just after you had lost your first good lady? I was able to comfort you, then! I knew what to say; but now . . .'

Then, his chest heaving in a deep, long groan:

'For me, you see, this is the end! I've bid farewell to my wife . . . then to my son . . . and now, today, to my daughter!'

He wanted to go home to Les Bertaux immediately, saying he wouldn't be able to sleep, not in that house. He even refused to see his granddaughter.

'No, no! I just couldn't stand the sorrow of it. But you must give her a big kiss from me. Goodbye! . . . you're a good lad! And don't you worry, I'll not forget,' he said, slapping his thigh; 'you'll still get your turkey.'

But on reaching the top of the hill he turned round, just as he had done long ago, on the road to Saint-Victor, when he parted from her. The sun was setting beyond the meadow, and in its slanting rays every window in the village blazed with fire. He shielded his eyes with his hand, and saw, on the horizon, a walled enclosure with clumps of trees dotted about like black bouquets among the white stones. Then he continued on his way at a slow trot, for his nag was limping.

Although they were worn out, Charles and his mother sat up very late into the night, talking. They talked about the past, and of the future. She would come to live in Yonville and keep house for him, they would never again be parted. She was tactful and tender, privately rejoicing at regaining an affection of which she had been deprived for so many years. Midnight struck. The village, as usual, was silent; Charles lay awake, thinking only of her.

Rodolphe, who, to take his mind off things, had spent the day in the woods with his gun, lay peacefully asleep in his chateau; down in Rouen Léon, too, slept.

But there was another person who, at that late hour, was not asleep.

Beside the grave, among the fir trees, a young lad knelt, weeping in the darkness; sobs rent his breast and he gasped for breath, oppressed by an immeasurable sorrow that was more tender than the moon, deeper than the night. Suddenly the gate creaked. It was Lestiboudois, coming to fetch the spade that he had forgotten earlier. He recognized Justin as he climbed over the wall, instantly concluding that he could finally put a name to the scoundrel who was stealing his potatoes.

CHAPTER XI

The next day Charles sent for his little daughter. She asked for her mama, and was told that she'd gone away, and would be bringing her some toys when she came home. Berthe mentioned her again several times; then, eventually, forgot about her. The child's cheerfulness broke Bovary's heart; he had also to endure the insufferable commiserations of the pharmacist.

Money problems soon resurfaced, with Lheureux again urging on his friend Vinçart. Charles signed his name to notes for exorbitant sums, for never would he even consider selling the smallest object that had belonged to *her*. His mother lost her patience with him, but he was far angrier than she. He was a changed man. She left the house for good.

Then everyone began scrambling for 'his share of the spoils'. Mademoiselle Lempereur presented her bill for six months' lessons; Emma had never actually taken a single one (despite that signed invoice she had shown Bovary), but the two women had had an arrangement; the owner of the lending-library claimed Emma had owed him three years' subscriptions; Mère Rollet demanded the cost of delivering a score or so of letters, and when Charles asked for details, was tactful enough to reply:

'Oh, I've no idea! It was business.'

Each time he settled a debt, Charles thought it was the last. But, always, there was another, and then another, on and on.

He wrote asking his patients to settle their overdue accounts. They showed him the letters his wife had sent, and he had to apologize.

Félicité went round wearing Madame's dresses, now; not all of them, because he had kept back a few, which he would go and look at, in her dressing room, first locking the door; the maid was more or less her size, and often Charles, catching sight of her from behind, would imagine she was Emma, and cry out:

'Don't go! Don't go!'

But, at Pentecost, she decamped from Yonville, running off with Théodore and carrying away with her everything that remained of Emma's wardrobe.

It was about this time that the widow Dupuis 'had the honour to inform him of the marriage of her son, Monsieur Léon Dupuis, notary at Yvetot, to Mademoiselle Léocadie Lebœuf, of Bondeville'. Charles, in his congratulatory letter to Léon, wrote these words:

'How delighted my poor wife would have been!'

One day when, wandering aimlessly round the house, he had climbed up to the attic, he felt something under his slipper: it was a crumpled-up sheet of thin paper. Opening it out, he read: 'Be brave, Emma, be brave! I can't let myself wreck your life.' It was Rodolphe's letter, which had fallen on the floor between some boxes and, after lying there for a time, had now been blown near the door by the breeze from the skylight. Charles stood there, open-mouthed, transfixed, on that same spot where Emma, in despair, her face whiter even than his, had once longed for death. Eventually, he noticed a tiny 'R' at the foot of the second page. Who was it? He remembered Rodolphe's attentiveness, his sudden disappearance and his constrained manner on the two or three occasions when they had subsequently met. But he was deceived by the letter's respectful tone.

'Perhaps their feelings were purely platonic,' he thought.

In any case, Charles was not a man given to examining anything too closely; he shrank back from concrete proof, and his wavering jealousy melted away into the immensity of his pain.

Everyone, he thought, must have adored her. Every single man, without a doubt, must have lusted after her. Because of this she became, in his eyes, only the more beautiful, and he conceived for her an unremitting, raging desire that fed his despair, and was unbounded, because it could never be satisfied now.

To please her, as if she were still alive, he adopted her preferences and her ideas; he bought himself patent-leather boots and began wearing white cravats. He waxed his moustaches, and, like her, signed his name to promissory notes. She was corrupting him from beyond the grave.

He was forced to sell the silver piece by piece, and then he sold the parlour furniture. All the rooms were stripped; but the bedroom, her bedroom, remained just as it had always been. After dinner, Charles went up there. He would push the round table in front of the fire, and draw up *her* armchair. He took his seat opposite. A candle was burning in one of the gilded candlesticks. Berthe sat beside him, colouring pictures.

The poor man hated seeing Berthe so badly dressed, her boots with laces missing and the armholes of her smock gaping open to below her waist, for the daily woman never bothered about her. But she was so sweet, so good, with her little head bending so gracefully over her work and her thick blond hair falling over her rosy cheeks, that he was filled with immeasurable delight, with a pleasure tainted by bitterness, like those wines of poor quality that taste of resin. He would repair her toys, make puppets for her from cardboard, and sew up the torn stomachs of her dolls. Then, if his glance chanced upon the workbox, or a ribbon left about, or even a pin lying in a crack of the table, he would lapse into a daydream, and look so sad, that she would, like him, become sad as well.

No one, now, came to see them. Justin had fled to Rouen, where he had found employment as a grocer's boy, and the apothecary's children spent less and less time with the child, for Monsieur Homais had no wish to encourage the relationship, given the difference in the social status of the two families.

The blind beggar, whom he had not succeeded in curing with his ointment, had returned to his former haunts on the Bois-Guillaume hill, where he entertained travellers with accounts of Homais's futile efforts, with so much persistence that the pharmacist, on his trips to the city, would cower behind the curtains of the Hirondelle to avoid encountering him. The pharmacist loathed the wretch; and wanting, in the interests of his own reputation, to be rid of him at all costs, he mounted a covert campaign against him, thereby revealing the depth of his intelligence and the unscrupulousness of his egotism. For six consecutive months, readers of the *Fanal de Rouen* were treated to paragraphs like the following:

'Every traveller heading for the fertile fields of Picardy cannot fail to have observed the presence, on the hillside of Bois-Guillaume, of a wretched creature afflicted with a hideous lesion of the face. He pesters and persecutes wayfarers, and quite literally exacts a toll from each one of them. Have we then not progressed beyond those horrendous Middle Ages, when vagabonds were permitted to display, in public places, the leprous sores and strumae they had carried back with them from the Crusades?'

Or again:

'In spite of the laws forbidding vagrancy, the outskirts of our large cities continue to be infested by bands of paupers. Some of them— and these may well not be the least dangerous—operate single-handed. Whatever can our Aediles be thinking?'

Then Homais began concocting anecdotes:

'Yesterday, on the hill at Bois-Guillaume, a skittish horse . . .' And he launched into the description of an accident caused by the presence of the blind man. His campaign was so effective that the offender was incarcerated. But, later, he was released again. He resumed his former occupation, as did Homais. The battle was joined. The pharmacist emerged victorious, for his enemy was condemned to spend the remainder of his days in an asylum.

This victory emboldened him: from that moment on there was not a dog run over, nor a barn burnt down, nor a woman beaten up in his district but Homais, inspired always by his love of progress and his hatred of priests, promptly reported the event to the public. He drew parallels between primary schools* and those run by the

Ignorantine Friars* (to the detriment of the latter), wrote about the St Bartholomew Massacre in connection with a 100-franc grant to the church, denounced abuses, and shot off some damaging broadsides. At least, that was the way he put it. Homais persisted with his undermining operations, and grew dangerous.

Stifled by the restrictions of journalism, however, he soon felt the need to produce a book, a major work! So he wrote his *General Statistical Study of the Canton of Yonville, followed by Various Climatological Observations;* then, from statistics, he quickly progressed to philosophy. He became preoccupied by the great questions of the day: social reforms, raising the moral standards of the poor, pisciculture, rubber, the railways, etc.* He even grew ashamed of being a bourgeois, and began to affect the appearance and lifestyle of the artist; he began smoking! He bought himself two chic Pompadour-style statuettes to decorate his parlour.

He did not abandon the pharmacy: quite the contrary! He kept abreast of the latest discoveries, and followed every phase of the spreading fashion for chocolate. It was due to his efforts that *cho-ca** and *revalentia** were introduced into the department of the Seine-Inférieure. He became a great devotee of Pulvermacher electric belts;* he wore one himself; and at night, when he removed his flannel undershirt, Madame Homais would lie there quite dazzled by the golden spirals that almost obscured him from her view, feeling her passion redouble for this man who was more heavily girdled than a Scythian and as magnificent as any of the Magi.

He had some splendid ideas for Emma's tomb. First he suggested a broken column with drapery, then a pyramid, then a Temple to Vesta, perhaps in the shape of a rotunda . . . even 'a heap of ruins'. Every single plan specified a weeping willow, which Homais considered the mandatory symbol of grief.

Charles and he went to Rouen together to look at tombstones made by a mason who specialized in memorials. A painter accompanied them, one Vaufrylard,* a friend of Bridoux's, who spent the entire time regaling them with puns. Finally, after examining about a hundred designs, obtaining an estimate, and making a second trip to Rouen, Charles decided on a mausoleum that would display, on its two principal walls, 'a guardian spirit bearing an extinguished torch'.

As for the inscription, in Homais's opinion nothing could match '*Sta viator*' for beauty, but no matter how hard he racked his brain,

he could not come up with the rest; he kept repeating '*Sta viator . . .*'
At last, he remembered: '*amabilem conjugem calcas!!*'* and this was
adopted.

It was a curious fact that Bovary, while constantly thinking about
Emma, was actually forgetting her; and he was filled with despair at
how this image kept fading from his memory at the very time when
he was struggling so hard to retain it. Every night, however, he
dreamt of her; the dream was always the same: he came up to her, but
just as he took her in his arms, she dissolved into dust in his embrace.

During one week he was seen entering the church every single
evening. Monsieur Bournisien even paid him a visit or two, but
eventually gave up on him. In any case, the priest, according to
Homais, was becoming increasingly intolerant, in fact almost fanatical; he ranted on against the spirit of the age and never failed, every
couple of weeks or so, in his sermon, to describe the death of
Voltaire, who died devouring his own excrement,* as everybody
knows.

In spite of his frugal ways, Bovary was still quite unable to pay off
his old debts. Lheureux refused to renew any of the promissory
notes. Seizure became imminent. At that point he turned to his
mother, who wrote agreeing to let him take out a mortgage on her
property, but used the opportunity to revile Emma, and demanded,
as compensation for her sacrifice, a shawl that had escaped Félicité's
plundering. Charles refused to give it her. They quarrelled.

She made the first attempt at reconciliation, by suggesting that
the child be sent to her; it would make things easier for her at home.
Charles agreed. But, when the moment came to part, his courage
failed him. This time the breach was final, irrevocable.

As he became increasingly alienated from others, the love he felt
for Berthe bound him ever more closely to her. But she worried him;
she coughed intermittently, and patches of red would colour her cheeks.

Always on display in the house across the square, the pharmacist's
boisterous family prospered. Everything was going right for Homais.
Napoléon served as his laboratory assistant, Athalie made him an
embroidered smoking cap, Irma cut out the paper rounds to cover
his jams, and Franklin could recite the entire multiplication table at
one go. He was the happiest of fathers, the most fortunate of men.

But no, not so! A secret ambition tormented him: Homais yearned
for the cross of the Legion of Honour. His claim was not without

foundation: (1) he had distinguished himself, at the time of the cholera epidemic,* by his complete and unconditional devotion to duty. (2) He had published, at his own expense, various works of public utility, among them ... (and he cited his treatise entitled: 'Cider: Its manufacture and its effects ...'; also some 'Observations on the woolly aphis, submitted to the Academy';* also his statistical opus, and he even included his pharmaceutical thesis); 'and that's leaving aside the fact that I belong to a number of learned societies' (he belonged to only one).

'And,' he exclaimed, giving a hop and a skip, 'even if they only looked at my outstanding record as a firefighter!'

So Homais began making overtures to Power. In secret, he rendered important services to the Prefect in the elections. In fact he sold himself, prostituted himself. He even addressed a petition to the sovereign in which he begged him to 'see justice done him', addressing him as 'our good king', and comparing him to Henri IV.

And, each morning, the apothecary would grab the newspaper, expecting to find his nomination in it; but it was never there. Finally, unable to bear it any longer, he had a grass plot laid out in his garden in the shape of the star, with two narrow strips coming from the apex to represent the ribbon. He would stroll round it, his arms crossed, meditating upon the ineptitude of government and the ingratitude of men.

From feelings of respect, or from a kind of sensuality that made him want to spin out his investigations, Charles had not yet opened the secret drawer in a rosewood desk that Emma had always used. But finally, one day, he did sit down at it, turned the key, and pressed the spring. All Léon's letters were there. There could be no further doubt, this time! He devoured them all, to the very last one, then ransacked every corner, every piece of furniture, searching every drawer and even behind the panelling, sobbing, howling with rage, frantic, quite demented. Discovering a box, he kicked it open. There lay Rodolphe's portrait, staring straight at him, on top of a jumble of love letters.

His deep despondency caused general amazement. He no longer went out, he saw no one, he even refused to visit his patients. People began saying that he 'shut himself away to drink'.

Occasionally, however, an inquisitive passer-by would peer over the top of the garden hedge, and stare in astonishment at this long-bearded, wild-looking man in filthy clothes who paced up and down, weeping noisily.

On summer evenings he used to take his little girl with him to the cemetery. By the time they returned, darkness had fallen, and the only light showing in the square would be the one shining from Binet's attic window.

But something prevented him from fully luxuriating in his grief—he had no one close to him to share it with; and he started dropping in on Madame Lefrançois simply to talk about *her*. But the innkeeper only listened with half an ear, having troubles of her own, for Monsieur Lheureux had finally started his own coach service, 'Les Favorites du commerce',* and Hivert, who had made quite a name for himself carrying out errands in town, was demanding better pay and threatening to go over 'to the competition'.

One day when he had gone to the market at Argueil to sell his horse—his last remaining asset—he bumped into Rodolphe. On seeing each other, both men turned white. Rodolphe, who had merely sent his card, at first stammered some excuses, but then, growing bolder, had the nerve (it was August, and very hot) to invite Bovary to come to the tavern for a beer.

Sitting opposite him at a table, Rodolphe leant on his elbows and chewed his cigar while he talked; and Charles drifted off into a daydream as he gazed at this face that she had loved. He felt he was seeing some part of her again. He was filled with wonder. He would have liked to be that man.

Rodolphe chattered on about farming, livestock, manure, plugging with small talk any gaps where an allusion might slip in. Charles was not listening to him; and Rodolphe, noticing this, watched the other's mobile features record the successive passage of memories. Slowly Charles's face grew crimson; his nostrils pulsated rapidly, his lips trembled; there even came a moment when, filled with sombre fury, he focused his gaze upon Rodolphe with such intensity that the latter almost felt afraid, and stopped what he was saying. But soon Charles's habitual expression of dismal lassitude returned.

'I don't hold it against you,' he said.

Rodolphe sat there in silence. And Charles, his head in his hands, went on, his voice flat, his resigned tone heavy with infinite suffering:

'No, now I don't hold it against you any longer!'

And then, for the only time in his life, he even uttered a memorable phrase:

'Fate is to blame.'

Rodolphe, who had orchestrated that fate, thought him remarkably tolerant for a man in his situation, a trifle comical, even despicable.

The next day, Charles went to sit on the bench in the arbour. The sky was blue, and the sunlight, filtering through the trellis, traced the shadows of the vine leaves on the sandy floor; jasmine scented the air, cantharides beetles droned busily round the flowering lilies, and Charles sat sobbing like an adolescent, overwhelmed by the nebulous wafts of love that swelled his sorrowing heart.

At seven o'clock, little Berthe, who had not seen him all afternoon, came to fetch him for dinner.

His head was leaning against the wall, his eyes were closed, his mouth open, and his hands held a lock of long black hair.

'Come on, papa!' she said.

Thinking he was playing a game with her, she pushed him gently. He fell to the ground. He was dead.

Thirty-six hours later, at the request of the apothecary, Monsieur Canivet arrived. He opened him up, but found nothing.

When everything had been sold up, there remained twelve francs seventy-five centimes, which paid Mademoiselle Bovary's fare to her grandmother's house. The good woman died that very same year; and, as Père Rouault was now paralysed, Berthe became the responsibility of an aunt. She is poor, and sends the child to earn her keep at a cotton mill.

Since Bovary's death, three doctors, in turn, have tried, and failed, to build up a practice in Yonville, so promptly and thoroughly did Monsieur Homais demolish their attempts. He is doing devilishly well; the authorities treat him with great circumspection, and public opinion is on his side.

He has just been awarded the Legion of Honour.

EXPLANATORY NOTES

The following abbreviations have been used:

MB n.v.   *Madame Bovary*, nouvelle version, ed. Jean Pommier and Gabrielle
            Leleu (Paris: José Corti, 1949)
OC   Flaubert, *Œuvres complètes*, 2 vols, preface by Jean Bruneau, ed.
            Bernard Masson (Paris: Éditions du Seuil, 1964)
DIR   *Dictionnaire des idées reçues*

Translations of passages from Flaubert's letters are mostly taken from the
Steegmuller edition (see Select Bibliography).

The originals of letters cited or referred to in the notes may be found, if dated
up to the end of 1858, in

Flaubert, *Correspondance*, ed. Jean Bruneau, 2 vols., *1830–1851* and *1851–8*
(Paris: Gallimard, 1973 and 1980)

and, if dated after 1858, in

Flaubert, *Correspondance*, nouvelle édition augmentée (Paris: Conard,
1926–33, with Supplément 1954)

Flaubert's most frequently cited correspondents are designated in references
by their initials, namely: LB Louis Bouilhet; EC Ernest Chevalier; LC Louise
Colet; HT Hippolyte Taine.

PART I

3 *Sénard*: the lawyer who conducted Flaubert's defence in the case brought
   against him, the publishers, and the printer after *Madame Bovary* had
   been serialized in *La Revue de Paris*.

5 *at prep*: Flaubert was at the Collège royal in Rouen between 1832 and
   1840, for the most part as a boarder. An almost exact contemporary there
   of Flaubert's elder brother Achille was Eugène Delamare, the principal
   model for Charles Bovary. The outline biography of Delamare fits rea-
   sonably neatly: he was medical officer in Ry, married a Mademoiselle
   Mutel five years older than he was, was soon widowed, and married the
   17-year-old Delphine Couturier who gave birth to a daughter, and died
   in 1848, aged 26. Delamare died in 1849. However, Delamare's character
   was apparently that of an active local politician who was an inconstant
   authoritarian husband. Less is known about his second wife. (See A.-M.
   Gossez, 'Homais et Bovary hommes politiques', *Mercure de France*, 15
   July 1911.)

6 *Charbovari*: the name Bovary (here slurred to evoke cart and ox and with
   perhaps a sly reference to Ry where Delamare married and worked) may
   derive from Mlle de Bovery, a local squire's daughter involved in a poison
   and adultery trial in 1844 and from Bouvaret, the proprietor in Cairo of a

hotel where Flaubert stayed in 1849 (see letter to Hortense Cornu, 20 Mar. 1870, and *OC* ii. 560).

7 *Quos ego*: a reference to Neptune's speech in *Aeneid* 1. 132 ff.

10 *Rouen*: the city was then the fifth largest in France with a population of 100,000, a considerable port and commercial centre.

Anacharsis: the Abbé J.-J. Barthélemy's very successful and influential book (1788) about fourth-century BC Greek civilization.

studying medicine: possible only to a preliminary level at the school founded in 1811 by Flaubert's father, who taught anatomy and physiology and was chief surgeon at the Hôtel-Dieu hospital where Flaubert was born. To qualify fully as a doctor it was necessary to go to Paris, but students could become an 'officier de santé' (see note to p. 12).

the Eau-de-Robec: a small tributary of the Seine in Rouen, then surrounded by dye works which discoloured the water, hence 'yellow, violet or blue' (p. 11).

12 *Béranger*: extremely popular liberal poet (1780–1857) whose writings, called *chansons*, attacked the monarchy and the clergy. Flaubert included 'admiration for Béranger' in a list of things he disliked in other people (letter to LC, 1 June 1853).

officier de santé: the position of *officier de santé* was created between 1803 and 1892 as something like the civilian equivalent of the military post held by Charles's father. No holder of this position could conduct important surgery without the attendance of a doctor nor practise medicine outside his *département*.

Tostes: now spelt Tôtes. Small town halfway between Rouen and Dieppe. Flaubert's father owned a farm at Saint-Sulpice-la-Pierre nearby between 1828 and 1839.

13 *Les Bertaux*: Eugène Delamare's second wife, Delphine Couturier (see note to p. 5), lived just outside Blainville-Crevon in the ferme du Vieux-Chateau, now named 'ferme Madame Bovary' on certain maps. The route through Longueville and Saint-Victor is fanciful.

17 *Yvetot*: the commercial centre of the pays de Caux with a population then of about 9,000.

18 *an Ursuline convent*: there were two in Rouen belonging to this order devoted to teaching, one in the Rue Coqueréaumont and the other in the Rue Morant.

19 *Ingouville*: to judge by the lawyer's actions this is probably the smart suburb of Le Havre, with exceptional sea-views, which was then being built as a fashionable residential quarter, rather than the village of the same name just south-west of Saint-Valéry-en-Caux.

25 *married at midnight*: a custom in some places rather than an eccentricity. Maupassant's grandfather, whom Flaubert knew, and Madame Schlésinger, whom he idolized, had both had midnight marriages in the *départment* of the Eure.

30 *Dictionary of the Medical Sciences*: this comprised sixty volumes (Paris: Panckoucke, 1812–22). Flaubert found in the work some fatuous assertions (which he added to his *Sottisier*, a collection of foolish comments made in learned seriousness), so it may not have been entirely to Charles's disadvantage to leave the pages uncut.

32 *truffles he has eaten*: when *Madame Bovary* appeared in serial form in *La Revue de Paris*, its editors worried about the propriety of this passage; it was to be raised by the prosecution at the 1857 trial in which Flaubert, the editor of the *Revue*, and the printer were accused of 'offending public and religious morality.'

Paul et Virginie: this novel of 1787 by Bernardin de Saint-Pierre describes the close friendship between two French children on the Île de France (Mauritius), a friendship which grows into adolescent love in the exotic world of the Indian Ocean and which ends in tragedy. It was a highly influential work of French Pre-Romanticism. Paul is of course not the brother of Virginie, but Emma's own brother had died young (see p. 29).

33 *Mademoiselle de la Vallière*: mistress of Louis XIV and his court favourite until 1667. She retired ultimately to a Carmelite convent.

Abbé Frayssinous's Lectures: originally given in churches, on theology and religion, these reflected the religious revival during the Restoration and were available in the *Défense du christianisme* of 1825.

Le Génie du christianisme: by Chateaubriand, who published in 1802 this famous attempt to understand Christianity through aesthetics and the senses.

34 *Agnès Sorel*: Charles VII's mistress.

La Belle Ferronnière: mistress of François I.

Clémence Isaure: this legendary lady revived the Floral Games for troubadours in Toulouse in the fourteenth century.

35 *under his oak*: Louis IX (1215–70) by tradition sat under an oak to give wise judgement.

Bayard: c.1473–1524. Fought bravely and chivalrously in the Italian wars of three French kings.

Louis XI: 1423–83. Noted for his pragmatic and unscrupulous methods to retain and further his power.

the Massacre of St Bartholomew: on the night of 23 to 24 August 1572 Huguenots were slaughtered mercilessly in Paris (and elsewhere in France in various massacres which went on until October).

Henry IV: 1553–1610. His white plume is frequently mentioned as his attribute.

Louis XIV: the plates are those mentioned on p. 33. The historical figures together form a collage of piety, beauty, love, bravery, and cruelty.

'keepsakes': Flaubert used the English word. These were a personal gift

to demonstrate one's affections in the shape of a book or album lavishly engraved.

Giaours: a derogatory term of Turkish origin, meaning non-Muslims, esp. Christians. Byron's poem *The Giaour* (1813), telling of a female slave in love with the Byronic title-personage, had given the term wide European currency.

36 *each engraving . . . these images of the world*: the Romantic literature read by Emma had some roots in northern Europe, popularized in *De la littérature* by Mme de Staël, who extolled the world of Ossian and the bards, Shakespeare, and Germanic and Scandinavian legend rather than the classical world of the Mediterranean. Byron (*Don Juan*) and Hugo (*Les Orientales*) were largely responsible for a new vision of Italy, Greece, and the Near East as places of warmth and exoticism. The classical view of the Mediterranean was of a literature and culture characterized by harmony and restraint. A letter from Flaubert to his mistress Louise Colet (3 Mar. 1852) describes his painstaking researches into some of the more ephemeral aspects of Romanticism: 'For two days now I have been trying to enter into the dreams of young girls, and for this have been navigating in the milky oceans of books about castles, and troubadours in white-plumed velvet hats.'

Lamartinian melancholy: Lamartine's poem *Le Lac* (published in 1820) regrets the passing of love, undermined by death but recalled in the beauty of natural scenery.

37 *travel far away . . . sweeter indolence*: Flaubert's brother Achille and his sister Caroline both travelled on honeymoon to Italy. Indeed Caroline and her husband were accompanied by Flaubert and his parents. The *Dictionnaire des idées reçues* includes Italy as a honeymoon goal.

some Swiss chalet: Rousseau was perhaps the first enthusiast for the Alps (*La Nouvelle Héloïse*, 1761).

42 *in the Italian style*: the visit to La Vaubyessard is based on a memory of Flaubert's visit with his parents to the Marquis de Pomereu's *fête seigneuriale* in 1836. The Marquis lived at the Chateau du Héron (now destroyed) just east of Ry and he had been a member of the Seine-Inférieure Conseil général between 1829 and 1833. So impressive was the occasion for the 14-year-old boy that Flaubert recalled it and his subsequent dawn walk through the park in a letter written years later to his friend Louis Bouilhet from Egypt (13 Mar. 1850). The description of a ball in chapter v of an early work, *Quidquid volueris* (1837), is a more immediate reflection of the event.

43 *Jean-Antoine . . . 1693*: the names are fictitious, the battles are historical.

44 *in their wine glasses*: in bourgeois circles Emma might have expected to see women refuse wine by placing a glove in their glass.

between Monsieur de Coigny and Monsieur de Lauzun: both dukes, soldiers, philanderers, and intimates of Marie-Antoinette.

46 *scarlet turbans*: the mothers are to some extent still following the style of
    their youth. Turbans were especially fashionable about 1820.

47 *jumping a ditch, in England*: a reference to steeplechasing, then less
    common in France.

48 *bisques*: soup made from birds, game, or crayfish.

    Trafalgar puddings: probably fictitious, though 'pudding à l'amiral'
    existed.

    cotillion: the final dance of the ball, here a waltz (for couples) by contrast
    with the earlier quadrille (danced as a foursome). The waltz was not
    always considered proper at this time.

52 *Pompadour*: the Marquise de Pompadour (1721–64) was a noted patron of
    the arts and an intimate of Louis XV. An elaborate rococo style is
    implied.

    'La Marjolaine': marjolaine is marjoram. The 'compagnons de la mar-
    jolaine', according to an old French song, are the keepers of the watch.

    Sylphe des Salons: there was a short-lived magazine *Le Sylphe: journal des
    salons* (1829–30), and another, *Sylphe: littérature, beaux-arts, théâtres*, was
    published in Rouen from December 1845 to January 1847.

    the Bois: the bois de Boulogne, which was already the most celebrated
    open space to be found in the capital.

    Eugène Sue: 1804–75. Popular novelist, and pioneer of the *roman-
    feuilleton* or serial novel. Best known for *Les Mystères de Paris* (1842–3).
    Flaubert wrote from Constantinople to Louis Bouilhet (14 Nov. 1850): 'I
    took Eugène Sue's *Arthur* from the reading-room. It's enough to make
    you vomit; there's no word to describe it.'

    Balzac: 1799–1850. Much admired by Flaubert (letter to LB, 14 Nov.
    1850), who saw his death as leaving a vast gap in the world of the French
    novel and who was influenced especially by the *Physiologie du mariage*
    and *La Muse du département* when he wrote *Madame Bovary*.

    George Sand: 1804–76. At the time Flaubert wrote *Madame Bovary* he
    had not yet come to know, befriend, and admire George Sand whose early
    novels stressed a defiance of conventional morality.

57 *Erard*: Sebastian Erard (1752–1831) was a pioneering piano- and harp-
    maker, and well known across Europe.

61 *Yonville-l'Abbaye*: a fictitious name (see note to p. 63), based on the Rue
    de la Croix d'Yonville to the west of the Hôtel-Dieu in Rouen and close
    to the house at Déville owned by Flaubert's father until 1844.

    a Polish refugee: after the Warsaw risings of 1830–1, when Russia crushed
    Poland.

PART II

63 *Yonville-l'Abbaye*: 'Yonville-l'Abbaye itself is a place which doesn't exist,
    so too with the Rieulle [*sic*], etc.' (Letter to Émile Cailteaux, 4 June 1857.)

Yonville has many of the spatial characteristics of Ry where the Delamare family lived, but the directions given are of a journey to Forges-les-Eaux where Flaubert, his mother, and his niece Caroline had stayed in 1848. They were taking refuge from Caroline's deranged widowed father Émile Hamard and they stayed with a family friend, Maître Beaufils (see letter to EC, 4 Aug. 1848). Ry is, for reasons of discretion and mystification, never mentioned in *Madame Bovary* and it is not known whether Flaubert ever went there. Some of the site characteristics of Forges (the Bray grazing district close by and the long red gashes of the iron-ore seams which help to create the spa waters) are evident.

Flaubert's imaginary Yonville lies about 20 miles from Rouen.

In the topography of *Madame Bovary* no place names outside Normandy are fictitious. Street and area names in Rouen also exist (or existed at the time). In Normandy, place names exist in the given geographical context with the exception of the following: Andervilliers; Banneville; Barfeuchères; Barneville; le Bas-Diauville; Les Bertaux; La Fresnaye; Givry-Saint-Martin; Côte des Leux; La Huchette; La Panville; the Rieule (river); Côte Saint-Jean; Sassetot-la-Guerrière; Thibourville; La Vaubyessard; Yonville-l'Abbaye; Yverbonville.

64 *in the area*: Maître Beaufils's house in Forges may still be seen today at 11 Avenue des Sources. It is a large, handsome, whitewashed building.

65 *the Charter*: the French constitutional charter accepted by Louis-Philippe was published on 14 August 1830.

Vichy . . . Waters: waters from spa towns in the Massif Central, Germany, and the Pyrenees respectively, though more generally *eau de Seltz* is soda water or artificial mineral water. *Robs dépuratifs* are purgative fruit juice extracts, *médecine Raspail* is a camphor-based cure, perhaps for worms (see *Bouvard et Pécuchet*, ch. iii). Raspail had been called to try to save Flaubert's sister in 1846 but had failed and he is mocked in Flaubert's *Sottisier*. *Racahout* was a food made of flour and starch introduced into France from North Africa in the nineteenth century. *Pastilles Darcet* are probably named after Jean-Pierre-Joseph Darcet, French chemist. *Pâte Regnault* was named after Victor Regnault, a French physicist. The evidence of Flaubert's early work *La Femme du monde* (1836) suggests it was a remedy for venereal disease.

66 *the cholera*: an epidemic crossed Europe in 1832. See also p. 309.

the tinplate tricolour: Louis-Philippe had revived this as the national flag. It is made of tin to be visible when the wind drops.

67 *Poland*: see note to p. 61.

the flood victims in Lyon: in 1840.

69 *behind my ear*: 'I have never written anything more difficult than what I am writing at present, trivial dialogue' (letter to LC, 19 Sept. 1852).

70 *a Supreme Being*: a deist cult introduced by Robespierre (who was especially influenced by Rousseau) on 7 May 1794 and publicly celebrated at

the *fête de l'Être suprême* on 8 June 1794, to combat atheism and excessive dechristianization by the institution of natural religion.

70 *and of Béranger*: Socrates had been condemned in part for the worship of his own deities. Benjamin Franklin was a freemason, Voltaire a somewhat sceptical deist. For Béranger, see note to p. 12.

the Vicaire savoyard: Rousseau's defence of natural religion, the *Profession de foi du vicaire savoyard*, is to be found in Book IV of *Émile* (1762).

immortal principles of '89: to be found in the *Déclaration des droits de l'homme et du citoyen* voted by the Constituent Assembly on 27 August 1789.

73 *fifty-four Fahrenheit*: this is 12.2 °C. Flaubert's notes stated 'Homais has rather a cavalier attitude to precision' (*MB* n.v., 60).

74 *'L'Ange gardien'*: a popular *romance sentimentale* by Pauline Duchambge (1778–1858).

75 *a lending library*: 'I am doing a conversation between a young man and a young woman about literature, the sea, the mountains, music, all the poetical subjects. It is something that could be taken seriously, and yet I fully intend it as grotesque. This will be the first time, I think, that a book makes fun of its leading lady and its leading man. The irony does not detract from the pathetic aspect, but rather intensifies it' (letter to LC, 9 Oct. 1852).

Voltaire ... Walter Scott: Flaubert seems to have acknowledged the greatness of both Voltaire and Rousseau whilst infinitely preferring the former (letter to Mme Roger des Genettes, 1859 or 1860). He had a low opinion of Delille, who was a popular eighteenth-century nature poet (see *Hommage à Louis Bouilhet*, III). Scott was seen as the archetypal Romantic novelist (see *Bouvard et Pécuchet*, ch. v).

76 *Le Fanal de Rouen*: Flaubert was asked by the *Journal de Rouen* not to use its name here, as had been his original intention.

78 *year XI*: 10 March 1803 is the Gregorian calendar equivalent of this Revolutionary calendar date. Flaubert is accurate about article I, though doctors and chemists were answerable to the *Prefect* and Homais might have expected a summons to the Prefecture.

79 *shattered into a thousand pieces*: the final disintegration of the statue follows its gradual decay. It is mentioned earlier on pp. 30, 51, and 58.

80 *Atala*: probably a memory of the Indian girl in Chateaubriand's work *Atala* (1801). Certainly there is nothing Italianate about the name.

Galsuinde ... Yseult or Léocadie: Galswinthe was Queen of Neustria (*c.*540–68), Yseult was Tristan's love in Arthurian legend, and Léocadie may be a memory of the heroine in a play of that name by Scribe and Mélesville (1824).

Irma: derived from an ancient Germanic root.

Athalie: Racine's last tragedy (1691), whose religious subject matter irritates Homais. 'Racine! Corneille! and other talents just as mortally boring' (letter to LC, 29 Jan. 1854).

81 *'Le Dieu des bonnes gens'*: an anticlerical piece of verse by Béranger (1817).

barcarole: a Venetian gondoliers' song.

La Guerre des dieux: Parny's blasphemous poem completed in 1799.

82 *her baby daughter*: worries over a similarity here with Balzac's *Le Médecin de campagne* were linked with further worries over comparison of the opening of the novel with Balzac's *Louis Lambert* and Du Camp's *Livre posthume* (letter to LC, 27 Dec. 1852).

six weeks of the Virgin: from Christmas until the Purification of the Virgin (2 Feb.) is six weeks. Mothers were traditionally expected to avoid physical exertion for six weeks after giving birth.

83 *Mathieu Laensberg*: a popular almanac first published in 1636 in Liège, which finally ceased publication in the middle of the nineteenth century.

87 *osmazoms*: liquid extracts of meat containing its taste and smell. The name *osmazôme* was coined by the chemist Thénard (1777–1857).

90 *flax mill*: flax cultivation and spinning were much developed during the nineteenth century in Normandy.

a bunch of straw . . . with tricolour ribbon: put up to celebrate the completion of the roof timbers.

91 *metric*: the metric system, approved after the Revolution, was spreading only slowly in the provinces.

95 *Notre-Dame de Paris*: Hugo's novel (1831) includes in it (as Esméralda's mother) Paquette-la-Chantefleurie. If Emma is doing the thinking here she is revealing a lack of accuracy while imagining herself to be sophisticated.

103 *diachylon*: a lead plaster to reduce swelling.

104 *Caribs or Botocudos*: tribes from the West Indies and from Brazil respectively.

105 *why not leave now?*: Flaubert read law in Paris in 1842–3; but his nervous illness which began dramatically on a journey to Pont-l'Évêque in January 1844 (and his failure in the second-year Law Faculty exam six months earlier) made him then abandon these studies.

107 *English style*: Emma considers the handshake too intimate initially, and then yields to the feeling that its Englishness prevents it from being a compromising action. This affair has ended platonically and without a formal declaration; Flaubert's early plans had sketched a full and passionate love.

108 *a Jesuit*: here meaning 'a hypocrite'.

112 *Emma was to be prevented from reading novels*: 'Novel—novels pervert the masses' (*DIR*).

113 *la Huchette*: Louis Campion has been considered the likely model for Rodolphe Boulanger. He lived at Villiers, a mile south of Ry, in a house

which has since become known on I.g.n. maps as La Huchette. His relationship with Delphine Delamare remains mysterious but suggestive. (See Gossez's article (note to p. 5 above), and *OC* i. 26.)

117 *the great Show*: this chapter set at the *comices agricoles* is the longest in the novel and took nearly five months to complete between July and December 1853. Flaubert had visited a *comice agricole* at Grand-Couronne, a little downstream from Croisset, in July 1852, which he described as 'one of those inept rustic ceremonies' (letter to LC, 18 July 1852). The record of the *Nouvelliste de Rouen* of 19 and 20 July 1852 shows that Flaubert drew much material from what he had witnessed. The *comice agricole* was instituted in the late eighteenth century as a free association for the improvement of agriculture. The term became transferred to the shows, which proliferated after 1830, and *comices agricoles* (covering either a *canton*, an *arrondissement*, or even a *département*) offered prizes for good use and development of agricultural implements, for breeding and cross-breeding, for soil use and for pasture development, for irrigation, and for upkeep of agricultural buildings. Hardworking and long-serving farmhands, shepherds, and farm servants could receive awards.

118 *rat in his cheese*: a reference to La Fontaine's fable *Le Rat qui s'est retiré du monde* (Fables, vii. 3).

120 *Agronomical Society of Rouen*: fictitious, but Rouen was the seat of the Seine-Inférieure Agricultural Society (see also p. 137).

125 *unable to come*: this had been the case at the 1852 Grand-Couronne *comice*.

132 *magnetism*: Rodolphe is referring to the hugely influential doctrine of animal magnetism propounded by Franz Anton Mesmer (1734–1815).

Cincinnatus: fifth-century BC Roman dictator to whom the lictors brought the insignia of office while he was guiding his plough.

Diocletian: abdicated as Roman emperor in AD 305, traditionally in order to cultivate his lettuces.

emperors of China: they took part in person in the sowing season.

133 *Leroux*: the *Nouvelliste de Rouen* recorded the award of a medal and sixty francs to a farm servant who had served for forty-five years. Flaubert is happy to exaggerate the evidence of hard-won reward.

137 *apostles of Loyola*: i.e. Jesuits. They had been re-established in France in 1814.

146 *on the night table*: Flaubert himself kept a pipe and a glass of water by his bedside. See the *Souvenirs* of his niece, Caroline Commanville (Paris: Ferraud, 1895).

149 *jujube box*: containing cough medicine.

155 *Doctor Duval's treatise*: this is the *Traité pratique du pied-bot* by Vincent Duval published in 1839. One patient, Cécile Martin, had been successfully cured by Duval after Flaubert's father, using irons, had failed over a

period of nine months to effect a cure. It is interesting to note that the next case in the book involves a patient whose first name was Hippolyte. Flaubert had consulted his brother Achille, a surgeon, about club foot surgery (letter to LC, 18 Apr. 1854). Charles as an *officier de santé* should have performed a club foot operation only in the presence of a fully qualified doctor.

the equinus . . . valgus forms: respectively a club foot taking the weight on the tip of the toe, an inward-turning club foot, and an outward-turning club foot.

156 *Ambroise Paré . . . Celsus . . . Dupuytren . . . Gensoul*: respectively famous French surgeon (1517–90), Roman doctor (25 BC to AD 50), French surgeon (1777–1835) for whom Flaubert's father had been anatomy demonstrator, and French surgeon (1797–1858).

tenotome: small scalpel.

159 *ecchymoses*: blotchiness caused by bleeding beneath the skin.

161 *Bon-Secours*: a pilgrimage basilica overlooking the Seine on the south-east of Rouen, consecrated in 1842.

branch of boxwood: it would have been blessed on Palm Sunday.

strabismus . . . lithotrity: (an operation to correct) squinting; an operation for removing gallstones.

168 *napoleons*: gold coins each worth 20 francs.

169 *Amor nel cor*: probably a quotation from Dante, *Vita nuova* xxiii. 31, which reads 'piansemi Amor nel core, ove dimora' ('Love wept in my heart where he abides'). Louise Colet had given Flaubert a seal with the identical motto. When she had read the novel, and because Flaubert had at his insistence ended their affair in 1854, she felt herself mocked. Presumably the wound smarted, for in 1859 she wrote a poem called *Amor nel cor* in which she half-openly derided Flaubert.

171 *a small brown beard*: in French, *un collier brun*. Beards of this type, following the line of the jaw, were among Flaubert's aversions as listed to Louise Colet (1 June 1852). Cf. note to p. 12.

175 *on the road to Genoa*: in 1845 Flaubert and his parents accompanied his sister Caroline and her husband Émile Hamard on their honeymoon through Paris and Marseille to Genoa. It was in Genoa that Flaubert saw in the Balbi Palace the *Temptation of St Antony*, which helped to inspire him to write his own versions of the work of that name. It was then attributed to Pieter Brueghel the Younger, but is now thought to have been painted by Jan Mandyn.

the fourth of September, a Monday: this may be a key to a possible chronology of *Madame Bovary* and would imply that we are now in 1843. This fits well with the other rather vague indications of time. But it may not be intentional and Flaubert is not always accurate about such details.

180 *manchineel tree*: a tree found in the West Indies and South America which

has a poisonous sap and whose shadow was popularly supposed to be deadly.

184 *a dead faint*: Flaubert may be remembering his own epileptic seizure when in a cab near Pont-l'Évêque in January 1844.

185 *sternutator*: (agent) causing sneezing.

186 *That is the question*: the English phrase (*Hamlet*, III. i) has become a fairly commonplace foreign phrase in France.

187 *130 francs*: 70 francs from the loan to Charles and 60 francs profit ('a good thirty-three and a third profit on the goods supplied', i.e. 'the travelling cloak, the hand-bag, two trunks instead of one, and a number of other items as well') which are valued at 'the one hundred and eighty already owing'.

190 *Monsieur de Maistre*: Joseph de Maistre (1753–1821). Flaubert in letters to Mme Roger des Genettes of 1859 or 1860 and of September 1873 scorned the writing of de Maistre's counter-attacks on the influence of the eighteenth-century *philosophes* and on scientific progress and scientific values.

repentant blue-stockings: i.e. who have turned their backs on free-thinking.

191 *La Vallière*: see p. 33 and note.

193 *Castigat ridendo mores*: 'It corrects morals by laughter', the motto composed by Santeuil for the harlequin Dominique (1637–88) to use in his theatre.

Voltaire's tragedies: there are some seventeen of these. Flaubert was scathing in his criticism of them (letter to LC, 2 July 1853).

Le Gamin de Paris: a light comedy by Bayard and Vanderbuch (1836).

Church Fathers: the early Christian writers (first to sixth centuries).

196 *the theatre*: this is the *Théâtre des Arts*, built in 1775 and destroyed by fire in 1876, facing the river opposite the suspension bridge. It had a capacity of two thousand. It even had a motto based on the words *Castigat ridendo mores*. (See G. Daniels, 'Emma Bovary's Opera', *French Studies*, July 1978, for a very sensitive and informative article on Emma's visit to the opera.)

Lucie de Lammermoor: Walter Scott's *The Bride of Lammermoor* (1819) had been adapted by Donizetti for his opera *Lucia di Lammermoor*. The French version referred to in this chapter had a libretto by Alphonse Royer and Gustave Vaëz with additional music by Donizetti. Flaubert had seen the original Italian version in Constantinople (letter to Mme Flaubert, 14 Nov. 1850).

197 *familiar books of her youth*: see p. 34. The plot follows that of *The Bride of Lammermoor*, but is much reduced. Henri Ashton wishes his sister Lucie to marry Sir Arthur Bucklaw. Lucie has pledged herself to Edgar Ravenswood, with whom her family has quarrelled. Ashton, helped by Gilbert his evil henchman, convinces Lucie that Edgar has abandoned her. The

wretched girl consents to marry Sir Arthur, when Edgar appears. Ashton's plot is revealed to Lucie. Edgar thinks Lucie is unfaithful and she, marrying Arthur, becomes mad and stabs him on her wedding night. Edgar challenges Ashton to a duel but he attends to his dying sister instead. Edgar learns the whole truth and kills himself in front of Ashton, who is now racked by remorse.

198 *Edgar Lagardy appeared*: Flaubert gives him the same first name as that of his role. Traditionally the model for Lagardy is the tenor G.-H. Roger.

201 *Guess who I ran into?*: originally Flaubert had planned that Léon and Emma should meet again in Paris but 'at the theatre' (*MB* n.v. 17).

202 *Her hair's all coming down*: the famous mad scene (III. vi).

203 *'O bel ange, ma Lucie!'*: song by the dying Edgar (IV. vi).

Tamburini, Rubini, Persiani, Grisi: famous Italian opera singers of the early nineteenth century. Léon had intended to hear 'the Italians' in Paris. Grisi was a prima donna; Persiani also composed.

204 *Passage Saint-Herbland*: opposite the west front of the cathedral.

PART III

205 *La Chaumière*: famous dance hall in Paris on the Boulevard de Montparnasse. Founded in 1787, it was very fashionable in the first half of the nineteenth century.

grisettes: young working girls of easy virtue.

the Code: a copy of the official statute books drawn up under Napoleon I.

209 *four prints ... La Tour de Nesle*: this is a melodrama by Dumas père and Gaillardet, first performed in 1832. The play, set in the early fourteenth century, evokes the debauches of the three daughters-in-law of Philippe le Bel which took place, by tradition, in the tower of Nesle (on the site of the present Institut de France opposite the Louvre). The prints with Spanish and French texts, a series of scenes from the play, were four lithographs by Lordereau published in 1840.

212 *the dancing Salome*: the thirteenth-century stone carving of Salome dancing before Herod which is on the tympanum of the Portail Saint-Jean. Flaubert's tale *Hérodias* (1877) was probably inspired in part by it.

stoups of holy-water: a feature not of the cathedral but of the nearby Saint-Ouen church is a 'marble holy-water stoup fixed to the first pillar on the right (on entering by the west door) in which, by a strange optical effect, part of the interior of the building is reflected' (Adolphe Joanne, *Itinéraire général de la France: Normandie* (Paris: Hachette, 1866), 49).

213 *boatmen carrying baskets*: in the Chapelle Saint-Nicolas in the north transept a window is dedicated to the Watermen's Guild.

Lady Chapel: built between 1302 and 1320, it forms the apse of the cathedral and is noted for its fine Renaissance tombs.

213 *the splendours of the cathedral*: there is a seventeenth-century carved wood reredos with a fine Nativity painted by Philippe de Champaigne (1629), which might have caught Emma's attention.

214 *without any kind of inscription or engraving*: this entirely unremarkable curiosity was in fact embellished with rose tracery in black flint decorated with representations of the four winds. It was destroyed in about 1883 at the time of the repaving of the square.

great bell: named after Cardinal Georges d'Amboise, Louis XII's first minister. It had formerly been hung in the Tour de Beurre, was one of the biggest bells known, and was melted down in 1793 in Rémilly.

Pierre de Brézé: the de Brézés were one of the most powerful families of fifteenth-century France and their fine tombs and brief biographies are accurately described and given.

Montlhéry: the battle between the forces of Louis XI and Charles the Bold.

215 *Diane de Poitiers*: mistress of Henri II.

the Amboise tombs: Georges d'Amboise (I) who died in 1510 and after whom the bell was named and his nephew Georges d'Amboise (II), died 1550, both cardinals. Georges I is the 'great benefactor'.

Louis XII: reigned from 1498 to 1515.

a chapel . . . cluttered with railings: that of Sts Peter and Paul in the north ambulatory of the choir, a temporary resting place for the statue of Richard Cœur de Lion, now placed near the choir railings.

its present condition: the statue had been rediscovered in 1838. The Calvinist disfigurement took place in 1562.

the Gargoyle window: this is at the south end of the south transept and depicts a legend of a miraculous and fantastic sort with a monster popularly thought to resemble a gargoyle.

fantastical metalworker: the spire, the tallest in France, was being reconstructed in iron to replace that destroyed by fire in 1822. From 1826 to 1849 building took place. A public row over the erection suspended further work until 1875. The finishing touches took place in 1884. The spire is in fact 495 feet high, but the statistics of the Great Pyramid, climbed by Flaubert on 8 December 1849 (see letter to Mme Flaubert, 14 Dec. 1849), are correct.

216 *the north door*: the Portail des Libraires has very beautiful carvings of the thirteenth and fourteenth centuries.

Pierre Corneille: the famous playwright (1606–84) was a native of Rouen. His statue was at this time on the western tip of the Île Lacroix. The bronze statue, 12 feet high on its plinth, was cast by David d'Angers and unveiled on 19 October 1834.

217 *in the middle of the day*: in fact, the cab-ride must have begun about midday.

the cab drew up: the cab-ride may have been based in part on a scene in chapter xi of Mérimée's *La Double Méprise* (1833). It can be followed quite clearly to 'the hill of Deville' after which it visits real places 'at random' (as the text states). The *Revue de Paris* serial publication of *Madame Bovary* in 1856 left out the cab-ride for reasons of discretion but Sénard defending Flaubert at his trial was not afraid to read it out in full.

219 *capharnaum*: it is unclear how Capernaum in Galilee (see John 6: 26–59) came to be associated with this particular disorderly feature of the French household, although one may suspect that a similar-sounding regional expression is involved somewhere. The closest English comes to a *capharnaüm* is 'glory-hole'.

220 *Fabricando . . . agis*: 'Whatever you do, practice makes perfect'

221 *Conjugal . . . Love*: the French text makes it clear that this refers to the *Tableau de l'amour conjugal* by Nicolas Venette (doctor and teacher of anatomy at La Rochelle) first published in 1686 and much reprinted. To use its own words, the work is one of 'initiation sexuelle'. Flaubert claimed this 'inept production' was one of the two annual best-sellers (letter to LC, 22 Nov. 1852).

222 *Doudeville*: 25 miles north of Rouen on the road to Saint-Valéry-en-Caux.

225 *a power of attorney*: this would give Emma the right to act for her husband in financial affairs.

228 *'Un soir, t'en souvient-il? nous voguions'*: from verse 4 of Lamartine's *Le Lac*, first published in the *Méditations poétiques* (1820). The poet is alone in his boat and reminiscing in the imagined presence only of his love.

231 *an idea of Rousseau's*: in *Émile* (1762), his novel of educational theory. 'I'm now reading the *Émile* of that Rousseau. What a strange set of ideas in the book, but "it's well written", I must admit and I don't find that easy' (letter to LB, 23 May 1855).

nursing her own child: see also *Émile* (Book I) and Rousseau's *Nouvelle Héloïse* (1761).

vaccination: in 1796 Jenner concluded his research into how to inoculate against smallpox. Flaubert and his friends Bouilhet and Du Camp had written a parody of a tragedy by Delille (see note to p. 75, which they called *La Découverte de la vaccine* and which was probably begun in 1845 or 1846.

232 *it sprawled . . . bridges*: this famous description would appear to be down the Rue d'Ernemont where it reaches the Route de Neufchâtel on the heights on the northern outskirts of the city.

234 *There was a smell . . . oysters*: 'I'm painting the places which were the "beloved theatre of your childhood games", that's to say: the cafés, taverns, bars and brothels which embellish the depths of the rue des Charrettes (I'm in the heart of Rouen). And I have even just left, in order to write to you, the brothels with their railings, the tubs of evergreen, the

smell of absinth, of cigars and of oysters etc. The word is out: *Babylon* is there' (letter to LB, 23 May 1855).

235 *Bathing Odalisque*: an odalisque was popularly taken to mean a woman of the sultan's harem. Odalisques figured frequently in early nineteenth-century French painting, for instance in the works of Ingres, Chassériau, and Delacroix.

'*pale beauty of Barcelona*': probably a romantic fantasy rather than a specific painting.

237 *Souvent la chaleur . . . l'amour*: from *L'Année des dames nationales* (1794) by Restif de la Bretonne (1734–1806).

242 *Emma found these calculations somewhat confusing*: so did Flaubert. 'I'm bogged down in explanations of bills of discount, etc., which I don't really understand' (letter to LB, 27 June 1855).

247 *for: I must go*: of the words Flaubert uses here, *turne* and *bazar* both mean 'a badly kept, dirty house', *chicard* means 'distinctive' or 'elegant', and *chicandard* is its superlative. *Je me la casse*, 'I go away', is based on the idea of bending or breaking the leg for forward movement. *Breda-street* (named after the Rue Bréda—now the Rue Clauzel—a centre of elegant night-life and prostitution at this time in Paris) gave its name to the slang coined by the *demi-monde* who frequented the quartier Bréda, other examples of which language are quoted here by Homais. Presumably the snobbery of all things English turned the Rue Bréda into *Breda-street*. In his letter of 23 May 1855 to Bouilhet written at about the time of the composition of this chapter Flaubert writes of Bouilhet's projected visit to Italy with Alfred Guerard and says: 'C'est une occâse [opportunity] (style Breda street).'

249 *Artists go for them*: 'I'm getting Homais to expose some bawdy theories about women. I'm worried that it will appear too *forced*' (letter to LB, 1 Aug. 1855. See also *DIR* under 'brunes' and 'négresses').

250 *Cujas and Barthole*: French and Italian jurists of the sixteenth and fourteenth centuries respectively. See *DIR* under 'Cujas' and 'Bartolo'.

seltzer water: Flaubert stayed with a chemist in Trouville who made his own seltzer water. He was something of a model for Homais (see letter to LB, 24 Aug. 1853).

258 *the banality of marriage*: this phrase was fiercely attacked at Flaubert's trial after the publication of the novel.

260 *some gardens*: probably the market gardens of the Prairies Saint-Gervais, a large open space west of the Hôtel-Dieu. Emma may well be in the Rue du Renard running along the northern edge of the gardens.

266 *cheminots*: 'It's essential that *cheminots* find a place in *Bovary*. My book would be incomplete without the said alimentary turbans since I intend to *paint* Rouen . . . I'll see that Homais is crazy about "cheminots". It will be one of the secret reasons for his journey to Rouen, and what's more his only human weakness . . . they will come from the rue Massacre'

(letter to LB, 23 May 1855). In the novel it is Mme Homais who dotes on *cheminots*. This patois word was usually spelt 'chemineau'. It is defined as 'cake of fine wheaten flour' in Henri Moisy, *Dictionnaire de patois normand* (quoted in Flaubert, *Correspondance*, ii, ed. Bruneau, (Paris: Pléiade, 1980), 1180).

murmuring . . . facies: 'Here now is the composition of the eye, as far as I remember it: 1st eyelids; 2nd sclerotic, or opaque cornea (it's the white); 3rd cornea proper or transparent cornea (it's the brown circle in the middle); 4th the pupil, in the centre of the cornea; 5th within, behind, the crystalline lens; 6th the optic nerve, etc. That, I think, is quite enough, beware of saying too much about it. Hommais [*sic*] is only a country chemist, he doesn't know any anatomy, he has remembered only a few words.' (Letter of 22 Sept. 1855 from LB to GF.)

267 *roast meat*: 'And in any case: as all these ailments are the result of a scrofulous defect, he will advise him, in a kindly way, to follow a good diet, good wine, good beer, roast meat, all of this volubly, like a lesson being recited (he remembers the prescriptions which he receives daily, and which end invariably with these words: abstain from *farinaceous* and *milk* foods, and *from time to time expose the skin to the smoke of juniper berries*). I think that these pieces of advice given by a large man to this wretch who is dying of hunger would have a fairly moving effect.' (LB to GF, 18 Sept. 1855.)

268 *Steuben's Esméralda*: i.e. a print of the painting *Esméralda et Quasimodo* (1839) (a scene based on Hugo's *Notre-Dame de Paris*) by Charles de Steuben (1788–1856).

Schopin's Putiphar: i.e. a print of the painting by Henri Frédéric Schopin (1804–80), perhaps his *Femme de Putiphar méditant sa vengeance*. Petrus Borel's *Madame Putiphar* had been published in 1839.

273 *Bautzen . . . Lutzen*: Napoleonic victories in 1813 over the Russians near Dresden and the Prussians near Leipzig.

French campaign: the 'Hundred Days' between the escape from Elba and the battle of Waterloo in 1815.

279 *among the branches of trees*: Flaubert's own hallucinations are somewhat similarly described in his letters: 'There's no day when I don't see from time to time what are like tufts of hair or Bengal lights passing before my eyes' (letter to EC, 7 June 1844).

281 *a sudden wave of nausea*: 'When I wrote the description of the poisoning of Mme Bovary I had the taste of arsenic so much in my mouth, I had taken so much poison myself that I gave myself two bouts of indigestion one after the other—two real bouts for I threw up all my dinner' (letter to HT, Nov. 1866).

285 *It was Doctor Larivière*: 'his former teacher' (p. 186). He had advised the move from Tostes for the improvement of Emma's health (p. 61). In Larivière there is something of a portrait of Flaubert's father, who

became a doctor in 1810 and worked at the Hôtel-Dieu in Rouen, of which he became Master in 1818. He died in office in January 1846.

285 *Bichat*: Xavier Bichat, famous French teacher of anatomy and physiology (1771–1802).

287 *cantharides, upas, manchineel*: the first is a species of beetle which includes the Spanish Fly. The dried beetle was used to raise blisters on the skin or, internally, to cause a discharge of urine. The upas is a tree whose poison was used by East Indian natives on their arrows. For the manchineel tree, see note to p. 180.

Cadet de Gassicourt: Charles-Louis Cadet de Gassicourt (1769–1821), French chemist. He wrote not only on chemistry but on travel and comedy as well.

288 *sudden cravings*: Flaubert himself suffered from these.

289 *The priest rose . . . the Almighty*: the extreme unction rite had been some-what similarly described by Sainte-Beuve in the death of Madame de Couaën in *Volupté* (1834). The defence at Flaubert's trial in 1857 linked Flaubert's description with Abbé Ambroise Guillois's *Explication historique, dogmatique, morale, liturgique et canonique du catéchisme . . .* (Le Mans: Monnoyer, 1851).

294 *read d'Holbach, read the Encyclopédie*: the Baron d'Holbach (1723–89), philosopher and theist, author of the *Système de la nature* (1770), was a contributor to the *Encyclopédie* edited by Diderot and d'Alembert between 1750 and 1780, which examined the universe through the use of the reason and which attacked—often covertly—superstition and dogma.

Les Lettres de quelques juifs portuguais: by the Abbé Antoine Gunéné (1769), a reply to Voltaire's attacks on the Bible.

La Raison du christianisme, by Nicolas: this defence of the Roman Catholic Church during the religious revival of the first part of the nineteenth century was by J. J. A. Nicolas. It is correctly called the *Études philosophiques sur le christianisme* (1842–5).

299 *It was time to start*: Flaubert had been to the funeral of the wife of Dr Pouchet on 7 June 1853. He anticipated the event in a letter: 'Since I must moreover *take advantage of all I can*, I'm sure that tomorrow will be a very dark drama and that this poor man of science will be pitiable. I will find there things for my *Bovary*' (letter to LC, 6 June 1853).

serpent player: the serpent was a musical instrument, a bass form of the cornet, shaped like a snake.

302 *an act . . . rather improper*: Flaubert, describing the funeral of his friend Alfred Le Poittevin, wrote: 'When the hole was filled in, I turned on my heels and came away, smoking, which Boivin [friend and lawyer] found lacking in taste' (letter to Maxim Du Camp, 7 Apr. 1848).

306 *primary schools*: instituted after Guizot's elementary education act of 1833, they multiplied slowly in the 1830s and the 1840s.

307 *Ignorantine Friars*: the monks of Saint-Jean-de-Dieu took this name out of humility. It later became a general insulting term for a Christian monk.

pisciculture, rubber, the railways, etc.: gradually we are brought up to the period of Flaubert's composition of the novel. Remy experimented with the artificial fertilization of fish spawn at La Bresse in the Vosges from 1842; Goodyear had invented vulcanization in 1837 and the uses rubber was put to multiplied subsequently in America and in Europe; the 1842 railway law had distinguished between and encouraged the coexistence and expansion of public railway companies.

cho–ca: a brand of cocoa powder.

revalentia: usually 'revalenta' or 'revalesciere'. The English industrialist Du Barry had invented this health-giving panacea made of lentils, maize, peas, beans, millet, salt, barley, and oats with cochineal colouring.

Pulvermacher electric belts: first marketed in France in 1852, this protective apparatus was worn next to the skin to cure and to ward off rheumatism, epilepsy, and other afflictions.

Vaufrylard: in Madame Sabatier's salon Flaubert was known as 'le sire de Vaufrylard'. Flaubert had taken to living some of the year in Paris from 1855 onwards and he presented Madame Sabatier with a copy of *Madame Bovary* in 1857.

308 *Sta viator . . . amabilem conjugem calcas*: 'Stop, traveller . . . a wife worthy of love lies beneath your feet.'

excrement: originally he was refused burial in sanctified ground, but in 1791, thirteen years after his death, his remains were interred in the Pantheon. 'Bournisien confuses Voltaire and Rousseau—who died devouring his own excrement, as everybody knows' (note by Flaubert in *MB* n.v., 128).

309 *the cholera epidemic*: see note to p. 66.

the Academy: i.e. to the Académie des sciences, belles-lettres et arts in Rouen.

310 *'Les Favorites du commerce'*: a 'favorite' was a small and presumably speedy cab in towns. Lheureux's service is designed as a fast coach or wagon service.

The Oxford World's Classics Website

www.worldsclassics.co.uk

- Browse the full range of Oxford World's Classics online

- Sign up for our monthly e-alert to receive information on new titles

- Read extracts from the Introductions

- Listen to our editors and translators talk about the world's greatest literature with our Oxford World's Classics audio guides

- Join the conversation, follow us on Twitter at OWC_Oxford

- Teachers and lecturers can order inspection copies quickly and simply via our website

www.worldsclassics.co.uk

American Literature

British and Irish Literature

Children's Literature

Classics and Ancient Literature

Colonial Literature

Eastern Literature

European Literature

Gothic Literature

History

Medieval Literature

Oxford English Drama

Poetry

Philosophy

Politics

Religion

The Oxford Shakespeare

A complete list of Oxford World's Classics, including Authors in Context, Oxford English Drama, and the Oxford Shakespeare, is available in the UK from the Marketing Services Department, Oxford University Press, Great Clarendon Street, Oxford OX2 6DP, or visit the website at www.oup.com/uk/worldsclassics.

In the USA, visit www.oup.com/us/owc for a complete title list.

Oxford World's Classics are available from all good bookshops. In case of difficulty, customers in the UK should contact Oxford University Press Bookshop, 116 High Street, Oxford OX1 4BR.

.